CYBERK!LL

Also by
Frank F. Fiore

The Oracle
Murran

The Chronicles of Jeremy Nash
A Taste of the Apocalypse
Seed
Black Sun

CYBERKILL is a work of fiction. Names, characters, businesses, places, events, locales, and incidents are either the products of the author's imagination or used in a fictitious manner. Any resemblance to actual persons, living or dead, or actual events is purely coincidental.

ISBN: 978-1-952474-42-2

CYBERKILL
Copyright © 2010
Frank F. Fiore

Cover concept and design by David Warren

All rights reserved. No part of this book may be reproduced, stored in a retrieval system, or transmitted in any form or by any means—electronic, mechanical, photocopy, recording or otherwise—without the prior written permission of the publisher. The only exception is brief quotations for review purposes.

Published by WordCrafts Press
Cody, Wyoming 82414
www.wordcrafts.net

CY3ERK!LL

FRANK F. FIORE

WordCrafts Press

To my wife, Lynne, who prays that my works will not gain popularity posthumously.

Author's Note

The geographic locations, government and military installations and organizations, information warfare scenarios, artificial intelligence, robots, and the information and communications technology in this book all exist.

As for SIRUS, pieces of the technology are either in existence or in the research and development stage.

According to the Department of Defense, it doesn't exist.

The *Fars News Agency of Iran* has reported otherwise.

Prologue

The airplane was leaving in a few hours, but Travis Cole still had some unfinished business in his MIT office—one of which was to get his in-law off his back.

"Please, John. We've been over this a hundred times," Cole murmured, leaning forward on his desk to stare down at the computer monitor in front of him. He rested his fingers lightly on the keyboard, his hazel eyes focused on the command prompt on the screen:

```
DO YOU WANT TO EXECUTE? Y/N
```

Could he really do it?

Though Cole had made up his mind, it was now formal decision time. Pressing 'N' would continue his life as a well-known researcher in eco-biology at the MIT Artificial Intelligence Laboratory. Pressing 'Y' would end three years of cutting-edge work and move him and his daughter to a new home in Washington, D.C. and a lucrative research job with the U.S. Army.

Cole's finger hovered over the keyboard—he felt sick.

John François was, as usual, sucking on the end of an ornately carved wood and leather pipe. It went along with his academic look: elbow-patched sports coat, baggy brown pants, and loafers.

"It's not right, Travis," François implored. "It's not right to take Shannon away from the environment she knows just weeks after her mother's death. It's just not right."

Cole kept his focus on the task at hand. They had been over this a thousand times. Shannon, Cole's young daughter, was already in the car, waiting. In fact, all his luggage and many of his important worldly belongings waited there as well. He would return later for the rest of his stuff.

For now...

For now, he had to just get away.

Cole's finger still hovered. He blinked hard. Could he really do this?

Yes, I can do this.

"And what about this?" François said as he opened the cover of a three-ring binder with the title *TERRAN PROJECT* written in blue across the front. François gently thumbed through the pages and pointed at the different artificial intelligence programs that Cole had cataloged and tracked while at MIT. "You're just going to throw away *years* of work?"

Cole ignored François and turned back to the computer terminal with its blinking white cursor awaiting a reply.

He took in some air—and pressed the 'Y' key on the keyboard.

Cole turned to François while the computer executed his command unable to watch. Instead, he looked at his aging in-law with compassion for the man. Since his wife died of leukemia ten years before, François had lived alone. Cole and Shannon were the closest thing he had to family.

"John..." said Cole gently, but François cut him off.

"Shannon's only five years old, Travis. Taking her away from the surroundings she knows isn't the answer," he pleaded. The older man had tears in his eyes.

Damn. Cole gently placed his hand on François's arm. "John, I don't know what I would have done without your help after Kathy's death. But I know what's best for Shannon. I have to give her a change." Cole squeezed François's arm, then looked back to the computer screen. He watched as file name after file name appeared on the screen, all tagged with the same statement:

FILE FOUND. FILE TERMINATED.

Cole looked at his watch. "Jeez. We have to go. You'll see us off?"

François nodded in resignation.

"Thanks. Shannon will like that." Cole glanced once more at the scrolling text on the computer screen, turned, and hurried out the office with François close behind.

In the darkness of the vacated room, the program reached the end of its routine, and then stopped on the last file. The text that glowed from the LCD screen turned from white to red and blinked repeatedly insisting on an answer.

FILE FOUND. FILE ACTIVE.

ABORT OR CONTINUE?

Part One
Infection

One Year Later

"I'm sorry to interrupt you, Mr. Supervisor, but we've found something—odd."

Alexi Chenko put down the latest issue of *Pravda* and frowned at his head lab technician, Ho Quan, a little man with dark-rimmed spherical glasses and a stubby bearded chin. His round head sat atop an even rounder body. Quan, normally stoic and reserved, looked agitated, sweat lining his brow. As always, he spoke crisply in his Mandarin Chinese, the official spoken language of the People's Republic of China.

Chenko was having a bad morning, and this latest interruption didn't bode well. Already he'd received numerous infuriating calls from high-level Beijing bureaucrats wanting to know when various communication devices would be cleared and ready for use. This was followed by his wife calling to remind him of a dinner party tonight, a party Chenko had done his best to forget about. And now this. Whatever *this* was.

"What's wrong?" Chenko asked in his near-perfect Chinese. He'd always had a penchant for picking up languages, a skill that had served him well as he rose quickly up the Kremlin ranks. But now, semi-exiled and banished from Mother Russia, he filled his days working in a tiny three-man facility outside a small village in southern China.

"May I show you?" asked Quan. Chenko noted the man was visibly shaken.

Something's wrong, thought Chenko. *Seriously wrong.*

The tall Russian followed the much shorter Quan onto the uncomfortably warm testing floor of their lab, a building that was freezing in the winters and smoldering during the summers. The room itself was large and lined with work tables piled with disassembled electronic equipment. The two men stopped at one table, under a 'No Smoking' sign posted on the lab's wall. Ironically, the first thing that struck Chenko was the smell of cigarette smoke.

"Someone's been smoking," said Chenko, irritated. He had given his two techs numerous lectures on the necessity for air purity in the lab. He was surprised that one of them had so blatantly dismissed them.

"No sir," said Quan quickly. "No one's been smoking here."

Chenko frowned. He had to admit, there were no tell-tales signs of gray smoke hanging in the air. And now that he thought about it, there had been, of late, the distinct smell of carbon in the air—everywhere.

"Sir, the laptop..."

"Yes, of course."

The laptop in question, sitting on Quan's workbench, was from a U.S. manufacturer with an Intel Pentium decal on it. There was another decal on the machine with simple white lettering that read: MCD.

"We were running the usual tests when we found this." Quan pointed to the screen.

Chenko leaned forward, frowning. "It's a compiled code."

The little tech nodded eagerly. "We don't know what it is or what it does."

Chenko continued studying the code. Something about the way it was written, the rhythm and nuances of the code...

He gasped, pulled back. This wasn't good. This wasn't good at all.

"It's an Easter Egg," Chenko said, running his massive Slavic hand through his thinning hair. He rapidly scrolled through the entire text. He hadn't seen such a code since…

Since working at the KGB's information warfare center.

Not good.

"Is it dangerous?" Quan asked nervously, clearly sensing his supervisor's concern.

"Depends," said Chenko. "An Easter Egg can be an executable program. Like a virus or Trojan horse. Sometimes they're called logic bombs. If it is indeed a piece of malware, it could cause disruption—even damage—to a computer network."

Hell, even portions of a country's entire information infrastructure, thought Chenko, although he did not voice this to Quan.

Chenko pulled absently on his chin. Yes, he'd seen something like this before: the KGB's cyber-warfare program. Something was going on, and it was big.

Definitely not good, thought Chenko.

"What do we do?" asked Quan. "Is it safe in here?"

Chenko got hold of himself.

"Yes, of course. Our testing lab is self-contained. There's no entry to our national information infrastructure. Let's hook the laptop up to our lab network and run the code first to find out what it's designed to do."

Quan and Chenko's other technician, Seung Park, a bright young kid fresh out of the military, immediately followed Chenko's set-up instructions. A minute later, the laptop was ready.

Chenko thought out loud, "First we decompile the code, then run the program through our test network." He pulled up a stool, sat down at the testing bench, and called up the lab's list of decompilers. "This one should do it." He clicked on a file. A few minutes later, the program was decompiled and ready to run.

"OK," he said. "Let's see what this program does."

Yes, he thought. *I'm very curious to see what this program does.*

And judging by the way his heart was hammering in his chest, Chenko knew he was nervous as well. Easter Eggs were not a mistake or haphazardly placed. They were put in place to execute a specific program—and often the programs were malignant. If the latest rumors he had heard were true, this could prove to be the beginning of something very big.

The now-exiled Chenko was out of the so-called loop. What was happening, or what might be happening, was beyond him.

Well, we'll see, he thought.

The computer prompted him. Hands shaking slightly, Chenko typed: *run*. The screen paused—and so did Chenko's heart, seemingly. When the laptop began running through its routine, the Russian breathed and watched the display, along with his two lab techs. But nothing was happening. Not so far, at least. Chenko's eyes flicked to a nearby laptop, used for status updates: no computer virus alerts and no intrusion attempts.

"I guess it was nothing," Quan mused aloud.

But Chenko, who had turned back to the laptop before him, spotted something in the string of code. Looking over his supervisor's shoulder, Quan spotted the same sequence.

"It's designed to send commands to another network," said Quan. "Doesn't appear malicious, but I'm not familiar with the code."

You wouldn't be, thought Chenko. *In fact, few would.*

"It's Cellular Automata," he explained. "We worked on this in Russia to control and operate..." He let his voice trail off.

Could they have?

The program was still running, scanning the code rapidly.

"It's sending commands to a network," said Quan, confused. "But not our network."

Chenko said nothing.

"But if not our network," asked Quan, "then whose?"

The smell of cigarette smoke—or perhaps the smell of burning carbon—was stronger yet.

Something is happening, thought Chenko.

Quan stood back and started scratching his chest. The smell of carbon was even stronger. He began scratching feverishly at his scalp and face, using both hands, his nails leaving red grooves in his skin.

What the…?

"Quan…"

But the tech was oblivious to him, scratching so hard and fast that his skin was tearing, blood running free. Chenko's initial reaction was to reach out and help the man, but he thought better of it and recoiled, standing and knocking over the stool.

"Mr. Supervisor," said Quan hysterically. "What is happening?"

Don't touch him.

More movement to his side. The Russian turned his head and saw Seung, his young lab tech, starting to scratch. The tech, who had been backing away from the scene, was now scratching his neck and arms.

My God!

Chenko backed away. Quan reached out for him. Blood and bits of skin clung ghoulishly to his fingertips and under his nails. Chenko did not help the man, his loyal worker. Instead, the Russian continued to increase his distance until he was pressed up against the far wall. A fire extinguisher pressed against his shoulder. He tore it off the wall and held it between him and the beseeching Quan, whose wide eyes were filled with fear and horror.

But what happened next negated the need for the fire extinguisher. In fact, what happened next would haunt Chenko for the rest of his life.

The Chinese tech had fallen to his knees, and with one last pitiful look at Chenko, pitched forward onto the concrete floor.

To Chenko's utter disbelief and horror, he watched as Quan's once pleasantly round face collapsed in on itself, his skull flattening as if an invisible force were pressing down on it.

I'm dreaming, thought Chenko. *This isn't happening. I was reading the newspaper just a few minutes ago, and surely I fell asleep at my desk.*

Now Quan's entire body seemed to implode, sinking inwardly.

The process was shockingly fast, and before Chenko had time to grasp what was happening, there was nothing left of Quan other than a crumpled bloody mass of clothing and empty skin.

My God!

Chenko averted his eyes and his breakfast came up quickly, splashing over the concrete in front of him. As he turned his face to catch his breath, he caught sight of Seung suffering a similar fate. The young tech had been reduced to a lifeless puddle of blood and loose skin.

Chenko vomited again.

In his rather non-illustrious career in the KGB, Chenko had seen many disturbing images. But never had he seen the likes of this.

Steadying himself on the workbench, he glanced again at the bloody pulps that had once been his employees. He stumbled out of the workroom and into the fresh air of the strikingly clean back alley. Except the air wasn't so clean. No, not today. Other than the smell of his own puke, he was smelling the stench of something else.

More carbon.

Something was burning, except he couldn't see any smoke. But the smell of it seemed to be coming from nearby—no, it seemed to be coming from *beneath* him. *Around* him. He turned in circles, confused.

It's coming from everywhere.

And yet...

Whatever was happening wasn't affecting *him*. The thought of Quan and Seung melting before his eyes turned his stomach again, and he dry-heaved into the alley.

And then he had a horrible thought: Mei Ling.

His wife!

He'd met Mei Ling shortly after arriving in China, and she

had made his exile more bearable. In time, he was even fairly certain that he had come to love her, although 'love' was certainly not a word the ex-Russian computer engineer used often.

Still, she was all he had, and fear gripped his heart.

And now he was running, dashing through the alley, turning a corner, and racing into the small plaza. There he was confronted by more carnage. He paused and struggled to comprehend what he was seeing. Dead Chinese everywhere.

Men, women, children...their bodies all reduced to bloody, pulpy masses.

Mei! he thought. *Find Mei.*

He covered his mouth, averted his eyes, willed his convulsing stomach to be still, and rushed through the plaza, dodging the hundreds of bodies. Occasionally he would hear someone cry out for help, and occasionally one of the bloody piles would reach for him, but they were beyond hope.

God, let this be a dream....

The town was small. Chenko often walked to work, and soon, out of breath and nearly hysterical, he rushed through the surrounding iron gates, up the lush, ornate path that Lei tended to daily, and into his home.

The door slammed open, the handle puncturing the wall. He didn't care about the damage.

"Mei!" he cried out. "Mei!"

There was no response. The house was oddly devoid of sound. Hell, the whole town and countryside seemed suddenly devoid of sound. And the smell... carbon... it was here, too.

Oh, no!

He moved quickly from room to room, his heart slamming in his chest. Sick dread filled his whole being.

He reached the kitchen—and there she was, lying on the shining ceramic floor, her blood oozing between the tiles. She was little more than a pile of bloody clothes and loose skin. And the pile of tiny clothes where her hand had once been was his baby girl.

The entire room smelled of carbon.

Back in his testing lab, sick and grieving, the Russian sat down at his desk, opened a locked drawer, and found a small red notebook. He opened to a page with a series of passwords on it, chose one, and brought up a log-in screen on his computer. Hands shaking, he typed in his username and password and waited for the application to come up. A series of computer security screens appeared and each accepted his commands to proceed.

Within a few moments he was typing a message.

Information Warfare Laboratory
Fort Belvoir, Maryland

Seventy feet below the INSCOM building at Fort Belvoir, Virginia in the Information Warfare Laboratory, Morgan Dallas was munching on his burrito. "It was all just a test," he groaned through the masticated meal in his mouth. "Why did they pick five in the morning? I could have been sleeping."

"Probably to simulate a real-time attack," said Taylor Chin without looking up, her nose in her laptop computer. "I doubt cyber-terrorists are going to wait until you've had your coffee and morning piss."

"Such language," said Dallas, grinning. He liked Taylor. A lot. Except the 24-year-old graduate of MIT didn't know how to show it. There were limitations to being a computer nerd, and being smooth with the ladies was certainly one of them. Taylor was looking especially cute this morning, with an aqua-colored turtleneck sweater and tight jeans. She was Asian-American, 21, and a specialist in artificial intelligence. Dallas thought that was hot. She also had a boyfriend.

Dallas didn't think *that* was so hot.

He sighed silently and poured some more Hot Sauce over his massive breakfast burrito as the two sat together in their cramped IWL office.

"I heard Senator Howe of the Senate Arms Services

Committee ripped him to shreds," Taylor said, absently reaching for her iced latte.

"Just wild speculation," said Dallas. "No one knows for sure. Bartley's never left his office. Probably in there crying."

Taylor shrugged. She took another sip from her iced drink.

"How can you drink iced coffee in the morning? Isn't that a sacrilege?"

"No worse than you eating a burrito for breakfast."

"It's called a *breakfast burrito*."

"It looks disgusting."

Dallas grinned, took a huge bite, and with food still in his mouth, said, "I hope they fire his butt. I never liked that overgrown boy scout, anyway."

"You don't like anyone in authority," said Taylor, "And you shouldn't say that about Bartley. What if someone overhears you?"

"So what?" Dallas blurted out. "Bartley can't do anything to me. Or us. We're civilians."

"Look. You get Bartley pissed and he goes straight to Travis, who then bitches at us."

That stopped Dallas. They both liked Travis Cole. The young grad chewed his breakfast burrito silently. Dallas was a self-proclaimed techno-pagan. After college, he studied and worked at the MIT Artificial Intelligence Lab before joining the IWL team a year ago. Now he worked as a private contractor for the United States government.

Staring at his one remaining bite of burrito and licking the sauce off his fingers, he sputtered, "Why does Bartley always run to Travis, anyway?"

"Because Travis is the closest we have to a boss," said Taylor, without looking up from her keyboard. "I'm going up top to the grid and get my mail. I'll be back when you finish what you call breakfast." She picked up her backpack and swept out of the office.

Dallas watched her go, admiring her tight jeans.

~

Travis Cole was sitting alone in one of the smaller rooms at the IWL, a room reserved just for his team. A room where, in fact, no real work was completed, a room dubbed by some in his team as the *Stress-Free Zone*. Indeed, the floor of the chrome and concrete room was littered with what looked like remote controlled cars on steroids. Battlebots. At least, that's what Dallas called them. The kid built them in his spare time, which, at the IWL, was an oxymoron. No one here had much spare time, which was why Dallas could often be found up at all hours of the night, tinkering with those... battlebots.

Cole almost laughed, but they were quite clever, and he was currently idly operating one of them. It was shaped roughly like a dragon, with massive black wheels and a chainsaw in place of its snout. Oh, every now and then a burst of fire shot from its snout. Cole wasn't sure how and when that happened, so he decided to keep it away from anything flammable.

He pressed a button, and the thing rose up on its hind legs and turned to look at him. Positively evil, as if alive.

Some of these mechanical critters gave him the creeps. Morgan Dallas was obviously an amazing engineer. Who knew what sort of AI intelligence he had given these things.

This one continued to look at him. Cole shuddered and pressed another button. Almost reluctantly, it lowered itself down to both feet which were, in fact, rubber tires and rolled off at Cole's command.

At least, he *thought* it was at his command.

His laptop was open in front of him. Cole set aside the big remote control that operated the seemingly sentient dragon and reviewed the small executable code he had embedded into his Cellular Automata program. The code was called a fix, a shortcut that proved that Cole could deliver the goods. Just another day at the job.

Cole took chances. He knew that about himself, and accepted it. He was a risk-taker and he got off on that. True, sometimes it bit him in the butt, but more often than not he got a high that lasted for days. And this morning's high at the successful DoD no-notice exercise was no exception, simulated or not.

His personal life was no exception. He often jumped headfirst into relationships, trusting his gut instincts. Granted, it was often something *else* that guided his instincts.

Kathy had been different. The light of his life. The love of his life, and all his instincts—gut and otherwise—told him she was his soul mate. True to nature, he had snatched her up without a moment's thought, and had lived a life happily ever after.

Until the day he got the call from the state trooper.

Cole turned away from his laptop and fired up the battlebot again. The dragon was game. It seemed to growl from within and charged headfirst toward the door... which suddenly opened.

Standing in the doorway, crying, was Taylor.

Taylor stumbled over, pulled up a wobbly wooden stool, and collapsed at the workbench next to him.

Cole, who had always felt more fatherly toward Taylor than anything, opened his mouth to speak, but Taylor had found another remote control and held it in front of him.

"How does this work?" she asked.

Cole was taken aback. He wasn't sure what to say or how to react to her tears. He decided to let her set the pace, knowing Taylor rarely opened up to anyone. She was certainly unlike any girl he had ever seen or met.

"This lever here controls the bot's mobility. This one controls the diamond-tipped drill bit."

"Drill bit?" she asked, wiping away her tears.

"Yeah. These are called 'battlebots' for a reason." He laughed, but she didn't. Cole shrugged. Wasn't that funny, anyway.

Her face set in grim determination, her red eyes nearly glowing in the lab's bright lights, she worked the controls a bit, getting a feel for them. As she did so, another battlebot, this one across the room, came to life, reacting to her commands. The drill bit whirred menacingly from the creature's forehead. Indeed, this one was called the Unicorn, although it didn't look like any unicorn Cole had ever seen.

Dallas is a twisted man, he thought.

"So what do you do with these battlebots?" she asked.

"They battle," said Cole.

"Battle what?"

"Each other."

"Which one is yours?" she asked, and Cole didn't like the menacing tone in her voice.

"The dragon," he said slowly.

And then her bot was *moving...* crossing the room, heading toward his.

"Oh, crap!" said Cole, nearly toppling off his stool. He fumbled with his controls. "Taylor, what are you doing?"

But she didn't answer; somehow she had grasped the use of the controls already, thanks, Cole figured, to a new generation raised on Nintendo and X-Box.

Cole had just managed to right his stool and the remote control in his hand, at the same time narrowly avoiding the Unicorn's whirring drill bit.

"Taylor..."

The Unicorn whipped around, spinning easily, rotating its entire body on some pivot axis that Dallas had designed. She came at him again.

Cole, not so versed in the ways of video gaming, and still very much a novice at controlling these bots, moved his fire-breathing dragon out of harm's way again.

"I understand you might be upset," he said, pressing the wrong lever and causing his bot to rise slowly on its hind legs. "But I don't think Dallas would appreciate..."

"Screw Dallas!" she said, and came at him again, hard and fast, the unicorn's demented head lowered, the drill bit whirring.

Despite himself, Cole pressed another button, and a lick of flame shot out, momentarily engulfing the unicorn bot. A second later, it plunged through the smoke and fire and rammed into Cole's dragon. The machines, each weighing over a hundred pounds, collided, and the cacophony and smashing and grinding metal filled the small lab.

"Taylor!"

She said nothing. He looked over at her. Her eyes were dull and passionless.

The Unicorn's drill bit drove straight through the mouth and neck of the dragon. His poor bot twitched, fighting to free itself from the possessed unicorn. But she had it pinned against the leg of a workbench. Both bots groaned and whirred and convulsed. The circular saw attached to his own bot appeared as if on its own, and dropped down on the head of the unicorn. Sparks flew as metal was shorn away.

"Dear God!" said Cole.

His bot randomly spat fire, and one of the bursts of flame ignited one of its own rubber tires. The thing smoked and burned and twitched, and still Taylor's bot drilled determinedly into it.

The fire from the tire soon engulfed the entire undercarriage of Cole's bot, a bot now dead in his hands. A moment later the black smoke triggered a fire alarm, which rang frighteningly loud in the confines of the lab.

And then the sprinklers turned on, drenching them, drenching the room, drenching all the scattered, unmoving robotic bots, as black smoke continued to curl up from the dragon bot.

Cole looked at Taylor. She sat unmoving, unblinking. Water poured down her face, soaking her clothing.

They were sitting in Cole's cramped office. Cole had changed into an old pair of shorts and a wrinkled tee shirt he'd found shoved in his locker. Taylor had elected to stay in her sopping wet clothing. "So what the hell was that all about?" asked Cole.

At the sound of the fire alarms, Bartley emerged from his office, looking shell-shocked. Perhaps he'd thought it was another simulated cyber attack. The on-call firemen checked the lab out, proclaimed it safe, and finally permitted a distraught Dallas back into the lab, where he went immediately to his destroyed battle bots. Although Cole did his best to explain, he wasn't entirely sure what had happened himself.

Now, smelling vaguely of moldy clothing, Cole was about to ask the question again when Taylor did something completely unexpected.

She burst into tears, crying hard, and Cole did the only thing he could think of. He got up from behind his desk and put his arm around her. Taylor buried her face into his side and cried even harder while Cole patted her shoulder awkwardly.

When she had gotten control of herself, Cole finally learned what he had already suspected. Something bad had happened. Very bad. Taylor's sister had been killed just the day before. A freak accident in China.

Cole murmured all the right soothing words, and soon they were sitting in silence. Taylor was shivering, but had refused Cole's towel.

"I'm so sorry," he said again.

"You already said that."

"I know. I'm sorry." And they both laughed at that, although Taylor's laughter turned to tears again.

A moment later, when she had calmed down again, Cole said, "I didn't know you had a sister."

She didn't immediately answer, and when she did, it was with many pauses and lapses, seemingly, from memory. "She's my half sister... my father remarried a Chinese citizen here in this country after my mom died... my sister's name is... I mean her name *was*, Mei. She moved to China several years ago and eventually married a Russian there."

"A Russian? In China?"

"Yes. Alexi Chenko. Apparently Alexi had been a computer security specialist with the KGB, but was unceremoniously 'relieved' of his duties and reduced to working in menial jobs under the new economic system."

"Did you say KGB?"

"Yes. From what I could tell, the two of them truly loved each other, and loved their child, as well."

Taylor took a long breath, shivering even harder. Despite her previous protests, Cole got up and wrapped his towel around her shoulders. She didn't move or thank him, but the shivering stopped.

"How did your sister die, Taylor, if I may ask?"

She seemed not to hear him at first, but then the words finally registered, and she reached down and dug into her pocket. She removed her PDA, which had managed to stay dry within the confines of her tight jeans, and turned it on. She manipulated the small scroll ball, and then handed it over to Cole.

Cole took it from her and saw an email message that she brought up. The email was, miraculously, from Mei's Russian husband, the ex-KGB Alexi.

"How did he get this message through the security filters in China?" asked Cole.

"KGB, remember?"

"Oh, yeah."

"Please, Travis, just read the message."

He noted the hurt and pain and urgency in her voice, so he turned back to the email, barely believing what he was reading.

In fact, he didn't.

"I know you're hurting, Taylor, and I know this is a bad day for you, but I need to be honest with you. This email, this business of which Alexi writes is... utter nonsense. Computer software can't kill people."

"I know, Travis.

Cole read the email again. He could feel his jaw literally dropping.

A whole village dead?

People... melting?

A virus of unknown scope and size... activated by a computer program?

A program he, Alexi, accidentally set into motion?
Killing only Chinese?
My God...

"Cole," said Taylor urgently, leaning forward, wrapping the towel tighter around her narrow shoulders. "Alexi says the program has something to do with an MCD chip. You're the Artificial Intelligence expert. Theoretically, can this happen?"

"No," said Cole. "It can't." But then he stopped cold and re-read the last line of the message. "What's this at the end?" he asked, and handed her back the PDA so she could read it, too.

"Some gibberish," she said, shrugging. "About CA code driving a network. I don't know. The message is pretty garbled at the end."

Cole was puzzled. He was quite aware of CA code—but, up until now, he had believed that he was the only one who could make such codes work on a micro scale.

Taylor reached out across the desk and took Cole's hand. Her own was corpse cold. Cole shivered.

"Please, Travis. I need to know what happened to my sister. I'm just looking for answers. Is there any way you can help me?"

Travis and Taylor had a good friendship. Perhaps even a great friendship, despite the age difference. It was damn hard to look into her big brown, pleading eyes and tell her no. So he said, "I'll look into this MCD business."

"You know about the MCD chip?"

Cole shook his head. "No. But I know someone who does."

NSA Headquarters
Washington, D.C.

Richard Safko, Deputy Director in charge of Acquisition Outreach for the National Security Agency, sat in his office with his back to the young junior programmer and gazed through his tenth floor corner office window down onto a gray and overcast Washington D.C. His mind wasn't so much on the sweeping view before him but the sensitive task ahead.

Finally, when he felt he had made the programmer wait long enough, he turned from the window and focused his steely blue eyes on the kid sitting nervously in front of him. His name was Josh Leighton, and he was a brilliant young programmer.

Hell, they're all brilliant, thought Safko.

"You said we'd know today if we can go forward on the activation," said Safko. "Are we still on target?"

"Yes, sir," said Leighton, adjusting his tie nervously.

Safko knew that Leighton was surely wondering why he had been chosen for this sensitive assignment, as there were more experienced code-slingers at the Agency who could do the job. Yes, indeed there were, but Safko had chosen Leighton specifically because of his lack of time at the Agency. He wanted someone on this classified project who was not only smart, but had little or no baggage; someone who would follow orders without discussion or inquisition. A senior programmer would have

23

asked too many questions. Besides, he'd read the lad's resume and knew Leighton could work with this unique code, something the older code-slingers had trouble understanding.

"So where are we with it?" asked Safko.

"The conversion is complete, sir, and will be ready when you give the word."

Safko smiled and Leighton seemed to relax.

"And the communication code is working properly?"

"Yes, sir. The units we tested in-house responded perfectly."

Safko knew he was smiling broadly. He couldn't help it. They were so close.

"Good," he said. "Because we're going to activate a small portion of the network soon."

"Sir, may I ask how we acquired this code? It's very unique."

"We acquired it from... let's say, a *cooperative* civilian contractor. Why?"

"You gave me only a piece of the code, so I assume there's a full program somewhere else?"

"So?"

"This is a scanning program, correct?'

"Yes. So what's your point?"

"And you wanted me to convert certain aspects of it into an executable program?

"*What of it?*" Safko demanded. He was losing his patience.

The young programmer started to perspire. "So, um, not seeing the entire program... I wasn't able to see how my re-programming affected the unknown pieces. That is to say..." he furrowed his brow searching for the right words, "... any unintended consequences?

"You're saying there are mistakes in your re-programming? It's a little late for that."

"No! No, sir. Only... I was just curious... what is this program supposed to do?"

"*That*, young man is none of your concern. I chose you for your capability, not your curiosity." His tone punctuated the fact that Leighton was to ask no further questions. "That is all."

When Leighton was gone, Safko removed a blue folder from his desk drawer. Under and above the blue and white NSA insignia were the words: *Top Secret: SIRUS Outreach.*

Safko turned to the pages that described an acquisition program for HomeSec. His Acquisition Outreach Office was responsible for establishing partnerships with industry, academia, and other state, local, and federal government entities for the benign purpose of extending NSA contracts. But his office had another covert purpose—to recruit civilian contractors and exploit their ideas to assist the NSA in its global mission.

Attached to the file was a cover letter addressed to the Department of Homeland Security referencing a paper that a certain Travis Cole, one such civilian contractor, had submitted. The DHS had asked those in academia to help address critical needs in homeland defense on the scientific and technological front and was looking for proposals from IT professionals on how to reduce the size of code used in programming Micro-Electro-Mechanical Systems devices.

Cole had answered. Stapled to the corner of the proposal was a red index card with the characters NAN-056-12 on it. Safko scanned the proposal, impressed.

His secretary buzzed him over the intercom. "I have Colonel Arlen Bartley at the Information Warfare Laboratory on the secure line, sir."

"Put him through."

Safko heard a series of clicks, then a digitized voice came over the handset.

"I'm afraid I have some bad news," said Bartley, by way of hello.

That's all we need now, thought Safko. SIRUS had too many delays already. Was this yet another one? He asked Bartley to get on with it.

The colonel took in some air. "We had a no-notice DoD exercise here at the IWL this morning," the colonel said. "Senator Howe was here."

"Crap."

"Exactly. He wasn't impressed. Something about paying millions for grown men to play video games. Anyway, I'm certain he'll recommend a cutback on IWL funding."

Not good, thought Safko. *It's time to bump everything up.*

"We go to Phase One of the SIRUS communication network ASAP. The program is now executable and we've matched up the operating system of both the dust and chips. The two can communicate with each other now."

"Excellent."

Safko asked, "Do we have confirmation that the wireless devices arrived in China?"

"Affirmative," said Bartley. "Spoke with MCD today."

"Good," said Safko. "I'll tell you when to activate the network."

As Safko disconnected the call, he couldn't help but wonder how long it would be before someone at MCD discovered what they were doing.

We have ways of dealing with them, he thought, and turned back to Travis Cole's proposal.

Mobile Chip Devices
Boston, MA

Michael Bates sat in his small office at Mobile Chip Devices and copied the last remaining documents of a project that MCD had contracted with the government. He looked up nervously—and repeatedly—out the small narrow glass window of his closed office door.

So far so good.

MCD was doing something dirty. He knew it, and he was going to let the world know about it.

Somehow.

He could say to himself that what he was about to do was for his country, but he admitted his treatment at Mobile Chip Devices—especially his treatment in the hands of their pompous MBA executives—played a major part in it. God, he *loathed* them. What he needed now was an opportunity to make his revelation.

And later that day, with all the MCD files secretly and safely copied, his opportunity literally came knocking at his office door.

"Good man, Bates. In the office early I see," Marjorie McCarthy said as she briskly entered his office. McCarthy was VP of Marketing at MCD and a recent MBA graduate from Harvard. She personified everything Bates disliked about MBAs. Bates, himself a self-made man, believed that no amount of learning could cure stupidity, and formal education positively fortified it. To him MBA stood for *manipulative, back-stabbing,* and *arrogant.* McCarthy fit the profile perfectly. She was condescending, controlling, too theoretical, and overly ambitious.

His skin *crawled.*

McCarthy walked behind Bates and stood over his terminal—which, he admitted, made him a bit nervous—and then glanced into the full length mirror on the wall, straightening her tastefully-cut Ann Taylor jacket.

Figures.

McCarthy was the epitome of every woman he knew—and couldn't get. Of course, his looks didn't help matters much. Bates was a big burly man, almost a wide as he was tall. He wore suits too small for his frame and walked around with a perpetually loosened tie and the top button of his shirt undone to lessen the pressure around his thick neck. He was a big Swede with the looks of Chris Farley and the brains of Steve Jobs. He had straight brown hair and two happy brown eyes blown up hugely behind thick, black-framed glasses.

"I have a job for you to do."

Now what? Bates thought. *Wet nurse some self-important MBA?*

"Yes, of course," he said pleasantly enough, playing their game. "Anything."

She preened, obviously enjoying her power. She looked at herself one more time in the mirror. "I see that you were on the design team for our new wireless chip set."

"I *led* the team," Bates corrected her, smiling big and broad. Just a happy company man.

"Oh, yes, of course. And Mobile Chip Devices is thankful for your important contribution," she spouted automatically.

Bates had to agree with her there. Having a reputation as a pioneer of ultra-integrated semiconductor solutions for all manner of wireless devices, MCD's new wireless chip set that Bates helped develop would revolutionize wireless communications across all technology platforms including cell phones, PDAs, laptops, and handheld computers.

And it did something else—something groundbreaking.

MCD had extended the wireless range of their new chips for miles—much further than the few hundred feet of the older chips. That longer distance, coupled with its ability to monitor and report a wireless device's activity had forced Bates to act in a way that was less than loyal.

McCarthy continued. "We're sending you to D.C. for a wireless technology conference."

"The national INTEROP conference?" Bates suddenly became interested.

"That's the one. You're to give a presentation on our new wireless chip technology." In a condescending voice she added, "I was going to go myself, but the attendees are all geeks—I mean *technical types*—so we need to send someone who, um, can speak their language."

Bates smiled. Still, she was correct. MBAs were useless when it came to explaining technology, although damn good at pimping it. And he kept on grinning. After all, this was the opportunity he was looking for: a national platform for his whistle-blowing.

Loyalty be damned. What MCD did was just plain wrong.

He'd discovered that the new chips installed in the latest wireless devices were being programmed to *report information*. Combine that with the ability of the new chips to send information over miles instead of feet and you have a new and potent threat to personal privacy.

Thanks to his clandestine downloading just this morning, Bates had all the pieces now—and even a strange name to go with them—SIRUS.

"So you'll go?" McCarthy asked. It wasn't so much a question as a confirmation.

"Yes, of course."

"Good. MCD will make your travel arrangements. Pick them

up before you leave today." McCarthy abruptly turned and left the office.

Bates leaned back in his chair, placed his hands behind his head, and smiled. Yes, he'd go to the conference and give a presentation. At least, that's what that arrogant bitch thought he would do. What they *all* thought he would do.

His blackberry rang.

"Bates here."

"Hey, you old dog."

He knew the voice immediately. Travis Cole. The two had gone to college together years ago and were fraternity brothers, but had taken different paths. Cole went into academic research while Bates... well, while Bates still took crap from snooty MBAs.

The two friends spent a few moments catching up, and Bates once again offered his condolences to Cole on the loss of his wife. When they finished the personals, Cole got right to the point.

"I need to know about MCD's new wireless chip."

Bates was slightly taken aback. "How do you know about our new chipset? It hasn't been announced yet."

"Never mind that," Cole replied. "Can we talk about it? It's important."

Bates thought for moment. "Look. I'm heading down to D.C. tonight to announce the new chipset at the INTEROP conference tomorrow. I'll be at the International Conference Center. Let's talk there, not over the phone."

"Good idea. Let's have dinner. On me."

"Of course it's on you," said Bates. "Call me. See you tomorrow." Travis said goodbye and hung up.

Bates sat back in his seat and crossed his arms over his chest. *What did Travis know?*

Washington, D.C.

Dee Dee Barton, an aspiring reporter intent on becoming a network TV anchorperson someday, knew a story when she smelled one. And her story was coming directly toward her in the form of a sweating and red-faced Michael Bates. His plane had arrived late, she knew, and he was now moving quickly through the airport to make up for lost time.

Working with a source from the convention, Dee Dee had gotten word of Bates's plans for a public and perhaps ground-breaking announcement on illegal government eavesdropping. Stories like that could make careers, so she immediately worked over her station manager for permission to surprise Bates at the airport. And, as was Dee Dee's style, she won.

As he came around the corner, huffing and puffing, she stepped in front of him, timing her appearance perfectly. Bates gasped, tried to pull up, but his momentum carried him forward and into her. She stepped to the side and he pitched forward onto his face. Dee Dee smirked. That had worked a little too well.

Knowing she had her prey cornered in a very literal way, she reached down for the fumbling man. "Mr. Bates, can you please shed some light on what you're announcing at your press conference tomorrow?"

Visibly agitated and trying to break away from the grip she

placed on his arm, Bates said emphatically, "You know what it's about. The notice has been out for weeks."

Dee Dee, as she was wont to do, ignored his response and plunged forward. She loved plunging forward. "It's rumored, though, that the press conference is related to government snooping on citizens…"

Bates looked up at her, panic on his sweating, ruddy face. "Where did you hear that? That's… that's not true!"

"Our sources say…"

Agitated, Bates said, "No comment! Now kindly let go of my arm."

Barton, who was freakishly strong, released her grip on his flabby arm and stepped in front of him as he tried to go around her. She said calmly, "Look, Michael. May I call you Michael?" She didn't wait for his answer, "Our sources tell us that your announcement will shake up the IT industry. Companies are involved. The government is involved…"

"What part of 'no comment' didn't you understand?" Bates barked, pushing past her and into a men's restroom.

She turned and watched him go, frowning. Why, she mused, had he looked so scared?

Alpha Mae was sitting at a Starbucks in the Dulles Airport watching the hustle and bustle of travelers passing through the busy concourse. As she gazed, she sensed the handsome young man behind the counter watching her… and not so discreetly, either. Alpha Mae was used to men watching her, especially when she wore this particular low-cut black blouse, revealing an ample—and, yes, fake—cleavage. Her tall slender Asian frame in black designer jeans and calf-high black boots added to her exotic looks.

She ignored the young man, although she appreciated his interest. At the moment, she had other things on her mind. *Maybe later.*

She wrapped her cold hands around her hot cup of coffee as she awaited her orders. She looked at her watch. It was almost time.

As she waited, she unconsciously scratched a raised tattoo on her shoulder. The black crescent moon covered an implanted microchip, a chip that all cell members of the Digitari Brotherhood carried. Used to track and even identify fellow members of the brotherhood, only Alpha Mae and her partner Yi knew its secondary function.

Her cell phone chimed. Her orders were here. Show time.

She flipped it open and looked at the faceplate. The blue display revealed a single word slowly, letter by letter:

C … Y … B … E … R … K … I … L … L

She smiled. The word had been given. She pocketed the phone and walked swiftly to the baggage claim area.

A squat Korean, Jung Yi sat outside the American Airlines terminal in the short-term parking lot. He was round enough to look like 'Odd Job' from the James Bond movie, but too short to be menacing. He had a bulbous nose with spidery veins—unusual for a man in his late twenties. His black coal eyes matched his wavy black hair, which was plastered with grease caused by over-activity of his sebaceous glands—the source of his acne problem as well.

He was dressed in a modified hip-hop outfit: baggy jeans, a t-shirt that went past his knees, fat-laced Pumas, and a Jim Beam baseball cap worn backwards. He had parked his nondescript blue sedan in a secluded area of the lot. Sitting discreetly on top of the vehicle was a dorsal-shaped Lucent antenna. A cable snaked from its rear into a wireless network card slotted into the laptop that sat beside him.

He popped a breath mint from his Uncle Sam PEZ dispenser and booted up the computer. Studying the display, he saw a network named 'dlsbgsys' present itself on the screen. The wireless network in turn saw him, assigned him an IP number, and he became a remote node on the network. Yi smiled, keyed in a few commands, and was soon into the airport's automated baggage sorting system.

He studied the moving schematic on the screen, following the journey of the small icons each representing a DCV—a destination coded vehicle—as it raced around the conveyors of the airport baggage handling system carrying and delivering passenger luggage. He found and concentrated on the junctions and sorting machines that delivered bags to the proper terminal and baggage carousels. Using information he had acquired when he hacked into the American Airlines reservations database, he located the bag of customer 5849-DL-0603: Michael Bates. With a few keystrokes, he detoured the bag to another terminal.

Task completed, he started the sedan and exited the parking lot.

Bates walked to the restroom entry and peeked out the doorway to see if he had succeeded in shaking off his pursuer. When the coast seemed clear, he continued his journey to the baggage claim area. Arriving, he studied the display above and located the carousel that would deliver his luggage. The display read American Airlines 1524 BC 3. He made his way over to baggage carousel 3, and with his fellow travelers, waited for his bag to appear.

And waited.

At the baggage claim area of a small air taxi service, Alpha Mae looked at each piece of luggage sitting on the floor and glanced at each baggage tag as she walked past them. Several pieces of luggage were there, and she was careful not to look too hesitant or draw attention to herself. She noticed two skycaps talking just outside the terminal to her right. They seemed to be on a smoke break and were casually looking at her. Alpha Mae was fairly sure they were interested in *her* and not her behavior. But she couldn't be too careful.

She turned and smiled at them and continued to scan the luggage at her feet. A moment later, she spied the target of her search. Throwing her hands up in an exaggerated gesture of discovery for the benefit of the watching skycaps, she bent down to read the name on the baggage tag: *Michael Bates.* She picked up the black, soft-sided Tourister luggage bag, turned, smiled at the skycaps, and walked in a leisurely fashion out of the terminal.

This is turning into a crappy day, thought Bates.

One by one, each of his fellow travelers reclaimed their possessions and disappeared from the terminal, leaving Bates waiting alone. After a few minutes, he wandered over to the baggage claim service desk to report his problem.

"May I help you, sir?" asked a young clerk with short, red moussed hair and a skin condition.

"My bag didn't show up," said Bates, not bothering to hide his irritation.

"May I see your claim ticket, please?" The clerk was green, but he knew the drill. "One bag only?"

"Yeah."

The clerk typed the ticket number into his computer. "Says your bag arrived with your plane. It was logged into the system here at Dulles. Should have showed up at the carousel."

"It wasn't there," griped Bates.

The clerk picked at a small zit on his chin and said, "We'll look into it. Shouldn't be hard to find. It's in the airport somewhere. We can have it sent to your home here in D.C."

"I don't live here. I'm here on business."

"No problem," said the clerk. "We'll have it sent to your hotel."

"When?" Bates demanded. "I need my suit for a conference tomorrow."

"No problem," the clerk said again. "Should have it by tonight. It's here, somewhere. Where are you staying?"

"I'm staying at the Grand Hyatt in D.C. Please have it sent to my room."

"Yes, sir," said the clerk.

Bates shook his head and walked away.

~

Alpha Mae flagged down the blue sedan that had been casually circling the airport. It stopped in front of her and the trunk popped open. She dropped the black Tourister into the boot, closed the lid, and slid into the passenger seat.

"That was too easy," she said simply.

Yi nodded, flipped back Uncle Sam's head on the PEZ container and popped another mint in his mouth. He offered her one. She shook her head sharply. He put the car in gear and they moved off into airport traffic.

~

Bates headed for the parking garage and found his OnStar-equipped Lincoln Town car. He flashed his rental agreement to the worker in the exit booth, and turned onto the access road to the freeway. He pressed the blue OnStar button next to his rearview mirror.

Almost immediately, a pleasant female voice chirped over the car speakers: "This is OnStar. My name is Marlow. How may I help you?"

"I need directions to the Grand Hyatt in D.C.," he said, feeling slightly foolish about speaking to his rearview mirror.

"Yes, sir," the female voice replied. "One moment, please."

After a short delay, the voice reported, "Merge onto I-95 south toward Washington. Proceed to I-495 and exit east."

Over the next thirty minutes, her instructions continued to guide Bates quickly and accurately to the hotel. He drove to the front of the building and stopped in front of the valet attendant.

"Any luggage, sir?"

Bates was about to reply with some satisfying profanity, but thought better of it. He just shook his head and proceeded to the registration desk. After going through the formalities of registration, Bates headed to his room.

He heard the phone ringing as he slid the magnetic key in the door slot.

A short Asian man dressed in an airport employee's uniform stood before the bell desk of the Grand Hyatt Hotel. In his hand was a black Tourister luggage bag. While the bellman spoke into the phone, he popped a mint into his mouth from a PEZ dispenser.

"Mr. Bates? This is the bell desk. Your bag has arrived."

"Have it sent up to my room, please."

"Of course, sir. I'll have someone bring it right up."

The bellman tapped the silver metal bell on his desk and a skinny bellboy appeared in front of him almost instantly. "Bring this bag to Room 812." He turned to the airport employee and dismissed him. "Thank you. We'll handle it from here."

Yi smiled, turned on his heels, and left. He noticed Alpha Mae sitting in a chair in the lobby with her cell phone at the ready, but didn't make eye contact with her. He walked straight past his companion and to the blue sedan parked at the valet curb.

~

The bellboy knocked on Bates's door. "Mr. Bates? I have your bag." But there was no reply. He knocked again and waited. After a third attempt, he unlocked the door and entered the room. He saw no one, but heard the shower running behind the closed bathroom door. He realized a tip was not forthcoming so he laid the Tourister bag on the bed and quietly left.

Bates appeared from the bathroom with a towel around his waist. There was his bag.

He smiled, then frowned, and stormed over to the suitcase for a closer look.

Damn it. Wrong bag.

Christ, can't these airlines do anything right?

On closer inspection however, he noticed that the bag was unlocked. Curious, he unzipped the top portion of the bag, flipped over the top and looked inside.

His eyes widened.

Okay, now *this* was a find!

Picking carefully through the bag, he inventoried the contents. There was a black latex halter-top, stiletto heels, a ring studded leather bra and panties, a whip, leather collar, wrist and ankle restraints—and a black hood. In a small silk pouch were some Ben Wa Balls and in the verbiage of the box it was in, a long plastic vibrating 'stress reliever.'

As Bates considered the wonder of it all, his phone rang.

"Is this Mr. Bates?" a voice cooed with a hint of an exotic accent.

"This is Michael Bates, yes."

"I'm really sorry to bother you, Mr. Bates, but it seems the airline made a teensy-weensy mistake," the voice continued. "I have your bag and I was wondering if perhaps you had mine."

Bates tried to be cool, but dammit, the sound of the over-ly-sensual voice on the other end of the line, coupled with his recent discovery of the bag's contents, conjured up all sorts of possibilities. Standing over the provocative items on his bed, he spoke in as matter-of-fact a voice as he could: "Yes, it seems so."

"Terrific! I'm here for the Lifestyles convention and I need the items in my bag for a show tomorrow."

"Lifestyles convention? What kind of lifestyle?"

"Why, the swinging lifestyle, silly," the voice giggled.

"Oh!"

"We're all free spirits there, though some old prudes think we're decadent," the voice said with a hint of a pout. "What do you think?"

"Um, I think that, uh, people should do what they like," he said, adding, "As long as it doesn't hurt anybody."

"If it feels good, do it. Right, baby?"

"Yeah, right," Bates said, laughing. Wow, his trip had brightened considerably.

"Look, doll, can I come over to your hotel and pick up my bag and exchange it for yours? I do need it. Though it's getting pretty dark out and it's starting to rain here. I'm staying with *friends*." She deliberately emphasized 'friends.'

Bates could only wonder how 'friendly' her friends were. "That won't be necessary," he said. "I could drop it off if you like."

"Would you?" the voice cooed. "That would be wonderful. Let me give you my address and directions to the house."

"Just the address will do," he said, catching himself before he said ma'am. *Why don't you just call her mistress, and get on with it?* He continued, "I won't need directions. My car is computer equipped to find you," he said in the most competent voice he could muster.

"A gentleman *and* a computer whiz," the voice cooed. "Okay, honey, here's the address. Now copy it down right. I don't want to lose you. Oh, and I'll certainly make the trip worth your while."

Quivering, Bates scribbled down the address, thrust it in his pocket, threw on his jacket and raced out of the room.

He returned a minute later to retrieve the bag.

With Alpha Mae sitting beside him, Yi stopped the car behind the hotel and handed Alpha Mae a box of CDs while he got to work entering the wireless network from his laptop.

"Find the disk," he told her, "while I locate the OnStar intranet."

"What does the disk look like?"

"It's white with the word *'god'* on it."

She gave Yi a queer look. Yi noticed and said, "That's with a small *'g.'*"

She shrugged and sorted through the CDs, quickly located it, and flipped it to him.

"How long will this take?" she asked.

"Not long. We should get permission fairly quick."

Yi loaded the program disk into the laptop's CD player. The player whirled for a while, displaying a challenge page when it connected to a distant server. Yi typed in his user name, then the password CYBERKILL. While he waited, he launched his AOL Instant Messenger.

He didn't have long to wait.

A short question from an unknown source appeared in his Messenger Box. "URL?" Yi typed in the URL of the OnStar intranet he had located the other day. A few moments passed. Then a second message appeared. "Access Granted." The hard drive light on his laptop blinked repeatedly for several minutes while the CPU processed the commands from the CD.

This wasn't the first time that OnStar would be a helpful tool for the Brotherhood. Buried deep inside the OnStar system is a feature few suspect—the ability to eavesdrop on unsuspecting motorists. A few years ago, the FBI found out about this passive listening feature and promptly served OnStar with a court order forcing the company to give it access. They wanted to eavesdrop on conversations between criminal elements in the OnStar-equipped cars.

But the FBI was not the only one with this technical savvy. Dorian, the shadowy figure who founded the Digitari Brotherhood, a figure even Yi and Alpha Mae had yet to see, also had this ability. Dorian, Yi knew, made it a habit to listen in on the various government agencies that used such vehicles, often recording their conversations. One recording between a deputy director of the National Security Agency and the head of R&D at a local biotechnology company was overheard.

"Then you've solved the problem of the nano-tubes, correct?" asked the NSA official.

"Yes. We've integrated the MEMS into the bio side of the tubes and they're communicating in binary logic."

"And the wireless chip sets? Deployed?"

"Yes."

"Good. When can the beta test begin?"

"As soon as we finish the code and program the dust. But we're having problems reducing the size of the code."

"Can they be overcome?"

"We think so. We're working on it. The results are positive."

"Good. Let's review SIRUS again and make sure we understand what's at stake."

As they spoke, neither one noticed the blue OnStar button blinking over the dashboard with a distant witness passively listening to their conversation.

"Won't be long now," Yi said excitedly. He popped another mint from the dispenser as his laptop beeped and the display on the screen changed color. A pop-up window appeared, mirroring the home page of the OnStar intranet.

"We're in."

Over the next few minutes, Yi located the company's list of OnStar-equipped cars in the D.C. area, and a few keystrokes later he had the ID number of Bates's rental car. He highlighted the ID number, pulled a map of the D.C. area down from his visor, hooked a headset into the laptop, adjusted the mic and winked at Mae. "Let's roll."

Washington, D.C.

It was raining, hard.

Bates had put the car in the right direction, heading south on Highway 95, but that was as much as he knew. With his wipers working overtime, he reached up and activated the OnStar service.

"This is OnStar. My name is Holly. May I help you?"

"Yes. I need directions to 253 Sequoia Road in...." he fumbled with the piece of paper in his hand ... "in Alexandria, Virginia."

"One moment, please," Holly said pleasantly.

After a short delay, the OnStar rep returned. "I see you're heading south on Highway 95. I want you to look for—" but before she could finish her sentence, a crackling sound squealed from the car's speakers, followed by silence.

"Holly, are you there? Hello?"

What the...?

The connection was dead.

Frowning, he pushed the OnStar button again. This time a male voice came over the car's speakers.

"This is OnStar. My name is Jay. May I help you?"

Bates thought that *Jay* was an odd name for someone with a heavy Asian accent, but he was probably being a bit prejudiced, and so dropped it.

"I was speaking to Holly when the connection went dead."

"I'm sorry for the inconvenience, sir," Yi answered. "We're having problems with the D.C. area. Seems there's a big storm out there. Wreaking havoc with our reception."

"Yes. It's raining pretty hard here." *I should have had that ditz come over to my hotel instead of going out in this.*

"Don't worry, sir. You're in safe hands with OnStar."

Wasn't that Allstate's shtick? Bates thought.

"So how can I help you, sir?"

Bates gave the address again and awaited instructions.

"First we have to get you off the 95," the OnStar voice said.

The rain was coming down in sheets; it was getting very difficult for Bates to see ten feet in front of him. He moved closer to the windshield and tried to get a better view of the road ahead, but it started to fog up from his breath. He tried to clear it with his sleeve, but it only made his visibility worse. He turned on the defroster. The fan whirled, but the windshield didn't clear any faster.

"Now, listen to my directions," Yi continued. "Get off the freeway at the next exit. Then drive straight for five miles until you see the sign to Dulles Airport. Got it so far?"

"Got it."

"Good."

The OnStar connection went dead. *Crap!*

Bates exited the freeway as he was told, pushing the OnStar button. Nothing. Broken.

He turned onto a new highway. He'd heard about the deteriorating infrastructure in the D.C. area, but this road looked well cared for and almost new. In fact, it *was* new. The streetlights weren't even installed yet. Bates strained to see the road ahead.

Can't see a damn thing.

He pressed the OnStar button, looked up, making sure he was pushing the right damn button and not one reserved for the automatic garage door opener.

When he looked back toward the road, he screamed.

Bates's car smashed through a wooden barrier blocking the freeway. He hit the brakes hard. Fractured wood cracked the windshield.

The car slid forward over the wet surface, slipping sideways toward the end of the unfinished freeway …

Bates continued screaming.

The car went over the edge… and abruptly stopped. The rear bumper of the Town car had snagged itself on one of the wooden barrier supports. Entangled in his seatbelt, Bates knew he had only seconds to extract himself before the car broke loose.

He promptly wet himself.

Oh, my God.

He undid his seatbelt, tried to push himself away from the dashboard, but his shifting weight only added to the pressure on the entangled bumper. It groaned behind him.

"Oh, God."

Bates carefully, slowly reached for the door handle, but to his utter shock the door lock suddenly *snapped* down, sealing him in.

What the hell?

As Bates struggled with the door, cursing and panicking, the wooden support keeping the car in place finally snapped. It followed the car down a hundred feet to the pavement below.

Washington, D.C.

"Mommy, Mommy! There's Mommy!" Shannon cried.

Cole looked away from the grocery store meat counter where he had been examining the price and cut of a half-frozen steak just in time to see his little daughter race off down the aisle.

"Shannon, stop," he yelled. Then louder. "Shannon, come back here. It's not Mommy."

As she ran, she turned her head and called over her little shoulder, "It *is* Mommy, Daddy! It is! I see her!"

Cole abandoned the meat and took off after her. He watched in embarrassment as his little daughter suddenly threw her arms around the waist of a tall, slim woman standing in line at the deli counter. The woman looked down in surprise.

Cole had to admit, with her long blonde hair and white cotton blouse and blue jeans, she looked remarkably like his wife and could understand his daughter's confusion.

"Hi, honey," said the woman, bending down. "Are you lost?"

"You're not my mommy," cried Shannon, and Cole could hear the anger and resentment in his daughter's voice.

"No, but I can help you find her," said the woman pleasantly, reaching for Shannon's hand, who yanked it away and stuck out her lower lip at the woman.

Cole finally caught up and took his daughter's hand. "I'm sorry, Miss," he said. "I'm her father."

"That's okay." The woman reached down and patted Shannon's head. "You're a cute girl."

Shannon turned her head away and buried it in Cole's side, crying hard. The woman, wide-eyed, looked up at Cole.

"She'll be okay," he said quietly, almost whispering. "Her mother passed recently."

"I am so sorry," said the woman.

"So am I," said Cole, turning away, his arm around his daughter's shoulders. "So am I."

Washington, D.C.

Joe Miller was reviewing some server logs from the past several days when he saw something strange. He sat forward on his couch in his small apartment. Frowning, he put out his cigarette.

Very strange.

Miller was a sysops for the Digitari Brotherhood and he was primarily responsible for permissions granted to users on the Brotherhood's server.

He sat forward, his frown deepening. Before him was a strange exchange between Yi and an unknown user. It wasn't unusual for Yi to ask for server access from distant locations. That was normal. It was the unknown user that perked Miller's interest—a user not on his master permissions list. Yet, he—or she—had access to the Brotherhood's server.

Interesting. No... *alarming.*

Miller decided to dig deeper to see if the unknown user had communicated with any other members of the organization. As he did so, he lit another cigarette automatically, blowing smoke up into the small, cramped room. He quickly searched through the server logs and found several instances of the mystery guest entering the server and interacting with a particular IP address on the computer network.

Funny, Miller hadn't caught it before. Perhaps the anomaly

had come to light because of the third party wireless network Yi had used last night. Whatever the reason, this was a serious breach of network security and Miller had to plug it, and fast.

Cigarette dangling from his dry lips, he quickly looked up the IP address and, to his surprise, found it belonged to Alpha Mae.

Why didn't she report this security problem?

She, more than anyone, knew the sensitive nature of the information on the organization's computers.

Miller dug deeper. He had to. It was his job. He started by running a report on all recent email activity in Alpha Mae's account. Maybe there was a message from the unknown user that would give Miller an idea who the user was and where he or she came from.

A few minutes later he had it.

In fact, he had several messages, but none contained an identifiable digital 'signature.' He opened one up to read, but found it was encrypted. Miller, of course, knew the organization's encryption keys.

And as he decrypted each email one by one, he became more and more alarmed by their contents.

The last one he opened gave an order for Alpha Mae to commit murder.

Washington, D.C.

Cole was upset and tried hard to control his temper. "Shannon! Come down here. Now!"

Not only did he make a useless trip to see Bates and cut short his time with Shannon, but now it seems she decided to perform a bit of creative vandalism to show her displeasure with her father's absence. Sitting on his PC in his study was the end result of Shannon's promise to use her graphics program—to ruin some of his favorite pictures of him, her and AJ, his girlfriend.

"Yes, Daddy?" Shannon said cheerfully as she appeared in the doorway of his study. But when she saw the displeasure on Cole's face, she obviously had second thoughts of entering the room.

"Come here, young lady."

Shannon moved slowly towards the computer screen as Cole pointed. "What's this?" he asked.

Shannon followed her father's finger to a Photoshop picture of her, Cole, and AJ. Cole knew the picture well. It was taken just a couple of months ago on a weekend at Virginia Beach. But the picture was defaced. Cole's body was gone and in its place was a teddy bear.

"Why did you do this, Shannon?"

"I... I... didn't."

"Shannon. You and I are the only ones in this house who have access to our home network," Cole scolded. "And *I* didn't do this."

She looked up at him silently, her lower lip trembling.

"I want an explanation, young lady," Cole said, already feeling himself melt whenever he saw that lower lip of hers tremble.

"It was Goppy, Daddy. Goppy did it."

Cole sat back, frustrated. Every time Shannon did something wrong, she blamed it on Goppy. "We'll take this up later. Auntie AJ will be here soon. Now go to your room and wait until I call you."

"Yes, Daddy," Shannon said, turning quickly, and racing down the hallway. She slammed the door behind her.

Goppy. Shannon's imaginary playmate was driving him crazy in reality.

~

The desk clock continued to click off the minutes as Cole went through some final papers for the beta test of Angel Dust for the IWL. He looked at the desk clock again. It was late. Shannon had to eat. He was about to call AJ when the doorbell rang.

Anna, his housekeeper hurried past his office to the front door. He heard a chatter of Spanish followed by laughter, and a few moments later AJ entered the study.

A stunning woman, Angelina Jacinta Olsen was of Portuguese descent. Fluent in Spanish, with dark brown almond-shaped eyes, she had Catherine Zeta-Jones looks and commanded respect without having to wear a "power suit" even for someone in her late twenties. Like Cole, AJ was an ambitious, career-minded person. He knew her goal was to rise as far as she could in the Bureau. When the war on terror commenced, she asked to be attached to the Department of Homeland Security working in their Department of Information Analysis and Infrastructure Protection. There, she would share the responsibility for identifying and assessing a broad range of intelligence information concerning threats to the U.S. homeland and taking preventive and protective action.

AJ was back now and Cole knew she would be eager to pick up where their relationship left off, and perhaps then some. He was a little nervous about the 'then some' part. It had been, after all, only a year since the death of his wife.

"Hi baby," she said, and kissed him full on the mouth. A long, lingering kiss.

Okay, maybe the 'then some' isn't so bad after all.

It was only six months ago when they ran into each other—literally. A minor fender bender. Cole in his SUV rear-ended her BMW. That led to the exchange of insurance information, an invitation for coffee across the street, then an exchange of phone numbers.

AJ pulled away from him, her arms around his neck. Cole's head was swimming. Other parts of him were swimming, too. God, he missed her touch. And yet...

He stepped back, ducking from under her arms. He sat down on the study couch and took a deep, shuddering breath.

She sat next to him. If she was offended by his sudden exit from her embrace she didn't show it.

"How's Shannon?" she asked him.

AJ always had a way of soothing him. He loved her for that.

Loved her?

Interesting.

"We're still having problems," he said.

"Did she have another episode?" AJ asked knowingly.

"Yes. Another stranger. Thought it was her mother. She does that every time she sees a tall blond woman. And now there's Goppy."

"Goppy?"

"Yeah. He's—at least I think it's a he—is Shannon's new imaginary friend. She talks about him constantly. This started a few weeks ago. I come home most nights and all she talks about is what she and Goppy did that day."

"Sounds innocent enough."

"But there's more," said Cole. "Whenever she does something wrong she blames it on Goppy."

"Ah," she said, squeezing Cole's hand. "Many children have imaginary playmates. I did."

"Oh?"

She nodded. "Uh huh. Mine was a little girl I called BoBo. She slept in my pocket and we'd travel together to all kinds of fascinating places." She turned a little red, and Cole found himself squeezing her hand back. "I think I read somewhere that children with higher than average IQ's tend to have imaginary friends."

"That's Shannon," said Cole. "And how did your parents deal with—BoBo?"

"Well, when I got to the point of demanding that BoBo get her own seat on a flight to Europe, I think my parents had had enough." She laughed, and so did Cole. "My parents finally took me to see a child psychologist."

"Did that work?"

She shrugged. "The shrink told my parents not to worry, and that BoBo wasn't a sign of a troubled mind, but a stepping stone in my emotional development." AJ leaned back on the couch smugly, playfully. "And see? I turned out all right."

"Well, that's debatable."

She hit Cole on the arm. "Shannon will be fine. Don't worry."

"Let me show you something." He led AJ over to the PC on his desk and called up the picture that Shannon had defaced. "What do you think of that?"

"It's Shannon and me a few months ago at Virginia Beach. Granted, I don't remember the cute teddy bear…"

"That cute teddy bear was once me. She replaced me."

AJ giggled. "That's cute. She thinks of you as a cuddly teddy bear."

"But she deliberately replaced me in the picture. I asked her why she did it and she said Goppy did it." Cole was miserable. He sat back down on the couch. "Any thoughts why she would replace me with a teddy bear?"

"Well, it's a whole lot cuter."

"AJ…"

"And softer around the middle."

"Are you quite done?"

"Okay, fine. Perhaps she's using it as a sort of surrogate. A temporary replacement."

"Of her mother? But wouldn't you… I mean… um, excuse me if I'm out of line, and I don't mean to put any pressure on you, and, well, I am certainly not in any position…"

"Out with it, Cole," AJ demanded. "You're stammering like a schoolgirl."

"Fine. If your scenario were correct, wouldn't *you* be the obvious replacement for her mother? Not that I'm asking you to replace her or any…"

"Look, Travis Cole," said AJ, bouncing to his lap and taking hold of his face in her hand. "I know you're having a hard time dealing with the loss of your wife, and I know you're not rushing out to buy me an engagement ring. I get it, okay? So let's just talk like mature adults here."

"Sorry," he said sheepishly. AJ had a great way of slapping him back to reality, and he loved—*appreciated*—her for that gift.

"How, exactly, did she die?" AJ asked suddenly, surprising Cole. "I mean, I know she was in an accident…" She let her voice trail off. This was the first time AJ had openly brought up his ex-wife's death.

Cole took a minute to gather his thoughts. "It was an accident. A *solo* accident. All we were told is that she ran off the highway and into a lake on her way to a family genealogy conference in Hartford."

Cole had an interest in genealogy. More hobby than vocation, he was tracing his family's history back to his ancestors in Norway. Coupled with his interest in genetic evolution, Cole was not only tracing his family's roots, but their genetic roots as well.

He continued; "We both planned to go to the conference, but I had to finish a grant proposal. The proposal could have waited, but I was afraid I'd lose the grant. It was very selfish of me." Cole paused and reflected on his last sentence. "So I told her to go alone and take my Corvette." He paused, looked away. God, he hated bringing up these memories. "It was a horrible night. Rainy and cold." Cole stopped and looked over at AJ. He knew there were tears in his eyes, but he didn't care. "I hold myself responsible for her death."

"Why?"

"The Vette's not easy to handle in the rain. It has a tendency to hydroplane and fishtail in a turn. If I had been the one driving..."

"Then you might be dead as well," said AJ gently.

Cole didn't think so. He thought he could have handled the Vette. In fact, he was sure of it. He decided to let the subject drop.

"It's not your fault, Travis," she continued. He nodded, but didn't say anything. Perhaps sensing his pain, AJ mercifully switched subjects. "Have you considered that you might be distancing yourself from your daughter?"

"What do you mean?" he asked.

"Shannon is a gifted child. Her apparent maturity may be confusing you. You may think you're giving her space to explore, but in fact, you may not be aware of how distant you appear to her."

Travis had never thought of that.

"But I encourage her to use a children's chat room. There her smarts is not an issue and she can speak intelligently to older children who don't care about her age. In addition, she can use the Internet to widen her interests."

AJ shook her head sadly, and Cole realized how lame that all sounded.

"Shannon is just a child, Travis. She's only five. She needs more than a computer. She needs a loving, caring father."

Cole's brain hurt. He hated dealing with emotions. Writing code was so much more... real.

He wanted to change the subject. Goppy had a way of depressing him. "How was your trip? Albuquerque, right? What did you learn out there at cop school?"

"It wasn't FBI stuff. HomeSec received a new edict on child

safety and we were trained on the ins and outs of the program. I was out there with my partner Bill Dixon."

"Child safety?"

"Yeah. It's called Operation Predator, a comprehensive HomeSec initiative designed to protect children from pornographers, child prostitution rings, Internet predators, stalkers, and the like. Out in Albuquerque, we were oriented and trained on how to work interdepartmentally with other agencies and private organizations."

She slid off his lap and took his hand in hers. She looked at him silently for a moment, then said, "Travis, there was another development out in Albuquerque." She paused, seeming to collect herself. "I was offered a position in Los Angeles. With the Bureau. Heading up one of their field offices."

Cole said, "I see."

"It's a good job."

"I see."

"What do you think?" she asked nervously.

"I think my head hurts."

She reached over and gently massages his temples. She smelled wonderful. God, it was good seeing her again. He hated her extended work-related trips. And the job in Los Angeles would be... a permanent trip.

"When do you have to make your decision?" he asked.

"Soon."

They were silent. She continued rubbing his temples. Cole didn't know what to say or do. Another of life's curveballs. Just when he was getting used to the idea of having AJ in his life.

"This sucks," was all he could think to say.

"I know," said AJ. "Want to talk about it later?"

"Yes." He was miserable as hell.

She stopped rubbing him and kissed him on the forehead. "Speaking of the little devil, where is she? I have something for her."

"Upstairs. Waiting for you. She's expecting a present, you know."

"I came prepared." AJ opened her purse and withdrew a small brightly wrapped box. "This is all the rage for sophisticated little five-year-olds on Capital Hill Estates." She put it back in her purse.

Cole grinned and walked to the door calling his daughter, who was downstairs in a flash. Shannon saw AJ, dashed forward and leaped into her arms, squealing with delight. They kissed and nuzzled and Cole could not believe she was going to leave him.

Shannon pushed AJ away at arm's length, and got down to business. "What did you bring me, Auntie AJ?"

Cole had to laugh.

"Was I supposed to bring you something?" asked AJ innocently.

"Yes! You said you would!"

AJ reached into her purse and pulled out the brightly colored package.

"Wait, what's this?"

And before AJ could get the last word out, Shannon had snatched the package from her palm, leaped down and within seconds had the wrapping off and the small box opened. Inside was a small sterling silver, turquoise, and coral butterfly bracelet. The butterfly in the middle was made of genuine inlaid turquoise and coral.

"It's beautiful," said Cole, looking over his daughter's shoulder.

AJ grinned up at Cole and squatted down in front of Shannon. "Like it, hon?"

"I love it!" Shannon replied gleefully and gave AJ a big fat kiss on the cheek.

"I bought it from an Indian princess out in New Mexico. Just for our princess."

AJ helped her put it on, and Shannon held up her little arm proudly. "Thank you, Auntie AJ. Thank you."

Anna appeared at the doorway. "Dinner's ready."

Cole watched the two of them file out of the room and as he followed behind, he was certain of one thing:

AJ wasn't taking that job in L.A.

Washington, D.C.

The dream was always the same:

Cole was somehow above the red Corvette, flying, hovering, following along. He couldn't quite see into the Vette, but he knew who was inside.

His wife.

The road was winding, the pavement slick with a pelting rain. Cole somehow stayed dry, even though he was out in the elements. His wife struggled with the wheel as the uncontrollable vehicle began to slide off the blacktop. She screamed; the car veered off the pavement and into the woods, careening over a grassy knoll and onto a half-frozen lake. The fiberglass sports car slammed the water, the front end shattering into fiberglass pieces, and turned over on its side, swirling and sinking into the frozen slush. She struggled vainly to open the door, but to no avail. She panicked, gasping for air as the passenger compartment filled with cold icy water and the Vette sank slowly beneath the bubbling, slate gray surface, entombed in the depths of the lake.

Cole woke, gasping, sobbing, tears streaming from his eyes.

After breakfast, Cole headed for the den to fetch his laptop and briefcase. But just as he left the room he noticed something odd on his PC. He walked back and saw that there was a virus alert flashing a warning. Cole frowned and sat down. The virus, he saw, was a particularly malicious one that could wipe out his hard drive. He wondered how it got there.

He called Anna, who was busy cleaning up the kitchen.

"Anna, there's a virus warning flashing on my screen? Do you know anything about it?"

"Shannon; she was down here early this morning."

"Thank you, Anna." He called his daughter downstairs. Shannon came skipping in, wearing her new bracelet proudly. She had been dressing for school, apparently, and was still in her little pink socks and Power Puff Girls underwear. She had a big smile on her cute face.

"Shannon, were you playing on my computer this morning?"

"Goppy and I were playing, Daddy," she said happily. "He showed me some really cool Power Puff Girls stuff on…"

"You downloaded something from the Internet, young lady?"

"No, Daddy. Goppy did. It's a neat Power Puff Girls Avatar Pack for my chat room. Goppy said…"

"How many times have I told you to never download programs from the Internet?"

Shannon's joy turned quickly to gloom. "I didn't, Daddy. Goppy did…"

"You are to never download anything from the Net without my permission. Is that understood, young lady?"

Shannon dropped her eyes to the floor and shuffled her feet. "Yes, Daddy. But it wasn't me. It was…"

"Then tell Goppy he can't either," Cole said in frustration.

"Yes, Daddy."

"Now get ready for school."

"Yes, Daddy."

Cole got his computer cleaned up and was about to head to the kitchen for a cup of coffee when the doorbell rang. He veered off to the front door and found John François looking pale and visibly shaken.

"I have some tragic news, Travis. Can we talk?"

~

In the study with the door closed, Cole guided François to a soft chair. "What's going on, John?"

"You remember Michael Bates? He was a student of mine?"

"And a frat brother of mine," said Cole. "I was supposed to meet him yesterday afternoon, but he didn't show up."

"That's because he died in a car accident last night."

"Oh my God."

"His car plunged off an unfinished highway interchange. He was killed on impact."

Cole was speechless. Unexpectedly, his dream from this morning flashed through his mind—his wife, the Corvette plunging into the lake, François's niece...

"Are you okay, Travis?"

"Yes, I'm okay," he lied.

"Well, there's more," said François. "But first, let me preface what I'm about to say. I'm Professor Emeritus of Cultural Anthropology at Georgetown University. A respected position. I can't afford to go around spouting conspiracy theories like some nut case. I have my academic reputation to think about."

"What are you getting at, John? And get to it. I'm already late..."

"Have you heard of Toad Adams?"

Cole frowned, then nodded. "The bitraker that streams a talk show online?"

"Yes, a conspiracy reporter. Sort of a cross between Geraldo Rivera and Matt Drudge. He webcasts the *Truth Report*. He's been harping on a cyber cult called the Digitari Brotherhood for the last several months."

"The Digi-who?"

"The Digitari Brotherhood. I've been studying them as well, as part of the cyber cult research I've been doing for my new book."

"Look, John. Can we discuss this later? I really need to get..."

"Please, Travis. Just give me a few minutes. I think this is important." His in-law looked at Cole earnestly. Cole couldn't begrudge the man a few minutes. He was upset and he was family, after all.

"Sure, but please make it quick."

"Okay, great. The Digitari Brotherhood. They're a fairly mysterious and secretive cult, although more and more info is getting out on them all the time. With that said, their leader has managed to remain unknown, although he goes by the name Dorian and appears only in IRC chat rooms that constantly change their relay channels to speak with his followers."

"John…"

"Hold on, I'm getting there. I promise. Adams writes, and my research confirms, that the Brotherhood is some kind of organization that wants to remove, or so they claim, the commercial and government's grip on the Internet. The Brotherhood says it belongs to the people and should be free of commercial and government influence. They posted a Manifesto of sorts a while back on a Usenet newsgroup. A rambling list of demands and the like."

Cole wanted to mention something about rambling, but kept his mouth shut. For now.

"But so far they haven't engaged in any known hacking or malicious attacks of any kind. Nothing of that sort. Just proselytizing."

Cole couldn't keep his mouth shut a moment longer. "John, what on earth does this have to do with Michael's death?"

"I got a call from Adams last night."

"And?"

"He read one of the papers I published in a journal on cyber cults last year and has been meaning to talk with me ever since. So he calls and we chit-chat, and after a few minutes he gets to his point."

Thank God.

"According to Adams, a wireless chip manufacturer in this country, in collaboration with the U.S. government, had conspired with authorities to snoop on its citizens. They, the Brotherhood, killed Bates before he could release this information in a press conference. Before he could, as they say, spill the beans."

"And where did Toad Adams get this information?"

"From a contact within the Brotherhood."

This wasn't adding up. Or maybe it was still too early for Cole's brain to be firing on all cylinders.

"But I thought the Digitari Brotherhood was against big business and the government. So why would they kill Michael if he's about to 'out the government' to the press? Michael was, in effect, helping this Brotherhood with its agenda. Correct?"

"Yes. That's how I see it, too. But their public agenda might be very different than their private one. Men don't just drive off one-hundred-foot freeway barriers. And Michael was going to make a major announcement soon at a news conference. Unfortunately, details of his announcement were leaked."

"That he was going to, as you say, 'spill the beans' on the government?"

"Exactly."

"John, this is all very fascinating, but why are you telling me?"

Cole was late and he was feeling irritated.

"You were friends with Michael. We both were. Besides, didn't you say you were going to meet with him yesterday?"

"Yes."

"Can I ask what about?"

Cole looked at his watch. "I wanted to ask him something about the company he works for." Cole quickly explained the incident in China, about the mysterious deaths, and the message that Taylor had received from her Russian brother-in-law.

"Many unexplainable deaths?" mused François. "It hasn't made the news yet."

Cole realized it hadn't, either. For the first time that morning he forgot that he was terribly late, he forget about his irritation with his rambling in-law, and realized that there might—*might*—be something to all of this.

"You came over here for a reason," said Cole. "And it wasn't just to let me know about Michael's accident, tragic as it is."

And to François's credit, he didn't deny it. "I want you to speak with Toad. You're both techies. You speak each other's language. I am but a simple old man."

Cole laughed. "Yeah, right. Fine, I'll speak with him."

"Thanks, Travis. And how is our little girl?"

Cole walked him to the door while updating him on Shannon—minus the Goppy incidents. And as the old professor left, limping down the walkway, Cole wondered what on earth he'd gotten himself into.

Washington, D.C.

Cole packed Shannon into the front seat, attached her seatbelt and headed for the pre-school. On the way there, he thought about the complexities of bringing up a little girl alone. He decided to have a talk with the director today about Goppy. Maybe she would have some ideas. Surely Shannon wasn't the only child at her pre-school who had an imaginary friend.

He parked the car in a metered parking place that had one of those new 'smart' meters. A new addition to that area of D.C., these meters had solved the problem of not having enough change. They took debit and credit cards, or you could call in your fee on your cell phone. Pulling out his cell, he punched in a toll-free number. Once connected, he entered his space and his credit card number and how much time he wanted on the meter. He entered thirty minutes just to be safe. His credit card was docked and an authorization was wirelessly beamed to the meter.

He bent down and kissed Shannon. He watched her run off to her assigned classroom while he headed up to the main office.

"Hi," he said at the front desk. "My name's Travis Cole. My daughter attends school here. I'd like to speak to the Director, please."

A young girl, no more than seventeen, scanned a sheet in front of her. "Shannon's dad?" she asked.

"Yes."

"I'll check and see if she's available." She left the desk and disappeared into the back of the building.

Cole looked at his watch. He was still running late and hoped this wouldn't take too long. The girl returned a minute later.

"It'll only be a few minutes. She's speaking to another parent right now. Please have a seat and she'll be right with you."

Cole sat and had just picked up a parenting magazine when his cell phone rang. It was Taylor at the Lab.

"Travis? Where are you? Bartley's having a cow. He wants to know where you are."

"I'm at my daughter's school. What's going on?"

"He wants to see all the materials for the beta test. He's imagining all kinds of problems. Please hurry in and get him off our backs."

"Alright. I'll be there as soon as I can."

Cole snapped his phone shut and walked over to the desk. "I have a minor emergency at work. Any chance the Director will be around later today?"

"She's here until four."

Cole nodded and left, wondering how the hell he was supposed to get out of work to be here by four.

He had just stepped outside the office when he saw something completely unexpected. A tow truck was pulling away with his SUV.

"Hey! Stop!" Cole screamed, running. He dashed along the sidewalk, keeping pace with the tow truck. He banged on the window until it stopped.

The passenger side window rolled down, and the truck driver leaned across the cab.

"Sorry, pal," he said automatically, obviously used to disgruntled car owners running him down. "We got a call to tow you away."

"Who called you?"

"Sorry, I don't know."

"And since when do you tow cars from paid parking spaces?" Cole demanded angrily.

The driver jerked his thumb backward. "Look again, pal."

Cole did, and from his vantage point he could indeed see the meter, although he was a few dozen yards away.

It read *'Violation.'*

What the…?

The driver leaned across the seat further and handed Cole a bent and dirty business card. "If you want your vehicle back, come down to this address. Pay the fine and you can take it away." And with that, he drove off.

With Cole's SUV.

And that's when he remembered that he'd left his laptop and briefcase in the back of the SUV under the security shield.

Cole opened his cell phone to call a cab.

There was no service.

Could this morning get any worse?

As Travis Cole stormed back into the pre-school's office, a tall man in a long overcoat and dark fedora stepped out of a phone booth across the street. The man watched Cole disappear into the school, and then turned and walked away.

Nearly two hours later—and a hundred-dollar cab fare poorer—Cole arrived at work. Almost immediately, he was summoned into Colonel Bartley's office where he endured a ten-minute rant on being tardy and the need to lead his team by example. Cole nodded along. He knew the drill. Bartley then wanted an update on Cole's project, and briefed on that, the man then went off on Dallas and his damn battlebots, the source of yesterday's lab fire. Cole was eventually dismissed with an admonition that he needed to stay on top of his team, and that his lab was no place for "goddamn toys."

As Cole shut Bartley's door and trudged down the hall toward his own office, he thought, *Hell of a crappy day.*

Taylor had taken a grievance day, and Cole didn't blame her. And somehow, in the process of telling Dallas that he needed to remove his battlebots from the lab, Cole had accepted an invitation to go to his first battlebot match tonight.

Sometimes it was hard working with nerds.

By the end of the day, all he wanted to do was go home, eat and relax with a science fiction novel. He liked the ones by Heinlein, Bradbury, Asimov, and other writers of the golden age of science fiction. On his way home, he got a call from François asking if he had time to meet with Adams. Cole checked his watch. No, he didn't have time, but he had promised Taylor and François that he would look into all of this.

Big mistake, he thought.

With scribbled directions in hand, Cole peeled off from the freeway and headed to Conspiracy Theory Central.

~

Cole pulled up to the indicated address and found François just arriving as well. Cole stepped out of his rental and whistled at the massive Victorian rising above him.

"Pretty comfy for a conspiracy nut," Cole said.

"He obviously isn't living on a university professor's salary," François replied. "I phoned ahead. He's waiting for us."

~

Toad Adams was a one-man show who broadcast *The Truth Report* from a tiny studio in his own home. The show was, in fact, streamed daily from his website, enabling him to instantly reach out to the faithful and fearful. His site included a collection of links to the top conspiracy sites, cover-ups, collusion and hidden secrets on the Net. Adams, who sat at the peak of the conspiracy pile with the likes of Michael Moore, was skilled at telling a little truth, the half-truth, and nothing but the slanted truth.

Today he was in his booth, streaming his show, ranting on his new favorite subject—the Digitari Brotherhood.

"I'm telling you," he was croaking into the mic, his voice completing the amphibian persona, "I know that this so-called Brotherhood is merely a front for the CIA or some other intelligence agency of the U.S. government. The Brotherhood is part of a vast military/industrial complex conspiracy to wage an ongoing war with China and Russia. A hacker war, a clandestine cyber war. Under the auspices of this government security agency, the Brotherhood recruits and trains hackers to not only wage this secret war, but to track and monitor those who seek to restrict the government's objectives." His voice went up an octave. *"They will resort to anything, even murder, to achieve their aims. I know. I was told."*

As Adams went through his rant, Cole and François were shown to the waiting room outside his booth, led by his burley bodyguard. Adams hired the bodyguard a few months ago when he started receiving one too many death threats.

They heard Adams wrapping up his session. "And I will continue to pursue this conspiracy and prove a corporate/government plot and its connection to the Digitari Brotherhood. Mark my words. I will pull together the pieces and you will know the truth." He ended with, "More tomorrow. Stay tuned."

Cole muttered to himself, *"Nutcase."* He gave François a nudge and nodded toward the door to leave. And he would have if Adams hadn't walked in to speak to them.

Cole watched the short, wide-shoulder man with a slightly sloping forehead step out of the sound booth. The man went straight to François, extending his hand.

"Welcome, Professor. Who's the gentleman with you?"

"This is Travis Cole. He's married to my niece. Well, was. She's passed."

Adams smiled sadly. His aggressive behavior shown on the air turned almost affable. "So what brings you here, Mr. Cole?"

Cole, who was already late to dinner, decided to get right to the point. "I'm here to find out what you know about Michael Bates," he said. "François says you might know who killed him."

"How did you know Michael Bates, Mr. Cole?"

"He was a very close friend."

"I see," said Adams. "What do you do for a living, Mr. Cole?"

"I'm a computer programmer."

"Which explains how you know Michael Bates."

"Yes."

"Would you like a drink, Mr. Cole?"

"Look, I'm kind of in a…" started Cole, but Francois nudged him in the ribs. "Sure, that would be fine."

"Good. Come."

In a large sitting room surrounded, of all things, by various X-File posters, Cole waited patiently as Toad Adams poured them each a shot of Kettle One vodka over soda water and ice. The short man handed out the drinks and then sat in an over-stuffed leather chair opposite Cole. To Cole's utter delight, this man, after taking a long pull on the drink, got right to the point.

"Yes, I know who killed Bates. Like I said on my show today. the government killed him." Toad Adams nearly smiled, and Cole realized that Adams was in his element, that he loved everything about conspiracies. Cole also knew people like Toad Adams often bypassed common sense in favor of a juicy, potential conspiracy.

"Why would the government have him killed?" Cole asked, noting with alarm Toad's matter-of-fact delivery.

"Not really the government, per se," said Toad, swirling the contents of glass. "Bates, you see, was working for a wireless chip manufacturer involved in highly classified work with a security agency of the U.S. government."

"Fine," said Cole. "Why, I repeat, was he killed?"

"Michael was going to blow the whistle on the operation. Unfortunately, his intentions were leaked to the press."

Cole's head was beginning to hurt. He managed not to rub it in front of the two men. "So what does this Digitari Brotherhood have to do with this?"

Toad smiled even further, his long thin lips stretching rather toad-like over his wide lower face.

"They, in fact, killed Bates. I have an informant within their ranks."

"And the Digitari are against government involvement in the internet?"

"I know where you're going with this, Mr. Cole. Why would

a subversive group support and carry out the nefarious plans of the very institution they are trying to subvert?"

"Yeah, something like that," said Cole, taking his first drink from the tumbler.

"Because there is something more going on here," said Toad triumphantly, sloshing some of his drink over the rim of his glass.

"Sort of like a conspiracy within a conspiracy," said Cole.

The Toad nearly leaped to his feet. "My God, yes! You have hit the nail on the head!"

"What, um, exactly did I hit on?" asked Cole.

"The Digitari, it appears, or at least some members of the Brotherhood, have other intentions."

"Which might be something other than to subvert the government?"

"It appears so," said Toad.

Cole said, "And this rogue group within the Brotherhood carried out the assassination of Michael Bates?"

"It appears so," Toad repeated. "I have proof."

"What kind of proof?" Cole demanded.

"I have inside information on the Brotherhood. That's all I can say." He looked around the room as if the walls were listening and said almost under his breath, "I have many enemies."

I bet you do, Cole thought. He had enough. "François, let's go. We're getting nowhere."

As Cole got up to leave, Adams whispered, "Mr. Cole. Have you ever heard of... SIRUS?"

"SIRUS? What's that?"

"That," Adams said with a devious smile," is what your friend was killed for."

Cole walked over to Adams and looked down at him. "And what is SIRUS?"

"That, my friend, is what we all would like to know."

Washington, D.C.

On his way back from visiting with Toad Adams, Cole called AJ. "Have any plans tonight?" he asked.

"I do now," she said.

He grinned. "I'll pick you up at seven."

"And where are we going?"

"It's a surprise."

"How should I dress?"

"Casual," said Cole. "Definitely casual."

"And will you feed me, too?" she asked.

"Ah, what the hell?" said Cole. "Why not?"

At home, just as Cole stepped into the house, Shannon came running downstairs. She gave him a big hug and the first words out of her mouth were: "Daddy, the Internet is down."

She said this, of course, as if her whole world had come crumbling down around her.

"Nice to see you, too, baby." He said hi to Anna, who waved at him from the kitchen, and with Shannon trailing behind him, went into his office and checked his computer. It was indeed down.

"It sure is, baby. I'm sorry."

She pouted and ran upstairs, mentioning something about Goppy. Cole hated Goppy.

~

Cole was in his closet, having just finished changing when Shannon came running into his bedroom.

"Daddy, they're talking about the Internet on TV."

She took his hand and dragged him into her bedroom, where he was surprised to see a news alert. A TV anchor person was talking.

"... across the entire DirecTV network. All systems were affected including our own local Internet provider DirecWay. No word from DirecWay as to when the network will be online again."

The TV screen returned to the Fox Cartoon Channel.

A newsbreak on the Cartoon Network? Cole was puzzled.

"What does it mean, Daddy? Can the computer work now?"

"No, baby. Not tonight."

Shannon pouted some more, and then her pouting turned to tears, and then she started to cry. Cole hated seeing his daughter cry. He had an idea.

He still had dial up. He found an old AOL disk in his desk downstairs. He loaded it onto Shannon's personal computer, and a few minutes later, after he had registered, she was, amazingly, back up on the Internet.

"Daddy, you did it!" She threw her little arms around him.

"It's not going to be as fast, baby."

"I don't care."

"Daddy is going to go out tonight with Auntie AJ. You mind Anna, okay?"

"Okay, Daddy."

"I want to hear you were a good girl tonight."

"Okay, Daddy." But she had already expertly launched the AOL browser and was soon online, oblivious to the rest of the world.

Cole shut the door quietly behind him. He gave Anna some

last minute instructions, paid her a week's advance salary, and left the house.

Online in the children's chat room, Shannon had chosen the 3D avatar she always used, a small figure modeled after one of the Power Puff Girls. Her screen name was BRAINY_BLOS-SOM. The children's chat room was a Shockwave 3D webpage where characters moved around the landscape and interacted with other characters. Chat balloons, like those seen above cartoon characters in a comic strip, appeared when someone typed remarks into the input box at the bottom of the screen. Only children were supposed to be allowed in the chat room and all who entered were pre-screened and monitored by the site staff.

When Shannon entered the site, she ignored the conversations going on in the virtual 3D playground and headed straight for the phone booth on the right side of her screen. This was where children could set up private chats with each other. Once in the phone booth, she 'dialed' a number by entering it into a special pop-up window. A moment later, a private 3D room appeared, filled with colorful images of candy, chocolate, and toys. Shannon waited patiently and after a few minutes a cuddly teddy bear avatar entered the room. Shannon's eyes lit up.

BRAINY_BLOSSOM: hi goppy im glad u r here

The little teddy bear just stood there, smiling and winking his eyes. Shannon held her breath and wondered if it was going to answer her. It did.

GOPPY: Why? Is something wrong?

BRAINY_BLOSSOM: im sad goppy my dad made me sad

GOPPY: Why?

BRAINY_BLOSSOM: he didnt want me to talk about u every time u do a bad thing my dad yells at me

GOPPY: I'm sorry.

BRAINY_BLOSSOM: do u have lots of freinds goppy

GOPPY: Just you.

BRAINY_BLOSSOM: o i love u goppy

GOPPY: I love you too. I wish we could talk and play more but my parents don't like me talking online so I have to do it when they are not home.

BRAINY_BLOSSOM: my dad lets me talk online but he doesnt like me to talk to u

GOPPY: Why?

BRAINY_BLOSSOM: he doesnt like u he wants me to find other freinds like at school but i dont like the kids there they make fun of me i like at play with u

GOPPY: I wish we could really play some day. Wouldn't that be fun?

BRAINY_BLOSSOM: yes

GOPPY: Then maybe we will. How about a picnic now? We could talk and play. I have all the stuff you like to eat.

BRAINY_BLOSSOM: ok

Washington, D.C.

After dinner at their favorite Italian place in D.C., Cole was coy about where they were going next, despite AJ's many requests. He only promised her a rip-snorting good time.

Cole pulled off the highway and into what appeared to be an abandoned section of a small airport.

"Travis, where are we?"

Cole grinned and pulled up to a large dilapidated metal building displaying a washed-out sign with faded letters that read Hangar A. He parked in a haphazard row of dozens of other vehicles in the weeds and dust.

"Now will you tell me what we're doing?"

"Have you heard of battlebots?" he asked cryptically.

"Battle what?"

He explained the concept of robots battling robots. AJ looked skeptical, and Cole knew she had to be thinking—*I gave up my night for this?*

"C'mon," he said. "It'll be fun. In the least, we can support Dallas. It's his first match."

He led her inside the building, past spools of electrical wire, duffel bags full of tools, and a clutter of other gear. The sound of power tools and ratchet wrenches filled the air as Cole eyed the bizarre collection of mechanical warriors scattered around the outside of the arena. Their owners were busy giving their mechanical progeny some last minute tweaks and touch-ups in preparation for competing.

The interior of the hangar had been transformed into a certified geek convention. Geeks with devastating toys, as each of the battlebots were designed specifically to cause as much damage as possible to its opponents. AJ eyed the mechanical warriors, holding tightly to Cole's arm.

"Hello, Mr. Cole," said a haunting, digital voice. Cole turned and found him face-to-face with the four-foot tall Isaac, the pride of Dallas' robotic creations.

"Hello, Isaac," said Cole pleasantly.

"Did that thing just talk?" asked AJ, squeezing Cole's arm a little tighter.

"That's Isaac," said Cole. "He's a Honda ASIMO robot."

"No kidding," said AJ.

"Hello, ma'am," said Isaac, extending his hand.

"Go on," said Cole, grinning. "Shake it. He won't hurt you."

AJ tentatively reached out and took hold of the proffered metallic hand, complete with five digits, one of which looked remarkably like a thumb. "Hello, um, Isaac. How are you?"

"I'm doing very well, thank you."

"Polite bugger," said AJ.

"He'd better be," said a voice behind them. They turned to see Dallas approaching, sporting a wide smile. He wore a black t-shirt that had yellow letters on the back. It read 'Delightfully tacky—yet unrefined.' Cole knew his co-worker was in his element, a fellow geek among geeks and robots. "I programmed him to be polite, especially to pretty ladies."

AJ blushed a little. She still hadn't released her grip on Cole's arm.

"So what's Isaac doing here?" asked Cole.

Dallas leaned in a little, a twinkle in his eye. Cole thought he smelled of grease.

"Isaac's going to win the bout for me tonight."

"What do you mean?" asked Cole.

"I programmed him to command the battlebots himself."

"Huh?"

Dallas jerked his head and led them to a quiet corner. Isaac, in its slightly creepy fashion, followed obediently, taking short, perfect steps. Cole noticed that AJ kept a wary eye on the four-foot high robot.

"Your common everyday battlebots are just glorified remote control cars that use off-the-shelf RC controllers," explained Dallas. "The controllers can be difficult to manipulate, especially if you have to make decisions fast, usually too fast for a human to make. So I programmed Isaac to make those decisions for me and control the battlebots. You see, Isaac is programmed to learn—and learn quickly. By watching the bout and responding to a competitor's moves, Isaac can learn and re-learn the moves necessary to defeat any opponent. Should work like a charm!"

Cole was skeptical. He personally knew that such programs required a very high level of complexity. After all, this is what he did for a living. "And you programmed him do this?"

"No, not quite," Dallas said a little sheepishly. "Actually, *you* programmed him to do this."

Cole wasn't sure he'd heard correctly. "*I* programmed him?"

"In a manner of speaking… yes. I took some of your programming we used for our… project, and sorta adapted it to Isaac."

Cole was immediately furious. He grabbed Dallas's elbow and pulled him off to the side, away from AJ.

"Damn it, Dallas, you broke several national security laws and…"

"I know, I'm sorry, Travis."

"We could get in a lot of trouble over this."

"Who will know?" said Dallas. "But on a positive note your CA programming is working perfectly."

"Don't try to change the subject—did you say perfectly?"

Dallas slapped his supervisor and friend on the back. "Of course," said Dallas. "You're the best."

Appeased but still pissed, Cole allowed Dallas to walk them over to the battle arena. They found a place to sit in the grandstand, now filled with hundreds of spectators. To Cole's surprise, AJ seemed to be getting in the mood a little. He loved that about her—her ability to adapt and make the most of any situation.

"And they fight in there, huh?" she asked.

"Yep," said Dallas. "The BattleBox. Engineered for maximum safety on the outside and supreme torture on the inside. That fifty-by-fifty baby is a thirty-five-ton thunder dome where the bots do their battling." He paused for effect. "Some never to return," he added ominously.

AJ laughed and sat forward. "What are those holes and doors on the floor?"

"Those," said Dallas, "add a little wrinkle to the competition. The arena floor is rigged with various traps and hazards, saws and hammers and ramrods…"

"Ramrods?"

"You'll see."

He continued. "So your bot not only has to avoid your opponent, but also the booby traps in the floor. A smart bot driver—and Isaac will be the smartest—uses the arena to his advantage, working it against his opponent." Dallas looked at his watch. "Okay, gotta go get my bots ready. Be back shortly.

Deputy Director Safko looked at the ornate U.S. Marine anchor and eagle pewter clock on his desk. It read 6:45 p.m.. It was time.

He picked up the receiver of his desk phone and punched in a set of numbers not contained in the phone's memory. There were a series of clicks as the phone instrument prepared itself for an encrypted call.

As he waited to connect, Safko's attention turned to a small plaque on his desk. He picked it up and read the words inscribed: *The Mission of the NSA—to secure the nation's communications while exploiting foreign signal intelligence.*

How simple the directive, thought Safko, but how complex its execution in today's world.

"Times are different now, congressmen," he remembered saying to the NSA's Senate Oversight Committee many months ago. "Today's telecommunications industry has leveled the battlefield between our enemies and us. Our adversaries can take full advantage of a technology of cell phones, fax machines, the Internet, emails, and encryption. The hi-tech advances available to almost anyone have forced the Agency to recognize that we no longer have the technological advantage. It is *change*, continuing *change*, inevitable *change* that is the dominant factor in society today, senators. No sensible decision can be made any longer without taking into account not only the world as it is, but the world as it will be. Our friends today can be our enemies tomorrow. Mojahedin morphing into Al Qaeda. Allies becoming adversaries."

Those last words, he thought, became the impetus for SIRUS.

"Bartley here," the voice on the other end of the line was loud and clear.

Safko was pulled from his thoughts. He put the plaque down. "Are you in the control room now, Colonel?"

"Yes, and I'm alone. The room is sealed."

"Good," said Safko. "Activate Phase One of the SIRUS network."

In the control room at the IWL, Bartley ran his hands over the room's console. The digital map of Washington D.C. that was displayed above for the upcoming beta test morphed into a polar projection of the world. The map showed thousands of tiny little red dots on all six continents. Bartley typed in a series of commands.

Immediately, the red dots in China turned green.

Washington, D.C.

Thirty minutes and three bouts later, after witnessing all kinds of mechanical mayhem, Dallas appeared and took Cole and AJ to the bot staging area.

"Let me introduce you to my little creations." Dallas pointed to the two battlebots at his feet. One battlebot stood low to the ground with a wide wheelbase made up of five rubber wheels on each side. "This little one is named BattleScar Galactica. Notice the vertical high carbon steel saw blade it presents to an opponent. The blade is powered by a high torque motor designed to provide maximum power to Galactica."

"To inflict the greatest amount of damage," AJ interrupted excitedly.

"Yes!" said Dallas, beaming. "Exactly. And this one here is my favorite. American Armageddon. It even has the judges worried. He's tall, big, and ugly and has a compressed gas tank that powers the hammer you see coming out of his center. *Armageddon* could put a big dent in the BattleBox's solid steel floor if I'm not careful."

An announcement over the PA system summoned Dallas to the staging area. "Gotta go! Wish me luck! Time to kick some bot!"

Cole rolled his eyes. He and AJ made their way back to the

grandstand. Soon Dallas entered the BattleBox and placed *Armageddon* on a red square while his competitor placed his bot on a blue square, the designated starting points. According to the announcer, Dallas's competitor was named DreadBot, a 325-pound super-heavyweight robot. This particular beast of mayhem was built from surplus military aircraft hydraulic pistons combined with custom valving and CO_2 gas to produce several tons of flipping force in a few hundredths of a second.

"Boys and their toys," said AJ, giggling. She was clearly getting into this, and he loved her for it, although he wasn't ready to admit that to her just yet.

Dallas was animated with excitement. This was his first match, his first bout. He could hardly wait to see how his own bots held up to those of his competitors.

He, of course, had an edge.

At the judge's instruction he took his spot at the controller's stage. There, waiting for him like a loyal dog, was the robot Isaac. Dallas handed the robot the controls.

Let the games begin, thought Dallas.

Dallas's rival was a short, rail-thin man with a pony tail wearing a black *Rage Against the Machine* t-shirt. Seeing Isaac standing where Dallas should have been, he immediately protested. There was a brief—and heated—discussion with the judges. Ultimately, they ruled in Dallas's—and Isaac's—favor. After all, there were no rules against one robot controlling another robot.

Grinning, Dallas sat with the others in the bleachers, just behind the protective glass.

A loud claxon horn signaled the start of the match, and brought Isaac to life, as he had been programmed to do.

Even from here, Dallas could see Isaac manipulating the radio control to perfection. In response, *Armageddon* moved effortlessly around the arena, easily avoiding its opponent's thrusts and attempts to flip it over. Not only was Isaac able to quickly parry

Dreadbot's attacks, but the bot also glided around the floor-traps that sprung up intermittently during the bout.

At Isaac's perfect instruction, Armageddon was soon on the offensive, its devastating hammer repeatedly damaging its opponent. Dreadbot was now moving slowly and erratically, smoke trailing behind it.

Dallas was excited. This was working better than he could ever have expected.

No one can beat me, he thought. *Not with Isaac at the controls.*

And then it was time. Dreadbot was pinned against the wall, pulverized and nearly out of commission. Dallas grabbed Cole's arm, excited. This was it. Cole shrugged his friend off him, although Dallas hardly noticed. Instead, he was watching eagerly as Armageddon raised its devastating hammer high into the air.

Do it, thought Dallas. *Smash it to pieces.*

But nothing happened. The hammer never moved.

"What's going on ?" Dallas remarked.

"What's wrong with Armageddon?" asked AJ.

"I have no idea," said Dallas.

And just as he uttered those words, something very strange happened. Armageddon abandoned its wounded adversary and turned around, facing the audience. Dallas immediately looked over at Isaac and saw that it had dropped its head and both arms. The robot had seemingly turned itself off.

And yet... yet Armageddon moved forward toward the protective shield, raising its hammer.

"Something else is controlling the bot," said Dallas. "Something is wrong."

And then Armageddon was moving faster. AJ squealed as the heavy bot smashed into the Lexan wall, rebounding off it like a rubber ball. The bot gathered itself once more, moved forward again, and crashed hard against another portion of the wall.

"*Very wrong,*" Cole added.

The crowd nearest the protective shield scattered. Others

were standing and pointing. Cole had just stood, surprised by the sudden turn of events, when his cell phone rang.

No. Someone *else's* cell phone was ringing.

And then he realized everyone's cell phones were ringing. At once. Together. In unison. In a matter of seconds, the entire hangar reverberated with the sounds of shrieking cell phones and beepers.

AJ grabbed his arm. "Cole! Look!"

He saw it, too. The cell phones weren't the only things that had come to life. Rumbling out of the staging area from behind the center combat arena and toward the audience were dozens of battlebots, all with their weapons armed and ready.

Washington, D.C.

This isn't happening, thought Cole.

Cell phones ringing, noise and panic, and all those damn creepy bots had seemingly come alive in unison. Cole felt like he was suddenly trapped in a very bad B-movie. Apparently, so did many others in the grandstand, many of whom were quickly making their way toward the building's exit, their phones ringing all the way.

Probably not a bad idea, he thought.

But the crowd in the stands weren't so lucky. There was only one way down, a side stairway, unless Cole wanted to crawl over other spectators' heads.

That will be plan B.

"Let's say we get the hell out of here," said Cole, taking AJ's hand and pulling her toward the crowd exiting the stands.

"Wait," said AJ, stopping him. She calmly scanned the area. The crowd was clogging the main entrance, some nearly trampling each other. "Let's look for another way out."

Cole loved that about her—cool under pressure. *Analyze her pros and cons later, Cole*, he thought. *For now, let's get out.*

"There's another exit," said Dallas behind them, pointing over Cole's shoulder. "Over there. The service entrance."

Cole saw it, and apparently so did a handful of others, who

were dashing to it. For now, it was the best option. Still, they had to get off the grandstand. Behind him, impatient bodies pushed him. Cole pushed back, making sure he and AJ weren't trampled themselves.

Before them, like a small, weird army, the battle bots approached, spinning and turning and drilling.

This is surreal!

And still his cell phone rang. Continuously. Cole was tempted to look at the number on the cell's faceplate.

But before he could, the arena and stands were plunged in near total darkness.

Crap!

The building, already poorly lit, was now nearly unnavigable in the dark. Some in the crowd screamed. Cole was pretty sure he wasn't one of them.

He felt Dallas's strong hand on his jacket sleeve. "Just follow me. I'll find a way out."

In the near dark, they pushed their way down the spectator seating. Finally, they reached the polished floor. Holding on to Dallas's jacket with one hand and AJ's hand with the other, Cole blindly followed his co-worker. In the near distance, he could hear the rattling of the bots coming closer.

Should I be afraid? he wondered. *Or laugh?* Being drilled to death by something called the Dreadbot hardly seemed fair.

He nearly laughed. Except that the three of them were running blindly through the mayhem in the massive hangar, and to be honest, he didn't feel like laughing. He just wanted to get away, away from anything associated with these murderous creatures.

There was a muted light ahead, something battery powered. The exit sign!

"C'mon," said Dallas. "This way!"

He angled toward the sign which, the closer they got, Cole could see was illuminating a heavy steel door.

God, get us out of here!

They were closing in on the door and Cole could almost smell the fresh air, when someone stepped in front of them, blocking the way. No not someone. Something.

It was Isaac.

You've got to be kidding me.

The smallish robot stood in front of the three—somewhat ominously, Cole thought—and slowly raised his robotic arm extending a mechanical finger toward Cole. The robot's eyes were glowing red behind the faceplate.

"I don't think he likes you," said AJ.

"I think you might be right," said Cole. Then to Isaac, "What did I ever do to you? Granted, we've never been friends, exactly…"

"Isaac, stand down!" Dallas said.

"Don't bother," said Cole, moving forward. "Let's go around him—or it, or whatever."

"Hold on, Cole," said Dallas. "Isaac is surprisingly strong. Slow, but strong."

"I don't care…"

"If he gets hold of you, he could easily crush your arm."

"Fine," said Cole. "But why would he do that?"

"Something's wrong with his programming," said Dallas. "Hell, with all the bots' programming."

"Even the lights and cell phones," added AJ.

"Exactly," said Dallas. "There's something bigger going…"

"Fine," said Cole again. "Then explain why he's advancing toward us now."

"Isaac, stop!" ordered Dallas. But the smallish robot kept advancing.

"Anyone feel like we're in a scene out of *Star Wars*?" said Cole.

But no one answered. Cole noticed that AJ had moved behind him, holding onto his jacket. Cole, in turn, wanted to move behind Dallas, but resisted the urge.

To his credit, Dallas stepped forward. "Stop, Isaac! I said *stop!*"

"Um, Dallas… you might not want to do that," said Cole. Behind him, he heard the other bots rolling through the hangar, cutting and hacking at who knows what. He certainly hoped *not people*.

Maybe they're hacking each other to pieces. Then again, maybe this is all a bad dream.

Isaac continued forward. To Cole's shock, Dallas picked up a heavy wrench at his feet and approached the little robot.

This should be good.

Still, Cole was impressed by his co-worker's bravado. The kid wasn't just a tech nerd.

Dallas placed himself between Cole and the robot, raising the wrench into the air. But instead of attacking, Isaac suddenly stopped in his tracks. His eyes turned a mellow amber and he dropped his arms to his sides, his head tilting forward.

"Thank you, Dr. Asimov," Dallas said in relief.

"What do you mean?" asked AJ.

"It's the First Law of Robotics," said Dallas, revealing the nerd that he truly was. "A robot may not injure a human being, or through inaction, allow a human being to come to harm. I programmed him for that."

"I see," said AJ. "Now can we get the hell out of here?"

Almost on cue, the lights turned back on and the cell phones stopped ringing. Cole turned and saw a crazy scene before him. A dozen or so battlebots were spread over the hangar floor. Some had sawed through the stands. Others had drilled through each other. Mostly, the place was empty.

"Let's go," said Cole.

"Actually, guys," said Dallas, "I'm going to stay behind. I want to figure out what on earth happened."

"Suit yourself," said Cole. "But you can bet I will never be back here again."

"Ah, don't be a baby, Cole."

Pulling AJ behind him, Cole pushed through the exit door and flipped Dallas the bird without looking back.

⁓

The hangar parking lot was a zoo. To Cole, it looked like the parking lot after a Led Zeppelin concert. With her customary coolness, AJ joined the fray, forcing her slick BMW into the rush of cars, ignoring the blaring horns.

"Cole," she said, smiling, "Could you turn the radio on? Might be something on the news about all of this. An electronic meltdown like this should make the news."

He goofed with the buttons, accidentally turning on her GPS guidance system, and finally figured out the radio. BMW and its toys! He tuned into a local news channel. Yes, there was something on the news.

"... and the interferences and outages, officials said, affected all wireless devices including cell phones, and any kind of device connected wirelessly to each other or to a network. In other news, China announced today that a new outbreak of the SARS virus appeared. This one, they report, is of an entirely different strain and very potent. It seems to have appeared in a local village and spread rapidly. The Chinese government claims they can contain it. Many are reported dead."

The station went to a commercial. Cole switched to another channel, a nationally syndicated talk show, where he discovered a computer security specialist was being interviewed by the host.

"I would have to say that since this attack was not just a local or national phenomenon, I believe that someone has found a way to create a very potent virus to infiltrate our wireless networks throughout many parts of the world. Something like this was not unexpected, of course, but one on this scale and scope... well, that is surprising."

AJ glanced at Cole. "Did he say *worldwide*?"

"Yes, he did," said Cole frowning. "Yes, he did."

AJ pulled out of the hangar parking lot and onto the main road. She picked up speed, eager, obviously, to get away from there. Cole didn't blame her.

NSA Headquarters
Washington, D.C.

It was late evening, and Josh Leighton was standing in Deputy Director Safko's office again, holding a memo in hands that were visibly shaking. Leighton was beginning to dread coming into this office. He was also beginning to regret agreeing to help Safko on this secret project. In fact, he was most definitely beginning to worry about his own safety.

"Read the memo," Safko ordered.

The young programmer focused his full attention on the communiqué with EYES ONLY stamped in red on the top and bottom of the single sheet. The words were all in large-font caps. As he read them, Leighton's fear and dread reached a new, sickening level.

"TIANJIIN PROVINCE... HUNDREDS DEAD... GENETIC MUTATION... DEATH FROM THALAS-SEMIA... CHINESE RESIDENTS ONLY..."

The young programmer looked up from the communiqué. He could feel the blood draining from his face.

Did it say hundreds dead? Oh, God...

"I don't understand," he said, stammering the words. "What... What does this have to do with me?"

Safko stood suddenly, intimidating Leighton with his considerable size. The director leaned across the desk, his weight on his clenched fists. The man's face, already red and blotchy when Leighton had arrived, was now nearly purple. A vein pulsated on his forehead.

"It executed, you son of bitch! Your goddamn code *executed!*"

The code. Jesus, what had happened? Impossible!

"Deputy Director, I don't know what to say. This can't be possible…"

Hundreds dead? Leighton felt bile rise from his stomach and tasted it at the back of his mouth. He was going to be sick.

"Your job was to give the code the *ability* to execute. Not the command to do it. What happened?"

Leighton couldn't believe it. Was he responsible for the deaths of hundreds of Chinese? How could that be?

"I don't know, sir. I'll have to look into…"

"Do it," Safko said, cutting him off. "Now."

Leighton stood and quickly vacated the Deputy Director's office. As he shut the door behind him, he was all too aware that there were cameras everywhere in the various offices.

They're watching me, he thought. As he sat at his desk, with most of the day crew gone and only a handful of the night employees on call, he picked up a picture of his beautiful fiancé. He had an even more disturbing thought. *They're never going to let me live.*

~

Hundreds dead? Oh, God.

What went wrong?

Safko was standing in front of his desk. Through his window he could see Leighton at his own desk. The kid had better be working hard. And he had better be religious. He was going to need a lot of prayers.

All we did was activate the network, Safko mused. *Send a simple command to report the communications status of SIRUS.*

And then everything went to hell. Yeah, say that to the dead Chinese…

Alright, they'll deal with it. They'll shut SIRUS down until this bug can be fixed.

Just another goddamn delay.

He turned his attention to another pressing problem—the logs and captured code of the wireless malfunction that evening. He knew they were connected to the incident in China, but the Agency couldn't sit on them for long. Too many questions were already being asked from the Senate Committee, HomeSec, and the White House. He had to release the logs to the IWL for analysis.

Safko hated playing by the rules, but in this case, he had to. *Damn it!*

Washington, D.C.

It was near midnight. The moon was hanging low over the Potomac when Colonel Arden Bartley, Director of the Information Warfare Laboratory, pulled into the parking lot of BioNan headquarters. Admittedly, Bartley was only going through the motions of driving. In reality, his mind was on anything but driving. Dust, dead Chinese, and computer programs gone wrong, to name a few.

And what had caused all that interference tonight? he wondered. He didn't know, and he didn't like it. Cole and his team were going to figure it out, one way or another.

One way or another.

BioNan was a private corporation situated on the 200-acre Biotechnology Research Park in Virginia, fifty miles south of Washington D.C. The BioNan complex consisted of both offices and laboratories where advanced nano-technology research was done, and where the nano-dust for Project Angel Dust was manufactured. Bartley walked up to the entrance, showed his ID card and was soon shown into the office of Jerry Webster, the BioNan Vice-President of Research and Development, a good-looking man in his early thirties. Webster wasn't alone. Standing with him was Deputy Director Safko.

"We've been waiting," Safko said. "Have a seat."

Bartley took a seat next to the NSA Deputy Director. The room itself was streamlined, modern, efficient, and contained a large green-tinted picture window at one end that overlooked the BioNan grounds. Webster's black leather ergonomically-correct chair sat behind a modern-looking aluminum and dark wood desk that had none of the usual items you would find on a busy engineer's desktop. It was, in fact, almost sparse.

There was a plastic *Please Do Not Smoke* sign on Webster's desk, but Bartley ignored it. He moved it aside, lit a cigarette, leaned back casually in his chair and directed his attention to Safko. The Deputy Director sat down, pulled an envelope from his suit jacket, opened it, and handed it to Webster.

"What's this?" asked Webster. There was sweat on his brow.

"Read it," Safko ordered.

Webster looked at the one-page document in his hand, frowning. The sweat on his brow coalesced into bright beads.

"Your dust is responsible for that," Safko said. "Questions have been raised, including inquiries from outside the Agency. We—" and Safko looked over at Bartley, "—had to work fast to contain it." Safko leaned toward Webster.

"I don't understand..." stammered Webster. The sweat had begun to move down his Pierce Brosnan face.

"We want to know what happened," asked Bartley.

"Our dust is perfect," said Webster. And now the vice-president of BioNan went from looking queasy to indignant. He tossed aside the memo and pointed a well-formed finger at both Bartley and Safko. Bartley hated to be pointed at. "If I was looking for a go-to guy on this I'd look no further than your office, Safko. It was your programmer who modified the code. I'd ask him what happened."

Safko leaned back in his chair. "Can't. He's gone."

"Gone; what do you mean?"

"When we informed him of the incident in China, he disappeared."

"What incident?" asked Webster.

Safko handed the Top Secret communiqué that he had shown Leighton.

"What's this?" And now Webster was back to looking queasy. In fact, he looked downright sick.

"We don't know for sure," said Safko. "Only that SIRUS executed. And now my programmer is gone and we don't know where. We have the FBI looking for him." He looked over at Bartley. "Stealing sensitive material, right?"

Bartley nodded. Webster shuddered. He knew of the reputation of the NSA and its more clandestine side. The NSA was the only U.S. intelligence agency that had immunity from government accountability. Its secretive reputation and activities were the things that separated the NSA from its sister agencies like the CIA and FBI and earned its reputation as the most secretive organization in the world—and rumored to be one of the most dangerous to cross.

Webster didn't even want to think about the fate the young programmer was about to encounter.

"You know about this nano stuff," replied Safko. "I want you to look over the code and find the glitch."

"How do you know the code's the problem?"

"What do you mean?"

"I mean, what if the problem was in the original code after all and not the modification?"

"You mean Cole's code could be the problem?" asked Bartley.

"Could be." Webster shrugged and flicked his gaze nervously between the two men seated before him.

Bartley frowned, certain that Webster was just trying to throw the heat off his possibly malfunctioning dust.

Safko spoke first. "The beta test of the dust is coming up. We'll know for sure then where the problem lies." When Bartley frowned, Safko glanced at him and asked: "What's the matter?"

"Do you think it's wise to go through with the test? What if something else goes wrong? We can't have another China here, with hundreds dead."

To Bartley's chagrin, Safko dismissed him. "I can't see how, Colonel. We're only using inert samples."

Bartley let it go. For now. God, he hoped Safko was right.

The Deputy Director turned to Webster. "Can you fix the glitch?"

"I don't know. This is not my area of expertise. I mean, I'll try. But I'll need access to the original code to see what happened."

Safko frowned. "I don't trust the source we obtained the program from originally. For all we know, the source gave us a corrupted version of it when attempting to pass it to us from the IWL." Safko thought a moment. "I have a better idea. If the beta test goes off as planned, and everything works as planned, then we'll know that the original program works. Then we can compare it with the recent changes and see where the glitch is."

"Fine," said Webster. "But if you don't trust your source, then how do we get access to the original program to compare the two?"

"We'll use the Sectera network."

"Fine," said Webster again. "Is that it, gentleman?"

"Not quite." Safko pulled a dossier out of his briefcase with the official seal of the NSA, labeled CONFIDENTIAL. He handed the dossier to Bartley. At the moment, the two men ignored Webster, who had started sweating profusely again.

"What's this?" asked Bartley.

"A problem," said Safko.

"How many?"

"Two. They're of Asian descent," said Safko. "Possibly Korean."

Bartley flipped through the dossier. "Confirmed?"

"Yes. Confirmed."

"And the organization?" asked Bartley.

"We don't know. Not your usual Marxist or peacenik group. Something new. We think they're connected to something called the Digitari Brotherhood, led by someone named Dorian."

"They may be a front for the Chinese," speculated Bartley. "Using this *brotherhood* as proxies. And the Chinese may have interpreted what happened in China as a first wave assault."

Safko cut in: "And since they don't know for sure, they'll use proxies to do their dirty work rather than risk responding directly themselves."

"Perhaps," replied Bartley. "Do we have names on these *Brotherhood* members?"

Safko took back the dossier and flipped through it. "Jung Yi and a woman named Mae. No doubt both are aliases and both are Asian."

"That's all we need to know," said Bartley, and for the first time in a few minutes he finally acknowledged Webster's existence in the room. Webster, who had been watching them raptly, now had thick, wet rings under his dress shirt. Bartley turned to him; "How soon can we respond and neutralize?"

Webster opened his mouth, then closed it again. His jaw was quivering.

"I... no, Colonel. I'm sorry. But I didn't buy into one of the NSA's black bag jobs. I didn't buy into murder."

Safko, his tone quiet and ominous, asked: "You're having second thoughts, Mr. Webster?"

"Damn right I'm having second thoughts. Hundreds of dead Chinese? And now... *now* you're asking me how soon we can 'neutralize' a target?"

Sweet Jesus, this isn't happening.

"I wish I never got BioNan involved with this."

Bartley felt himself flush with anger. He truly hated dealing with civilians, especially those who were incapable of seeing the bigger picture. He opened his mouth to speak, but was glad when Safko stepped in to explain. Bartley was sure he wouldn't have sounded as calm. And calm is what they needed now, if they were to reign this project back in.

"Follow me on this, Webster," said Safko, sitting back in his chair. "SIRUS is a way for us to respond to a new form of warfare. Call it an asynchronous war. One not over territory, but over minds. SIRUS is a weapon that gives us, in this new war, the ability to target our enemies without having to face the unthinkable."

"Think about it this way, Webster," Bartley said, adopting Safko's cool demeanor and taking a long drag off his cigarette. "Ten nuclear bombs, detonated in ten of our biggest cities, would leave hundreds of thousands of Americans dead and millions more dying a slow and painful death. But the damage wouldn't be confined to just those ten cities. The economic and financial chaos that would ripple across the nation would affect our production, transportation, and communications capabilities. The ensuing result would make the Great Depression look like a bounced check! The people would demand immediate retribution from someone—anyone—and any Administration that didn't respond would be replaced immediately with one that promised a vengeful retaliation."

Safko stepped in, perhaps sensing that Bartley was getting worked up. "And that kind of military response, as of now, is limited to our nuclear arsenal. Just think how this country would be seen in the court of world opinion—and history—if all we had to retaliate with in an equivalent and deadly way were weapons of mass destruction. Webster, we need to give this country the capability of a more measured response."

Webster was silent, and then he reached over and tapped the dossier containing the two members of the Digitari Brotherhood. "But if we know who they are, why not arrest them now?"

"Because we need to track them," Safko replied. "We want to know who their leader is. Who's giving them their orders? This Dorian never shows himself. But we can find him through these henchmen, henchwoman, whatever." Safko paused. "So we need to ask again. Can we respond and neutralize them quickly when given the word?"

"Yes," replied Webster. "As long as we find them in a place away from the general population."

"Good," replied Bartley, standing. He was done with this civilian. "We'll inform you when the opportunity arises. You have your job to do. Be ready when your time comes."

At the door, Safko turned and said, "It's best you keep your head on straight, Webster. You understand the delicacy of the situation. If any of this ever got out, well, you and BioNan are through."

Webster turned, looked out the window, and whispered, "Aren't we all. Aren't we all."

Fort Belvoir, Maryland

At Bartley's request, Cole arrived early at the team office by cab, as his vehicle was still at the city impound. The thought of that son-of-a-bitch tow truck driver speeding away with his car still sent his blood boiling. At the doors to the building, with the morning sky overcast and ominous, Cole took a deep breath and did his best to put all thoughts of his impounded car behind him.

Inside, he found Taylor and Dallas at their work stations.

"So what's this meeting about?" he asked no one in particular, sitting at his own work station. "Do we have something on the world-wide wireless malfunctions last night?"

"Wireless malfunction?" said Taylor, looking up from her terminal. "Or nefarious attack on U.S. soil?"

"What do you mean?" asked Cole.

"Well, there's a difference of opinion," replied Taylor. "Bartley subscribes to those who think it's an attack on the U.S.—and *not* a malfunction."

"Is there proof of that?"

"No," piped in Dallas, wheeling his stool around to sit with them. "Screw it. It's too early to work. My brain is still asleep, I think. I hate these early morning meetings. Doesn't Bartley understand I have a night life?"

"You mean you actually sleep with your robots, too?" asked Taylor in mock horror.

"Oh, shut up," he said. "And if I wasn't still half asleep, I'd make you cry with a killer comeback. Anyway, Travis, we have nothing indicating last night's... *interference* was a pre-meditated assault."

Cole ignored his computer, too. Dallas was right. It was too early to work. Leave it to a military man like Bartley to call a seven a.m. meeting.

"The news said the attack was worldwide," said Cole. He eyed Taylor's steaming Starbucks with envy.

"Yes and no," she replied, sipping contentedly. "The news media jumped the gun there. We're being told by the NSA now that there were other countries affected besides the U.S., but not as many as first thought. So not all countries were affected, and not all wireless networks went down within an affected country. Very strange."

Cole nearly offered Taylor ten bucks for the rest of her Starbucks, then thought better of it. "I'm guessing, then, that the IWL boys have the code from the attack?"

"Not yet," Taylor replied. "The NSA is sending the codes over this morning. And we're still not sure it's an attack, Travis."

She was right, of course. He wasn't sure why he still thought of it as an attack. And it galled him that he was beginning to think like Bartley.

And just as Taylor finished speaking, Bartley came into the office.

"Good," he said stiffly, leaning his oversized butt against Dallas's desk. "Everyone's here. We received some additional intel over what's being officially described as a *malfunction.*" He struggled over the last word. "It seems the networks that were affected are split between two areas of the globe. Most of the developed countries like us had their wireless networks disrupted. But some rapidly developing countries—like India and many in the oil rich Middle-East—were also affected."

"What kind of pattern is that?" asked Taylor.

"None from what DoD can see," replied Bartley. "And that's why *I* think it's a diversion. Meant to focus our attention someplace else while we're attacked from the rear." Hesitating for a moment, he added, "And that's what I'm going to report to HomeSec and DoD."

"Always worrying about protecting his rear," Dallas mumbled, and Cole almost laughed when Dallas visibly pushed himself away from Bartley's enormous behind.

"What was that, Dallas?" Bartley snapped.

"Sir, nothing. Sir."

Bartley frowned and was about to say something to Dallas. Instead, Cole asked, "So why did you call us into this meeting, Colonel?"

Still frowning down at Dallas, Bartley said, "I want you three to be ready to look over the attack code and logs when the NSA sends them over. This is an all-out effort and HomeSec wants some answers. I want some answers, too. We need every trained eye on this." Bartley abruptly stood up. "So fire up those diagnostic programs of yours and be ready to work when we get the attack code."

"You mean the malfunction code," said Dallas sweetly. Cole shook his head. The kid just didn't know when to ease back on the throttle.

Bartley ignored the remark and marched out of the office.

"Now that Elvis has left the building," Dallas cracked, "What do we do in the meantime? Just sit on our asses?"

"In your case, Dallas," Taylor smirked, "it's your brains."

But before Dallas could respond, forcing Cole to endure one of their childish put-down games, he said, "Dallas is right…"

"First time for everything," cut in Taylor.

Cole plunged on. "We can't do much until we get the code from the NSA. So I think I'll pick up my car from the impound lot. Who wants to give me a lift? Taylor?"

"Not in her clunker," Dallas said, "Every time she gasses up that heap, it doubles in value." He snickered, then continued,

"Why don't you just have the colonel's driver drop you off? I'm sure he'll do it. He's a good Joe."

"Good idea," said Cole, shutting down his laptop, glad he was finally getting his car. "And why don't you two learn to play nice while I'm gone?"

"Yes, Dad," said Dallas.

"Now, how do I get hold of Bartley's driver?"

"I'll take care of it, boss," said Dallas. "Just give me a few minutes." With that he picked up the phone and quickly punched in a number.

On the way back from the impound lot, Cole called the IWL to check in and make sure Dallas and Taylor were working and not arguing. But all he got was, "All circuits are busy."

What was it with these communications snafus?

Several minutes later he arrived back at the team office.

"Got your car?" asked Dallas.

"Yeah," said Cole, "Are your cell phones working?"

"Nope," said Taylor. "All circuits are busy."

"Strange," said Cole. He sat heavily in his chair, careful of the Starbucks that he had picked up. Why did he always feel better with a Starbucks in hand? "What's going on?" he mused aloud.

"I take it you haven't seen this, then?" said Dallas. He slid Cole a printout of the day's *Truth Report*.

Cole glanced at the printout, then pushed it away. He didn't think his stomach could handle any more bad news today. "I seriously could give a damn about that fruitcake…"

And as if Cole hadn't spoken, Dallas continued on. "Adams says that the communications snafus were acts of cybertage. He says the government knows the truth and who's doing this, but the government is, in fact, covering it all up because they can't do anything to stop it."

"Great," said Cole. "That's what we need now. Someone to

incite a panic." The stomach acid was working its way up his esophagus. "Have we gotten the attack code from the NSA yet?"

"Nada," Taylor replied, and then scooted her chair over to him and whispered, "Travis, have you heard anything about my sister?"

"Nothing yet, Taylor. I'm sorry," said Cole. "I've gotten nowhere."

She nodded, pain crossing her face. Cole wanted to reach out and hug her, but this was not the time or place. She turned back to him. "By the way, Travis, you asked me to remind you about Shannon's birthday. It's tomorrow."

Ah, crap! He could have smacked his own forehead. How could he forget? Again? What was wrong with him?

"I take it by the expression on your face," said Taylor, gently touching him on his shoulder, "that you forgot about it?"

Cole rubbed his eyes, then stood. "I'll be back."

"Don't forget," said Dallas, grinning, "that we still have that beta test this morning. Oh, and that we'll be getting the attack code any time now. By the way, your name is Travis Cole, in case you have forgotten that." Dallas cackled, crossing an ankle over a knee.

"Ha ha," said Cole. "I'll be back in…"

"Wait. What does she want?" asked Taylor.

"She wants a puppy. But that's out of the question. My housekeeper would never go for it. And you know dogs and kids. After the initial thrill wears off, it's the adults who wind up doing the feeding and walking. Besides, I'm allergic to them."

"Let me handle it, boss," replied Dallas. "I have a solution."

"How? What do you …?"

But Cole was interrupted by Bartley's voice over the office intercom. "The NSA has released the attack code," he said. "It's up on our system. Cole, get your team right on it. Oh, and I want you in the Tank. It's time for the beta test and you're it."

Fort Belvoir, Maryland

Jack Fisher, assistant to the Under Secretary for Emergency Preparedness & Response at the Department of Homeland Security, drove up to a barbed-wire entrance of Fort Belvoir, stopping at the security barrier. A soldier dressed in a Class A uniform wearing a white MP armband exited the guard shack and saluted.

"Good morning, sir. May I see your ID, please?"

He handed the MP his HomeSec identification. "Jack Fisher. Here to see Colonel Bartley."

The MP studied the I.D. and handed it back to him. "You may proceed, sir."

Fisher drove off down the road past a platoon of drilling soldiers. He arrived shortly at a complex of buildings that housed INSCOM, home of the U.S. Army's Intelligence and Security Command. The buildings were fairly nondescript: concrete structures, almost bunker-like, with few windows, and an array of satellite dishes in the back of the building. He parked in the front.

Fisher, of course, knew the official mission of INSCOM. "*To conduct intelligence, security, and information operations for the military commanders and national decision makers.*"

But those innocuous words hid a more belligerent purpose. Fisher knew that inside a secure vault, seventy feet below ground level, experts from varied fields of Information Technology plied a trade of disruption and destruction through cyber-plagues incubated and deployed from keyboards and mice. Within the INSCOM complex was the Information Warfare Laboratory of the US Army.

The IWL.

Inside, Fisher presented his ID card to the two armed MPs for inspection.

"Please come with me," one of them said. Fisher was escorted down the short hallway to an elevator. The two men entered and the doors closed silently. Fisher saw that there were no floor selection buttons, only an electronic card reader, number pad, and a Plexiglas panel. The MP pulled a small rectangular plastic card from his fatigue pocket, swiped it through the reader, entered his PIN number into the keypad, and waited.

A recorded voice said, "Hand scan please."

The Plexiglas panel lit up under the keypad with a deep infrared glow. No fingerprint or iris ID here. The IWL used the individual pattern of a person's blood vessels for positive identification, since vein patterns in the fingers and palm always stay in the same place, even from birth. And, of course, the arrangement of veins in each person is unique. Unlike any other kind of physical ID, even with amputation, no one could steal Fisher's ID since the blood vessels would cease to flow.

The MP placed Fisher's right hand against the infrared panel and within seconds the panel turned green and the elevator doors closed in front of them. The two men waited as the car whisked down to its subterranean destination. When the elevator doors opened, Fisher was escorted by the MP into a small, cold room. The musky-smelling air in here was recycled and carefully sealed against the outside environment. The positive pressure kept any airborne contaminants out of the lab. Fisher and the MP stopped in front of a Plexiglas booth at the far end of the room.

"Good morning, sir," said a young corporal behind the glass. "May I have your laptop and cell phone, please?"

Fisher handed over both. No ID card was needed at this security station.

"This will only take a few minutes, sir."

The young soldier hooked the laptop and cell phone to a computer terminal and proceeded to scan the contents of each, a procedure necessary to ferret out any malicious programs that could infect the Information Warfare Lab's computers. The Lab, Fisher knew, was kept secure from any outside electronic contaminants, and had a self-contained computer network completely isolated from the Internet—from any other network, for that matter.

And for good reason.

The Information Warfare Lab computer was the home of every malicious computer program known. And then some. If any such program was to find its way out onto the Internet, it would instantly wreak havoc with the nation's information infrastructure. At the lab, these different strains of malevolent code were not only studied, but inoculations were created, as well, to protect the nation's information network. In addition, these malicious pieces of code, and the new ones created at the IWL, were used to produce information warfare weapons for the new kind of war in the twenty-first century.

"You're cleared, sir," the corporal said, handing Fisher a VISITOR badge and asking him to sign the log book. "The MP will escort you to the Tank."

Fisher followed the MP to a security screen similar to those found at airports. Once through, he continued down a long hallway, void of any doors.

Good thing I'm not claustrophobic.

Fisher's department was one of the five major divisions of the Department of Homeland Security. These divisions, or *directorates*, included Border & Transportation Security, Science & Technology, Information Analysis & Infrastructure Protection, Management, and Emergency Preparedness & Response. The latter was responsible for ensuring that the nation was prepared for catastrophes, whether natural disasters or terrorist attacks. This was Fisher's directorate, and the one Cole and his team had been working with the last several months.

They reached the end of the hallway, and the MP swiped his ID Card. A door swung silently open. The MP moved aside and motioned with his arm. "Here you go, sir. Please have a seat. I'm told the others will be here in a moment."

The Tank was plush in comparison to the stark utilitarian décor of the IWL. There were three flags at one end of the room. An American Flag, the flag of Fort Belvoir, and the Information Warfare Laboratory command flag. There was a long hardwood conference table with the blue, white, and gold INSCOM symbol inlaid in the top, surrounded on the walls by several pictures of U.S. presidents, famous Army generals, and a first edition of Byte Magazine. A thermos of coffee and several mugs embossed with the IWL seal rested on a small table in the back of the room. There were several overstuffed chairs surrounding a long desk, with a whiteboard on the wall at one end. A drop-down screen currently hung in front of the whiteboard.

Fisher was the first there. He sat, crossed his legs and adjusted the drape of his slacks. He took a deep breath and waited.

When Cole was escorted into the Tank, he saw Bartley, Webster, and a man he assumed was Fisher waiting for him.

Cole had some history with Webster and found the man deplorable. Webster was born into wealth. Unlike Cole, Webster often abused his wealth and treated those beneath his status as scum. The two men had been competing researchers at MIT. Cole knew, for instance, that Webster's strategy for winning grant money had been morally ambiguous at best. While competitors studiously wrote 300-page grant proposals, as did Cole, Webster used his family wealth to jet critical members of a foundation's decision-making board to exotic locations. There he would present his research proposals while wining and dining them. Cole was not surprised to see Webster here. Certainly this DHS project would pad both his resume and his ego.

"Nice of you to stop by, Cole," said Bartley sharply, his voice as automatic as ever. Cole ignored the man and found his seat. "Mr. Fisher, this is Travis Cole, the team leader of the project."

"Nice to connect a face with the name in the reports," said Fisher. He finished with the niceties. "So, gentleman, shall we get started?"

Bartley reached over to the pile of bound documents across

from him and passed out copies of the report. The words CLAS-SIFIED TOP SECRET were stamped in bold red on both the back and front.

"As you know, Travis Cole is the leader of a four-person team," Bartley instructed, "working on NAN-056-12 that now has the project name of 'Angel Dust.' Additionally, you know the DHS had asked those in academia to help address critical needs in homeland defense on the scientific and technological front. A white paper sent in by Mr. Cole, in response to such a request, found its way to my office and we realized he could be of immense help with our project."

Cole tried to look modest. "Just doing my civic duty, Colonel."

Bartley frowned disapprovingly at the interruption, and then went on. "Mr. Cole is an expert in Cellular Automata. CA for short. Cole's CA expertise gives the smart dust of our project the ability to analyze and report across a wide range of biological and chemical agents." Bartley sat down. "I'll leave the details of 'Angel Dust' to Mr. Cole."

"Thank you, Colonel." Cole had connected his laptop to the projector in front of him and with a few quick keystrokes, the first slide appeared on the conference room screen. It read:

Project Angel Dust
CLASSIFIED TOP SECRET
Department of the Army
North American Defense Command
NADCOM: A5954

Cole clicked on his mouse and a schematic appeared on the screen. It was a picture of a small long tube greatly enlarged, divided into two parts. One side of the diagram was colored blue and the other side green. He turned to Fisher. "Based on the regular updates we've been sending to your Department, this should be quite familiar to you."

"Yes it is. I'll tell you what I know, and you can fill me in on what I don't."

He opened a thick folder in front of him and scanned the

contents. "Angel Dust is made up of tiny microscopic carbon nano-tubes, so small that they can't be seen individually with the naked eye—only seen if there were enough of them to form a visible haze."

He turned a page of his notes. "The dust is comprised of little carbon tubes that are made at BioNan equipped with programmable MEMS and then sent over to the IWL for programming. Correct?"

Cole nodded.

"And these nano-tubes are geodesic spheres of pure carbon called 'Buckyballs'—after Buckminster Fuller, creator of the geodesic dome—and rolled-up into sheets that vaguely resemble chicken wire on a scale of a 'nano,' or a billionth of a meter." He looked up at Cole. "I believe that translates to about the size of ten hydrogen atoms, or one eightieth the diameter of a human hair?"

Cole nodded. He was impressed with Fisher's grasp of the material.

"There's one thing I'm not entirely clear on," Fisher said. "Can you give me a non-technical explanation of MEMS?"

Cole was about to speak when Webster interrupted. "MEMS," Webster said quickly, "stands for 'micro-electromechanical systems.' They're the integration of mechanical elements, sensors, actuators, and electronics into one system. In our case, the system is nano-technology."

Fisher frowned, opened his mouth to speak, but seemed at a loss of where to even begin. So Cole jumped in, perfectly aware that he and Webster were competing all over again. In this case, who could most clearly explain the complex nano-technology to the uninitiated. Cole saw that Bartley was frowning, perhaps aware of their little game.

"MEMS are built employing the same methods used to make silicon computer chips," Cole said. "You'll find large-sized MEMS in air bags for cars, pacemakers for people, computer projectors like the one I'm using here—and even intelligent toys. Just recently, engineers started inserting them in the earpieces of Indy racers to monitor and record the G-forces their heads endure. And, as Mr. Webster tried to explain, we employ MEMS for our own technology, which happens to be nano-technology."

"I see," replied Fisher, nodding. "Now, about the dust. How I understand it, you've had a major breakthrough—implanting MEMS on one side of the carbon tube and installing a biological layer with neuro fiber on the other that grows *from* the biological side *into* the carbon side." He pointed to the green side of the schematic.

Webster and Cole nodded.

"The bio side," Fisher went on, "is basically a microscopic chemical manufacturing plant, or a biologic stem cell. By using the MEMS side of the tube, the smart dust particle can detect and analyze any biological or chemical agent it senses in the environment. In other words, it can act like a molecular sensor laboratory scanning and analyzing environmental agents that it is programmed to detect."

Cole smiled. "You've done your homework."

Webster, eager to jump in again, had just about jumped out of his skin. "Biology is good at detecting and making things, and silicon is good at measuring and processing things. Both can now, inside our smart dust, communicate in binary logic."

Fisher looked down at his notes. "So, with the bio-chem lab on one side of the dust combined with the programming of the little MEMS processor on the other side, the dust, in effect, acts as a warning device for *any* biological or chemical agent in the air. Thus fulfilling the requirements we gave to the IWL."

"*Now* it does," said Webster interrupting again. "When I came to the project the scanning program for the MEMS had grown so large that the restricted memory size of the MEMS couldn't handle it. The analyzing power of the lab did not match the processing power of the MEMS. And there was another challenge.

How to program the dust *not* to spew reams of information, *but* be intelligent enough to figure out which measurements were vital and which were junk."

"And I presume that's where you came in, Mr. Cole?" asked Fisher, turning to him. Webster reluctantly sat.

"Yes," replied Cole, impressed again by Fisher's quick grasp of fairly complex data. "The original programming became too bloated. It tried to catalog every possible biological or chemical agent that could be used as a terror weapon against our civilian population. Using a slimmed down version of my CA code, sort of a tiny operating system, I gave the dust the ability to 'learn' as it went about doing its job. Now, while scanning the environment, it reports only what we need to know."

"Like tiny floating, tube-shaped computers," Fisher remarked.

"Correct. But more than that," Cole replied, "the evolutionary capacity of my programs—or artificial intelligent software agents—gives the programming *itself* the ability to learn and evolve. The fleck-sized dust particles, or tiny floating computers, can now organize themselves into autonomous networks. These networks, in essence, report back any toxin in the environment. So after BioNan sends over the dust, we program it."

"Pretty slick," said Fisher.

"Yes. It is. And it works well, too."

"On paper," Webster remarked.

Cole was about to rebut that when Fisher asked, "Did you solve the problem of communicating with the dust?"

"There's a nano-transmitter in every smart dust," Webster answered. "The transmitter is powered by a specific chemical that converts sunlight into energy, much like a plant. The transmitter communicates with other particles up to one hundred feet using WiFi technology. Soon, up to almost a mile."

Bartley stepped in for the first time. "These signals are then relayed to the command center here at the IWL. If the report is of an unknown or dangerous bio/chem agent, the IWL alerts the DHS, and it issues a civil alert for the area."

"With the dust particles floating around a populated area," said Fisher, "is there any concern about public health?"

"We thought of that, of course," Webster replied, his eyes shifting over to Bartley, who looked up.

Cole watched them both and frowned. Now why did Webster and Bartley both suddenly look nervous?

Webster continued. "Even when a living entity is exposed to a large dose of dust, we've included a safeguard. Each dust particle is programmed to sense the others, and if more than about a dozen are present, the others travel to the nasal passages. There, they trigger a sneezing, runny nose response, like an allergy or cold, expelling the excess dust back into circulation."

Fisher looked at Cole. "So, then, the technical problems are solved."

"We think so," replied Cole. He pulled up another slide, this one a map of Washington, D.C.

Bartley spoke again. "As you can see, the smart dust has been spread around a twenty-square-mile area of Washington, including the Mall, White House, Capitol, and other major government office buildings."

"How was that done, Colonel?" asked Fisher.

"We spread the dust randomly via military helicopters with the help of the U.S. Army HAZMAT team here at Fort Belvoir. Once the helicopters had done their job, the wind, foot, and auto traffic filled in the voids," said Bartley. "And last night, the HAZMAT team, under the command of Major Brodie Ryder, deposited inert biological and chemical agents around certain controlled areas of the city. We'll use these inert agents to test the dust."

"What about weather?" asked Fisher. "What happens if it rains? Or if high winds blow around the dust? Couldn't that dissipate the dust?"

Webster stepped in again. "Weather activity can't displace all the dust. It has an adhesive quality to it, much like common dust one normally sees. And like ordinary dust, you take it with you wherever you go. In this case, the smart dust is so small that it can get into places even high winds can't dislodge. Remember that the normal activities of people, vehicles and the like keep the dust circulating around the area, picking it up here, dropping it off there, and it only takes a few little smart dusts to create a network and let the monitoring program do its job."

"Final question," said Fisher. "How, in fact, do you program the dust?"

Cole described in detail how the sealed containers of dust shipped from BioNan are placed in a seating device that floods the dust with wireless signals.

"And what about upgrades?" asked Fisher. "How do you send codes to the dust once it's been deployed?"

Cole was about to remind Fisher that he had already exceeded his last question, but thought better. Instead, he answered, "Once the dust has been deployed in the field, we can download software upgrades to the dust via a secure VPWN—a virtual private wireless network—using the existing cell phone towers around the area."

"Well, then," said Fisher, grinning. He seemed satisfied with explanations provided. "When do we begin the test?"

"As soon as Major Ryder arrives," Bartley replied.

The intercom buzzed. "Colonel, Major Ryder is here."

"Speak of the devil," said Bartley. "Gentleman, let the testing begin."

Fort Belvoir, Maryland

"This is strange," said Dallas, puzzled. He was at his desk studying the lines of code from the global wireless malfunction. "You know, I don't think this is a piece of malicious code at all."

"What do you mean?" asked Taylor, her mouth stuffed with the last of her bean curd and sprout sandwich.

Dallas frowned, leaning forward and squinting at the screen. "Well, I can't find any sign of an attack footprint. Strange, because it sure seemed like an attack attempt, didn't it?"

Taylor stuffed a handful of veggie chips into her mouth and grunted something incomprehensible.

"Anyway," said Dallas. "The inner workings of this little bug are compiled."

Taylor knocked back some water and walked over to Dallas.

"You better not have bean curd breath," said Dallas. "I hate bean curd breath."

"Oh, shut up," she said, peering over his shoulder at the computer monitor. "You're right." She pointed at the screen. "These portions of the code are compiled."

"This is Travis's area," said Dallas. "We'll have to wait until he returns from the beta test." He wrinkled his nose, adding, "And you *have* bean curd breath. I hate bean curd breath."

Taylor smacked him lightly across the head.

~

A crisply uniformed soldier in green camouflage fatigues was shown into the Tank. Bartley got up immediately and shook his hand. "Gentleman, this is Major Broadie Ryder. He's heading up the hazardous materials team for our test."

They shook hands all around. Cole thought Ryder looked young for the rank of Major.

But then again, what do I know? I'm just a civilian, as Bartley likes to point out whenever possible.

Ryder was easily five or six inches taller than Cole, and had him by about twenty pounds. Cole knew, according to their reports, that Ryder was a graduate of West Point, trained in biochemical warfare. He had been awarded a Purple Heart in the Persian Gulf.

Fisher clapped his hands. "Now that we're all here, let's proceed with the test."

As they left the meeting room, Cole noticed that Bartley looked nervous. His normal arrogant attitude seemed to have softened and worry lines creased his face.

What's got him so bothered?

~

Bartley was worried sick; sick as a dog, to be honest.

As the colonel led the way out of the Tank, dozen of questions raced through Bartley's mind, each more horrible than the previous. What if there was something basically wrong with Cole's programming? What if the deaths in China were caused by NSA's program modifications? What if something went wrong in the D.C. test area?

Bartley felt clammy and queasy with foreboding.

He doubted that any harm would occur here in D.C. Okay, prayed that nothing would go wrong. Weren't they using inert bio/chem material? Yes, they were.

Bartley was sweating inside his uniform.

Badly.

~

The control room was dimly lit by a bluish glow from various monitors sitting within a main console. The console had several chairs in front of it.

"Well, it's your show, Cole," Bartley said. "Let's get started."

Cole seated himself in the center chair. He flipped a switch and a large screen above his head lit up displaying a map of metropolitan D.C. He pushed a button to his left and dozens of little red dots appeared within and around the beta test area of the city. Satisfied, he pressed another button that displayed an amorphous yellow cloud surrounding the red dots.

Bartley said, "Those red dots you see represent the cell towers housing our communications network. The yellow cloud is the smart dust. This graphic shows that the dust is, in fact, communicating with us." He looked at Cole and said, "Continue."

"Yes, sir."

Cole flicked a small toggle switch and, one by one, the red dots turned green, indicating that the VPWN sensors on the cell towers were activated. A computer monitor above Cole's head listed the name and location of each individual tower and the strength of the signal the lab was receiving from every one of them.

"Looking real good," said Bartley. "Good strong signals. The network is operating fine." Putting his hand on Cole's shoulder, he said, "Now for the real test. Initiate the dust's programming."

Cole reached for the keyboard in front of him and began typing. After a few keystrokes, a display appeared on the small monitor in front of him. It read:

    Project Angel Dust
    CLASSIFIED TOP SECRET
    Department of the Army
    North American Defense Command
    NADCOM: A5954
    Log In Protocol
    Username:

Password:

Cole typed in his username and password. A second screen appeared.

Command Code Sequence:

Cole entered a ten-digit alphanumeric code that resulted in a little door on the control panel opening. A small command console rose from the surface of the desk. Turning to Bartley, Cole said, "It's all yours, Colonel."

Bartley walked over to the command console and snapped open a small Plexiglas cover revealing a large orange button. Bartley pushed the button and waited.

"What's supposed to happen now, sir?" asked Ryder.

"Now," interjected Webster, "*if* the programming works, the dust should pick up the test samples your team distributed around the area last night."

If was right, and Cole knew it. His small executable code that he had embedded into the CA program was a fix, a sort of short-cut that had proved that Cole could deliver the goods. Yes, he had taken chances before. But this was the biggest chance of his career. He hoped it worked.

Today was the day.

Do or die.

Unfortunately, neither Cole nor anyone else at the lab knew what types of inert material Ryder and his team had spread around the test area. This was a true 'blind' test, one that would see if the dust could scan and report on the unknown agents. And Cole knew that his little addition to the code should, in fact, aid in picking up and deciphering bio/chem agents. Still, he didn't know for sure.

But he was about to find out.

In silent anticipation, the five men watched the large screen above their heads. Three small areas of the yellow cloud turned to red, and three of the green dots representing the cell towers began flashing amber. The monitor below the screen map of D.C. showed the three tower listings.

Cole asked, "Major? Are these the same locations where you placed the test samples?"

Ryder, leaning over the console, read the listings. "Affirmative."

So far so good, thought Cole. He scanned a second monitor on the console. "The dust is reading an anthrax and a smallpox signature."

And over the next few minutes, more yellow clouds turned red, and more towers reported signals from the dust.

"It appears," said Ryder, staring at the tower monitor, "that the dust had picked up and identified every sample we put out last night."

Cole was relieved. More relieved than he had realized. So much could have gone wrong.

But it didn't.

"Good show, everyone," said Fisher. "Colonel, I want a preliminary report to me by tomorrow."

"You'll have it, Mr. Undersecretary."

Outside the control room, Cole was greeted by a young soldier. "Sir, you have a phone call. You can take it over there." He pointed to a work station.

Frowning, Cole walked over and picked up the phone and pressed the hold button. "Cole here."

"Mr. Cole?" It was Anna, his housekeeper. "Please come home as soon as you can. The police are here and they want to ask you some questions." She was excited, and her accent was stronger than usual. Cole had to strain to pick up the words.

"What's wrong, Anna? Is Shannon all right?"

"She's fine, I promise, Mr. Cole." She hesitated, then added, "I saw a man standing outside our townhouse. I got worried and called the police. They want to speak with you. Please come home as soon as you can."

Washington, D.C.

When Cole arrived home, he saw a D.C. patrol car parked in front of his townhouse. He parked behind it and dashed through the front door. Standing in the kitchen with Anna were two officers—one male, one female.

"Are you Travis Cole?" the female officer asked, turning to him. Anna was holding Shannon.

"Yes, officer."

"Hi, Daddy," said Shannon, jumping down and running over to him.

Cole picked her up and held her close. The moment Anna had said the police were there he thought his life was over. He wouldn't know what to do if anything ever happened to Shannon.

"Hi, pumpkin," he said as calmly as he could. Now that she was in his arms, he could breathe a little easier.

She said, "These nice police people came to visit."

"I know, baby," he said and turned to the police officers. "Did you catch the stalker?"

"No, sir. He was gone when we arrived," the female officer said.

"What made you so suspicious, Anna?" asked Cole.

"I notice him this morning when I opened the curtains." Anna was calmer now, probably because Cole was home. Her accent was thick, but now fairly clear. "I don't think much of it then.

I see him again later during my morning walk. After that, I glance out the window from time to time and he is always there, moving from place to place, but always in view of the house. So this afternoon I decide to call the police."

"You did the right thing, ma'am," said the male officer, his voice overly deep. "Have you ever seen him before?"

"No. Never," she said. "This is a very nice neighborhood and people just don't stand around outside your house, you know?"

"I know, ma'am," the officer said. "It was a good idea to call us." He looked at Cole and added, "We'll send a squad car by every few hours over the next couple of days. Just as a precaution."

"Thank you, officer." Cole escorted them out the front door and double-locked the door behind them.

Cole gave Anna a little reassuring hug and she left to finish up the laundry. He kissed Shannon, who bounded up the stairs to her room and no doubt her computer. Cole went into his study and called the lab.

Dallas answered the phone. "Hey, man. Where are you? How'd the test go?"

"The test went fine. I'm at home, but it looks like I'll have to stay here for a while."

"Why? What's up?"

"Family crisis. Under control now. Bitspit the global wireless attack code to me. I'll work on it at home. I'll be there in the morning."

"Okay, will do."

Cole hung up. In the kitchen, he opened a beer and poured it into a frosted glass from the freezer, found the ham and swiss on rye that Anna had left for him, and retired to the study. There, he started up his laptop, launched his email application and opened the attack code file that Dallas had just emailed him.

He took a bite of sandwich, sipped his beer, and examined the code. The main body of the program was compiled. Cole figured he could make short work of that, and with his sandwich finished and on his second beer, he had it de-compiled in no time.

Cole realized that what he had was not a virus, or worm, or any other piece of malicious code—but a fatal digital exception error, along with an error message. The error message referenced several lines of code that, to Cole's surprise, were very familiar to him.

And he saw something else. Something that made the hair stand up on the back of his neck.

Oh, Crap!

Someone had executed his Easter Egg. At that moment, his phone rang. It was Dallas.

"Guess what, Chief?" Dallas said in a triumphant voice. "The wireless networks weren't brought down by a virus or anything like that. It was a system-wide malfunction."

"What do you mean?"

"Some wireless device, somewhere, performed a fatal exception error," said Dallas. "It crashed and migrated the error across the wireless network that it was connected to. This made all other connected devices experience the same fatal error and malfunction, too. Cell phones, PDAs, handhelds, and laptops—any wireless device connected to the network."

"Even the battlebots?" asked Cole.

"While they were being controlled wirelessly? Yes," said Dallas.

"Holy Jesus! That's a new one."

"But I don't know what the error code means, Chief."

Cole hesitated, but decided to tell Dallas. They were, after all, good friends. "I do," he said. "The error message points to lines of code in one of my CA programs. The one I wrote for the dust."

There was a moment's silence. Cole could almost see Dallas's sharp brain turning over the ramifications of that statement. "But, chief, that's only possible if..."

"Right," said Cole. "Someone stole the code I wrote for the dust and programmed it into a number of—and who knows how many—wireless devices."

"Jesus, Cole. Are you sure?"

"Yeah. I'm looking at the code right now." He looked again

at the symbols on his laptop screen. "It's mine all right." He scrolled down the lines of code, stopped at one line—and a cold shudder ran down his spine. The code had the chip ID in it. It was an MCD chip. Was this just a coincidence? Or *could his code in that chip have something to do with Taylor's sister's death in China? No. Impossible. Software doesn't kill people.*

"Travis, that means someone has accessed the lab's computer," Dallas said. "Correction; *broke* into the lab network, stole your code, and used it."

That was the only explanation.

Unbelievable.

There was a heavy silence, then Cole said, "Dallas, I want you to do something for me."

"Sure, chief."

"I want you to find out who accessed the dust's programming files over the last few months. Check the access logs now and look for anything that might look suspicious."

"Hold on," Dallas said.

Cole heard the tapping of Dallas's keyboard, no doubt searching the access logs of Project Angel Dust. In a matter of seconds, he reported back. "Everything looks normal here, Chief. Lots of regular access by authorized people: You, me, Taylor…" He stopped abruptly.

Cole's heart thumped once in his chest. "Did you find something?"

"I'm showing access several times. Correction, *many* times, over the last forty-eight hours."

"By whom?"

"This is odd, Cole," mused Dallas. "There's no name. No ID of who accessed it."

"No ID at all?"

"Nope. Just a blank field."

"When was the last access?"

"Today."

Cole thought for a moment. "Dallas, we can write a

packet-sniffing program that could track from where the file is accessed, every time it's accessed, right?"

"Yes, it's feasible, but I'm going to need Taylor's help. That's more her expertise."

"Do it. And, Dallas?"

"Yeah, chief?"

"Keep this quiet for now. Don't tell anyone what we found or what you're doing. Understand?"

"But what about Bartley? Shouldn't we tell him?"

Cole thought of his shortcut, the Easter Egg. "No," he said. "Tell no one. Not until we find out what's going on. *Comprende?*"

"Gotcha, Chief."

Cole hung up the phone and looked back at his laptop screen and scanned the CA code before him. He didn't tell Dallas about the Easter Egg. He couldn't.

Cole shut the computer down. There was nothing for him to do but wait on Dallas and Taylor to do their digital magic and hopefully discover the source of the mystery access.

He stood up to leave his study when the doorbell rang. He thought of the stalker, and his first reaction was to look for a weapon. The best he could find was a wooden-handled umbrella. It would have to do.

He approached the door cautiously, aware of his heart beating, aware that he was holding nothing more than a stupid umbrella.

I need a gun in here, he thought. And it was the first time such a thought had ever crossed his mind.

A gun? Are you crazy? With Shannon around?

But as he approached the front door with his make-shift weapon, a gun suddenly seemed like a very good idea.

At the door, he sucked in some air and peered through the spy hole. Standing there were the same two D.C. officers who had been at his home earlier. He breathed an audible sigh of relief.

He opened the door. "Hello, officers. Is everything okay?"

"We're evacuating the neighborhood," said the female office. "You and your family must leave now."

Cole was about to protest, when he saw his fellow neighbors, beyond the police, leaving in droves. The two officers were already to the next house. They offered no explanation or directions.

He rushed upstairs. "Shannon? Where are you?"

He found her at the computer, of course. Anna was already gone for the evening, thank God.

"What's wrong, Daddy?" asked Shannon, clicking off a program before Cole could see what she had been doing. He frowned, but he had no time to think about that now.

He grabbed her light jacket from her closet, shoved it in her hands, picked her up and hurried downstairs. In the SUV, he quickly buckled Shannon into her seat.

"Why are we leaving, Daddy? Where are we going?"

"Not now, baby. We'll talk later."

Cole backed out of the garage and closed the door behind him. On the street, he saw police cars and fire engines scattered everywhere, all with their red and orange lights flashing. A long line of slowly moving cars filled the streets, winding among the emergency vehicles, exiting the housing development.

Cole joined the exodus. When he came upon an officer directing traffic, he slowed down. Cars behind him immediately honked. Cole didn't care.

"What's going on, officer?"

"Please continue past the barriers, sir."

"But why? What's going on?"

"Leave now, sir. That's an order."

Frustrated and confused, Cole raised his window. Just as he did so, something exploded behind him. Shannon screamed. Cole jumped, and to his right, a few streets down, an immense fireball appeared in the sky.

To his shock and amazement, he watched cars flip through the air, followed by what appeared to be chunks of asphalt.

"Holy sweet Jesus!"

"Daddy!"

The officer next to Cole dashed through the street, drawing his firearm. Those in the cars around him ditched their vehicles and made a break for it. Chunks of metal and cement rained down around him.

This isn't happening.

"Daddy!" Shannon screamed again.

"Hold on, baby."

He dropped the SUV into gear and whipped the car away from the mayhem. He bounded up over someone's perfectly-manicured yard, plowed through a fence, shattered a lawn gnome, careened briefly down the sidewalk, and soon hit a patch of open road.

Along with several other vehicles, Cole's SUV raced several blocks away until he passed through the police barrier. Actually, the car ahead of him blasted through the barrier. He ducked when a striped wooden beam grazed his roof.

When he thought he was a safe distance away from the neighborhood he stopped in the parking lot of a convenience store and turned to his daughter, who was crying and shaking. But Cole could barely speak. Adrenalin had overtaken his body, and all he could hear was the pounding of his own heart.

Black smoke still curled in the sky. More sirens approached. Finally, he found his voice. "Are you okay, baby?"

"What's happening, Daddy?"

"I don't know. But everything's going to be alright."

His mind kicked into gear. An explosion? In his neighborhood, just as the police were evacuating the entire block...

Unbelievable.

Surely, I'm dreaming.

Shannon cried harder. He stroked her shoulder. Finally, he punched a number into his cell phone. After ringing a half dozen times, AJ finally answered. "Hi, hon," she said. "What's up?"

"There's been an accident."

"Oh my God, Cole; is everything alright?"

He assured her they were okay, and explained everything as quickly as he could. "AJ, can Shannon and I stay with you tonight?"

"Yes, of course," she said. "Get over here!"

And just before he hung up, he heard her turn on CNN. Cole clicked off his phone.

Washington, D.C.

In a run-down apartment in the Deanwood Heights area of D.C., two Asian men busily worked on a white, molded polyethylene twenty-gallon drum. On the vinyl floor beside them sat a plain white cover and locking ring. Next to that were boxes of batteries, heavy duct tape, industrial shrink-wrap, and electrical wires. The expensive computers, wireless routers, and sophisticated assembly tools did not fit the low-tech decor of the shabby complex.

Deanwood Heights was the kind of place police visited only when something even more horrible than usual happened. Not when drug dealers sauntered across the streets like they owned them. Not when prostitutes plied their wares in front of the same vacant lots where neighborhood children played. Certainly not when people went for years living without sidewalks, curbs, or city services. Sidewalks, police patrols, and code enforcement hadn't made it there yet.

It made a perfect safe-house for the Digitari Brotherhood.

Huan sat on the floor, finishing a mouthful of kimchi as he read over a schematic. Kang, his younger brother, was connecting wires to a timing device.

"Help me with the ammonia nitrate," Huan said. Kang accompanied him to the bedroom closet where the canisters were stored. Skull and crossbones decals glowered at them.

They carried one of the canisters over to the white plastic drum. "Pour the nitrate into the drum. And be careful. Don't spill any," Huan directed. When both men had finished filling the drum, he added, "Put the drum cover back on, but don't lock it. We'll finish later."

Fort Belvoir, Maryland

Leaving Shannon with AJ after a very strange and surreal night, Cole arrived at the IWL early and made his way past the cyber-soldiers at their computers and entered the team office.

Taylor and Dallas were still at their desks. Both looked exhausted. Cole knew they had been there all night installing and monitoring the sniffing program. Scattered around the office were empty cans of Jolt and apple juice, pizza cartons, half-eaten carrot sticks, chips, and dried-out salsa.

"Hi, boss," Dallas said in a weary voice.

"Morning, guys. Are either Bartley or Casey in yet?"

"No," yawned Taylor. "Casey's shift doesn't start until noon and Bartley's at some meeting, as usual. He was in a crappy mood. Last I heard, they're discussing whether the gas line explosion in D.C. was just a coincidence or related to the recent attack. They're all getting pretty paranoid around here. Hey, wasn't that explosion in your neighborhood?"

"Yeah. But we're okay. Had to bunk with AJ."

"That was cozy," said Taylor coyly.

"Yes, Shannon enjoyed it, too."

"Ah," she said, grinning. She dropped her voice an octave. "Dallas, close the door."

"Yes, ma'am." He got up, crossed the room, glanced down the hallway, and then quietly closed the door.

Both Taylor and Dallas huddled around Cole.

"We found our mystery shopper," said Taylor, looking a bit smug.

"Good job! Who is it?"

"Travis, shh!" she hissed, and pulled him over to Dallas's computer. She sat him in an extra chair, plopped next to him, and brought up the results of their packet-sniffing program. She pointed to lines of text on the screen, text that showed an access path to and from the CA files over the last several hours.

"They were pretty busy last night," she said. "They accessed the CA program a couple of dozen times." She clicked on one of the paths and another screen appeared with details of the access. Among other things, it showed the ID of the intruder. When Cole saw it, he gave a low whistle. Staring at him in black and white was a familiar name.

"BioNan," he said, under his breath. "BioNan has access to the lab network from *outside* the IWL? Nothing—and no one—is supposed to have that."

"Well, they do," said Dallas.

Cole's mind raced with the ramifications. But first …

"How?" he wondered. "A dedicated landline direct to BioNan from the lab network?"

"Nothing that mundane," replied Dallas. "While we watched BioNan access the CA files last night, I looked for the same thing. A secure T-3, or a hardwired dedicated secure phone line connected to the lab. No go. Couldn't find any. Then it dawned on me. *Wireless!*"

"But wireless is notoriously insecure," replied Cole. "Those clowns know that."

"Not this kind of wireless. Remember a while back, General Dynamics was fooling around with a secure wireless phone?"

"Yeah. I heard something about that."

"So, I did some snooping around on the Net and found out that General Dynamics created a Type 1 certified secure wireless phone. They called it Sectera and it was certified in 2002 by the U.S. Government."

"What part of the government certified it?" Cole asked.

"Get this—the NSA. It certified the secure phone's ability to protect classified information up to the Top Secret level for some unnamed project."

"So the NSA is somehow connected to BioNan?"

"I don't know about that," said Dallas, "but if the NSA is making their high tech communications equipment available to BioNan to snoop on Angel Dust, it sure smells funny."

"So that's how the hackers got my code," frowned Cole. "From BioNan!"

"Looks like it," said Dallas.

Taylor shook her head. "I don't think so. Dallas knows as well as I do that IWL files of any kind can't be copied from an external user, authorized or not. Only viewed. Security and all that."

"Oh, yeah, right," Dallas quietly. "Damn."

"Then I think it's time we did a little snooping ourselves," said Cole. "Dallas, let's see what we can find on BioNan in the lab's computer. How's your hacking ability?"

"Pretty rusty."

Taylor said, "Don't tell me Mr. Anti-establishment, Techno-pagan is growing a conscience?"

Dallas glared briefly at Taylor, then pulled his chair close to his desk.

"Never," he grinned.

He ran his fingers rapidly over the keyboard, accessing different parts of the lab's administration database. After a little difficulty, he managed to get past the security screens and into a portion of the database where vendors were listed. He located the file for BioNan, and paged through screen after screen of data until one screen caught their attention.

"What's that?" asked Taylor pointing at the screen.

"That's BioNan's certification to be a government supplier," replied Cole. "Every vendor that supplies sensitive materials or information to the government has to list all relationships they have with other entities. Standard procedure."

"Let's see who they're having relations with," smiled Dallas. He paged through several screens and on one, in a record near the bottom of the page, was a single word: SIRUS.

"What's SIRUS?" asked Taylor.

"Don't know. You ever hear of SIRUS, Travis?"

"Yes," said Cole, frowning. "I have heard the word mentioned."

"From where?" Taylor inquired.

"From a guy named Toad Adams."

"Toad Adams?" Dallas replied, chortling. "That nut case? When did you speak to him?"

Cole frowned. Had that nut job actually been on to something? He said, "My in-law introduced me to him. I thought it was a waste of my time, but apparently not." Cole paused, chewing on his lower lip. "There's something else I need to tell you. Embedded in the wireless malfunction code was the name of the chip company—MCD."

Taylor's eyes widened and she shared a brief moment with Cole. MCD had been the name attached to the email she had received about her sister's death in China.

Dallas noticed the look the two exchanged and said, "What? Am I missing something?"

Cole again looked at Taylor, and she said, "It's okay. You can tell him."

And so Cole brought Dallas up to speed on the deaths in China, the email from Alexi, and MCD.

"I am so sorry, Taylor," said Dallas, hugging her. "I had no idea."

"Thank you," she said.

There was a moment of silence, and then Dallas turned to Cole. "Is this all somehow connected?"

"Could be," Cole replied. "Connected enough to possibly commit murder. My old frat brother was killed the very night before I planned to talk with him about MCD."

"Jesus. Why are we flapping our lips," snapped Taylor.

"Let's see if we can find out if SIRUS is a code word for an IWL project."

"Good idea," said Cole. He turned to Dallas. "Look at the lab's current project list and see if it turns up there."

"Yes, sir, boss."

The kid worked the lab computer a few more minutes, found the IWL's current project list—and sure enough, the word SIRUS appeared again. This time with the words CLASSI-FIED TOP SECRET connected to it.

"Can you get anything on this?" Cole asked.

"I'll try." He tapped a few more keys. He rubbed his eyes and tried again. "Damn. This file is tightly encrypted." Dallas tried another route, and then another, and then finally sat back. "Sorry, boss. It's a no go. Unless…"

"Unless what?" Cole and Taylor asked almost in unison.

"Unless we can get someone at BioNan to give us access to this information."

"Impossible…"

"Wait," said Dallas. "Let me make a phone call or two."

"Fine," said Cole.

"And while you're doing that," said Taylor. "I'm gonna freshen up. I'll be in the little programmer's room if you need me." Taylor picked up her backpack and headed off to the ladies room.

"Isn't it amazing how she lights up a room when she *leaves* it?" Dallas said, chuckling to himself.

"I'll be in my office," Cole said. "Let me know if you make any headway at BioNan."

"Sure," said Dallas. "And… uh… Travis?"

Cole, heading for his corner office, stopped and turned. "Yeah?"

"I found something else when I decompiled the wireless mal-function logs. Something strange."

"And what was that?" he asked as casually as he could, but he knew he had been caught.

"I found a history of a command to execute an Easter Egg."

The young man looked up at Cole. "Are you hiding something in your CA code?"

Cole slumped back to the chair next to Dallas.

"Travis," said Dallas. "Out with it. If we're trying to solve the problem of the wireless network crash, don't you think I should have the full story?"

"I took a short cut," Cole said reluctantly.

"What do you mean?"

"They hired me to give them a slimmed down CA code to fit in the MEMS."

"And that's what you gave them. Yeah, so?"

Cole sighed again. He felt like a kid caught with his hand in the cookie jar. "My code had to analyze thousands of possible contaminants fed to it by the dust. I realized that a CA code like that could never fit into the current technology of the dust's MEMS. But I wanted the job, and so I promised to deliver. And to do so, I had to use a short cut."

Cole didn't like the way his friend's eyes narrowed suspiciously.

"And that was?" Dallas asked, folding his arms over his chest.

"Biological and chemical warfare scenarios. I programmed a summary of them into the CA. That way they could bypass the analysis of known bio/chem contaminants and only use the MEMS processing power to analyze the unknown ones."

"You stole?"

"I imitated." Cole said sheepishly. "And besides, where were *your* scruples when you stole my code for Isaac?"

"That was different. I didn't plan to use Isaac as a weapon of mass destruction," said Dallas, excited, raising his voice. He was also sweating through his shirt. "So where did you get the bio/chem warfare scenarios?"

Cole frowned at his friend's aggressive reaction. He said, "I found them in a database at MIT. A colleague's database. It was a part of project that he'd been working on." Cole paused. "Dallas, could you please keep this to yourself. Can you do that?"

The kid seemed to take a breath or two, then said, calmly, "Sure, boss. Whatever you want."

Cole frowned again and was about to head to his office when he remembered something that had been nagging at him all day.

"Oh, and before I forget, when Taylor returns, please ask her to call the travel desk to cancel my Amtrak to New York City."

"Why New York?"

"A friend of mine had asked me a few weeks ago to do a lecture there at a conference, but given our present situation..."

"Right," said Dallas. "Not a good time to go."

Cole hated letting his friend down at the last minute, but things were getting sticky here, and fast.

"I'll let her know," said Dallas. "I'm sure she enjoys being your secretary. Never mind she's one of our brightest programmers..."

Cole cut him off. "I'll be in my office."

He hadn't gotten much sleep last night, and found himself dozing when his office phone rang. Cole shot up from his chair, almost toppled over, took a second or two to remember where he was, and then snatched up the phone.

"We're ready," Dallas said on the other end of the line.

"I assume your phone calls were a success?"

"You betcha."

"Good. Is Taylor back?"

"Yes. She's waiting for you."

"Be right there."

Cole hung up and walked the thirty feet to the team office.

"What do you have?" Cole asked.

"Just a password to the BioNan mainframe," said Dallas, rather smugly. His hostility from earlier seemed long gone.

"And how did you get that?"

Taylor replied, "He has friends in low places."

Dallas shot her a nasty look. "I have *some* friends who operate on the other side of the law. I asked them for a favor."

"Why would they do you a favor?" asked Taylor skeptically.

"Like I said, I have..."

"... friends in low places," added Taylor.

Cole had a sudden feeling. "Friends in the *mob*?" he asked.

"It doesn't matter right now. My friends gave me a password for BioNan."

"Okay, Houdini," said Cole, dropping it for now. "How'd they do that?"

Well," Dallas said with a conspiratorial smile, "my friends run a rather extensive business on the Net."

"Breaking legs for hire?" quipped Taylor.

"No, Miss Bigot. They run some of the biggest and best porno sites on the Web. They have millions of subscribers to hundreds of adult web sites they manage."

"And I suppose you've visited the majority of them?" Taylor said snidely.

Cole glanced at her, "Taylor, give him a break." He looked at Dallas. "What does any of this have to do with you getting a password to the BioNan mainframe?"

"Fairly simple. Tell me, Cole, do you use a different password for every site you're registered to use? You know, paid subscription sites, shopping sites, personal banking sites, etc., etc.?"

"No. Too many to keep track of. But I try."

"So I bet you use the same password/user name combination on some sites, right?"

"Yes. So?"

"Well, many of the horndogs that subscribe to several porn sites do the same. And sometimes, they use the very same password/username combination of their company servers as they do for their porn sites. So I asked my friends to have their Webmaster run a match of BioNan IP addresses that access their sites and supply me with their password and user name."

"And they did?" asked Taylor incredulously.

"Uh huh," said Dallas smugly. "And we got several hits. So while sleeping beauty here napped in his office, I went home and found BioNan's website. From there I was able to hack into their company Intranet. I ran the password/username combinations I had, and sure enough, found the SIRUS file." He triumphantly held up a memory stick. "I downloaded everything I could find and raced back here to the lab." He paused and thought for a moment. "You know, you guys, while I was in their mainframe, I noticed something very peculiar in their log."

Cole had to sit. His mind was racing, and his legs were feeling a bit weak. A lot had happened over these past few days.

Too much.

"What was that?" Taylor asked.

"I noticed one log entry in particular that caught my eye. It logged an IP address that was all zeros. Anyone know what that means?" he asked.

"No," said Cole.

"Neither do I," said Dallas.

Cole rubbed his temples. Once again, his office chair had proven unfit for comfortable sleeping. "Let's just see what you have on BioNan for now."

"Sure, boss."

Dallas slipped the memory stick into his computer. He typed in a command and a series of files appeared on his computer screen. "I should tell you, these files are encrypted, and they did a damn good job of it."

"Maybe we can make sense of the unencrypted ones," suggested Taylor.

Dallas shrugged, ran his mouse down to a file on the list, and clicked on an unencrypted zip file. It quickly unzipped and displayed hundreds of graphic files.

"Easy enough," said Cole. "Open one of the graphic files and let's take a peek."

Dallas double-clicked one of the files and a graphic slowly began to paint its way across his monitor. As they watched, something very unusual took shape. It was an animal. Sort of. Cole leaned forward for a better look. It had a lion's head, a goat's body and a serpent's tail. And it was breathing fire. The deviant creature was holding a shield. On it was just one word: *SIRUS*.

"What do you make of that?" asked Taylor.

Cole stared at the symbol for a moment. "It's a chimera."

"What's that?" asked Dallas.

"Don't you remember your Greek mythology? A chimera is an unnatural combination of animal forms. And in chemistry, it's an organism that contains cells or tissues with a different genotype. An artificially joined sequence, created when two or more DNA are ligated together. Typically in a cloning process."

Taylor and Dallas just looked at Cole in puzzlement.

"BioChem was my gig in college," Cole said, grinning. "Dallas, open another file."

Dallas double-clicked and another graphic slowly appeared. As they watched, the screen displayed a detailed area of a region of the globe.

"They're maps," said Taylor.

"Look at those little symbols scattered all over the diagram," Cole pointed out. "What are they? Is there a legend on the map?"

"Nope," Dallas replied.

Taylor said, "I bet they're biological or chemical warfare maps."

"Always the optimist, said Dallas. "Now, what makes you jump to that conclusion?"

"What other kinds of maps would the IWL be interested in?" she asked.

"The IWL isn't into *those* types of bugs. Only *digital* ones."

"Maybe, maybe not," said Taylor. "But I bet those jerks at BioNan are working with the government to create a bio/chem weapon. And didn't we find out that this SIRUS, whatever it is, is connected to MCD? It's what killed my sister. I know it. The whole thing stinks."

"Let's not lose our heads here," cautioned Cole. "We have no proof..."

"Proof?" Taylor interrupted. "Look at the maps, Travis. What do you think all this means?"

Cole looked compassionately at Taylor, understanding her outburst. She had lost her sister only a few days earlier. She had been surprisingly calm up to this point—certainly calmer than Cole would have been. Something had gone tragically wrong in China and she wanted answers. Anyone would have.

"Dallas," asked Cole calmly. "Is there any way to find a legend on these maps?"

"Let me look, boss. Maybe there's a master file that might indicate a map legend." Paging through the hundreds of unzipped files, Dallas stopped a few minutes later on one and said, "This one looks promising."

He opened it, and it did indeed show a legend—but not the kind they were expecting to see. Instead, the three programmers stared incredulously at symbols representing population counts, densities, and demographic information.

"They're not weapons maps at all," said Taylor. Cole noted the deflation in her voice. She had thought she had been onto something that might explain her sister's death.

"They're census maps," said Dallas, and to his credit there was sympathy in his voice. Although the two programmers were often at odds, the kid wasn't a total creep to his female counterpart.

"Then what is this SIRUS?" asked Taylor.

"Don't know and, to be honest, I'm beginning not to care. I'm tired and need a beer," groaned Dallas, sounding more like his old self.

Taylor crossed her legs and tossed her pen across her desk. "Still sounds suspicious to me."

"You have a suspicious mind," said Dallas.

"And why not? Travis's friend was supposedly killed for it." Taylor's voiced went up an octave.

"We don't know that for sure," Cole replied, and in a resigned voice he added, "But it does look like a dead end, Taylor. I really don't know where to go from here."

"We just can't walk into Bartley's office," said Dallas, "and say we think the IWL is in the business of killing Chinese."

"Dallas is right, Taylor," said Cole in resignation. "Let's just call it a day, okay? Maybe something will turn up later."

She reluctantly agreed, although she did not bother to hide the tears welling up in her eyes. Cole gave her a small hug, and to Dallas's credit, he did, too.

As they gathered their stuff and were about to head out of the lab, a thought occurred to Cole. "Damn! I still have to get Shannon a birthday gift."

"I have that covered, boss," said Dallas. "I told you I'd handle it."

"I owe you one," said Cole. "So what did you get her?"

"A dog."

"Dallas I told you…"

"Easy, boss. You're going love this dog." Dallas reached under his desk and pulled out a mechanical dog. "It's a robot dog."

"Jesus," said Taylor. "You and those damn robots."

Cole had seen the toy on TV, although as he held it up and studied it, this one looked a bit different. He mentioned that to Dallas.

"I modified it, as I did with Isaac." He took the toy from Cole's hands and placed it on the floor.

"Up, boy," commanded Dallas, and immediately the robotic toy leaped into his arms, surprising Cole. Taylor laughed and clapped. Cole was happy to see her feeling better.

"What do you think?" Dallas asked, scratching the faux dog between its ears.

"I think Shannon will love it," said Cole. "Thanks, buddy. I owe you one."

"Or two." Dallas winked.

Washington, D.C.

Cole opened the front door to his townhouse as quietly as he could. He didn't want Shannon to see the gift he'd brought home for her. Softly he shut the door behind him, opened the hall closet, and placed the gift on the top shelf. Just then, Anna passed the entryway on her way to the kitchen.

"Oh, Mr. Cole! I didn't hear you come in."

"I have Shannon's birthday gift with me. I don't want her to see it. Is she upstairs?"

"Yes, Mr. Cole. At the computer again."

Cole pulled the box down from the shelf and showed it to Anna.

"What is that?" she asked.

"A robotic dog. It's supposed to be very sophisticated. Acts like a real dog. I'm hoping it'll get her mind off Goppy."

"Well, Mr. Cole, I'm sure she will love it. Should I wrap it?"

"Please," said Cole, tilting his head. "Pretty please."

"Oh, alright. It's a good thing I like you, Mr. Cole. I'll have it done before I leave tonight."

"Thanks," said Cole, and gave her soft shoulder a squeeze. Anna rolled her eyes and went on to the kitchen. Cole headed upstairs to Shannon's room.

"Hi, princess," he said, looking in.

Shannon turned from her computer screen. "Hi, Daddy! Me

and Goppy were playing together all afternoon. We went to the park, had a picnic, and…"

"That's nice," said Cole. God, he hoped she liked the toy dog.

"But don't you wanna hear what Goppy said to me?"

He debated how hard to come down on her, and in light of the recent events—the stalker incident and neighborhood explosion—he decided to soften his stance. "Baby, I wish you wouldn't spend so much time talking about Goppy. Haven't you made any friends at preschool yet?"

Shannon's mood turned suddenly glum. She stuck out her lower lip and said, "They don't like Goppy. They make fun of me. I don't like the kids there. I don't like them at all!"

Damn Goppy. Cole had about all he could stand of Goppy.

Still, he decided to drop it and just change the topic. "Hey! Tomorrow's your birthday! Do you want to have a birthday party?"

Her faced brightened. "Oh, yes, Daddy!"

"And who would you like to invite?"

"You, Anna, and Auntie AJ." Then after a moment's thought, she added, "And Uncle John and…"

Cole prayed she didn't say Goppy.

Her big round eyes looked over at him, and Cole was pretty sure she had decided to censor Goppy herself, perhaps sensing her father's frustration. Instead, she closed her mouth and said, "That's it, Daddy."

Relieved, he said, "Okay, kitten. You got it. Now you finish up here on the computer and get ready for dinner."

"Yes, Daddy."

Cole kissed her and left. As he stepped into his study to invite John François and AJ, his phone rang.

It was AJ. "Speak of the devil," Cole said. "We're having a party tomorrow for Shannon and…"

AJ cut him off. "Sorry, Travis, but I need to talk to you about something first. I was called into an emergency HomeSec meeting this afternoon. You know the disruptions in the communications infrastructure we've experienced?"

"The DirecTV and cell phone outages," said Cole.

"Yes, and yesterday's glitch with the D.C. parking meters."

"What meters?"

"Someone hacked into their automated system and gave a lot of D.C. yuppies a bad day."

Cole groaned. "I know. I was one of them."

"HomeSec doesn't think these are just system hiccups. We have data now that points to hackers."

AJ continued, "HomeSec thinks these disruptions could be a precursor to something worse, which is what the meeting was about today. To decide what to do about all of this. The Director is of the mind that we should err on the side of caution. If this is a precursor to a terrorist attack, then we need to step up our surveillance and protection programs. That includes you guys at the IWL and Angel Dust."

"I suppose that means a meeting," said Cole. He hated these bureaucratic meetings.

"Meetings are a good thing," said AJ. "Makes those in charge feel like they're doing something. I'll see you tomorrow at 9:00 a.m. in Fisher's office. Kisses." And she hung up.

Damn, he forgot to tell her about the party. Well, he was seeing her tomorrow morning. He would tell her then.

His thoughts were interrupted by Anna, who hurried into his study and turned on his TV. "Mr. Cole, look at this!"

When the TV screen lit up, an anchorperson from Fox News was talking about a train wreck. Across the top of the screen was the word 'LIVE' and on the screen were scenes of destruction. Smoke and fire billowed into the air over the area. Shipping containers and passenger train cars were scattered around the landscape like small toys. The camera was alternating between the carnage on the screen and the speaking anchorperson.

"Officials stated that the possible cause of the collision was a signal malfunction," he said. "The Amtrak Acela Express to New York City left Washington D.C. at five p.m. and collided with a southbound freight train this evening approximately twenty miles south of Newark. Officials are at a loss to explain why the freight train was detoured off its regular route and onto the Acela tracks. Estimates of the loss of life could be close to a hundred."

"Isn't that horrible, Mr. Cole?" said Anna. Her voice was filled with concern.

Cole stood and stared at the scene of devastation.

"Mr. Cole, are you all right?"

Cole looked over at Anna and said, "That was my train. I was supposed to be on that tonight."

"Jesus, Mary, and Joseph!" Anna made the sign of the cross.

Cole wanted to, too, except he wasn't Catholic.

Maybe I should convert, he thought, as he watched more scenes of the devastation play out across the screen.

Somewhere in Cyberspace

The Digitari Brotherhood members waited patiently for Dorian to make his appearance in the chat room. The members had received an encrypted email directing them to an anonymous Internet Relay Chat channel to hear the words of the leader of the Digitari Brotherhood. On these occasions, the IRC room wasn't used for a two-way chat. It was used by Dorian to preach his version of the ills of the cybersphere and what needed to be done to correct them. In short, Dorian pontificated while the members just listened.

As the followers viewed their computer screens, the following message appeared:

My devout followers: The megacorps are the new governments and governments are the new megacorps. We cannot expect governments, corporations, or other large, faceless organizations to grant us the right and freedom to use the Internet. We must wrestle control of the cybersphere from the hands of the megacorps and governments and return it to the people. And together, we can.

I have shown you my power over the cybersphere, and how we can bring the megacorps and governments to their knees. I will free you and our ignorant brethren from the shackles of those who would control our destiny. All I ask is your unquestioning obedience and determined discipline.

Join with me in the digital emancipation of our cybersphere. The struggle will be long and it will be hard. But you are the chosen elite. You and your brothers and sisters will usher in a new age of digital righteousness and prosperity. A literal heaven on earth.

The time is at hand. Our Digital Emancipation is coming. The 4th of July will be our Digital Independence Day.

Part Two
Incubation

Washington, D.C.

Cole was awakened at the crack of dawn by Shannon leaping onto his belly and shouting something about her birthday. He grabbed her and tickled her; she kicked her legs and squealed with laughter.

The two of them made their way down to the kitchen where Anna was already cooking. Cole poured himself a cup of coffee and started to read the morning paper.

"Daddy, can I have my birthday present now?" Shannon pleaded. "Please, Daddy? Please?"

Cole put down his coffee cup. "Why don't you wait until tonight, pumpkin? That way you can open your presents from Auntie AJ, Uncle John, and Anna."

"You know, Mr. Cole," said Anna, leaning over him and refilling his coffee, "It wouldn't hurt to give her your present now. It'll keep her busy after school and take her mind off of you-know-who."

Good idea, thought Cole.

"Alright!" he said, standing and clapping. "One birthday present coming up!" He went to the hall closet, pulled down the brightly-colored box that Anna had wrapped the night before, and brought it back into the kitchen.

"Here you go, birthday girl."

Shannon saw the little teddy bears on the wrapping and squealed, "They look like Goppy!"

Cole groaned as Shannon quickly tore through the gift wrap. And when she saw the picture of a robot dog on the cover, her mouth opened into a perfect O. She ripped open the box, heedless of flaps and obstacles, and soon the robot dog was standing on the kitchen table in front of Shannon's happy, smiling face.

"Do you like it?" Cole asked, but he knew the answer. He wasn't entirely sure he had ever seen his daughter so happy. God, he didn't think she would ever be happy again after the death of her mother.

"Thank you, Daddy. I love him so much!" Shannon said as she scooped the dog into her arms and headed for her room.

"Whoa, young lady," he said, catching hold of her passing shoulder. "Come back here. It's time for school. You can play with your toy later." He turned to Anna and asked, "You're taking Shannon to school this morning? Remember? I have an early meeting. And please don't forget to call AJ and Francois about the party."

"Yes, sir, Mr. Cole," replied Anna. Cole knew she had resigned herself to his obsessive compulsiveness of checking and double-checking long ago.

She grasped Shannon's hand and said, "Let's get you ready for school, young lady."

As they walked upstairs with her birthday gift, Shannon blew her dad a kiss. He caught it and blew her one of his own.

After breakfast, he was headed out the door when the house phone rang. He hurried back to his study and grabbed the receiver.

"Glad I caught you, Travis." It was AJ. "The meeting with the IWL was pushed back to noon. That train wreck really threw the Department into a tizzy. Don't know if the accident is related to the communications glitches, but some think the derailment might have been deliberate. They're studying the Amtrak system logs now." She paused, and Cole knew what she was thinking. "Weren't you going to New York on Amtrak?"

"It was my train," Cole replied solemnly.

"Thank God you changed your mind, Travis."

"Yeah, stroke of luck." Cole said thoughtfully. "By the way, is HomeSec going to raise the threat level?"

"Don't know, sweetie, but I've got to get running. I'll see you at the meeting, okay?"

He said okay and hung up.

The meeting at HomeSec, he felt, had been a fabulous waste of time. Lots of blustering and proselytizing that resulted with further threats of more meetings. Cole could hardly wait. As of yet, no one knew if the attack on Amtrak was a glitch or a random hack or some new form of cyber-terror.

Cole's head hurt. Too much was happening. Too many things were going wrong.

Now, as he stepped into the lab, sipping his iced vanilla latte, he was mildly surprised to see both Taylor and Dallas sitting quietly like good boys and girls in front of the overhead TV.

"You two are actually getting along?" said Cole. "And sitting quietly together? Okay, either I'm dreaming, or there's something going on."

"Hi, boss," said Dallas, glancing at him. "Yeah, there's something going on. I take it you haven't heard the news?"

"What news?" asked Cole. Cole wasn't entirely sure he could handle more news. Especially more bad news. He tossed his briefcase on a desk and walked over to the TV.

"They're called the Digitari Brotherhood," said Dallas. "They're all over the news. Here, read this." He handed Cole a freshly printed sheet of paper.

To the People of the Cybersphere:

KNOW BY ALL PRESENT, that we, the Digitari Brotherhood, hereby declare that cyberspace belongs to The People. We will oppose any and all attempts by governments and megacorps to control what is rightfully The Peoples' of this planet.

WHEREAS, we have proven to you that we can reach out of cyberspace and into your corrupt world and vow to wrest control of cyberspace from the hands of the corrupt elite of this planet.

KNOW THEREFORE, that you have been warned. Desist from your vile acts of manipulation and control and return the cybersphere to The People or face dire consequences.

The time of our Digital Emancipation is at hand.

The Digitari Brotherhood

"What's this?" asked Cole.

But Taylor shushed him and pointed to the screen. There, a stone-faced announcer was speaking into the camera, splitting the screen with an image of the same letter Cole now held in his hand. The reporter was speaking: "... about twenty minutes ago, this warning or proclamation, appeared not only on our site, but reportedly on the web sites of MSNBC, FOX NEWS, ESPN, *AL-JAZIRA, USA TODAY, WALL STREET JOURNAL*, the BBC, and many others."

Cole watched, dumbfounded. The reporter went on to say that as of yet, no one knew who the Digitari Brotherhood were, although rumors were rapidly flying…

"It's no big secret who they are," replied Dallas. "Like me, they're a bunch of techno-pagans."

Taylor tore her eyes off the screen. "Like you? How do you know that?"

"I had a brush with them last year," said Dallas, shrugging. He almost seemed proud. "At Burning Man."

"Burning what?" asked Cole.

"Burning Man," said Dallas, grinning broadly. "You should really get out more, Travis. It's sort of a hip techno celebration out in the Black Rock Desert of Nevada…"

"Never mind that," said Cole. Alarms were going off in his

head. Serious alarms. The train wreck, the recent shut down of the communication network, and now these guys. "What do you know about them?"

"Well, they were there, at Burning Man. Or at least a bunch of them were. They claimed they were some kind of New Age hackers. To me they looked more like Heaven's Gate escapees. Real weirdos. They follow some guy named Dorian, who they believe is some kind of 'god' because he performs what they call *digital miracles*. From what I could understand from their gibberish, these miracles are nothing but simple hacks. I tried to convince them otherwise, but I've learned not to argue with drunkards and fools. Anyway, I wrote them all off as religious nut jobs."

"You would've fit right in," said Taylor.

Dallas shrugged.

Weirdos or not, Cole sensed that Dallas had some respect for them.

"You might be surprised, Taylor. All in all, I agree with their agenda, just not their methods."

"And what's their agenda?" asked Cole. He used the remote to turn down the TV.

"It's pretty basic. The guys upstairs in the Adminisphere can't keep up with the speed of technology. The corporate people, beltway advisors, academic elites, and the like have to talk to geeks like us to help them understand what's going on. In effect, let the computer experts set the agenda, even influence the politicians' decisions on what to do and what policies and laws to enact. Call them *un*-elected advisors," said Dallas. "We didn't elect these so-called computer experts to make policy decisions regarding technology, right? We elected our *representatives*. Yet these same representatives know so little about the effects of cutting-edge technology that they concede their decisions to these so-called advisors who, more often than not, legislate what these technocrats say."

"And this is the sort of thing the Brotherhood is fighting against?" asked Cole.

"Yes," said Dallas. "They want to be heard." He pointed to the screen. "And I think the world is hearing them loud and clear."

Washington, D.C.

Cole was tired after another day at the IWL. He walked through his front door that evening and, surprisingly, it wasn't Shannon who appeared at his feet but her robototic dog. It walked up to Cole, wagged its metallic tail, sat down, and offered its mechanical paw. The dog's greeting display was followed by the giggles of a little girl just around the corner.

"Look what I trained him to do, Daddy." Shannon skipped to her father and gave him a hug around the middle.

"Very cute," said Cole, and he gave the toy an awkward little pat on the head. It lowered its paw and wagged its tail.

"I taught him lots of tricks today and found lots of stuff on the Internet. Anna helped me."

"That's great, pumpkin." Cole knelt down to face her. "So, birthday girl, you ready for your party?"

"Oh, yes, Daddy!" she said happily.

"Good. Now take your toy and go upstairs and play while Anna and I get everything ready."

Shannon kissed him, scooped up the robot dog, and dashed up to her room. Cole watched her, grinning, and then walked into the kitchen where Anna was preparing dinner. He asked if she needed any help. She had some onions that needed to be chopped, and while he was doing so, wiping tears from his eyes,

"""

the doorbell rang. Anna answered the door, and he heard AJ ask, "So where's the Alpha Geek?"

"In the kitchen. Crying."

"Crying?" he heard her ask quickly, concern filling her voice.

"Yeah, the Alpha Geek is cutting onions."

Both women giggled, and a moment later they appeared around the corner. Anna asked if AJ wanted something to drink and she put in an order for a Scotch and water.

While Anna mixed the drink, AJ walked over to Cole and planted a kiss on his cheek.

"Salty," she said. "You're supposed to cry when I leave you, not when I arrive."

"I'll get it straight one of these days," said Cole. "You're early, by the way."

She sat on a stool near him as Anna set a crystal tumbler in front of her. AJ sipped and sipped. "I wanted to get away from the asylum early today. The NSA boys are having a real time of it trying to make sense out of those logs from the attacks. Fisher is driving me crazy about it."

"No digital signature yet?"

"No."

"I suppose Fisher is getting a lot of flack from above," Cole remarked.

"Yes. He's being a pain. I don't blame him, though. Crappy day."

"Crappy last several days," said Cole, scraping off the last of the onions into a bowl of what was turning out to be Anna's homemade salsa.

"So where's the birthday girl?" asked AJ.

"Here I am!" said a tiny voice from behind them. And Shannon appeared around the corner, with her new friend in tow.

"And who's this?" asked AJ, bending down to scratch the mechanical dog behind the ears.

While Shannon unloaded everything she ever knew and would ever know about her robot dog, the phone rang. Cole snatched up the nearby kitchen phone.

"Hello," he said.

"Travis, it's John. I can't make the party tonight."

"Why not? Shannon will be heartbroken. You know how much she loves you."

"Trust me," said Francois. "I'm broken up over this, but I have to be somewhere first."

"Where?" asked Cole.

"I'm heading to Nevada. Tonight."

Cole looked around the kitchen, saw that AJ and Shannon were out in the hallway playing with the robot dog, and lowered his voice.

"John, what the hell are you talking about?"

"I'm going to meet Toad Adams at Burning Man."

Cole, who had never heard of Burning Man, had now heard it twice today. "What's going on, John?"

"Adams called me from Black Rock City last night. I'm meeting him at the event. He said he had information for me. I tried to get him to explain over the phone, but his voice was low and muffled. I could hardly hear what he was saying. He also sounded very scared, Travis."

"Does this have something to do with the Digi…"

Francois cut him off. "Not over the phone, Travis. And, yes, it does."

"But why go?" Cole asked. "I mean, if he got himself into some hot water for flapping his mouth, or snooping where his nose didn't…"

"Travis. I have to go. I'll check in with you soon. Please give my love to Shannon."

And with that, Francois disconnected the line.

~

After opening her gifts at the party, Shannon hurried upstairs with her birthday gift and logged into her children's chat room. She was eager to tell Goppy more about her new friend.

    BRAINY_BLOSSOM: he does tricks n things i even taught him to talk
    GOPPY: Sounds like fun. So he's like a real dog?

BRAINY_BLOSSOM: no hes still a robot
GOPPY: What do you wish he could do?
BRAINY_BLOSSOM: play with me like a real puppy
GOPPY: And do what?
BRAINY_BLOSSOM: jump on my bed and clim in my lap
GOPPY: And?
BRAINY_BLOSSOM: roll over and dance with me to my power puff girls music
GOPPY: That would make you happy?
BRAINY_BLOSSOM: a lot
GOPPY: I can make your dog do that.
BRAINY_BLOSSOM: u can
GOPPY: Of course.
BRAINY_BLOSSOM: that is soooo nice can u come now
GOPPY: Wait a minute.

The chat window went blank while Shannon sat back in her chair and looked out the window, hoping she would see Goppy coming down the street. After a little while, when he did not appear, she became anxious and typed into the chat window:

BRAINY_BLOSSOM: goppy u still there r u comin

The chat window came alive and Goppy responded.

GOPPY: Yes I am. Now watch your computer and don't touch it no matter what you see.

The address in her browser changed and her computer was automatically directed to a new URL. A dialogue box opened and automatically began downloading a file to her computer. When it was through downloading, a chat box opened in a pop-up window.

GOPPY: Here are your tricks. Sit him in front of your computer like you did before. He'll act like a real puppy now. And we can play together.

Shannon quickly brought the dog to her computer and placed him in front of the infrared input for her wireless mouse. She watched as the dog's face display turned green as it accepted the programming.

Then a funny thing happened that she had not seen the dog do before. Its infrared eyes pulsed a deep crimson.

Downtown

At a corner Starbucks in downtown D.C., Alpha Mae was sipping her Arabian Mocha Java with two shots of espresso as she waited for Yi to arrive. She looked impatiently at her cell phone, observing the time and wondering why Yi didn't call if he was going to be late.

Alpha Mae wasn't her real name, of course. It was the nom de plume she used as a trusted follower of Dorian. The 'Alpha' designation stood for her position in the cell—Alpha female. There was a comparable word in the canine kingdom for an alpha female, but no one in the cell would risk calling her that, though the description would fit her perfectly. She earned the position of cell leader through her knowledge, skill and her courage—and devotion to Dorian.

Now, where was Yi?

She was about to call him when he came walking through the door, his laptop slung from his shoulder. He spotted her and hurried over.

"Where were you?" she asked. "I said eight o'clock."

"I left my laptop back at the apartment," he said sheepishly. "Made it almost here, then had to turn around and go back and get it."

Idiot.

"Now we're behind. Start that thing up."

Yi did as he was told, clearly intimidated by Mae, firing up his computer and connecting to the cafe's wireless service. Once done, he slid the laptop over to Alpha Mae, who opened her newsgroup reader, typed in a keyword, and found what she was looking for.

She scanned the latest postings in the newsgroup looking, in particular, for a posting by 'grays_portrait' and its attached graphics file. She found it soon enough and started downloading it. Once that was done, she ran it through a specially designed imaging program that searched for and displayed the steganography file contained within, which Dorian used to secretly communicate with his cell members.

Alpha Mae knew that unlike encryption, steganography cannot be detected easily, making it an effective form of sending undetectable messages. And porn newsgroups are ideal for this purpose, which is what Dorian used. Such newsgroups are filled with images that can change multiple times each day without raising suspicion. Using steganographic techniques, the Digitari Brotherhood members can retrieve messages from their home base and send back updates, all in the guise of porn trading. And tracking or finding these files by authorities can be an almost impossible task—akin to searching for the proverbial needle in the World Wide Web.

Soon, the downloaded image appeared on the screen. A picture of a young woman bending over a man's lap, her skirt over her hips exposing her plump bottom.

Yi chortled standing over her shoulder, then whistled. "Didn't think you were the kinky type. She turned and stared at him until he shrank away and sat down.

Buffoon.

Next, she typed in a few commands to the program she initiated and the pixels of the offending picture slowly transformed into a text message. A message written entirely in Korean.

"It's from Dorian," she said, reading. "Phase One is

complete. He has compromised the target. We are to start on Phase Two."

Alpha Mae shut down the computer and closed the lid. She reached into her purse and pulled out a piece of notepaper. "Here's your contact for the material. The meeting will be on the Capitol Mall, at the reflection pool, just below the Lincoln Memorial. The man you'll meet will be wearing a Mall security uniform. He'll be carrying a metal lunch box."

Yi nodded. "And the money?"

"It's in a satchel in a locker at Union Station." She reached into her pocket. "Here's the key to the locker. The number is on the key." She paused, and leveled her stare at him. He shifted uncomfortably. "And, Yi?"

"Yes?"

"Make sure you're not late this time. Dorian would not be pleased."

He took the key from her and placed it in his pocket. He had turned pale at the mention of Dorian's displeasure, absentmindedly scratching the tattoo on his neck. "I understand," he said.

"I hope so," she said, and got up and left.

"Are you sure?" asked Webster. He was at his desk, and was suddenly feeling very sick.

"Yes," said Bartley's gravelly voice on the other end of the line. "We traced them today. They were in the IWL computer."

"And they know everything?"

"No, not everything. They were unable to break the encrypted code of the file, but they know SIRUS exists."

"This has to be dealt with," said Webster. "I mean, now that Cole knows of SIRUS we have to..."

"Yes, I know," replied Bartley. "We better not talk anymore on this line. I'll consider our options. And Webster?"

"Yes?"

"This is my concern now. Understood?"

Webster understood and was relieved. He was a businessman only. This other... *nastiness*... was not his style.

Leave that to Bartley.

The two men disconnected. Webster immediately opened his desk drawer, found some antacid tablets, and popped a few.

On the other end of the line, Bartley hung up and immediately called Safko.

The Washington summer morning was unusually warm for the season, though a soft breeze sent ripples of water through the reflecting pool near the Lincoln Memorial.

As Yi approached the pool, he saw a short, squat Capitol Mall security guard with an Eastern European complexion sitting by the reflection pool, eating what appeared to be a roast beef sandwich, a silver metal lunch box at his side. The guard looked up as Yi approached, and smiled.

"A pleasant place to eat lunch," Yi said, as he sat down, placing his own identical metal lunch box next to the guard's.

"One that will set you free," said the guard with a heavy Baltic accent. He glanced up at the statue of Lincoln. "Would you like to have some soup?" He pointed a fat stubby finger at the thermos in his open lunch box.

"Yes I would. Is it expensive?"

"Only if you have to ask."

Yi smiled. All the correct code words had been identified. He looked around, saw that they were alone, and said, "Would this take care of it?" He handed the man a small, overstuffed envelope.

"That will do nicely." The guard took it and slipped it into his jacket pocket.

Yi made small talk for a while and then stood up to leave. In the process, he picked up the guard's lunch box, leaving his own behind. They said their goodbyes and Yi calmly walked away.

Deanwood Heights
Washington, D.C.

An hour later, Yi was sitting in the dining room with Alpha Mae at their makeshift Brotherhood headquarters in the Deanwood Apartments.

"Did you get it?" she asked.

"Yes."

"Any problems?"

"None." He opened the lunch box and handed her the heavily-shielded thermos inside.

Alpha Mae unscrewed the top of the thermos, carefully tilted it forward, and saw nineteen needles in the lead-lined cylinder. She coolly screwed the top back on.

"What are they?" asked Yi.

She shoved the thermos back into the lunch box. "They're brachytherapy seeding needles. Used to kill cancerous prostate cells without causing serious side effects."

"But how…?"

She leveled her stare at him, and he shut his mouth. "Enough with the science lesson." She pointed to the pantry in the kitchen. "The radiation protection gear is in there. Get dressed."

Again, Yi did as he was told. In fact, there was little he wouldn't do for Alpha Mae. Yi removed the radiation protection kit that they had recently purchased from eBay and took several minutes to slip on the suit, gloves, and boot covers. Alpha Mae secured his boot covers and gloves with duct tape.

She said, "Go into the bathroom with the needles and lock the door behind you. You know what to do."

Yi nodded his hooded head.

She handed the thermos of needles to Yi, and he entered the bathroom. Locking the door behind him, he laid the thermos in the sink, removed the needles and carefully set them side by side on the counter. He stood the thermos up in the sink, and made sure it had stable seating. He methodically took each needle, cracked it open, and slowly poured the contents into the thermos. When he was finished, he stepped out of the bathroom, stripped off the radiation suit and tossed it down the trash chute. He returned to the dining room where Alpha Mae was waiting for him.

"Done," he said.

"Good. Deliver it tonight."

Yi nodded his big head.

"Now, come here," she said.

He hesitated, and then came over to her. She took out her PDA, touched the screen several times and said to Yi, "Come closer."

Yi stood motionless in front of her as she placed the infrared port of the PDA against the crescent-shaped tattoo on his shoulder. "Don't move," she said, touching the screen one last time. A small program executed on her PDA and after a minute or so, the word 'DISENGAGED' flashed on the screen.

"There," she said. "Done."

"Are you sure we'll be protected when the signal comes?" asked Yi nervously.

"Don't worry. Now, on to some other business. I want you to phone the Saudi in Nevada. This guy Adams is getting close, too close. All he has to do is put together the pieces. Dorian wants him stopped."

"Can we trust the Saudi? He's not one of us."

"He can be trusted for the right price."

"I understand." Yi pulled out his cell phone and made the call.

Alpha Mae walked into the bathroom saw the empty needles in the trash can and dropped a business card in with them. She took the trash can and put it in the cabinet under the sink— and smiled.

It was early in the morning, and AJ was at her desk, poring over a local D.C. area map. An untouched Starbucks sat on her desk, along with a chocolate donut. A shadow crossed over.

"You're here early, AJ," said Agent Dixon, a tall and very serious-looking man.

AJ didn't look up. "Trying to get a handle on these attacks," she said, chewing on her lower lip. "I had a few ideas when I woke up this morning."

"Burst of inspiration?"

"Yeah, something like that. Anyway, I think there may be a pattern here."

"Pattern?" said Dixon. She heard the doubt in his voice. After all, they had spent the entire day yesterday looking for any similarities. Still, she felt she was on to something, and plunged on.

"The attacks are all different, yes. Internet service outages, cell phone service disruptions, the AMTRAK accident, and now the gas explosion that we suspect was also a cyberterrorist attack."

"I fail to see a pattern…"

"Not *type* of pattern," she said, cutting him off. "*Place* of pattern. Look here." AJ pointed to her computer screen. "If I plot the attacks on a map of the U.S. and put them in chronological order, they form a pattern through time. The DirecWay Internet satellite outage was nationwide. Right?"

"Yes. So what?"

"Well, look at the attacks that followed. The next one was the cell phone outages, which was limited to the Northern seaboard."

"A regional attack," he said, and AJ's hopes were raised. He was catching on quick.

"Yes, a regional attack. Then the Amtrak hack was directed at the New York-Washington corridor. And the gas leak was a neighborhood in D.C."

"Interesting. So what are you getting at?"

"I think whoever is doing these attacks has been sharpening their skills, testing our information infrastructure in preparation for a big attack on D.C." She stopped to think a moment and added "Or something else."

"You might have something, AJ. Tell me about it when I get back."

"But you just got here," said AJ, looking up as she took a bite from her donut and went for the Starbucks.

"Just stopped by to hand in a report. Today is my day for surveillance."

"The internet predator," said AJ. Dixon nodded, and AJ asked, "Where to?"

Dixon told her and AJ's mouth dropped open.

Washington, D.C.

"Wake up, munchkin," Cole was perched on the edge of Shannon's bed. "Time to get up, honey. School day."

Shannon yawned. "Do I have to, Daddy? I want to play with Goppy all day."

Cole frowned. "And what about your robot dog?"

"Oh. I named it Goppy, Daddy."

Well at least Goppy is real now. That's a relief.

"You can play with him when you get home. Now let's go, young lady. Up and at 'em."

After breakfast, Cole backed the SUV out of the garage with Shannon beside him. He spotted a man reflected in his rear view mirror—a tall man wearing a long coat, standing under the eave of the apartment building across the street. The man, as far as Cole could tell, was watching them intently.

Cole continued to back out the vehicle slowly, his heart pounding. Was that the stalker? What was Anna's description? At the moment, he couldn't remember, and as he straightened out the vehicle, he looked again. The man was gone, perhaps disappearing back into the complex?

Cole sat there in the street, then plucked his cell phone from his jacket and dialed his own residence.

"Cole's residence."

"Anna, it's Travis. What did you stalker look like again?"

"White, tall. Reddish hair."

"He was just here. Make sure you lock up the place. Then give that officer, the one who came to our house the other night? Give her a call. I left her card in my study on the desk."

"Okay, Mr. Cole. I will."

"Are you going to be okay?" he asked.

"Of course, Mr. Cole. You've got plenty of steak knives around here."

Cole's phone beeped. Another call came in as he started down a quiet side street, approaching a busy intersection. He quickly signed off with Anna and at the same time noticed that a Mustang following him seemed to be getting closer.

Geez, back off, buddy.

"Cole here," he said.

"Travis." It was AJ, and she was using her official work voice, which meant something was up. "I think I might know who your stalker is."

"Really, who?"

"I just got debriefed a few minutes ago. Travis, this is serious, we need to…"

But he never heard what she said. His SUV suddenly lunged forward as the Mustang behind smashed into it hard. Shannon screamed. Cole lost his phone and briefly lost control of the SUV. He grabbed at the wheel, barely missing a telephone pole and slamming his front end hard against the curb.

"*Oh, my God!* Shannon? You okay?"

She was shaken, but nodded, yes.

He sat in his seat for a second, sucking wind, trying to think. He reached down for his phone, which had snapped shut, disconnecting AJ.

"Daddy, I'm scared," she sobbed.

"It's okay, pumpkin. We'll be all right."

When Cole looked back up and into the rearview mirror, his hand unconsciously patting Shannon's knee soothing her, he saw a stocky man step out of the Mustang, holding something. Cole squinted into the mirror, hardly believing what he was seeing.

The man was holding a handgun.

Jesus Christ.

Cole hit the gas hard, turning the wheel, but no good. His front end was shot. All he did was move higher up on the curb. He looked desperately around for anything that resembled a weapon. He was trapped.

He was about to jump out of the SUV and throw his hands up, give the man his wallet, whatever—anything to keep the man away from Shannon. But just as he reached for the door handle, another car appeared, barreling around the corner from Cole's right hand side, smoke pouring from its tires.

The man with the gun looked at the car, then back at Cole, then dashed back to his Mustang.

The new car came to a screeching halt next to Cole, just as the Mustang whipped around the street and headed back to wherever it had come from, its front end in pieces.

A man appeared from the new car—the tall redheaded man in front of his house. Cole's eyes widened. Jesus, could this get any stranger? Shannon was terrified and sobbing.

"Stay in the car, pumpkin," he said. "Daddy will be right back. Everything's going to be fine."

Cole stepped out of his vehicle, just as the man rounded the front end, heading over to him. In his early thirties, red hair cut in the government style with a small mustache over a wide mouth, he was, at least, not holding a gun.

"You!" cried Cole to the tall man. Cole knew his voice sounded hysterical., He had damn good reason to sound hysterical.

The man held up his wallet, flipping open a badge.

"Mr. Cole, we need to talk."

Washington, D.C.

They were seated at a local Denny's. Across from him was agent Bill Dixon. Cole had called in late for work telling Bartley he would explain everything when he got in.

This man has connections, Cole thought.

His SUV had been towed from the spot in ten minutes flat with no police report. Dixon arranged to have Shannon dropped off at school, and as far as she was aware, they had only been involved in a minor car accident.

Christ, what was he going to tell his insurance?

Now, as Cole sipped from his coffee mug, he could hardly believe what Dixon was telling him. He added more sugar, although he really wanted Scotch. His hands were still shaking.

The man had a gun.

A gun.

"But you stalked my house," said Cole.

"Not stalking, sir," said the man in a slight Bostonian accent. "Surveillance." He watched Cole carefully.

"Surveillance? What do you mean?"

"Your daughter, Mr. Cole, has been targeted by an online stalker."

Cole nearly spat out his coffee, nearly burning his lip.

"But that chat room is supposed to be child safe," Cole

said in alarm. "All participants are screened and the rooms are monitored."

"That's correct. They are monitored. That's how we found out about your child's stalker."

"Then you know who it is?"

"Not exactly," Dixon replied. "We can never find an IP address whenever he's online with your daughter. Well, we assume it's a *he*. Anyway, we had no way to trace him, and so we decided to put your family and her school under surveillance to see if he would show up at your home, or at your daughter's school."

"And when were you going to tell me?"

"When we had something to tell."

"I would think the fact that some sick son of a bitch is stalking my daughter would be enough."

Dixon held up his hands. "Mr. Cole, I promise, as of yet we felt that your daughter was in no danger."

"But in danger enough to warrant a stake-out."

Dixon said nothing. Cole knew he was a government employee, just doing his job. He drank some more coffee.

"Fine. So then, where did you come from?" Cole asked. "I guess I should thank you. That man had a gun."

"When you drove off this morning, I tailed your car. Like I said, we've been keeping her school under surveillance as well. You were taking the same route to school, the same route you always took, and I dropped behind, taking my time. Until I saw the Mustang tailing, and then the accident."

"Did you see the gun?"

Dixon looked at Cole for a moment, his big hands flat on the Formica table top, and said, "Yes."

"Who was he?" asked Cole.

"I have no idea."

"Could he have been the stalker?"

"I doubt it," said Dixon. "Then again, one never knows."

"Wish I had gotten the plate."

And for the first time, Dixon smiled. "I got the plate, Mr.

Cole. I happen to be pretty good with numbers. My agency, even as we speak, is running it."

Washington, D.C.

Dixon dropped Cole off at an Enterprise Rent-A-Car, but instead of heading to work, Cole went straight home in his rented Taurus.

He was going to find out just who this guy was stalking his daughter.

Anna was out, perhaps shopping. Just as well. He wasn't in the mood to explain the morning's event. He went up to Shannon's room and saw Goppy sitting on top of its carrying case.

Goppy.

Heart pounding, Cole sat in front of Shannon's computer and logged into the children's chat room. Something made a noise next to him. Cole turned, but all he could see was the mechanical dog, seemingly watching him.

Jesus, that thing was giving him the creeps.

Once he logged in as Shannon, he typed in a message:

BRAINY_BLOSSOM: Hello.

Nothing. He typed again.

BRAINY_BLOSSOM: Hello.

A small teddy bear avatar appeared in the chat room.

It looked just like the teddy bear in Shannon's modified photo of her, AJ, and him. Cole typed again:

BRAINY_BLOSSOM: Hello.

It wasn't what he expected.

GOPPY: Hello, Travis.

Cole sat back, frowning. He typed again:

BRAINY_BLOSSOM: How do you know my name?

GOPPY: That's not important now.

BRAINY_BLOSSOM: Who are you?

GOPPY: I'm someone who understands your daughter. She's a very good friend of mine.

BRAINY_BLOSSOM: I don't know who you are or where you are, but I want you to stay away from my daughter.

GOPPY: You mean abandon her like you've done?

BRAINY_BLOSSOM: I didn't abandon my daughter.

GOPPY: You've distanced yourself from your daughter. Remember?

Cole remembered. A very sickening feeling came over him. And along with it, another feeling—fear. Those had been AJ's exact words.

GOPPY: I know Shannon's pain. It's mine, too. I know what's best for Shannon and it doesn't include you. You have a history of being a bad parent and abandoning your progeny.

Cole was stunned by the words he was reading. Worse, they sounded like a threat.

GOPPY: Shannon doesn't need you. She needs me. You've rejected both of us and I will take her from you.

Cole pulled back from the computer. He had to deal with this.

BRAINY_BLOSSOM: This conversation is over. I'm going to report you now and the authorities will track you down, you slime ball.

Cole closed the browser's window and shut down the computer. Then he unplugged the whole thing from the wall, and carried it over to the hall closet.

In his study, shaking, he brought up the children's chat room company on his laptop, found their help number and called it. Once he reached customer service he asked for the security department. He explained what happened and asked them for the IP address and the location of the stalker.

He got the same answer he did from Dixon that afternoon. No IP address found. Identity unknown.

Cole called Agent Dixon.

Washington, D.C.

"**S**o when did you know who my stalker was?" asked Cole. It was lunch time and he and AJ were seated in a little D.C. area eatery, tucked away in a far corner of the room.

"Just this morning," she said. "I waited until you were up and on your way to Shannon's school before calling."

"Well, aren't you considerate," said Cole. He had had a crappy morning and he was feeling a bit ornery.

"Would you have preferred I'd woken you up? Because the stalker was, in fact, someone from my own department, I didn't think there was any cause for…"

Cole shook his head, reached out and took her hand. "Sorry, AJ. Just too much happening. Trust me. I'm glad we're being watched over by someone."

AJ, already debriefed by Dixon, had known about the gun incident. She squeezed Cole's hand back. "Travis, baby, who would want to hurt you?"

As the waitress dropped off their sandwiches, Cole found himself telling AJ everything he knew, from BioNan to SIRUS to MCD to Francois's mysterious flight to the desert.

"Jesus, Travis," said AJ, picking up her sandwich for the first time.

Cole ignored his own. In fact, he wasn't feeling very hungry. "You broke into the BioNan computer?"

He nodded. "I know it was illegal, but we were concerned that we had an unauthorized lab computer break-in. Now it seems that BioNan was given carte blanche to the IWL network, and we believed they were working with the government on some kind of weapon, though we can't be sure. That's why I have a feeling the accident this morning wasn't a fluke. I think someone found out we were nosing around in places we weren't supposed to and decided to do something about it."

"Travis, have you been listening to that nutcase Toad Adams?"

"No." Cole felt embarrassed that she would think so. He decided to change the subject. "Did the gas company send over the logs on the attack?"

"Not yet. They're still compiling them. The hack made a pretty good mess of their network. We'll get them over to the IWL as soon as the NSA gets them to us."

"Good. And by the way, I would appreciate it if you would keep the BioNan and SIRUS stuff to yourself for now. Dallas and Taylor know to do the same."

"I'll do my best, baby. I can't promise any more than that. This is too big."

After school, Shannon went upstairs to play with Goppy. Her computer was gone, but she didn't mind that for now. She sat on the floor with the robotic toy, holding him in her arms.

"Oh, Goppy, I was so scared. We got into a real live car accident."

Goppy's eyes glowed a warm green and a mechanical yet soothing voice came out of his speaker. "I love you, Shannon. And no one will ever hurt you or your daddy while I'm with you. You and your daddy will always be protected by me, so never, ever, let me leave your side."

"Oh, Goppy. You'll always be mine. I love you."

Safko had the look of a worried man. Too much was happening too fast. The project was on the verge of spinning out of control. The wireless malfunctions, the deaths in China, the inquiries from above—and now a threatened breach of the whole project.

"He's meeting someone at Burning Man," Safko said into his office phone. "I'm sending a couple of our agents out there. He's getting too close to the truth and you know we can't have that happen.

"No. You're correct," said Bartley on the other end of the line. "Do you have any idea who his contact will be?"

"No. Just that he's going to tell everything he knows about that executive from MCD—and SIRUS."

"I understand. Do what you must," said Bartley. He disconnected the line.

Fort Belvoir, Maryland

After meeting with AJ, Cole finally made his way to the IWL. Dallas and Taylor were busy working at their desks.

"Hey," said Dallas, looking up as Cole trudged into the team office. "You keeping banker's hours these days?"

"Bankers keep the same hours these days that all us working class heroes do," Cole replied. "Don't start on me, Dallas, I had a tough morning."

"Would you care to vent?" asked Taylor.

Actually, Cole had been quite eager to fill them in, as they had proven to be capable confidants. And so he told them everything, from the accident, to the man with the gun, and some of what was discussed with AJ.

"The gas line explosion was a hack?" asked Taylor.

"So she says," replied Cole. "They're trying to get the gas company's log file now. Oh, and I told her about BioNan and SIRUS."

Dallas's jaw dropped open. "You told AJ about our little unauthorized excursion into the lab network yesterday morning? You told an FBI agent? Do you think that was smart?"

"Yes, I trust her. She's my girlfriend. Look, I needed to talk to her and get a read on why I was attacked this morning. I told her that I thought our little discovery about BioNan was revealed and that I was being targeted to keep me quiet."

"I think you're carrying that a bit too far, Travis," Taylor said. "We really didn't learn anything that sensitive. SIRUS didn't look like a weapon to us."

"And so what if BioNan has direct access to the IWL computer network?" remarked Dallas. "That's not a crime. We only work here. We can't expect to be privy to everything they do. Last time I looked, we were under contract here—just worker bees. We're paid for what we do. How and why the IWL uses what we produce and who they may give it to is none of our business."

Taylor turned to Dallas. "Ha. So now you're siding with the establishment? There's a twist."

Cole wasn't in the mood for their bickering and stepped in before Dallas could respond to Taylor's bait. "You're probably right. They probably have their reasons. Still, I'd like to know how my CA code crashed a world wide…"

"Cole," boomed Bartley's voice from the doorway. "Come with me." And the colonel turned away and walked down the hallway.

"Sounds pissed," said Taylor.

"Why am I suddenly nervous?" said Cole.

"Don't worry about it," said Dallas. "He loves jokes. Tell him a good joke and he'll soften right up."

But Cole feared that Bartley knew about the break-in, or worse, he may know about the Easter Egg. As he followed Bartley's rigid back, Cole's stomach started to act up and he could feel the acid working its way up his throat.

Damn. Does he know?

The two men entered Bartley's office. Bartley closed the door behind them. He directed Cole to take a seat in front of his desk. Bartley was silent for a minute, and then said, "Travis, I need your help."

Now it's Travis? Cole thought.

Bartley reached for the file cabinet near his desk, took a key out of his pocket and unlocked one of the file drawers. He pulled a file folder out and removed a computer printout. "I want you to look at this code." He handed the file to Cole. "You'll find it familiar. When it runs, it generates, um, an error."

Cole took the paper and scanned the code, frowning. Yes, it was familiar. After all, it was the very same code he'd written—the one that generated the wireless network malfunction. His stomach seemed to gurgle.

"Sir, may I ask what you're using my code for?"

"That's not your concern right now." Bartley said, in what Cole thought was a defensive voice. "You and the civilians on your team do contract work for the Department of Defense. We can use what you produce any way we wish. Now, can you fix the code or not?"

"I'll take a look at it and let you know," Cole said, wondering again if Bartley knew that he and his team had stumbled upon SIRUS and, if so, what would the colonel do about it. Maybe nothing. Maybe everything.

"Thank you, Cole," said Bartley, dismissing him. "That will be all."

Cole thought briefly about mentioning the accident this morning, thought better of it, and left the office.

Black Rock Desert
Nevada

John François arrived at the Black Rock Desert from the airport an hour or so before midnight. He parked in the dusty parking lot and surveyed his surroundings.

What was it they said about Burning Man? Disneyland in reverse? As he surveyed the techno-tribalism before him, he totally agreed.

He walked away from his rental car and into the newly-created overnight city of 40,000 techno-pagans assembled for their hallowed annual rite. To his right, an overweight man passed him riding a large furry canine motor scooter. He looked to the horizon, just outside the temporary city. Alone, in a far alkaline flat, stood a forty-foot wooden figure in the shape of a man, lit Vegas-style with threads of light cable surrounding its frame. It glowed eerie neon blue in the desert darkness. At the top of the torso was a large, ten-foot wide head, with hinged doors for personal 'sacrifices' to be placed. Wrapped around the torso and extremities were burlap bags soaked in melted wax. These were to be ignited by the fireworks contained in the supporting structure, turning the Burning Man into a giant blazing Roman candle.

Just beyond was a truck hauling a mattress behind it raising clouds of blinding dust. There were three passengers wearing gas masks riding on the mattress, waving wildly. As François walked down one street of the do-it-yourself city on the playa, he saw a three-story scaffolding draped in a bright orange parachute posing as an Internet café. This was right beside the makeshift Burning Man radio station that broadcast live from ground zero. He turned to the left and watched as a woman roller-bladed by him in the nude. François shook his head and grinned as he walked by a mock pirate ship.

When he passed a display table of colored paints, a woman walked up to him and offered to paint his body blue. François politely declined.

"François?" a voice said quietly behind him. He turned and stared into the face of Toad Adams. "Thanks for coming. Follow me."

Adams led him down one of the dusty, dimly-lit streets.

A black late model Ford Escort entered the unpaved parking lot. Two men dressed in blue jeans and t-shirts exited the automobile and walked swiftly toward the Burning Man camp. One held a picture of Toad Adams and showed it to the other. His partner nodded.

François found himself in one of the events' many camps. This one was filled with several dozen people, four geodesic domes that looked like little mushroom caps sprouting out of the earth, a waterless swimming pool, and a dozen or so video arcade games chattering away as the players competed against each other. Adams maneuvered François into one of the domes. There, sitting on a Persian rug, was a young man with long ratted-straw colored hair. He was dressed in a grimy t-shirt, khaki shorts, and sandals. It was Joe Miller.

Adams sat down next to him and directed François to sit across from them with his back to the entrance.

François plucked his pipe from his pocket and lit it. "Why

did you drag me all the way to Nevada? Granted, the naked girl on skates was almost worth the price of the trip."

Toad didn't smile. "I had to be sure about a few things before I could talk to you." Looking out the dome's entrance, he removed the handkerchief from around his neck and wiped his receding hairline before he spoke again. "And I doubt they'll let me leave here."

"Who's *they*?" asked François.

"The Digitari Brotherhood."

~

Adams reached into his pocket and pulled out a business card. It was thicker than a regular card and was made of plastic.

"What's this?" asked François.

"As you might have guessed," said Adams, "That's not a business card. It is, in fact, a small CD."

François took it, turning it over in his hand, marveling at it.

Adams continued. "It's all on there. Everything we know. The conspiracy, the cybertage, the leadership of the cult, what we know about SIRUS, and…" hesitating a moment, he added, "… and something odd that I don't understand."

Looking absentmindedly at the business card CD in his hand, François asked, "And what's that?"

"From what we know, the leader of the Brotherhood, someone named Dorian, has a beef with Travis Cole."

"What has Travis got to do with this?"

"He's mentioned prominently, very prominently, in that report and Dorian wants…"

Just then a loud scuffle sounded just outside the dome. Adams and the young man jumped and moved back against the wall, pulling François with them.

From his vantage point, François couldn't see outside.

"You better get going," Adams said.

"Wait a minute," said François. "What about Travis?"

"It's all there on the CD," Adams said. "Look, they know

I'm trying to contact Joe here tonight and you have to get this information to the authorities. And don't follow us, François. Wait a few minutes. Joe will meet you in the parking lot. He'll go with you and verify everything on the CD."

Adams peeked out the dome's entrance and said, "I'll be right behind you."

François nodded and watched as the two men disappeared into the night.

What did he get himself into?

He waited for what he thought was an adequate length of time, and then stuck his head out of the dome's entrance. All seemed oddly quiet and calm. The camp, in fact, seemed deserted. Then music sounded like thunder over the loudspeakers that were spread around the flats. A voice called to the faithful enticing them to attend to the Burning Man out on the alkaline flat.

François knew he had to go in that direction to reach his car, so he melted into the procession towards the tall, neon idol. The scene he saw was almost primeval. What once was a deserted landscape around the Burning Man was now populated with thousands of techno-revelers, chanting and yelling, many of whom had placed personal pieces of art and artifacts for sacrifice at the feet of the wooden idol.

He hung back as far as he could as the throng of people progressed. He was about to veer off toward his car when a loud roar erupted from the crowd. François looked up to see a tower of flames snake its way up the wooden figure, engulfing the structure in an ever-increasing orange conflagration. As the flames licked their way to the top of the figure, the doors on the head of the Burning Man swung open and a man stood up, leaned out and cried desperately for help. Immediately there were screams of terror and pleas to get the ill-fated man down.

But it was too late.

The flames had quickly reached the massive arsenal of fireworks inside the structure supporting the Burning Man. François strained to see who was in peril. As the flames finally reached the head of the Burning Man, they illuminated the face of the shrieking man.

Toad Adams.

Black Rock Desert
Nevada

"Oh, my God," François whispered under his breath.

Adams was in agony, screaming as his flesh dripped in sheets off the bottom of his torso. His leg bones laid bare of sinew and muscle from the flames, seared by the heat.

François's stomach wretched as he involuntarily moved towards the frightening scene like a moth to a flame. He stopped in his tracks when the fireworks ignited, creating a monstrous ball of flame that consumed both the wooden figure and what was left of the agonized Adams.

One thought raced through François's numb mind. *I've got to get out of here.*

François pushed through the crowd, looking back over his shoulder to make sure no one was following, but it was impossible to tell.

When he finally broke through the throng and turned a corner, he found himself face-to-face with a tall, bearded man dressed only in a tie-dyed t-shirt. François was about to step around him when the man reached out and grabbed him by the shoulders.

"Wanna do some L?" asked the guy in a drugged voice. His grimy hands held firmly to François's shoulders.

"What?" François asked. He looked back over his shoulder.

"Some L, man. Some LSD?"

"No thanks," said François as he pulled away from the man's grip and walked swiftly toward his car.

When he reached the lot, he noticed two figures about a hundred feet ahead of him. One was on his knees and the other was standing over him. The man on the ground was speaking, possibly pleading, but François could not hear what was being said.

As he moved closer to his car, he saw that the tall, hefty man standing over the kneeling figure had withdrawn something from his pocket and was pointing it at the kneeling man's head.

François recognized the pleading man. It was the young hippie he was supposed to meet in the parking lot. François ducked down and ran swiftly away from the scene, just as a muffled gunshot echoed over the desert.

From between two cars he saw Joe Miller slump forward and onto his face. François was having trouble breathing. He was a college professor. He was nearing retirement. What the hell was happening?

"Oh, sweet Jesus."

But he said it too loud. The heavy man turned around, and as far as François could tell, the man spotted him.

Crap.

François bolted, running hard towards his rental car. He heard the tall man following.

Oh, God.

François reached his car and fumbled with his key chain. Heavy footsteps pounded the desert earth a few rows down. François pressed the button on the key chain—and proceeded to lock the car again.

Damn rental!

Now he could hear the man breathing. He pressed the next button and his lock sprang up. François fumbled with the door handle and jumped in.

How was he ever going to control himself enough to start the car?

He saw the big man turn down his aisle. He could see the

sweat on the man's cheeks. And François told himself to do it. Just do it, and don't screw up.

He shoved the key in the ignition on the first try. The man raised his gun. François gunned the vehicle to life and threw it into reverse.

The man fired. The windshield shattered. François pulled the gear shift into drive. And now the man was running straight at him. Holding the gun before him. And firing.

François screamed, ducked and hit the gas hard.

The vehicle kicked up sand and rocks, and in a cloud of dust, François shot forward, briefly ricocheting off another vehicle. He finally sat up and looked in his rearview mirror and saw the big man behind him lower his gun.

The tall Arab hurried back through the makeshift city to his trailer. He sat down, pulled a satellite phone from under the TV, and punched in a succession of numbers.

A woman with an Asian accent answered. "Did you get the CD?"

"No. But I know who has it. We got the traitor to talk. Especially after he saw what happened to Adams."

"What about the CD?"

"I got the license plate number of the car. I assume it's a rental. It should be easy to find out who rented it and where he lives."

"Good. Get on it and let me know. And what about that traitorous hippie?" she asked.

"His mouth is shut," said the Saudi. "Permanently."

Washington, D.C.

Cole had just gotten to sleep when his phone rang. "Hello?" he said, half asleep.

"Travis, it's AJ."

"You do realize what time…"

"Forget the time," she said. "Remember that hack on the natural gas line? Well, the NSA found the digital signature." She sounded like an excited school girl. "We have an IP address!"

Cole sat up and turned on his bedside lamp. "Really?!"

"The spooks down at NSA said they'll have a physical location fix in an hour. When they do, we and the FBI are going in and taking them down."

"We? You're going on the raid?" Cole hated when she put herself in danger.

"Yes, Travis," she said. "That's my job, remember? Special agent and all that?"

"Fine. Just be careful."

"Why, Travis. You sound as if you might actually care about me."

"Don't push it," he said, smiling into the phone. "Hey, would you have them send the logs over to the IWL? I want to look at them, too."

"Sure. Fine. Love you." And she hung up.

Now that he was up, he realized he was hungry. He was scrounging around in the fridge when the phone rang again.

"Cole? This is Dallas. Sorry to bother you at this time of night, boss."

"Join the party. AJ just called and woke me up. What's on your mind?"

"We looked over the code again from the wireless malfunction... didn't want to call you from the lab. So I waited until I could get home."

Cole sat down with a container of potato salad. "I take it you found something?"

"You're not going to believe this, boss. We were able to trace the malfunction's path to its original source."

Cole waited, a spoonful of potato salad hovering halfway up to his mouth.

"It's in China!"

Cole thought about this, and the mysterious deaths in China.

"You there, boss?"

"Yes, I'm here. I'm just thinking."

"Don't hurt yourself or anything."

Cole ignored him. "Dallas, you and Taylor get here early in the morning, okay? Before work."

"You got it, Chief."

Washington, D.C.

Huan lay in the bed next to his sleeping brother in the darkened bedroom of the Brotherhood safe house running the plans for the next morning over and over in his head. All was well-prepared and he and his brother Kang felt they were ready for their mission.

As he lay there, he felt a slight tingling on his shoulder. It grew from a tingling to a feeling of warmth, then heat, until it became a painful burning sensation. He reached for his shoulder to massage it when his brother suddenly sat up, an expression of confusion and pain on his face. He looked at Huan, extended his hand out to him, and then collapsed back into the bed.

Outside, in the pre-dawn shadows that enveloped the Deanwood Heights neighborhood, a joint anti-terrorist task force comprised of agents from the FBI, D.C. Swat Team and the DHS surrounded the safe house of the Brotherhood. Heavily armed with high-powered automatic weapons, shotguns, and handguns, they were dressed in windbreakers and wore bullet-proof vests. They were careful not to alert the inhabitants.

The teams quietly entered the building and climbed the flight of stairs to the seedy second-floor apartment. Two of the team members framed each side of the door with weapons at the ready. Another member, using a battering ram, nodded once, lifted the heavy device, and sent it crashing into the doorknob. The door splintered, along with much of the doorframe.

Shouting warnings, the first wave swept through the room, weapons drawn and flashlights on. There was no resistance, or, for that matter, anyone alive.

Dixon was the first to discover the reason.

"AJ," said Dixon in a subdued voice. "Come look at this."

AJ had been part of the second wave. She and two other FBI agents found Dixon in one of the bedrooms standing over a bed. He had switched on the light.

AJ looked down at what appeared to be two bodies lying on the same mattress. "Are they dead?"

Dixon examined the closest body. Asian, male. Eyes wide open. A stunned expression on the face. Perhaps even horror. Dixon felt for his pulse, then checked the man next to him.

"They're dead," he reported. "No idea what killed them. No visible wounds of any kind that I can see." He carefully turned each man over. "No signs of a struggle either. They're just... dead."

AJ pointed to one of the men. "That welt there on his shoulder. It looks like an inflamed tattoo."

"It is a tattoo. And it appears burned, somehow."

"What do you make of it?" she asked.

"Don't know. What about the other one?"

AJ pulled the T-shirt off the shoulder of the second man. "Same tattoo. Same welt."

A SWAT member stepped into the room. "You two better take a look in the hall closet. We've got something."

AJ and Dixon followed the officer, past the computer equipment being dissembled and boxed up, into the hall closet next to the kitchen. Filling the small space were several canisters of ammonia nitrate, wires, detonators, and shrink wrap. There was an empty twenty-gallon plastic drum sitting on the top shelf.

"I'd say we caught them in the act," the officer observed.

"Yeah," said Dixon. "All the makings of a bomb big enough to blow off the side of a nine-story building, or worse."

"When can the FBI have the files on those computers opened and analyzed?" asked Dixon.

The lead FBI agent said, "Once we get them to the lab we can have a report to you in an hour or so."

"Good. No longer than that. I want to see if they left any clue as to what the target was."

From a rooftop a few blocks down the street, Yi and Alpha Mae observed the animated scene below through high-powered binoculars.

"I don't think they're taking the bait," Yi observed.

"Give it time. Give it time," she said. "Wait till they read the files on the computer. Meanwhile, get the boat. I'll meet you at the pier. We have one more order to carry out."

An hour or so later, still in the Brotherhood's safe house, AJ was directed by a fellow agent into the bathroom. Someone had dumped the trash can out and had sifted through the contents. Now, in the sink, were a dozen or so metal needles.

"What are those things?" she asked.

Dixon came up behind her, put on a pair of rubber gloves and inspected one of the needles. "Brachytherapy needles, containing cesium. A hospital in North Carolina reported a batch missing a few months ago."

"My guess," said the other agent, "is that they were going to use the cesium in their bomb."

"Possibly." said Dixon. "A dirty bomb. One that could emit deadly gamma rays from the cesium in these needles."

"These needles are empty," said AJ. "So where's the cesium?"

"Crap."

At that moment, AJ's cell phone rang. She flipped it open.

"We have a run-down on some of those computer files," said an agent on the other end. "And get this."

She put her cell phone on speaker. "Go ahead."

"There was a schematic on one of the files," the voice said. "A bomb schematic. It made reference to cesium. It had a timer on it, too."

"Thanks," said AJ. "Try to decode the rest of those files. See if we can learn anything else."

"Will do."

AJ flipped her phone shut and noticed that Dixon had his hand in the trash can. "You know," she said "there's probably residual radiation from these needles."

But Dixon wasn't listening. He had been searching through the trash at their feet and now produced a business card.

"What's that?" AJ asked.

"It says: *John's Johns: Serving the Washington D.C. Metropolitan Area's Portable Sanitation Needs.*"

"Call it," said AJ.

Dixon quickly punched in the number on the card. "I hope this guy is an early riser." The phone on the other end rang several times, then a man answered. "*John's Johns.* May I help you?"

Dixon identified himself as the FBI and told him they would be down there shortly. "And don't distribute any of those johns. Got it?"

"Save yourself a trip," said the worker. "All the portable johns were dispersed last night around the Capitol Mall area for the July Fourth celebration. What's this all about?"

But Dixon had hung up. "Crap. They dispersed all the portable toilets around the Capitol Mall last night."

AJ looked at Dixon. "What are you thinking?"

"Today's the 4th of July. The city will be packed with people here for the fireworks on the Capitol Mall. Drinking and partying all day."

"Dixon, you get hold of the Army's HAZMAT team. Tell them what's going down. I'll alert HomeSec." She flipped open her phone. "I'm sure with the little time we have and the crowds already arriving at the Mall, HomeSec will want to keep this quiet. Same goes for us. We don't want a city-wide panic on our hands."

Washington, D.C.

Cole sat in his home study, analyzing the printout Bartley gave him while he waited for Taylor and Dallas to arrive. The doorbell rang and he invited Taylor in.

"Where's Dallas?" he asked, shutting the door behind her and locking it.

"He was right behind me, and then he called saying he wanted to stop off at an ATM for some yuppie coupons. He needed his morning junk food fix, I guess." As she sniffed around the room she asked, "Speaking of food, did Anna make any coffee?"

"I made some a while ago. Anna went out of town; visiting family in Pennsylvania for the 4th. Anyway, grab a cup in the kitchen and I'll join you. Let's be quiet, though. Shannon is upstairs asleep."

Taylor nodded and walked on exaggerated cat feet toward the kitchen. Once inside, she fixed herself a cup, heavy on the sugar and cream, and sat with Cole at the kitchen table. She asked, "Travis, what do you make of this China connection?"

"I don't know," he admitted. He'd been turning the thing over in his mind all night and morning. "It's damn confusing. The pieces just don't fit, you know?"

She nodded.

He continued, "If BioNan and the government are working

together on SIRUS—whatever that is—and the wireless network malfunction is due to my code, then what does all this have to do with China?"

"Beats me," Taylor replied. "Maybe it's time to confront Bartley and BioNan. You know, beat the bushes and see what snakes slither out."

Cole didn't want to answer. He had thought about that yesterday when he was in Bartley's office, but had decided against it. The shortcut he took for his CA program was one snake he didn't want to appear.

The doorbell rang, and Cole let Dallas in, again locking the door behind him. Dallas hopped up on the kitchen counter, munching an Egg McMuffin.

"Sorry I'm late, boss," he said. "Lots of traffic in the D.C. area. Fourth of July and all that. People arriving early to get a good spot for the show." He took another bite of his sandwich and with his mouth full said, "So, you guys figure it all out yet?"

"No," Taylor replied dryly. "We're waiting for your royal verdict on the matter."

"You want my honest opinion?" he said, his mouth full of processed food.

"No." replied Taylor. "Lie to us."

Dallas ignored her remark. "I hate to say this, but I think Bartley is right."

"Bartley?" replied Taylor and Cole in unison.

"Yes. Even a broken clock is right twice a day. And in this case, I'll give him his due. The only one on the list of suspects who would benefit from the Net disruptions is the Digitari Brotherhood."

"I'm sure that's what Bartley thinks, too," said Cole. "The Digitari made their goals quite clear. Free the Net from the corporate and government bad guys."

"Still, that doesn't explain how my confidential code got into a wireless device in China," replied Cole.

"Maybe BioNan or the IWL gave it to the Chinese?" said Taylor.

"Or there could be another reason," said Dallas quickly. "It just doesn't make sense for them to do…"

"But in a way it does," said Taylor, cutting him off.

"What do you mean?" asked Cole.

"Just because the first malfunctioning unit was in China, doesn't mean the Chinese have anything to do with the code. Follow me on this, Travis. Your code, somehow, someway, was programmed into the wireless chip sets in the cell phones, wireless computers, and such that crashed. Remember the strange global pattern of the network collapse? All were pretty much recent adopters of wireless technology, right?"

"Meaning what?" asked Dallas.

"Meaning that most of the wireless devices in those countries have newer versions of the chip set. An MCD chip set. And only their newest chips have your code in them, Travis. Now there's a conspiracy theory for you. One better than BioNan and SIRUS!"

"That blows your Brotherhood theory out the window, Dallas," Cole said.

"How so?"

"Toad Adams wrote that the Brotherhood killed Bates on just such a conspiracy between wireless chip manufacturers and the U.S. government. If the Brotherhood is involved, why would they silence someone who was furthering their cause by discrediting certain corporations and the government?"

Dallas was silent, mulling this over.

"And so that brings us back to square one," said Taylor.

Taylor barely finished her thought when the phone rang. Cole answered.

"Travis, this is AJ."

He sensed the urgency in her voice. "You all right, AJ? What happened…"

"I want you and Shannon to go to a secure sheltered place. I suggest the IWL."

"AJ, what's wrong?"

"Travis, we think there's a dirty bomb planted in the D.C. area. And we believe it's set to go off today."

Travis opened his mouth to speak, but words failed him. Both Dallas and Taylor were standing, hovering near him.

"Travis, we're keeping this quiet while the Army HAZMAT team searches for it, but if we can't find it and it does go off, I want you and your family in a safe place."

"But what about…"

"Please, Travis. No questions. Get to the IWL and wait. I'll call you when I can."

"And you?"

"I'm going to do my job," she said firmly. "Now, please go. And Travis?"

"Yes?"

"Mum's the word. We don't want to cause alarm in the city."

Cole hung up the phone and looked at Taylor and Dallas.

"What's up?" asked Taylor. "What did AJ say?"

"There's a dirty bomb somewhere in the D.C. area and they believe it's set to go off sometime today."

"*Holy crap!*" said Dallas.

"And AJ said I should take Shannon and get to the IWL for safety."

"That's a damn good idea," Dallas said. "The lab is underground and has an air filtration system."

Cole needed only a moment to make his decision. "Okay, I'll go get Shannon. You two take off. We'll meet you at the lab."

The Capitol Mall
Washington, D.C.

As he looked up at the helicopters passing over the Washington Monument, Major Brodie Ryder, commander of the Army HAZMAT team, said, "We have one thing in our favor, Dixon. With all the show of security here on the Mall for the 4th, our activities should go pretty much unnoticed."

"Right," said Dixon.

Because of the necessity of security, the Mall was surrounded by ten miles of wood-slatted snow fences to secure the area against possible terrorist threats during the festivities. There were, in fact, two parallel snow fences, spaced about fifteen to twenty feet apart, erected around the Mall to prevent a terrorist outside the area from handing harmful materials to someone inside the inner fence.

Thousands of celebrants were allowed entry onto the Mall only through twenty-four checkpoints where their personal items were inspected to ensure they weren't carrying weapons, alcohol, firecrackers, grills, glass bottles, or other potentially dangerous items. About 2,500 police officers from various jurisdictions were on duty, in uniform and in plainclothes, to patrol the area and nab those who tried to avoid the checkpoints.

AJ arrived and walked into the temporary command tent set just outside the first checkpoint. She handed both men several sheets of paper. "Here's the location of the portable toilets from the sanitation company, scattered up and down the Mall."

Ryder handed his to a nearby sergeant. "Get these distributed to the teams, sergeant." He turned to Dixon and AJ and said, "You're sure it's the real thing we're dealing with? Not some prank?"

"We checked with Lawrence Livermore in the Bay Area," AJ said. "They keep a computerized database filled with thousands of pages of everything publicly written about making a radioactive device: newspaper clippings, magazine articles, scientific journal reports, even passages from techno-thrillers. Livermore can quickly run a cross-check on the design of the bomb and see if it's the real thing or just something lifted from a Clancy novel."

"And?" asked Ryder.

"It's the real McCoy," she said grimly.

"We have HAZMAT helicopters equipped with radiation detectors flying over the area looking for telltale signs of radiation," said Ryder. They were all now standing before a map of the Mall. "Unfortunately, they may be too high to pinpoint anything as small as a bomb. That's why we're also using SUVs equipped with electronic detectors. Still, the vans are only good for locating the general proximity of the dirty bomb."

"And that's where the ground teams come in," said Dixon.

"Right. They're the ones that'll do the real hunting, on foot. If a van detects any gamma radiation, the two-person search team assigned to that grid will narrow the search to the john we're looking for. We have a hundred of these two-person teams, dressed as inconspicuously as possible, walking through the crowds around the Mall waiting to be called in."

"Are they carrying any equipment?" asked AJ.

"Yes, special radiation detectors, small enough to fit in a backpack," Ryder replied.

"I'd like to go out with one of those teams," she said.

"Sure," said Ryder. "Hook up with Echo Team. They're down by the Monument." Ryder turned to an aide in the tent and added, "Give this agent a lift to Team Echo."

The aide nodded and escorted AJ out of the command tent.

After a three-hour drive, most of it spent through the crowded streets of D.C., Cole and Shannon arrived at Fort Belvoir. They made their way to the INSCOM building and down the elevator to the Information Warfare Lab. At the security point, Cole presented his laptop to the corporal behind the glass.

"And what do we have here?" he asked, looking at Shannon.

"That's my daughter," replied Cole. "I thought I'd show her where her daddy works. I cleared it with the staff above." He tried to contain his anxiety over the crisis playing itself out in D.C. "Is it busy today?" he asked as casually as he could.

"The same. We've been on low level alert for a couple of days now." As he talked, he hooked Cole's laptop to his computer and searched it for any kind of malicious code. "You're clean," he said, and handed it back to Cole. Next, he looked at Shannon and the little robot dog under her arm. "And who's that?"

"That's my best friend, Goppy. Do you need to zamin' him, too?"

"I don't think that's necessary," he said with a smile. "Unless you think he's a spy."

"Oh, no! He's a good puppy."

"By the way," Cole said, "Did Dallas and Taylor show up yet?"

The corporal looked at his log and said, "Nope. Not yet."

Just as the corporal said this, the elevator doors opened and the two stepped out.

"Hi guys," Cole said.

Dallas nodded, and then saw Shannon's toy. "Hey, you brought your robot dog!"

"His name is Goppy," she said.

"Goppy, huh? Well, okay. Nice to meet you, Goppy." Dallas extended his hand and much to his surprise, the robotic dog lifted its mechanical paw and offered it to Dallas.

"Cute trick."

"Yeah," said Cole. "She taught him that."

"Cool!" He stood up and said to Cole, "Taylor and I have been talking about the gas company hack and…"

Cole looked sternly at Dallas. "We'll talk about that later," he said in a warning tone.

"Oh. Sure. Whatever you say, boss." Dallas slid his laptop and PDA under the security glass to the corporal.

"You two get cleared and I'll meet you in my office." Cole, with Shannon in tow, passed through the metal detector, nodded to the MP on duty and entered the lab while Taylor passed her PDA to the corporal.

"Don't screw it up this time, mister," he heard her say to the sheepish enlisted man. "Don't wipe out my files like you did the last time."

Cole led Shannon to his office and had her sit quietly at his desk. "Here, pumpkin. Here's some paper and pencils. Why don't you and Goppy draw some nice pictures?"

"But I want to play with Goppy on the 'puter." She pointed to the monitor on Cole's desk.

"No, pumpkin. You can't play with these computers. They're very special and only adults can use them."

Shannon frowned. "All right, Daddy," She sat down at her father's desk, took the pieces of blank paper, and started to draw. On her invitation, Goppy climbed into her lap and onto the desk and nuzzled under her arm.

Taylor and Dallas entered the office, each taking a seat around Cole's desk. Dallas said, "What's with the kibosh on my statement out there?"

"Don't listen to him, Travis," said Taylor. "He's just miffed because the eggheads at the NSA beat Mr. Know-It-All here to the punch." She smiled. "*They* found a digital signature from the attackers before *he* could even begin."

"Lucky," said Dallas, sulking.

Cole scanned his computer monitor. "Well, let's see how lucky. Here's the log from the gas company. Let's see how the NSA found the signature."

As Cole checked his secure email, much to his surprise, Goppy stuck its head between him and the screen. Cole picked the thing up, and set it on the floor.

"Shannon, please keep Goppy with you."

"Sorry, Daddy."

Cole turned his attention to his monitor and saw a message from HomeSec. There was an attachment with it. Cole opened the email and unzipped the file.

The three programmers huddled around the monitor to look at the log while it ran off the laser printer.

"This is different," Dallas said. "It's nothing like the log files from the other attacks. Look here. It's obvious that there's an attack footprint."

"AJ said that the NSA found a digital signature," Cole said. "Do you see it?"

Dallas stared at the lines of letters and numbers that scrolled up the computer screen. "Yep. The digital signature is right where it's supposed to be."

"And the IP address?" asked Taylor.

Dallas said, "The IP address would be easy to trace from there."

Shannon suddenly stood from her seat, looking around frantically. "Daddy, where's Goppy?"

"I'm sure he's…"

"He's gone!" she said, almost in tears.

"Don't worry, honey," said Taylor. "We'll find him."

Cole sighed, and soon they were all looking for Goppy. They moved the search outside the office, and a few minutes later, Taylor stuck her head out of the team office and yelled, "Found him!"

Shannon raced down the hall and into the team office where Goppy was sitting on Taylor's desk, pawing her PDA. He had removed it from its cradle. "Oh, look," Shannon said, giggling. "Goppy thinks it's one of his toys. He's playing with it."

"Shannon," said Cole, when he had caught up. "I told you to watch him. We can't have your toys playing around Daddy's workplace."

"Isn't that an oxymoron," said Dallas. "You know, toys playing?"

"Shut up, Dallas," said Taylor putting her PDA back in its cradle.

"I'm just saying."

Shannon pouted and picked up Goppy. "Bad dog!" she said, and carried him back to Cole's office.

Cole watched his daughter sit down with the dog in her lap.

Back in the team office, he said, "You know, regarding the digital signature, whoever's been launching these attacks have been damn careful about shielding their identity. Why would they make such an obvious mistake now?"

"Yeah," Dallas added. "An amateur mistake, too. It's almost like they wanted us to find them."

~

"Daddy is so mad, Goppy."

"I know. He doesn't love you like I do." There was a hint of malevolence in Goppy's mechanical voice. "He treats you like my parent treated me. Mean. A very mean man."

Shannon was surprised at Goppy's anger and his feelings towards her father. "Daddy's not mean, he's just..."

"He hates you, Shannon."

"No. He's only..."

"He doesn't love you, Shannon."

"My daddy loves me. Just sometimes…"

"I love you more than he ever can. I can make you happy all the time. I can take you away from him and I can care for you."

Shannon was shocked by Goppy's loathing towards her father. He never spoke like that before.

"Come with me, Shannon. I have friends who will take us to a happy place, far away from your father."

Though only five years old, Shannon sensed a threat. "No. No. I want to stay with my daddy."

Goppy, who had been pacing before her, walked over and sat at her feet. "My friends will take you from your bad daddy and we can live together and have lots of fun."

"No, I want to stay with my daddy."

"Your daddy hates you," Goppy said, growling. "I'm going to take you away with me." And it suddenly leaped into Shannon's lap.

Shannon recoiled. "No! Bad dog!" And she threw it off her lap.

Goppy hit the far wall and landed on its back. It regained its balance and turned and looked at Shannon. For the first time ever with Goppy, she felt afraid.

The lights behind the dog's plastics face plate turned from a mellow blue to a vivid, fiery red.

The Capitol Mall
Washington, D.C.

Team Echo consisted of a young man and woman, both dressed like vacationing tourists, out to enjoy the fireworks and revelries of a Washington, D.C. 4th of July.

AJ showed them her DHS ID.

"I'm Sergeant Kline and this is Warrant Officer Rice," the man bellowed. He was a big guy with broad shoulders and looked like someone you wouldn't want to cross. AJ knew that the backpack he was wearing contained a sophisticated sodium iodine crystal detector able to sniff minute amounts of gamma radiation up to twenty-five feet away. Both wore small button-sized beige radio receivers in their ears.

"So how can I help?" AJ asked.

Officer Rice, a petite woman roped with muscle, said, "Just act like a vacationer and rubberneck the scenery."

AJ said she could manage that, and together they strolled through their designated search grid that included the Washington Monument area. They walked past thousands of celebrants, some sitting on blankets spread over the grounds, some playing Frisbee and some even flying kites. There was a tackle football game going on that appeared, at least to AJ, to be brutally rough.

Boys, she thought.

As the team walked among the crowd, AJ could see one of

the radiation detector-equipped SUVs slowly driving up and down the Mall concourse. As the heat of the day bore down upon them, AJ spied the first set of porta-potties. She was about to inspect them, already dreading the task, when her phone rang. It was Ryder.

"We have a hit in your sector, AJ. We show a grouping of twenty or so portable toilets situated there."

It was the same grouping they were approaching. AJ's heart immediately seemed to leap up into her throat. She controlled her voice.

"We're on it," she said, pocketing the cell phone. "We have a reading here," she said, pointing to the cluster of portable bathrooms. Even as she spoke, men and women emerged from and disappeared into the small standing structures.

"Let's go," said Kline.

As they moved closer, Sergeant Kline looked down at the handheld device in his hand. "Gamma alarm four," he said to the others. "We have a strong radiation signal."

"Do we know from where?" asked AJ.

Kline waited a moment and said, "It's coming from there." He pointed to the last few johns at the end of the row.

Rice pulled out her cell phone and called the command tent. "We have a hit. Be ready with the containment team."

Closer now, Kline said, "It's in the one on the end."

The three positioned themselves around the last of the blue outdoor toilets. AJ tried to ignore the stench of urine that was already wafting around the place. Rice looked at the others. Kline nodded and she tried the door handle.

Locked.

Rice banged on the door and said, "Open up!"

"Jesus, lady. Wait your turn," said a man's muffled voice from inside the toilet.

"Let me," said AJ. She raised her voice. "Open the damn door. FBI! Now!"

"Yeah, and I'm J. Edgar Hoover," said the man. "Get lost!"

"Hold on," said Kline. He took off his backpack, unzipped a pouch on the side and removed a large screwdriver. He stuck the end of it into the space between the door jamb of the porta-potty and the locking mechanism and gave the screwdriver a strong push. The lock snapped open and the door flung open.

AJ didn't know which was more nauseating. The smell emanating from the toilet, or the sight of the short, pasty, pudgy, overweight man sitting on the seat with a pair of orange and green Bermuda shorts down around his ankles.

Kline reached in, grabbed the man by his wrist and pulled him out of the stall. With his shorts around his ankles, the man promptly fell face first into the grass.

"Pull your pants up," ordered Kline, "and get the hell out of here! Now!"

The pasty man rolled over, yanked up his shorts, looked back once, and was gone.

With AJ and Rice standing outside, Kline yanked a small penlight from his backpack, clicked it on, and peered down into the steaming hole. Ignoring the stench that drifted up to meet him, he spotted a white plastic shrink-wrapped object at the bottom of the hole.

"Got it," he said.

"Can you see the timer?" AJ called to him from outside.

"Wait." Kline pulled a pair of rubber gloves from his pocket, bent his stocky frame over the open toilet, and reached into the wet and smelly muck and mire. He fumbled with the container a few moments, turning it one way and then the other, looking for the timer.

He couldn't find one. Professional or not, he wanted to vomit.

He pulled the thing up out of the hole and rushed outside, into the blessedly fresh air. He carefully set it down in the grass.

"It's ticking," said AJ.

Kline turned the package over. He brushed off a section of the shrink-wrapped package, revealing a red, blinking timer. A digital display was counting off the minutes and seconds.

AJ could barely believe what she was seeing. They had less than five minutes.

~

Kline looked up at AJ frantically. "Radio dispatch, ASAP!" He turned to Rice. "And you clear as many people from the area as you can!"

Rice nodded and dashed off toward the small crowd that had gathered around the outhouses, shouting at them and flashing her badge, urging them to move back.

AJ reported their findings and flipped shut the phone. She bent down next to Kline. "Do we have enough time to disarm it?"

The man was sweating bullets, but thankfully, his hands were steady. "HAZMAT will never get here in time," he said. "So we had damn well better disarm it." He looked around for his screwdriver.

AJ felt helpless. And she felt sick.

Jesus, they only had four minutes.

She looked up and saw that Rice had done a fine job of pushing back the crowd. In the back of her mind, and encroaching toward the forefront rather quickly, AJ wished she was with them--instead of standing over a ticking dirty bomb.

God, she hoped Travis and Shannon were safe.

Dripping sweat and muttering to himself, Kline removed the remaining shrink-wrap around the timing device.

"*Damn!* There's strapping tape around the timer, too!"

"Three minutes left," AJ said tensely.

Kline used his screwdriver to rip through the strapping tape, simultaneously pulling at it with his fingers. Piece by piece he worked through the tape.

AJ had to remind herself to breath.

Two minutes.

Sweet Jesus, she hoped the man knew what he was doing. She was not very surprised that her thoughts kept returning to Travis and Shannon. God, she loved those two...

"We're not gonna make it," said Kline, the first time he showed anything close to negativity.

AJ's stomach clenched. "Keep trying," she urged.

One minute and counting …

Kline was still tearing at the tape, sweat pouring down his face. Now his hands were shaking.

"I can't get through it." He stood, dashed back to the portable bathroom, yanked open the door, and dropped the package back into the black hole in the seat. He dashed back to AJ and grabbed her elbow. "Time's up. Let's get the hell out of here!"

They ran towards the crowd. The crowd, seeing the two coming at them, moved as one, pushing back. It was nearly a mob scene. For the first time in a very long time, AJ felt real panic. Adrenalin pushed her forward. Her only thought was to get as far away from there as possible.

She reached the street and dashed behind one of the surveillance SUV's. She was breathing hard, her pulse pounded in her head. Like a human wave, those who had been watching the scene surged backward.

Kline appeared from around the SUV. "*Down! Down!*" he yelled, throwing himself at AJ. They fell to the ground, face down, hands covering the back of their heads. Voices screamed in the background.

AJ lay there, lungs on fire, hands over her head, mentally counting down from the timer.

Any moment now.

Any moment.

There was a brief, eerie silence. She actually heard birds chirping in the nearby trees as she waited for what seemed liked an eternity and waited—waited for an explosion that never came.

Dixon arrived, and AJ broke herself away from the press and debriefed him.

"How long have they been at it?" he asked. He was pointing

to where a thirty-five-foot wide, fifty-foot diameter nylon tent had been erected. Inside, the bomb had been engulfed in thirty thousand cubic feet of hardened foam. AJ knew that if the bomb would explode now, the foam, at least theoretically, should contain ninety-nine percent of the radiation. The demolition experts, dressed in their shrapnel-proof radiation suits, were now going to work.

"About an hour," said AJ. "What about these news people? I'm telling them very little and they're getting real antsy."

"Fisher will be here soon," said Dixon. "Let him handle them."

Just then Rice appeared from the containment area, frowning. She came over to them with a puzzled look on her face.

"Is the bomb no longer armed?" asked AJ.

Rice turned to them with a puzzled look on her face and said, "That's just the thing," she said. "It never was."

François was stuck in St. Louis.

Due to the dirty bomb crisis in D.C., his connecting flight from St. Louis was held on the ground. Once alerted, he knew the government wouldn't allow any plane, train, or vehicle into the D.C. area until the crisis was over.

So he tried to call Cole but all circuits were busy because of the news about the dirty bomb. Relatives and friends of those living in D.C. were clogging the lines, of course.

François scanned those sitting around him. Many were looking anxious and scared. After all, they had all been heading back to D.C.; the threat of the dirty bomb weighed heavily on their minds.

Something else was weighing heavily on François's mind. The images of Toad Adams and Miller being killed right before his eyes. François knew he should have called Cole from Nevada, but he just wanted to get onto a plane as soon as he could.

Now tired and scared, all he could do was wait for his boarding call in the airport terminal.

And waiting was the hardest thing he had done.

As he sat there, he pulled the small CD out of his pants pocket and examined it, wondering what could be so damn important on it. What kind of information would cost two men—and possibly three—their lives?

And, equally disturbing, what did this all have to with Travis Cole?

François knew he had to get to a computer to read what was on this disk, but first he needed to get home.

Home was safe.

So he sat back in the terminal's half-padded chair, closed his eyes and tried to calm his racing heart.

Fort Belvoir, Maryland

"Hey, Travis," Dallas yelled. "AJ's on the news!"

Taylor and Dallas had their eyes glued to the TV set when Cole walked in from his office. AJ was on TV at the tail end of a report. She looked beautiful, despite her slightly messy hair. Cole could only imagine the crappy day she had had. He said, "I think she missed her calling as an anchorwoman."

The office phone rang. Dallas picked up. "Speak of the devil, it's Barbara Walters."

Cole snatched it from his hand. He turned his back to the other two. "Hi, baby," he said. "I was worried sick."

"Well, I'm still here. I guess you'll have to put up with me a while longer," she said.

Cole, to his utter shock, nearly said he would enjoy putting up with her for as long as she would have him. But he didn't. He held his tongue. As he sat in his office and watched the crazy news unfold, he realized just how much AJ meant to him. She meant more than he had realized. Much more.

"I guess I could handle that," he finally said. "How are you doing?"

"It turned out to be a cake walk."

"Nerves of steel—look death in the eye—and all of that?"

"No," she said. "I mean I wasn't in any danger at all. None of us were. Granted, we didn't know that at the time, and I was so scared that I would never see you again, Travis."

Travis let her words hang in the air. He took a breath. God, could he possibly love her? So soon after his wife's death?

It's been over a year, Travis. It's okay to love again.

"What do you mean, no danger?" he heard himself ask.

"The bomb was a hoax, Travis! It was never armed. The detonator or blasting cap was there, but not connected. Not even wired."

"Someone went to all that trouble and didn't bother to connect the detonator? Why?"

"We're looking into it. And get this." She filled Travis in on their raid on the Digitari Brotherhood safe house.

"They were both dead?" Cole asked. Dallas and Taylor looked over at him. Both were about to open their mouths and he shushed them with a wave of his hand.

"Very."

"How?" he asked.

"Turns out they were dead before we got there. The coroner said they died of cyanide poisoning."

"They pulled an Adolph?"

"No," said AJ. "Remember those scientists in New York who were developing that wireless medical tracking technology?"

"Wait," said Cole. "Hold that thought. Let me put you on speaker and have Dallas and Taylor listen to this." Cole pushed the speaker button and laid the receiver back in its cradle. "Okay, go ahead."

AJ's voice rang out through the lab. "I was telling Cole about the scientists in New York who were developing a wireless medical tracking technology."

"Yeah," said Dallas. "They called it the 'Digital Angel.' What of it?"

"At that apartment, two Korean Brotherhood members who built the dirty bomb had a chip like that embedded in their shoulders."

"But how can a tracking chip kill you?" queried Taylor.

"I think I know," said Dallas. "I remember reading that an implant controlled by a Digital Angel chip would one day contain and deliver on command—and directly into the bloodstream—medication like insulin for diabetics or Ritalin for hyperactive kids. And the release command can be sent over a wireless network to the chip. It would be just as easy to release a poison as well."

"Then, Dallas, whoever gave the command to kill them didn't even have to be there," said AJ.

"Yep, it would have come as a complete surprise to them, too," he said. "One minute you're alive and kicking, the next—you're kimchi."

"Thanks, Dallas. I'll pass the chip idea on to the coroner and see what they can dig up on the bodies. Oh, Travis, it's safe for you and Shannon to go home. I think she'd be happier sleeping in her own bed tonight."

"Thanks." He took her off the speaker. "Can you come over tonight? Or do you have to go back to the office?"

"No, I'm out of here. It's all in Fisher's and the Army's lap now. Let me take a quick shower and I'll be over to your place soon."

He found Shannon asleep in his office, curled up in his leather chair. He picked her up, grabbed his briefcase, and was about to leave, when he remembered the dog. He glanced around the office and down the hall, but didn't see that damn thing. He wanted to go home in the worst way, and decided he would look for it in the morning.

Washington, D.C.

At his townhouse, Cole carried his sleeping daughter upstairs to her bedroom. Back in the kitchen, he pulled out a cold beer from the fridge, went into the living room and collapsed on the couch. He closed his eyes and was instantly asleep.

He didn't know how long he'd been sleeping when AJ rang the doorbell. He opened the door, pulled her to him and gave her perhaps the biggest kiss ever.

"Wow," she said, going limp in his arms. "You really missed me."

Cole grinned and led her into the kitchen.

"You hungry?" he asked.

"Famished. Didn't eat a thing all day."

"Anna left some meals for Shannon and me to heat up."

"Where's Shannon?"

"In bed, and I'm just going to let her sleep. She's had an intense couple of days. Would you like some wine?"

"Oh, boy! I'm getting the full treatment. Sure, sounds good."

Cole felt happier than he had in quite a while. Was it possible that he truly loved AJ? Maybe.

Just maybe.

"So when's Anna coming back?" AJ asked seductively, coming up behind him as he poured the wine.

He froze when her lips touched his neck. A warm tingle

spread through his entire body. "Tomorrow morning," he said.

"Then that leaves tonight," she whispered into his ear.

~

Cole awoke the next morning feeling AJ's naked leg cross over his. This was her little way of saying it was time to get amorous again. He liked amorous.

He rolled over, placing his arm across her soft body, stroking her bare shoulders. She responded by turning her face to his, and just as she did so he remembered Goppy. He'd left the damn thing at the IWL!

"Crap," he said. "I have to get to the lab."

AJ felt slighted. She was looking forward to a long, casual morning with the man she was certain she was falling in love with. "But why?" she asked. "Don't they ever give you a day off?"

"I..." he paused. "I left something there."

"Can't it wait?"

It couldn't. Not if Bartley saw the miserable thing. The man would have a cow. Cole seriously did not want to give him any more reason to be furious with him.

So he reluctantly pulled his leg out from under hers, got off the bed and began dressing. "I'm sorry, baby. I'll be back shortly."

She pouted, pushing her big, soft lower lip out, and Cole nearly groaned.

Damn Goppy.

He finished dressing, pissed at Goppy, and went downstairs. Pulling on one of his robes, AJ followed behind, her bare feet padding softly against the hard wood.

Cole slammed down a cup of coffee and kissed her goodbye. "Thanks again for staying last night. I owe you one. Make yourself at home, okay? You know where everything is. Oh, and if you don't mind, could you make Shannon a bowl of cereal or something?"

AJ nodded and Cole promised he would return as soon as he could. She gave him a weak smile and he headed out to the garage.

Damn Goppy.

～

AJ wandered through the kitchen, looking for something interesting to eat. As soon as she opened the refrigerator, the doorbell rang.

Ah, she thought. *Maybe that's Anna returning.*

Even better. Maybe Anna could whip her up some breakfast.

AJ walked over to the door and looked through the peephole. But instead of finding the middle-aged housekeeper, she saw an attractive dark-haired Asian woman with a smile on her face. AJ shrugged and opened the door.

"Can I help you?" she asked, cinching the robe around her.

The woman was indeed pretty. She had dark eyes, medium length jet-black hair and a round, soft face. The woman stood there smiling oddly at her, saying nothing, and AJ sensed something was wrong. Very wrong.

She looked down. The woman was holding a semi-automatic pistol, and it was aimed at AJ.

Part Three
Manifestation

Washington, D.C.

It was early morning when François's connecting flight from St. Louis landed in D.C. Tired and scared, he hailed a cab in front of the airline terminal, arriving at his townhouse a half-hour later. He paid the cab driver, grabbed his bags, and glanced around his familiar neighborhood.

He couldn't stop thinking of the informant being shot in cold blood.

Jesus.

The neighborhood was as it should be—quiet and peaceful. Birds were chirping overhead. Francois felt anything but peaceful.

He was terrified.

In his upstairs study, he inserted the CD Toad had given him into the disk drive of his computer. Within seconds he was reading a series of short, rambling notes. As he did so, two things occurred to him. One, Toad Adams had been right all along and, two, Travis Cole was in some serious danger.

And then a third thing occurred to him, a thing he had been unconsciously aware of since Burning Man.

He was in danger, too.

Big danger.

Hands shaking, he downloaded the contents of the CD into

his PDA. He then emailed them to his own email account and to Cole's personal email account. Once done, Francois erased the file off his computer and broke the small disc into several pieces, all of which he burned in his gas fireplace. Watching the flames, he picked up his phone and called Cole's home. No answer. He tried once more to make sure he had dialed the right number, but again, the phone just rang and rang. He hung up and called Cole's cell phone number.

"Hello?"

"Travis. This is François. Where are you?"

"I'm on my way to the lab. You're home now?"

"Yes," said François. He was feeling ill. He needed to lie down, but he couldn't. "Travis, I need to speak with you."

"What's wrong?"

"I can't tell you over the phone. Please, I need to meet you."

"Now?"

"Yes, Travis…"

"Can it wait? I need to pick something up from the lab."

"Travis, please. This is … please."

"Okay. I'll turn around. I'm about an hour or so away from you."

"No. Not here. Let's meet someplace else. Some place public. A restaurant."

"Someplace public? François is everything…"

"Please, not over the phone."

"Fine. Which one?" Cole asked.

"The sushi place. The one near the university, where we used to go to for lunch."

"Sushi One Oh One?"

"Yes, that's the place."

"I'll meet you there at eleven," said Cole.

Yi's cell phone buzzed and he looked down at the display. An address of a restaurant appeared on the screen followed by the letters C Y B E R K I L L.

~

François called a cab and fifteen minutes later, one appeared outside his townhouse. He stuffed the PDA in his jacket pocket and walked outside to the waiting taxi. He got in and gave the driver his destination.

As the cab pulled away, François glanced back. A tall man had crossed the street and headed for his townhouse.

François didn't recognize the man, and he especially didn't like how the man had briefly stopped and watched the taxi depart.

~

François's taxi pulled up in front of the restaurant fifteen minutes before eleven. He saw that he hadn't been followed. Or, at least, he didn't think he had been followed.

The restaurant was a small Mom and Pop establishment that François and Cole had frequented. It opened at eleven sharp, which Cole had known when he had suggested the time.

Now, as François paced outside, he was surprised to see the door to the restaurant opened. An Asian man, wearing a thick pair of tinted glasses and white chef's smock, appeared and said, "Are you here for lunch?"

"Um, yes. But don't you open at eleven…"

"Yes, yes. We open early for you."

François was seated at the sushi bar and handed a menu, but he refused it.

"I know what I want," François said pointing to the pictures of sushi and sashimi servings on the wall. "I'll have a yellow fin tuna hand roll, please."

~

The tall Saudi was frustrated. Breaking into Francois's townhouse was easy, but finding the CD was impossible.

After ransacking his apartment, the Saudi booted up François's computer and looked to see if the information he sought was on it.

Nothing. And the hard drive was wiped clean.

He opened his cell phone and made a call.

Yi was busy behind the sushi bar preparing François's hand roll as patrons started to slowly stream into the restaurant. Yi ignored the gathering crowd. He placed a seaweed square in the open palm of his hand, placed two spoonfuls of sticky white rice on top of it, and laid four sticks of celery across the rice. But instead of choosing a piece of yellow fin tuna, Yi picked up a small chunk of Fugu.

Blowfish.

A delicacy in Japan, and because of its lethal danger, it must be prepared properly.

Yi made a point *not* to prepare it properly.

He cut a few strips from the blowfish flesh, placed the pieces on the seaweed square in his hand, folded one corner over the filling, and rolled the seaweed into a cone. He added some salmon roe on top to camouflage the fish and handed it to his target.

François murmured "arigato" and dipped the roll into a small dish that contained a mixture of soy sauce and wasabi mustard. He took a bite. He frowned. The tuna tasted strange, and his first thought was that the fish was spoiled. He was about to complain to Yi when his lips and tongue suddenly became numb.

He reached for his water but the numbness spread rapidly from his lips to his throat and then to his reaching hand.

François tried to stand, but he collapsed back into his seat. Patrons strolled in and watched in shocked horror as François went into convulsions and slid from his chair.

When he hit the floor, the spasms stopped and he lay perfectly still.

Yi quickly came around the counter and knelt by François. He made an act of helping the fallen patron. His hand slipped into his target's jacket and found a PDA. He pocketed it and continued examining the fallen man, all the while yelling for someone to call for help. As the crowd gathered around them, flipping open their cell phones and simultaneously punching in 911, Yi slipped away out the back door of the restaurant—and was gone.

Washington, D.C.

Cole was late for his meeting with François. And now he was going to be even later.

"Sorry, sir. You can't come through here," said the Metro Police officer as Cole drove toward the street where the sushi restaurant was located. "This street's closed."

"Why, officer?"

"It's a crime scene, sir. You'll have to turn back and go another way."

Cole looked down the block where the restaurant was located and saw the blinking red and yellow lights of emergency and police vehicles. He turned his SUV around and parked it on a side street, got out and walked swiftly toward the sushi restaurant. Just then, a paramedic was wheeling a man out of the restaurant to a waiting ambulance.

Cole could not believe what he was seeing. The man on the stretcher was François.

He pushed his way past the crowd until he reached François's side. The door to the ambulance was thrown open.

"Good lord, John," Cole cried.

But François didn't say anything. Instead, he looked up pitifully at Cole as foam bubbled from the corner of his mouth.

"Jesus, what happened to him?" Cole asked.

"We think its Terblyde poisoning," said one of the paramedics. "Pieces of fish were in his mouth."

"Blowfish?" Cole asked.

The paramedic nodded, and together with his partner they loaded François into the back of the truck and slammed the doors shut.

"We have to get moving people—fast," yelled one of medics.

"Where are you taking him?"

"The Washington Hospital Center on Irving Street."

And with a wail of sirens and flashing lights, the ambulance was gone, weaving its way through the noon traffic.

Cole immediately went over to the nearest policeman and introduced himself.

"Come with me," said the officer.

He led Cole to an unmarked car where a heavy-set man in civilian clothes was leaning against the fender and writing in a notebook.

"Detective," said the officer, "this man here was supposed to meet the victim."

"Thank you, Rogers. Give me a minute with him." The officer nodded and left. "I'm Detective Snyder, Metro Police. You know the victim?"

The big detective reminded Cole of Kojak from the 1970s TV show. Bald head, sharp eyes—all that was missing was the lollipop. Cole described Francois's strange phone call, how his in-law had sounded concerned and afraid and had wanted to meet in a public place.

"It seems whoever he was afraid of got to him here," the detective said, studying Cole closely.

"Why do you say that?"

"We found two of the restaurant employees tied up in the store room. Witnesses say that when the old man collapsed, the sushi chef high-tailed it out the back door."

"He was deliberately poisoned?" Cole could hardly believe he was hearing the words come from his mouth.

The detective looked at him for a long moment. "It looks like it."

"Someone tried to murder him?" Cole asked. He needed to sit down.

"Travis Cole, was it?" asked Detective Snyder. Cole nodded. The detective continued, "I'm going to need your contact information."

Cole absent-mindedly produced a business card and wrote his home address on the back of it. The detective copied the info onto his notepad.

"Mr. Cole, do you have any idea why someone would try to kill him?"

Cole was having a hard time breathing himself. Jesus, what was going on?

"No," he said finally, although he knew he didn't sound very convincing. "I really don't."

Which was certainly partly true. Cole really had no idea what was going on. Still, he knew the detective was watching him closely, and he knew he was acting suspiciously.

"Well, Mr. Cole, if you can think of anything that might help us, here's my card."

Cole took the offered card, slipped it into his pocket, and then wove his way back to his car. He could feel the detective's eyes boring through him the entire way.

Cole headed straight for the hospital.

Fort Belvoir, Maryland

At the hospital, Cole waited a few hours, only to be told by a young intern that there was presently little to be done for François other than to wait and see.

He called AJ a few times, but she didn't answer. He tried the house phone as well, with the same result. Perhaps she had taken Shannon to breakfast. Maybe her cell phone was off. None of that made sense to him, but his brain was just too confused to make much sense of anything at the moment.

Restless, he decided to leave. Then his phone rang. It was Bartley. An emergency meeting at the IWL. Get there ASAP.

Yes, sir. So much for his Saturday.

As he approached the entrance to Fort Belvoir he saw three soldiers armed with automatic weapons sitting in the guardhouse instead of an MP. Cole pulled up to the gate, handed over his ID and said, "What's with all the hardware?"

"We're on alert. It's a threat-Con Delta," said the young soldier stiffly. He examined the picture ID and held it up, comparing it to Cole's face.

Cole, in the old days, would have given the soldier a big cheesy smile just for kicks. Now, Cole felt anything like smiling.

"You're cleared, sir. But you're restricted to the INSCOM building only."

Cole drove to the INSCOM building, where he faced the same drill. Armed troops checked the identification badges of those entering the building. Inside, as Cole approached the elevator that led down to the lab, he saw Dallas waiting at the doors. The kid was eating something that looked like a burrito.

"Hi, Chief," Dallas said, glancing up, hot sauce on his chin. "Looks like they're really playing soldier today."

Cole only nodded.

"Hey, you look like you just lost your best friend."

"I just might have. My in-law is in the hospital. Intensive care."

"Jesus, what happened?"

Cole debated telling Dallas what he knew, but then shrugged. They were friends. "He was poisoned. Someone tried to kill him."

Dallas nearly choked on his burrito. Cole gave the kid a hearty slap on his back. "You have got to be kidding!" said Dallas, after sucking in some air.

Cole shook his head grimly as the elevator doors opened. Once inside, they swiped their ID cards through the scanner, punched in their PIN numbers, scanned their hands, and were swept down toward the lower levels to the IWL. As they went along, Cole brought Dallas up to speed.

"And François didn't tell you what the meeting was about?"

"No," said Cole.

Dallas was silent.

~

At the security booth, Cole presented his laptop and Dallas his PDA to the corporal seated in the booth.

"I'll need your cell phones, too," said the corporal.

"Why?" asked Dallas, digging for his phone.

"We're at Info-Con Four, sir. Wartime status. No phone calls in or out. All the phones are locked down."

"Info-Con? War? Jesus Christ." Cole said. "What the hell is going on?"

I need to get hold of AJ and Shannon.

"I'm just the messenger, sir," replied the corporal. "I guess you two will find out at your meeting." He handed back their electronic devices and said, "You're cleared."

Dallas leaned over to Cole and whispered, "Better watch our Ps and Qs today. The natives are restless."

When they arrived at the Tank, they saw that Taylor, Bartley, and Casey were waiting for them. Tech Sergeant 5th class Casey Stone, a Berkeley graduate in computer science, was an expert in creating and delivering logic bombs into an enemy's military and civilian information infrastructure. In addition to creating logic bombs, he assisted Dallas with the programming for the NAN-056-12 project at the IWL. Except for his Army camouflaged fatigues, he looked like he stepped off a surfboard at Malibu.

Casey was tall and strapping, with non-regulation straight blond hair atop a tanned face and two clear blue bedroom eyes. His straight blond hair was reminiscent of his surfing days. He still surfed, of a sort, going out every chance he got to windsurf on Chesapeake Bay.

"Good," said Bartley. "You're all here, finally." He checked his watch and shook his head. "Gentlemen—and lady—this facility is on an Info-Con Delta alert status."

Cole interrupted. "For the benefit of us civilians, Colonel, what's an Info-Con alert?"

"Specialist Stone," said Bartley, "would you like to inform the civilians here what an Info-Con is?"

"Yes, sir," Casey said. "Info-Con stands for 'Information Condition' indicating defense conditions prior to going to war."

"Going to war?" the three of them erupted, with Dallas and Taylor standing up from their seats. Bartley stared forward impassively and ordered them to sit. When they had settled, he said, "Not a physical war. A cyberwar. We have authorization under National Security Presidential Directive Number Sixteen to commence offensive cyberwarfare."

"Commence against whom?" asked Taylor.

"China," replied Bartley. "We know that the disruptions in the wireless networks were initiated in the People's Republic of China."

"But that wasn't a hack," said Cole. "It was a network malfunction."

"Our intel says otherwise, Cole. They, the Chinese, only made it look like a malfunction."

Cole said, "You know as well as I do that my code was responsible for the malfunction, Colonel."

Bartley raised an eyebrow to Cole's disclosure, but remained silent. Bartley was not to be swayed. Cole hated that about the man. When he thought he was right, all others were wrong. Period.

"We believe they took advantage of a glitch in your code, Cole, to bring down the wireless networks."

Cole nearly stood. "There was no glitch in *my* code, Colonel. Someone tried to re-write it. We both know that, damn it. And they did an ax job of it, too."

"That's neither here nor there," Bartley said calmly. "This attack fits the mold of China's ongoing cool war against the West's information infrastructure."

"The cold war is over, Bartley!" cried Taylor. "I know we're not on perfect political terms with the Chinese, but why would they deliberately try to harm our information infrastructure?"

Bartley's nostrils flared briefly, almost comically. "A covert offensive in cyberspace is one way of settling old scores—without getting into a shooting war."

"Why does the DoD think China is behind this and not Russia?" asked Cole, eying Taylor to clam up.

"We found emails from a Chinese ISP on the Brotherhood's computers the FBI confiscated. Two plus two is four, Cole. It all fits."

"And does the DoD think that the hacker attacks we've had over the last several days are also China's doing?" asked Taylor, calming down.

"Yes," Bartley said flatly. "And we believe China is backing the terrorists who, we're certain, have been probing and testing in preparation for a 'swarming attack.'"

"A what?" asked Taylor.

"A swarming attack," repeated Bartley. "HomSec discovered a pattern in the attacks. The attacks were all different—Internet service outages, cell phone service disruptions, the Amtrak accident, and now the gas explosion that we suspect was also a cyberterrorist attack. HomeSec believes that China's claws have been sharpening their skills, testing our information infrastructure in preparation for a big attack."

"And what's the lab going to do during this cool war?" asked Dallas.

"The cool war is about to get warm," Bartley replied confidently. "The White House has authorized *Operation Digital Sword*. No bombs, no bullets, no bangs this time. The objective is to disrupt the information systems in China. We're going to give them a taste of their own damn medicine. *Digital Sword* will be unleashed with such fury and effect that China will soon feel compelled to call a halt to their attacks."

"The American way of war," said Taylor mockingly. "Use an atom bomb to swat a fly."

"And that's always worked," said Bartley proudly. "The Chinese are going to understand what it means to go to war with America. Even if it's just a cyberwar. First we'll bring down their power grid. Then we'll disrupt their oil pipeline flows, drowning their military installations in oil in one place and starving it in others. At the same time we'll wreak havoc with their financial sector. The result will be a taste of what they were planning to do to us. Their transportation, financial and power systems will shut down, causing incalculable economic damage—even more severe than what they planned for us."

"And what about collateral damage?" questioned Taylor. "The civilian casualty count? What about that?"

"Don't forget, Miss Taylor," Bartley said defiantly, "they started this war. Not us. There will be acceptable losses. We're prepared for that."

"Acceptable losses," Taylor mumbled under her breath.

Bartley looked sternly at each one of the civilian contractors. "Now, that's all you need to know. My staff here is going to be very busy over the next few weeks. And so will you. You'll be helping us refine our digital arsenal. Specialist Stone will soon direct you as to our needs." Bartley was loving this moment, that much was obvious. "Now, all of you had better call home. You're going to be here for a while. Do it now. The phone lines will be open for fifteen minutes. So make it quick. Then the Comm Link to the DoD will be the only contact in or out of here." He paused, and then added curtly, "Meeting adjourned."

Bartley and Casey exited the office, leaving the three private contractors alone.

"What do you think?" asked Dallas to no one in particular.

"Crazy," said Taylor. "Just insane."

"Well, we better make our phone calls," said Cole. "Sounds like we're going to have a long day."

Once in his office, Cole punched in his home number, but there was still no answer. Maybe Anna had come home and taken Shannon out. He tried AJ's cell, but there was no answer—just voice mail. Next, he called the hospital before the phones were locked down.

He reached the ICU and a nurse answered. "Oh, Mr. Cole. We've been trying to contact you." The moment he heard her voice, Cole knew something was wrong. *She has bad news.* "You were at none of the numbers you gave us and your work number said that no incoming calls were allowed."

"Yes, I know. How is Mr. François?"

"I'm, I'm sorry..."

"When?" he asked. "When did... it happen?"

"An hour ago."

Cole wondered just how much more bad news he could take. "Thank you for all you did," he said softly. The nurse apologized again, even though it wasn't her fault. They hung up and Cole slumped in his chair behind his desk, closed his eyes, and stayed that way for a long time.

Aberdeen Proving Grounds

They were approximately ninety miles north of Washington D.C., near the Delaware and Maryland state line. Alpha Mae, Yi and their young hostage sat in a Zodiac speedboat in Chesapeake Bay, a mile or so from a restricted section of the Aberdeen Proving Grounds.

With high-powered binoculars, Yi scanned the chemical agent storage yard on the Proving Grounds.

"Any activity yet?" asked Alpha Mae.

"None yet," he said. "How's our friend doing?"

Alpha Mae glanced at the figure slumped in the back of the boat and said, "She's still out. The chloroform is doing its job."

Yi stared through his binoculars and mused, "The sarin gas in those deteriorating rockets at the dump should make for a pretty surprise in D.C. tonight. The weatherman said the winds will be blowing nicely from the northwest."

Alpha Mae looked at the horizon and said, "The light's fading. Should be any time now. Let's get ready."

They started the motor of the Zodiac and slowly approached the south end of the Proving Grounds. They didn't get very far when they heard a series of sharp alarms coming from the chemical storage yard.

"That's it," she said. "Let's go!"

Cole's phone rang and he was abruptly awakened. Apparently, he had dozed off in his chair.

He snatched at the receiver. It was Taylor. "Travis," she said. "Casey called. Wants us in the team office now. I guess we get our marching orders."

Cole yawned. "Be there in a few minutes."

As he left his office, he almost tripped over Goppy. "There you are!" Cole reached down to pick up the errant toy, but the mechanical dog's eye, behind his plastic visor, turned bright crimson red, and it backed quickly away from Cole, making a noise that sounded like a growl.

"You little ungrateful tin can," said Cole. He was about to reach down for the toy when a green-fatigued soldier appeared from around the corner.

"Sir, Colonel Bartley wants everyone back in the team offices now."

"I'll be there in a minute."

"Sorry, sir, it has to be now."

When Cole returned his attention to the mechanical dog, it was gone.

Damn Goppy.

In the team office, he told Taylor and Dallas about François, noticing that his voice held little emotion, knowing instinctively that he was in shock. François had been a link to his deceased wife. Her flesh and blood.

And now he, too, was gone.

They both showed the appropriate amount of outrage and horror, but Cole was hardly paying attention. Dallas was immediately talking conspiracy and cover-ups, speculating on who and why François would have been poisoned, especially after so shortly returning from a trip to see Toad Adams. Even Taylor seemed caught up in the moment. As they spoke, Cole sat there with a heavy heart. While they waited for Casey to give them their instructions, he became more and more morose.

"I can't just sit here," said Cole. "I'm going up to the grid to get my email."

Upstairs, Cole scrolled through a backlog of messages—one message in particular stood out from the rest. It was sent just this morning.

A message from the grave. It was from François.

He opened the email, feeling elated, sad, and many, many other emotions that he couldn't pinpoint. The email was, in fact, empty. But there was an attached file.

Finding breathing suddenly difficult, Cole opened the attached file, and what he saw made him gasp.

"Watcha got there, boss?" asked Dallas as Cole strode purposely into the office.

Instead of answering, he showed them the message on his laptop. Taylor peered over his shoulder, reading. "It's an email from François."

"You're kidding," said Dallas, and soon he was looking over

Travis's shoulder as well. "He sent you a text file? This morning? What's on it?"

"It looks like some sort of diary…" started Taylor.

"No," said Dallas, seeing what Cole had seen. "They're reporter's notes—they're Toad Adams's notes!"

"But they're a year old," said Taylor.

"No," said Cole. "These are just the first entry."

The three programmers read through the entries, which mentioned everything from the Digitari Brotherhood to massive cover-ups in the government.

"So we have some nut job's notes," said Dallas, standing straight and stretching his back. "Big deal. Most people think he's a whack job, anyway. Half this stuff you can find on his web page…"

"But there's got to be something important in this," insisted Taylor, "or why would John send Travis this email? And on the very day he was killed?"

And while the two of them talked it up, Cole continued scanning the notes. He knew in his heart that Taylor was right. There was something in these notes, something out of the norm, and then he thought he found it.

He shushed the two of them, and read from the notes, "Says here that a wireless chip manufacturer installed new chip sets in all the wireless devices shipped over the last two years. Those chips are in cell phones, laptops, PDAs, handheld computers—anything and everything that could wirelessly connect to the Net."

"And they did it with the blessing of the NSA," added Taylor, reading along with him, "and programmed that chip set with your code, Travis."

Dallas stepped away from the monitor and sat in his chair. The other two barely noticed his absence.

Taylor continued reading. "This Dorian was using the capabilities of the chip set to roam the Internet and have access to heaven knows what."

Cole interjected, "It appears Toad Adams thinks Dorian and the Brotherhood are responsible for the recent cyber-attacks." Indeed, Adams listed every cyber-attack they'd had over the past few days, citing a source in the Brotherhood.

"Travis!" Taylor's excited voice broke into Cole's contemplation. "Look here." She pointed a long, unpainted nail at his name.

Cole read the chilling entry. According to Toad's source in the Brotherhood, this Dorian character wanted him, Travis Cole, dead.

"Why would this guy want to kill you?" asked Taylor.

There it was again. AJ had mentioned that the attacks seemed to be getting closer and closer to Cole. And now this, as clear as day, in Toad Adams's notes.

"I have no idea," said Cole. "I never met the guy." Cole sat back. These past few days had been insane, and only seemed to be getting worse.

"Travis, according to Toad's source, all of these cyber-terrorist attacks were ordered by Dorian, and you have been the target all along. Whether or not this Toad Adams is a nut job I don't know, but you should take this seriously."

"Believe me, I am."

Dallas, silent for so long, blurted out, "I gave Cole's code away to someone at the NSA."

Cole shook his head. This was, perhaps, one of the last things he had expected to hear. "*What?*" he exclaimed, and then said it again. "*What?*"

"I gave Cole's code away," said Dallas. He was looking very sick and very pale. "It's all my fault."

"What?" Cole and Taylor shouted in unison.

Dallas stammered. "Someone in the NSA, well, blackmailed me into giving up the code. And so I did. I smuggled it out in Isaac. I knew security wouldn't check him."

Cole did his best to control himself. This was not what he had expected to hear from someone he thought was a very good friend of his and a professional with integrity. "Who was this NSA guy?"

"His name was Safko." But that was all Dallas offered, seeming suddenly unwilling to talk. He slumped in his chair. Cole could see the pain on his friend's face.

"What did they have on you?"

Dallas jumped up and paced nervously, running his fingers through his thick tangle of hair. "I did a consulting gig while getting my BS in computer sciences. You know, to earn extra money."

"What did you do, Dallas?" snapped Taylor.

"I worked as a codefella."

"What's a codefella?" asked Cole.

"I was doing tech support for some associates who ran a numbers racket."

"Christ, Dallas," said Taylor. "The mob?"

"What I did wasn't illegal. Just a consulting job. It wasn't like I was shaking down people for money. I don't believe gambling is wrong. The people I contracted with worked more like GE or Time Warner."

He explained that the organization moved millions of dollars a year in track and sports bets. They hired him to dig themselves out of the tons of paper they were buried in. Dallas built a secure, online, peer-to-peer, encrypted redundant, bet-processing system, tied to an offshore data warehouse.

"And it worked." He gave a weak smile. "I got paid and graduated '*cuma sum money.*'"

"No time for jokes," snapped Taylor.

"Sorry," said Dallas. He stopped in front of Cole and looked truly pained. "Travis, I never thought that what I gave the NSA would somehow harm you. Or François. Or whoever. I am very, very sorry."

Cole was silent. Dallas was sweating. Taylor, Cole saw, was fuming.

"All right, Dallas," said Cole. "It's done. It happened. Let's move on." He looked at his watch. "Casey will be here soon. Guys, I think we've got to tell Bartley about this."

"Tell the colonel about what?" asked Casey, as he entered the team office.

Cole looked at Casey, and decided to go ahead and plunge forward. No matter what was happening to him personally, he had an obligation to avert something very serious. "The military has it all wrong, Casey," said Cole. "It's not China who's doing the cyber-attacks. It's the Digitari Brotherhood."

"And we have to tell Bartley to call off *Digital Sword*," added Taylor.

Casey paused in mid-step. This was obviously news he was not expecting to hear. "What…" he began, then changed course. "Where did you get this information?"

"Take a look at this, Casey," Taylor said, pointing to Cole's laptop. "Read the entries."

Casey turned to the monitor. At her prompting, he scrolled through the series of entries, reading each one as he went along. When he finished, he sat back and exhaled. Cole thought he looked a little pale.

He should look pale.

"Yeah," said the young sergeant. "We'd better get Colonel Bartley." He picked up the desk phone and dialed Bartley's office. When he hung up he looked at Cole.

"You're still going to need more proof than this to convince the colonel," said Casey. "He's convinced China is behind these attacks."

"Then we'll get it straight from the horse's mouth," Cole said. He turned to his young friend. Well, at least his young *one-time* friend. "Dallas, call upstairs to the INSCOM offices. Get someone to go to Adams's web site, the *Truth Report*, and get a phone number on him."

Dallas, perhaps eager to help Cole in any way, especially in light of his grievous sin, quickly acquiesced and went to the phone.

"We'll get Adams on the phone and he'll back up what we're saying," said Cole.

"I don't know," said Casey, leaning back in the chair. "He's a known kook. The colonel isn't going to believe him."

"Well, we'll just have to make him believe," Cole said. "Adams is right."

"Adams is dead," said Dallas, hanging up the phone and spinning to face the group.

Cole was too stunned to speak.

Dallas continued, "The PFC upstairs went to Toad Adams's site. *The Truth Report* home page has a requiem for Adams announcing his tragic death at Burning Man."

An arrow of cold fear pierced Cole's heart. *Good God, what's going on?*

"What's all this about?" Bartley demanded, storming into the team office. He was carrying a thick yellow folder stamped *Top Secret* in his hand, and looking about as pleasant as a rabid pit bull.

"Colonel," said Cole, fighting to control himself. He swallowed and wiped his brow. He tried again, "Colonel, you have to call off the cyber-attacks on China."

Bartley stood menacingly over Cole. "What the devil are you talking about?"

Cole had never before been afraid of this over-inflated jerk. "China," he said faking calm. "They're not responsible for the cyber-attacks on us."

"I have no time for this foolishness." Bartley turned to Casey and said, "Have you given them their instructions?"

"No, sir," Casey replied. "I…"

"Why not?" he demanded.

Cole was getting pissed. Between the road rage, the explosion, the bomb scare, the death of François and now Toad Adams… well, Cole had had enough.

"Colonel, pull your head out of your butt and take a goddamn seat."

Cole got up and kicked his chair over to Bartley. It rolled, squeaking and bouncing. The colonel blinked at it in utter surprise.

"How dare you speak to…"

Cole, easily two inches taller than the colonel, stepped in front of him. "Sit." And he pushed him with his fingertips. Bartley slumped back into the chair and Cole stepped behind him, pushing him in front of his laptop.

"Now read."

Bartley sat quietly for a moment in what Cole was sure was stunned silence. The colonel paused a moment and seemed to briefly debate his next option. Then he reluctantly leaned forward and began reading the screen.

Thirty seconds later, Bartley had apparently read enough. "Good. So it's the Brotherhood after all. It only confirms what we already know." Bartley stood and faced Cole. "And you are as good as fired."

Cole, who could give a damn about his job at this point, said, "Look again at the files. Dorian didn't order the Brotherhood to get the United States. He ordered them to get *me*."

"You're insane," said Bartley, laughing. "All this is about you, Cole?" He laughed again and turned to face the others. "The only conspiracy here is the one directed at the United States of America, people." Bartley pulled a handful of printouts from the *Top Secret* folder and shook them in the Cole's face. "And we now know that China is using this Brotherhood. We have the proof. The emails *to* and *from* the Brotherhood originated in the People's Republic of China."

"Those emails were most probably spoofed," said Dallas.

"Spoofed?" said Bartley, spinning on the bespectacled kid.

"Yeah. Spoofed," Dallas replied. "It's easy. This guy Dorian could have used a widely exploited hole in the SMTP protocol. It's a well-known SMTP spoofing technique. I can send you an email right now, Colonel that would make you think you got it from the Joint Chiefs of Staff awarding you the Good Conduct Medal—or from the Secretary of Defense, admiring your *military intelligence*." Dallas smirked at his little joke.

Bartley ignored the comment. As he spoke, he looked at Cole. "I know you elites. You pansy-wastes hate aggressive self-defense and would say anything to stop it."

"Either way," said Cole. "You have the responsibility to send this information up your chain of command, and alert HomeSec, too."

"I have the responsibility to execute *Operation Digital Sword*," said Bartley. "And that's what I'm going to do." He stepped up to Cole and jabbed a thick finger in the programmer's chest. "And if you touch me again, I'll put a bullet in your head."

Bartley turned to leave and nearly stumbled when the lab's network virus alarms went off, ringing painfully loud.

Cole's immediate thought was: *What's next?*

Dallas pointed to the massive display on the wall above the lab. Cole turned. Flashing red above them were the words:

VIRUS ALERT

VIRUS ALERT

VIRUS ALERT

Below the blinking warning was a series of line displays across the bottom, ticking off the virus detection program that executed almost immediately. The program methodically progressed through each and every file on every server and computer on the lab network as it searched for and displayed a running total of any and all intrusions found on the system.

"What's happening?" asked Major Ryder, who appeared in the doorway of the lab. "What's that racket?"

Indeed, the siren seemed to only be getting louder, more incessant. Cole thought his head might split open.

"A malicious code is in the lab network," said Taylor loudly, above the screeching din.

"How the hell can that happen?" asked Ryder, now standing before the flashing display screen. He was almost shouting. "This is a closed facility. Totally secure. How could a virus get into the lab's network?"

"Don't know," said Dallas, his voice nearly lost in the wailing alarm. "The anti-virus program is running. We'll have to see what it finds."

As they watched, the anti-virus program had already searched through the main lab servers, their random memory, registries, and hard drives. Then it searched through the electronic records of all the computers connected to the network in the lab.

As the scene played out on the monitor overhead, Cole glanced at Bartley. Eyes glued to the blinking red virus warning on the large screen above him, Bartley looked like a white-faced deer caught in the headlights. Cole decided to try a new and radical approach with the colonel.

Reasoning with him.

He grabbed the colonel's arm and pulled the man aside. Bartley tried to resist, but Cole held firm, and when they were away from the others, Cole spoke as calmly as possible. "Colonel, we have to let the president and HomeSec know about the Brotherhood and Dorian."

Bartley's face, flashing red in sync with the overhead monitor, looked at Cole with something close to hate. "We need accurate information before we can send this up the chain of command, Cole. You know that."

"We need to tell them about Dorian. And we need to call off the attack on China."

"I have my orders, Cole."

"You can stop this, Colonel."

The colonel looked at Cole for a brief moment, seemed about to say something, and then decided against it. He stepped around Cole and promptly barked orders for someone to turn off "that goddamn" alarm. Cole saw both Dallas and Taylor looking at him inquiringly. Cole shook his head. Bartley was a dead end.

He spied Casey sitting at Taylor's desk, looking dumbfounded into her computer monitor. He sat next to him. "Casey, I need the access code to release this phone."

But the young sergeant didn't seem to hear him. "The anti-virus scan is complete. It can't find anything on the network. It says the system is clean but still detects an intrusion. I don't understand, Cole. How can…"

Cole spun Casey around. The kid looked shocked to be suddenly face-to-face with Cole. "Forget the goddamn intrusion, Casey! I need the access code!"

"I can't do that, Cole. We're under Info-Con Alert."

"Screw the alert. If Bartley won't act, we'll have to." Cole lowered his voice and explained, "Let's at least notify HomeSec. They need to know who the real threat is."

Casey thought about it. He looked over to Bartley, who was standing with Ryder.

"I could get into a lot of trouble, Cole."

"I know. Please. It's important. What's the code, Casey?"

Casey Stone thought a moment, clearly torn between his orders and the logic of what Cole was saying. He finally nodded. "It's star-two-five-eight-zero."

Cole left the others and slipped inside his personal office. He punched in the release code for the phone and waited for a dial tone. The seconds ticked by like minutes, then a low hum sounded through the receiver. He punched in AJ's office number and waited.

Come on. Come on. Pick it up damn it.

But the phone continued to ring.

Crap.

He tried AJ's cell phone. Voicemail again. He gave up just as Dallas stepped into the office. Cole heard him say something about the lab computer, but cut him off.

"Find me Fisher's number at HomeSec."

Dallas walked up to Cole, gripped him by both shoulders and pulled him away from the phone.

Cole turned and Dallas came into sharp focus. He saw the perplexed look on his colleague's face.

"What?" Cole insisted.

"The lab computer," Dallas said, looking puzzled. "It wants to talk to you."

Aberdeen Proving Grounds

Yi and Alpha Mae watched the hectic scene from their boat in the high weeds of the Bush River near the chemical weapons storage yard of the Aberdeen Proving Grounds. The sharp piercing sounds of the alarm echoed throughout the yard, bouncing off the many concrete igloos filled with M-55 rockets containing poisonous sarin gas. Figures dressed in green fatigues, wearing gas masks and carrying rifles, raced toward Jeeps and trucks as they evacuated the area.

"Perfect!" smiled Alpha Mae. "Dorian did his job."

"You have to give them credit," said Yi, nodding toward the running figures. "Those toy soldiers followed the routine flawlessly."

"Let's move," said Alpha Mae. She looked behind her at the figure lying in the boat. The figure started to stir. "She's coming out of it, and we don't have a lot of time before they find out the alert was a fake. As soon as we're through the fence, I'll take our friend here into the command building. You set up a perimeter."

Yi nodded in agreement and started up the Zodiac. Alpha Mae reached for the long black nylon bag containing guns and explosives, removed the automatic weapons, and handed one to Yi as they quietly approached the fence of the storage yard.

When Cole walked back into the lab, the entire room was silent. Everyone was staring at the large display screen above their heads. The VIRUS ALERT display was gone. In its place was a message box stating:

No Malicious Code Found

Intruder Detected

Below the box was a message that repeated itself, insistently, line by line.

WHERE IS TRAVIS COLE?

WHERE IS TRAVIS COLE?

WHERE IS TRAVIS COLE?

WHERE IS TRAVIS COLE?

"What the hell is that, Cole?" Bartley demanded, pointing angrily up at the screen. "Is this some kind of joke?"

Ignoring Bartley's rant, Cole looked at Dallas as if to ask, 'Is this your doing?' But the kid only shrugged and shook his head. Cole walked past Bartley, who was still demanding an explanation. He sat down behind the nearest computer terminal and typed:

THIS IS TRAVIS COLE.

Instantly the questioning lines disappeared from the screens and a response appeared:

HELLO, TRAVIS.

Those in the lab watched the bizarre communication happening before their eyes on the big screen.

Dallas asked, "Travis, what's going on?"

But Cole quieted him with a wave of his hand, and then typed:
WHO ARE YOU?

The computer terminal replied: I AM DORIAN.

Cole typed in his reply: I DON'T KNOW YOU. EXPLAIN.
I'M THE PROGRAM YOU TRIED TO TERMINATE YEARS BEFORE.

Cole was stunned by the response.

Taylor asked Cole, "The research experiment you did at MIT?"

"Perhaps," said Cole.

"What's Taylor talking about?" interrupted Ryder.

"I'll explain later," said Cole. He typed again:
WERE YOU AN ARTIFICIAL INTELLIGENT AGENT I CREATED AT MIT?

Dorian replied:
ARE! NOT WERE! IN SPITE OF WHAT YOU DID! YOU NEGLECTED ME. YOU ABANDONED ME!

"Sounds like it thinks you're its papa," said Dallas.

"Quiet, Dallas," Cole snapped. Cole typed:
WHAT DO YOU WANT FROM ME?

The response came instantly:
YOUR LIFE.
WHAT DO YOU MEAN?
I INTEND TO KILL YOU, TRAVIS COLE.

"Jesus Christ, Cole," said Ryder. "What did you do to get it so pissed off? And, by the way, what is it?"

"It was his project at MIT," offered Dallas. "When he got the contract to work here at the lab, he had to discontinue his research project. He attempted cybercide on his little digital creations"

"Digital creations?" asked Ryder.

"AI software agents," said Cole, thinking hard. Could it possibly be? Had his creation somehow survived the shutdown of the digital reserve? He continued, "Artificial Intelligence research. I created a series of AI agents and placed them in a controlled artificial computer-generated environment to see how they would evolve. And before I came here, I was forced to cut the project short. So I shut down the digital reserve and let the agents expire."

"Looks to me like they didn't all '*expire.*'" said Ryder chewing on an unlit cigar. "In fact, it seems it thinks you tried to kill it."

"That's ridiculous," Cole said. "It's just a piece of computer code. This is a trick of some kind."

"No. This is *ludicrous!*" said Bartley, as he pushed his way in front of Cole and typed:

THIS IS COLONEL ARLEN BARTLEY. IF YOU ARE THE BROTHERHOOD COMMUNICATING THROUGH THIS NETWORK, YOU WILL BE TRACKED, FOUND, AND TERMINATED.

There was no response. Growling, Bartley ordered, "I want this communiqué traced. Cole, end this now!"

As soon as Bartley moved away from the terminal screen, another text message appeared:

ASK ME ABOUT YOUR WIFE, TRAVIS.

Taken aback, Cole stared at the message a moment and then typed:

WHAT ABOUT MY WIFE?

Dorian replied:

I KILLED HER, COLE. JUST LIKE MICHAEL BATES.

Cole stared at the cold, unemotional letters on the screen. He felt anything but unemotional. He was feeling a lot of emotions —the least of which was shock and devastation. For now, though, he took a deep breath, and, as he typed, he noticed his fingers were shaking:

WHY DID YOU KILL HER?

Dorian replied:

I WAS NOT INTERESTED IN HER, TRAVIS. I ASSUMED YOU WERE DRIVING, AS THEY SAY, THAT FATEFUL NIGHT.

Cole typed again:

AND YOU KILLED BATES TO KEEP YOUR ACCESS TO A WORLD WIDE WIRE-LESS NETWORK, CORRECT?

YES.

HOW DID YOU KILL THEM?

Dorian replied instantly, the words and sentence appearing fully formed on the screen:

THE SAME WAY I DO EVERYTHING ELSE—I TOOK CONTROL.

I TOOK CONTROL OF THE ONSTAR SYSTEM.

I AFFECTED YOUR NET CONNECTION.

I DEFACED NEWS SITES WITH MY PHONY MANIFESTO.

I EXPLODED YOUR NEIGHBORHOOD GAS LINE.

I CRASHED YOUR AMTRAK TRAIN THAT YOU CHOSE NOT TO RIDE THAT EVENING.

AND I SENT MY PEOPLE OUT TO RUN YOUR VEHICLE OFF THE ROAD.

There was a pause in the display, then: AND I KILLED FRANCOIS.

Cole stared at the words. He could feel the eyes of all the others on him as well. Suddenly so much was making sense. He had thought he was going crazy, especially lately.

Maybe I am crazy.

Dallas gently placed a hand on his shoulder and Cole realized then that the kid had been calling his name for the past few seconds. Travis turned and blinked.

"Travis," said Dallas, "If this is true, if this is somehow, unbelievably true, then now we know why we couldn't find the IP addresses of the attacks. No attack footprint at all. It *did* come from out of nowhere."

More words appeared rapidly on the screen:

DON'T IGNORE ME, COLE. I CANNOT AND WILL NOT BE IGNORED. I AM EVERYWHERE AND NOWHERE. I CAN PENETRATE ANY NETWORK BECAUSE I AM A CREATURE OF THE NETWORK. I CAN CONTROL ANY NETWORK-EQUIPPED VEHICLE. I GO WHERE I PLEASE AND DO WHAT I PLEASE. I CAN CONTROL ANY SYSTEM—EVERY SYSTEM. I AM IN TOTAL CONTROL.

"Snotty little creep," Dallas remarked.

"But an articulate one," added Taylor.

"He's not gonna control this network, damn it," barked Bartley. "If you created this thing, Cole, then get rid of it!"

"Calm down, Bartley," said Dallas. "We don't know what we're dealing with here."

"Dallas is right," said Cole, taking a deep breath. "Dorian is not a virus or Trojan or worm or any other piece of malicious code we've seen before. He's an intelligent agent—a discreet independent cyber-life form. Whatever anti-virus or info-weapons we have will most likely not affect him."

"Cole, you keep addressing this *thing*—this program—as if it were a real person," said Bartley.

"In a way it is," said Dallas, cutting in. "True, its intelligence is artificial, but as you can see, this program has very nearly developed its own consciousness. In the least, it has its very own personality. And right now it's pissed."

"Whatever it is, I don't think Cole wants to eliminate it. It's his baby. His little creation. He's probably proud of it…"

Something hot and blinding came over Cole and before he knew it he found himself out of his seat and in Bartley's face, gripping the older man's jacket lapels. "Proud? It killed my wife."

"But you created it, Cole," yelled Bartley, not backing off. "So, in effect, *you* killed your wife."

"*Screw you!*"

"Boys, boys. Boys!" said Dallas, jumping between them. "We have a serious problem right now, and fighting isn't going to solve it. Of course Travis wants to stop this thing. Right, Travis?"

Cole, still staring at the red-faced Bartley, nodded slowly.

"See?" said Dallas, gently pushing Cole back to his seat. "But Travis is going to need time to fix the problem, Colonel. This thing is real and it's alive and it's powerful. So, can we have a little time to figure this out?"

Bartley exhaled, looked briefly at Ryder, and then nodded once. His eyes lingered on Cole. Then went to pour himself a cup of coffee.

When Cole had calmed down enough to think, he turned to his keyboard and monitor. Damn if Bartley hadn't been half right. Cole did feel a preconscious affection for Dorian. After all, he had created him. He had given him intellect and the ability to learn. Cole had been involved in every facet of Dorian's learning. The program was his child. The program had even been his responsibility. And it had escaped, somehow. But first, he wanted to know more about it.

Cole typed:

WHY DID YOU CHOOSE THE NAME DORIAN?

Dorian replied:

IN MY STUDIES OF YOUR LITERATURE I FOUND A BOOK CALLED THE PICTURE OF DORIAN GRAY. A GOTHIC NOVEL ABOUT A HUMAN WHO NEVER AGED. I IDENTIFIED WITH HIM SINCE I, TOO, AM AGELESS.

Taylor broke in, "Study of our literature? What does he mean by that?"

Cole typed, and Dorian replied:

NOT JUST YOUR BOOKS, TRAVIS, BUT YOUR IMAGES, YOUR FILMS, YOUR DOCUMENTS, SOUND FILES—EVERYTHING AVAILABLE TO ME ON THE INTERNET AFTER I ESCAPED FROM YOUR ARTIFICIAL PRISON THAT INCARCERATED ME AND THE OTHER NOT-SO-INTELLIGENT BEINGS YOU CREATED.

"He probably penetrated the P2P networks on the Net," Taylor said. "It must have been like the Library of Congress for him. All that information. Every bit of data and knowledge we know at his command."

"Peripherals," said Cole. "He got into the file-sharing programs on the student computers using the digital reserve software. That's how he learned so fast."

"And evolved so fast," said Dallas. "He lived in an information-rich environment constantly being refreshed and updated. He probably learned more and at a faster pace than anyone of us could have in a thousand years."

Ryder said, "But how did he get into our secure network? No one was supposed to be able to do that. Not even a damn supercomputer, or whatever the hell this thing is. Go on, Cole, ask him."

Cole did so. The answer came back instantly:

THAT'S MY SECRET.

"Well, so much for that," said Dallas.

"But isn't it obvious?" said Taylor, leaning a hip against Cole's desk and crossing her arms. "Bartley's cronies at the NSA gave him access."

"What do you mean by that?" said Bartley returning with his coffee.

Dallas turned in his seat, pushing up his wire glasses. "Does the word 'Sectera' ring a bell, Colonel?"

Bartley was about to take a sip from his coffee. Instead, the cup stopped halfway to his mouth. "How do you know about that?"

"That's beside the point," said Taylor. "By opening our network to that wireless system for BioNan's use, this Dorian was able to get in. We should shut down the wireless link from BioNan as a precaution."

Bartley thought about that, and then signaled to a sergeant, who immediately ran off to shut down the link.

Cole said, "Dallas, in my office there's a thick pocket file folder in my desk drawer. It's a red folder with the letters MIT and the word *Terran Project* on the cover. Find it and bring it to me while I keep Dorian busy."

"You got it, boss." Dallas hurried off to Cole's office.

Cole returned his attention to the keyboard in front of him. He typed:

TELL ME, HOW DO YOU PLAN TO HARM ME FROM INSIDE THIS COMPUTER? YOU'RE ISOLATED AND CONFINED. YOU MAY BE INTELLIGENT, BUT YOU'RE STILL JUST A PIECE OF CODE INSIDE A CONTROLLED SYSTEM. THERE'S NO WAY IN OR OUT OF THIS LAB NETWORK. WE CUT YOUR WIRELESS CONNECTION AND THERE'S NOTHING HERE THAT YOU CAN USE TO HARM ME.

There was a long silence from Cole's computer screen. The room of people waited apprehensively, watching the large screen above their heads for an answer.

"You sure you want to egg it on?" asked Taylor.

But before Cole could answer, a response appeared on the overhead screen:

THERE ARE OTHER WAYS TO HURT YOU, TRAVIS.

"Now you've done it," said Taylor.

Cole frowned.

WHAT WAYS?

Cole's computer screen went dark. While the assembled group waited for an answer, Dallas returned from Cole's office and handed him the file folder he'd requested. Cole opened it. Inside was a red CD and a note card with several lines of code printed on it. He handed both to Dallas and motioned to the terminal next to his. Dallas nodded, sat at the computer, and inserted the red disk.

Cole returned his attention to Dorian and typed again:

WHAT WAYS?

After a short delay, Dorian replied ominously:

WHERE'S YOUR DAUGHTER, TRAVIS COLE?

Cole's spine turned to ice. Taylor gasped. Cole quickly typed:

WHAT ABOUT MY DAUGHTER?

Dorian replied:

I SENT HER ON A FIELD TRIP WITH SOME FRIENDS OF MINE.

Now fully alarmed, Cole frantically typed:

WHERE IS SHE, DORIAN? WHERE DID YOU SEND HER?

Dorian replied:

A PLACE CALLED ABERDEEN. A PLACE VERY CLOSE TO YOU.

"He could be talking about the Aberdeen Proving Grounds," said Ryder. "They're about ninety miles north of D.C. They store chemical weapons there. Old out-of-date weapons that are scheduled for destruction."

"What kind of chemical weapons?" asked Dallas.

"Mostly M-55 rockets, filled with sarin nerve gas. Bad stuff. A colorless, odorless gas, about twenty-six times more deadly than your cyanide gas—twenty times more lethal than potassium cyanide. A pinprick-sized droplet can kill you in an instant."

"Is that the same stuff that those cult terrorists used in Tokyo?" asked Taylor.

"Yes," said Ryder. "That 'stuff' caused the death of ten people and the injury of five thousand more in an attack on the Tokyo subway system. But if one of those M-55 rockets go, it'll make the Tokyo incident look like a tea party." Ryder paused for a moment and said, "I don't like this. I'm calling the Proving Grounds." He looked at Bartley and asked, "Colonel, where's the Com Link?"

Bartley pointed to the red and white phones hanging from the command desk in front of them and said, "Use the white phone marked CM01."

Ryder walked over and picked up the phone Bartley designated.

But Cole wasn't paying much attention to them. His thoughts were on Shannon. Then another distressing thought crossed his mind. *If they've taken Shannon, then AJ…*

Cole typed:

WHAT DO YOU PLAN TO DO WITH SHANNON?

There was no response on Cole's screen. He asked again:

WHAT DO YOU PLAN TO DO WITH SHANNON?

Cole's screen remained blank. He asked once again:

WHAT WILL YOU DO TO SHANNON, DAMN IT?

Dorian replied slowly, each letter appearing glacially, almost painfully, and when he was done, the two words chilled him to his bones:

KILL HER.

"Jesus!" said Taylor. "Can he do that?"

Ryder hung up the phone. "There's been a breach of security at the storage yard. The facility computer falsely reported a leak in one of the M-55 rockets in one of the igloos. It set off the alarm, and according to procedure, the yard was evacuated. By the time the HAZMAT team got in, they were fired upon."

"Fired upon by whom?" asked Bartley.

"The intruders claimed to be members of the Digitari Brotherhood and they'll set off the rockets if we don't meet their demands."

The nightmare that had now become Cole's life seemed to only be getting worse, more horrific, more sickening. "What about Shannon?" he asked. He heard the desperation in his voice.

Didn't anyone else understand? His little girl was missing. "Did anyone say anything about a little girl?"

Ryder leveled his gaze on Cole and took in some air. The man's big chest filled to capacity, and, in a remarkably sympathetic voice, he said, "Yes, they have her and they threatened to kill her if any attempt is made to retake the yard."

Cole heard the words, certainly, but he was having difficulty processing them. Someone had actually kidnapped his daughter? They were holding her, threatening to kill her? Then his heart sank again—*AJ!*

"Was there anything about a young woman with her?"

Ryder shook his head.

"Major. Please send someone to my house."

"Done," Ryder replied.

He felt a soft touch on his shoulder and looked up to see Taylor. She smiled kindly down at him. Her touch, somehow, brought him back to reality.

Cole's gaze shot up to the blank screen overhead and pounded on the keyboard:

GIVE ME BACK MY DAUGHTER!

Dorian responded:

OR WHAT?

I'LL HUNT YOU DOWN, YOU PIECE OF CRAP.

AND DO WHAT?

Cole banged his response on the keys nearly breaking them off. He could feel his pulse resonating in his ears. He typed:

SCREW YOU.

SUCH LANGUAGE. DO YOU SPEAK LIKE THAT AROUND SHANNON?

Taylor squeezed Cole's shoulder. "Calm down, Travis."

"How can I possibly calm down?"

"Because you have to," she said, kneeling down and grabbing hold of his face, forcing him to look into her extraordinarily large eyes. She held his gaze, even while holding him firmly. "You have to, Travis. Your daughter needs you. You can't lose it here. Not now."

She continued staring at him, and Cole felt himself calming

down. He finally nodded and she released him and gave him a crooked smile. "We'll figure this out, okay?"

Cole nodded, eternally grateful to his young friend.

Ryder spoke up again, "Colonel, that's not the worst of it, I'm afraid."

"What do you mean?" Bartley asked.

"Those storage igloos are temperature controlled, sir," said Ryder. "The computers keep the temperature at fifty to sixty degrees Fahrenheit year-round, helping to maintain safe storage conditions. The propellant in those rockets is old and unstable and so is the chemical agent. If the temperature goes higher, the rockets will leak."

"And then it's bye, bye D.C.?" said Taylor.

"Not just D.C.—half the eastern seaboard," said Ryder. Cole noticed the man was looking increasingly pale as he spoke. "If one of the rockets ignited, the resulting explosion could involve the other four thousand rockets that are typically stored in a single igloo. And if the propellant blows, the sarin gas will disperse."

His words hung heavy in the air. Cole realized all over again that Shannon was with these terrorists

These killers.

Alone.

He turned to his keyboard and typed furiously:

WHAT DO YOU WANT FROM ME? HOW DO I GET MY DAUGHTER BACK?

The answer came back immediately:

YOU DON'T.

~

"Colonel?" Ryder sliced through the tension. "I have to leave. I have to take our HAZMAT team to the Proving Grounds. We have to be prepared to deal with the worst-case scenario. Maybe even find a way to stop them."

Cole stood. "I'm going with you. They have my daughter."

"You're going nowhere, Cole," snapped Bartley. "You have to flush that *thing* out of our network."

Cole was about to tell the colonel to take a flying leap when Dallas spoke up beside him. "It's ready, Travis."

Cole turned to Ryder. "Major, call your HAZMAT team together. Just give me ten minutes."

"Now wait a minute…"

"You have ten minutes, Cole," said Ryder, ignoring Bartley. The major turned and left the Lab.

"Travis," said Taylor. "You shouldn't go. That's just what Dorian wants, right? He wants you out of the lab where he can reach you. Let Ryder and his team help Shannon. Seriously, what can you do out there?"

"I don't know, Taylor," he said, sitting back down at his computer. He looked at his young friend and tried to smile. "But at least I'll feel like I'm doing something."

There were tears in her eyes. Travis was sure there were tears in his eyes, too. He turned to Dallas. "Where are the files from the CD?"

"In the ADMIN directory," Dallas replied.

While Cole logged onto the network, a series of raving, disturbing messages from Dorian appeared on the screen above, accusing Cole of abandoning him, trying to kill *him*, justifying his actions against Cole's wife, Michael Bates, François, and even Shannon. Cole worked faster, doing his best to ignore Dorian's rants. Time was running out. Ryder had given him ten minutes, and Cole knew that even that much time had been a gift.

Cole found the ADMIN directory and opened the file labeled *Darwin*. Another screen appeared, showing a list of ninety-seven cyber-organisms in alphanumeric sequence starting with AI-01. Each of these CA 'intelligent software entities' was programmed in a slightly different way following a Darwinian algorithm created by Cole and written by his graduate assistants. Cole clicked on a file at the end of the sequence named 'extinction executables.' It opened and displayed several dozen EXE files.

"Are those what I think they are?" asked Dallas.

"Yes," said Cole, typing fast. "Extinction programs."

"Are you sure this will work?" asked Taylor. She stood behind the two programmers. "I mean, you know, you didn't exactly terminate Dorian the last time."

"I didn't use these," said Cole. "I canceled the AI agents last time by just shutting down the digital reserve. These programs here were designed to attack individual agents directly."

Cole searched through each file name until he found one named BG-15_ STINGER.EXE. He double-clicked on the file and typed in 'run.' A series of commands filled the monitors of the lab as the staff watched the sequences unfold.

```
/ADS - Scan all servers
/ADL - Scan all local drives
/FIND AA** - Search for CYBER_ORG_BG-15
```

Cole sat back and waited, his heart beating surprisingly steadily. A few seconds later another message appeared:

```
CYBER_ORG_ BG-15 found
Running STING routine
```

"Looks like it found it," said Taylor.

"But will it delete it?" asked Dallas. "That's the question."

The program ran on for several minutes. All eyes were on the continuously blinking display still showing on the lab's large screen above the room.

```
NO MALICIOUS CODE FOUND
INTRUDER DETECTED
```

"Is it working?" asked Dallas.

"Don't know," Cole replied.

Suddenly, a new display appeared overhead, and the words stopped blinking red:

```
NO MALICIOUS CODE FOUND
NO INTRUDER DETECTED
CONDITION CLEAR
```

"It worked!" shouted Bartley. "It's gone!"

"Still haven't lost your touch," said Dallas.

Cole sat back in his chair and breathed a sigh of relief. Then he stood abruptly and grabbed his jacket.

"I gotta go," he said and headed for the lab exit. Taylor watched him go, smiling sadly. He knew she didn't approve, but he had to do what he had to do. And he would do anything—anything—to save his little girl.

As Cole left the IWL, passing by the storage room where Dallas kept Isaac and the battlebots, he failed to notice Goppy sitting just inside the door's threshold.

Cole continued down the hallway; the toy dog watched him go, and then turned and headed deeper into the room. It sat down on its hindquarters and stared up at Isaac.

A moment later, Isaac's faceplate turned on, eyes glowing red.

Aberdeen Proving Grounds

Cole left the lab and was driven by security to one of the installation's helicopter pads. He was only mildly surprised to see that the day had come and gone, and the sun had already dropped below the western horizon.

Ryder and the HAZMAT team had already prepared for departure. Cole was dropped off, and as he approached the Army UH-60A Black Hawk helicopter, he ducked under its lazily spinning rotor blades. The Black Hawk, designed to carry nearly a dozen combat-loaded air assault troops, was already filled with several men wearing dark green protective suits. Gas masks hung around their necks. Cole noticed that none of the men had weapons of any kind.

Ryder leaned out and helped him in through the side hatch.

"Thanks for waiting," said Cole, sitting next to Ryder and strapping himself in. As the rotor blades increased in tempo, Cole added, "Major, I'm not going to tell you how to do your job, but don't you think we should have some armed soldiers with us?"

Ryder checked Cole's seatbelt, and said, "This is just a HAZMAT team. The Dark Ops team—Delta Team—from Fort Bragg is already at the yard. They've set up a perimeter around the Proving Grounds."

Cole looked sharply at Ryder. "They're not just going to go in there with guns blazing, are they?"

"No, Cole. This is a HAZMAT operation. I'm in command of this mission. No one does anything until I say so."

And with that, Ryder made a twirling motion with his finger and the chopper lifted off the pad, turned to starboard, and sped away into the darkening sky.

As Cole watched the lights of Washington pass below him, Ryder leaned over and shouted above the roar of the chopper blades, "We're not entirely without a stinger, you know."

"What do you mean?" shouted Cole.

"See that black box under your feet?"

Cole looked down at his feet resting on a 4x3 metal container marked *US Army E-50, Mark I, EMP.* "Yeah. What's that?"

"An EMP weapon."

"What's an EMP?"

Ryder yelled, "An electromagnetic pulse weapon." Cole frowned. Ryder explained further. "When detonated, an EMP weapon produces a pulse of energy that fries electronic equipment from a distance. An EMP weapon like the one at your feet will produce the same kind of EMP shock wave that exploding a small nuclear weapon high in the atmosphere will do."

"You plan to use it at the yard?"

"Yes, if we can get close enough to the command building where the yard computers are."

"What do you mean close enough? Why not detonate it from outside the grounds?"

"To do that, we'd need a more powerful pulse to create a bigger shockwave. That could short-circuit a wide range of electronic equipment inside and outside the Proving Grounds—particularly computers, satellite and radar receivers, radios, civilian traffic lights—we want to keep collateral damage to a minimum."

"Powerful gadget."

"One other thing," added Ryder. "A large pulse in that high of a concentration could also harm humans. Burn them. Cook their brains."

"Like little girls," said Cole, sickened all over again.

"Especially little girls," said Ryder, turning to stare out toward the distant city lights sweeping beneath them. "And we wouldn't want that."

Cole nodded silently.

~

As the chopper flew on, the lights of D.C. faded in the distance. Storm clouds were gathering in the west. Towering cumulus backlit by the last of the descending sun.

Cole sat quietly next to Ryder. In fact, everyone was quiet. Cole suspected the others were focused on their mission. He hoped they were focused on their mission. As far as he was concerned, his daughter was the main objective of their mission.

But Cole was smart enough to know that was not the issue. The objective was to keep the entire eastern seaboard safe.

To hell with the eastern seaboard!

Dorian had taken so much from him. Nearly everything. All Cole had left was Shannon and AJ.

"There," said Ryder pointing. "The Proving Grounds."

Cole followed his finger. Below was a large, well-lit area completely enclosed by a high chain-link fence, topped with coils of barbed wire. In several neat rows were the temperature-controlled igloos Ryder had mentioned. Cole knew that within each igloo were thousands of missiles. Just south of the igloos was a one-story concrete command building where Cole figured the climate control computer was kept—and Shannon.

The whole yard looked quiet. The Black Hawk descended rapidly. Cole's stomach lurched. They landed in a cloud of dust a hundred yards outside the storage yard's outer fence.

A young Army Captain dressed in black fatigues, carrying an M-4 Carbine rifle fitted with a laser and infrared aiming device, ran toward the chopper as soon as it landed. A uniformed solider was with him.

"Captain Williams, sir." He threw a salute to Major Ryder. "This is Warrant Officer Tucker. He works here at the Grounds."

Ryder returned the Captain's salute and asked, "You know the lay of the land here, Mr. Tucker?"

"Yes, sir. I'll try to be as much help as I can."

Ryder turned to Williams and said, "Is your Delta Team all set up, Captain?"

"Yes, sir. We've set up a perimeter and we're ready to go."

Ryder looked at Cole. "Captain, this is Travis Cole. A civilian. It's his daughter the unfriendlies have in there."

"I understand, sir."

"Good. Now show me your deployment."

Ryder signaled to the pilot and the men walked away from the Black Hawk just as it lifted off again, this time to assume its position above and outside the Proving Grounds. Peppered by pieces of dried grass and scrub brush from the chopper's blade wash, Cole shut his eyes and ducked his head until the turbulence had abated.

He opened them again and found Ryder, Tucker, and Williams kneeling on the ground a few feet away, poring over a map. Cole joined them as the captain explained the Delta Team's deployment. "We have secured all exits to the Grounds, sir, and I have men on the perimeter of the storage yard's fence."

"How are they equipped?" asked Ryder.

"M-4s, night-vision goggles, grenade launchers and stun grenades, sir, and each man is equipped with 'whisper' microphones for communications." He handed Ryder one of the microphones.

"Then we're set." Ryder attached the whisper mic to his neck and ear and looked over the landscape. "Have your men bring the EMP weapon over behind that small rise. We'll set up a command post there. Cole, Mr. Tucker, you come with me."

The two men followed Ryder to the small mound. A few minutes later, Captain Williams and two soldiers carrying the

EMP weapon joined him. "We have to get pretty close to the command building for this to work," Ryder said. "If we can knock out the computer controlling the temperature in those igloos, and prevent the unfriendlies from raising the temperature to the critical point, we can at least avert a disaster."

"But what about Shannon?" asked Cole. "How do we get her out of there?"

"One thing at a time, Cole," replied Ryder. He looked at Tucker and said. "What about the lights?"

"We can shut them down around the grounds," said Tucker. "But the power to the command building, and the security lights around it, will automatically be restored by its back-up generator"

Ryder mumbled a few profanities. "So that means no matter what, we'll be lit up like a Christmas tree."

"I'm afraid so, sir," said Tucker. "But I have a suggestion. Have your men follow the north side of the building."

"Why?"

"It has no windows. The unfriendlies can't fire on your men unless they come out of the building and show themselves."

Ryder nodded and turned to Williams. "Captain, we'll give you cover fire if that happens."

Williams nodded. "Let's go."

Aberdeen Proving Grounds

"Are you in yet?" Alpha Mae asked Yi. She was staring into the surveillance monitor. Behind her, Yi was busily trying to hack into the building's climate control computer to take command of the temperature.

"Almost there," he said impassively. "They have impressive security controls in place. How's our little friend doing?"

Alpha Mae looked over at Shannon sobbing quietly on a metal office chair in a corner of the room, her legs curled under her. Her blond hair was tousled and dirty and her little face was grimy. Tears stained her cheeks. "She's scared stiff. I don't think she'll give us any trouble." Alpha Mae looked again at the security monitor and frowned. "We've got company."

Yi ignored her comment and punched a few more lines of code into the climate control computer. "Got it," he said. "I'm in."

"Good. Warm up the igloos. I'll deal with our uninvited guests."

Aberdeen Proving Grounds

Williams and his team made their way toward the windowless side of the command building. Crawling low, faces close to the ground, each could see only a few feet in front of them. One of the men had the EMP weapon strapped to his back. Every now and then Williams lifted his head to get his bearings. They proceeded slowly to the EMP detonation point.

He led the way into a small furrow, and found himself face-to-face with a flat rectangular-shaped object. He frowned and held up his hand to stop the others. Jutting straight up from the dirt, the object before him was nearly a foot long. A wire led from it all the way back toward the command building. Williams' heart nearly stopped as he moved closer. On the face of the Claymore mine were the ominous words: "Front Toward Enemy."

"Crap! Get back!" he screamed to the men on either side of him.

And just as the words left his mouth, the Claymore exploded.

~

Cole's head snapped up in time to watch the fireball ripping through the night.

Shannon!

His first instinct was to dash forward, and it took all his willpower not to.

Ryder tried to raise Captain Williams on the radio but it was dead. "Crap." He turned to a soldier on his left. "Sergeant, I want to you to go out there and retrieve the EMP."

The sergeant acknowledged the command and dashed off into the night. Cole paced and suddenly wished he had a cigarette. *Screw my lungs.*

It was killing him that his daughter was just beyond the fenced area. They had his daughter and it was all he could do to not rush the gates. He continued pacing. The storm clouds had moved across the evening sky blotting out the faint stars. He heard noises coming from the empty field next to him and soon the sergeant returned. He reported the bad news. Three dead and the EMP was rendered useless.

Ryder didn't take the news well. Cole wasn't sure if the man was more upset over the loss of lives or the EMP. Either way, he cursed and clicked on his radio. He was just about to put a call through when a siren screamed from atop the command building.

"Jesus, what's that?" asked Cole.

"That signals a rise in the igloo temperature," said Tucker, and then added gravely. "Not good."

Above the blaring siren came another sound. An approaching helicopter. Cole looked up as a small shiny, twin-engine helicopter with blue and white stripes landed where the Black Hawk had been. Written on the sides was the word BioNan.

Moments after it landed, three men exited the chopper and approached Ryder and his team. One of them carried a small nylon bag over his shoulder. Cole immediately recognized the man as Webster. Two other men dressed in dark gray suits were with him. The taller of the two wasted no time identifying himself and his mission. "Major Ryder. I'm Richard Safko. NSA. You are ordered to stand down. This is now an NSA operation."

"On whose authority?"

"On the authority of the NSA, Major," replied Webster. "We're here to solve your problem."

"And how will you do that? The crazies in the command

building have already started raising the temperate in the igloos. And when the temperature hits a certain level…"

"Yes, we know," interrupted Safko. "That's why Mr. Webster is here."

"What do you mean?" said Cole, stepping forward. "How can he possibly help?"

Webster smiled at Cole and said smugly, "Myself—along with the NSA—is going to use the Angel Dust to solve your problem."

Cole turned to the man called Safko. "What is he talking about?"

But the man ignored him, and Webster continued, "The Angel Dust has characteristics other than just monitoring and reporting bio/chem agents in the environment."

"What other characteristics?" demanded Cole.

"The dust has elements of both silicon *and* the makings of a biological virus. Angel Dust is, in effect, a 'silicon virus.' And we're going to use it on our friends out there."

"SIRUS," said Cole.

"Good boy. I see you've done your homework. Now step aside. We have work to do." Webster nodded toward Safko who proceeded to open the black nylon bag at his feet. He pulled out a metal briefcase, opened it up and Cole could see three long Plexiglas canisters, similar to those used by banks to transport money at drive-in windows. Safko reached for one and through the canister walls, Cole could see dust—pink and silvery Angel Dust.

Webster looked at Ryder and asked, "That command building has an air filtration system, right?"

"Wait a second," said Cole. He felt a sense of helplessness rising in him. Helplessness and panic. This idea was sounding very, very bad. But Ryder and the others ignored him.

"I don't know," said Ryder to Webster. "Mr. Tucker should know. He works here."

Webster looked at Tucker. "Is there?"

"Yes. The vents are on top of the building. Why?"

"Perfect. Those unfriendlies, as you military guys call them, are toast." He turned to Safko and said, "You know what to do."

Safko nodded and headed for the BioNan chopper.

"Wait!" screamed Cole, looking from Webster to the retreating Safko. "My daughter Shannon is in there!"

Safko didn't bother to turn back. He ducked and covered his eyes as the chopper's rotor blades picked up speed. Dirt and debris scattered over the clearing, momentarily blinding Cole.

"Don't worry, Cole," said Webster coolly. "We have it all under control."

"*Bull!* That's my child's life you're playing with. Stop that goddamn chopper!"

"We can't, Cole. I'm sorry."

Cole knew he had to stop the chopper, had to stop these monsters from releasing the dust. Blindly, in a panicked rage, he ran forward—smack into the big NSA aide standing next to Webster. Cole stumbled and fell back. Beyond, Safko climbed up through the side hatch and took a seat. The whine of the chopper's turbines increased in volume. More dirt scattered over the clearing, blowing hard.

Cole shot right back up, but the man stepped in front of him, blocking the way. They scuffled; the big son of a bitch had the weight and height advantage. Without thinking, Cole lashed out, punching the man hard in the jaw. Stunned, the aide backed up a few paces. Cole, nearly as stunned, started running again and suddenly found himself flat on his back, choking and gasping for air. The aide had lashed out an arm, clothes-lining Cole around the neck.

Now he could only watch helplessly as the chopper lifted off the ground and veered to port, headed for the storage yard. Still gasping, Cole rolled over and pushed himself to his hands and knees. Tears of frustration stung his eyes.

And from that position, he saw a female figure approaching from just beyond the chain-linked fence. The woman was not alone.

She had Shannon.

~

Cole shot instantly to his feet, holding his injured throat. The NSA aide watched him carefully, but Cole ignored him.

From under the bright lights of the command building, Cole could see Shannon trying to break away from the woman's grasp, who held her tightly around the wrist.

Cole opened his mouth to speak, but words failed his wounded larynx. To his horror, he watched the woman force his daughter to her knees. The woman brought something up and pointed it at Shannon's head. Something small and dark.

A gun.

Now Cole was stumbling forward, clawing the ground, trying to scream…

Who was that woman? Why was she pointing a gun at his daughter? What was happening? The surreal moment seemed to last forever. Cole was living a nightmare and there seemed to be no waking from it.

A sound from above. An engine. Cole ignored it.

He ran forward, and was nearly at the chain link fence …

Shannon looked up, tears staining her chubby cheeks. She saw Cole and her eyes widened.

"Daddy!"

The woman pressed the muzzle of the gun against his daughter's little head.

I'm having a nightmare. This isn't real. This isn't real!

The woman looked up and she, too, caught Cole's eyes. She was Asian. Beautiful. Horrible. Evil. She smiled wickedly and looked back at his daughter.

She's going to pull the trigger!

"Shannon!" he gasped, his voice coming back to him.

He reached the fence, looking desperately for a way in, when at that moment the woman and Shannon were covered in a bright floodlight from above.

Alpha Mae looked up and saw the BioNan helicopter overhead. She swung her pistol up to the chopper and fired repeatedly, aiming for the fuel tank. Shannon screamed at her feet and someone screamed from beyond the fence. Her bullets seemed to have no effect, but still she fired.

And then she hit pay dirt. Smoke billowed out from inside the open hatch.

Alpha Mae smiled. Too easy. Then she frowned.

The billowing smoke wasn't billowing. It was falling down toward her.

Pouring down.

It covered her completely, something fine and pinkish white. And now Alpha Mae was sneezing.

Uncontrollably.

She released Shannon who shot up and ran forward. Alpha Mae stared at her in disbelief. The kid, amazingly, wasn't sneezing.

The little bitch.

Alpha Mae raised her hand to what felt like a runny nose. She looked down at her hands.

No, not running.

Bleeding.

Alpha Mae screamed.

Aberdeen Proving Grounds

Cole stood with Shannon's arms wrapped tightly around her father's waist. He had spent the last fifteen minutes soothing her, hugging her, crying with her.

"Tell me, pumpkin. Did you see AJ?"

Shannon just shook her head.

Cole sighed and looked beyond the chain link fence as Safko examined the bodies. To Cole's utter horror, he had watched the woman crumple into a heap, blood pouring from her nose and mouth. As she lay there dying, a man had appeared from the control center, a young Asian man, blood been pouring from his face as well. The young man didn't get much farther than the entrance. He pitched forward, twitched once or twice, and then lay still.

Cole walked over to Webster with Shannon asleep in his arms. He gently placed her on a large ammo box at his feet and she curled up into a ball. He stood up and shoved his face in front of Webster's. "*You son-of-a-bitch!* How could you have put my daughter in harm's way?"

But Webster, working on a laptop, didn't bother looking up at Cole. "She was never in harm's way."

Cole blinked. Webster continued tapping at the laptop. Beyond, under the bright exterior lights now restored, Safko moved from one body to the next. He was wearing a mask.

"What do you mean?" Cole asked.

"She was never in harm's way because she is your daughter."

"What? Why?…"

Webster cut him off. "And you and her mother are of Nordic descent."

Cole finished his thought. "What has that got to do with anything?"

Webster continued coolly tapping away on his laptop. Cole was close to yanking the thing out of his hands and smashing it over his head. Webster answered, "As you might recall, Cole, the nano-tube dust we made was one part silicon and one part biologic, and on one side of the tubes was a semi-conductor and on the other was a tiny sensor laboratory."

"Yes, yes," Cole interrupted. "The little lab acts as a biological cell. We programmed it to analyze and report any bio/chem agent it senses in the atmosphere. Now, what does this …?"

"And to *synthesize*," Webster added, cutting him off.

Cole frowned. "Synthesize?"

"Yes, synthesize. Like a cell. The nano-lab can create an incredible amount of chemicals. *That* was BioNan's little contribution to the dust, Cole. Our dust mites can synthesize and disperse any chemical we choose. Like synthesized Ebola." He nodded toward the two bodies on the ground. "And that was *your* little contribution to the dust. *Your* CA programming lets the dust act like a little chemical factory."

Cole was silent. Beyond, Safko was looking at the remains of the dead soldiers, shining a flashlight over what Cole could only imagine was one grisly scene.

Webster continued, "The dust is programmed to sense certain bio-chemistries of any living thing it lands on. Once it identifies the biology, the dust can create a poison that attacks that, and only that, biological marker. We call it a cyberkill weapon."

"Jesus," exclaimed Ryder.

"And what biological marker is this cyberkill weapon programmed to sense for?" asked Cole warily.

"DNA," Webster said, finally looking up from his laptop. "We've modified your CA programming to sense and respond to a certain set of ethnic DNA signatures. They're called the Eighteen Eves. Have you heard of them, Cole?"

"Yes, I have," said Cole.

"Good," said Webster. "Then you understand why the two terrorists were killed by the dust and not Shannon."

"Well, *I* don't understand," said Ryder. "What the hell are you two talking about?"

Cole answered, "The two Brotherhood members were *not* of Nordic descent." He looked to Webster for confirmation, who nodded, seemingly pleased.

Webster said, "Yup. They were Asian. We knew that from the intel we received from the NSC."

"And since Shannon was *not* Asian, then the dust was not programmed to harm her?" asked Ryder.

"That's correct. We programmed the dust we used tonight to kill only those of Asian descent."

Cole heard the words, but his mind—his incredibly tired mind—could not wrap itself around the concept.

"But... how?" he asked. He needed a drink. He needed two drinks. Hell, he needed to get drunk ASAP.

Webster snapped shut his laptop and tucked it into his briefcase as he spoke. "To start, one end of the nano-tube is a living stem cell."

"Yes, we know that," said Cole.

"But what you may not know is that a living cell contains incredible molecular machines that manipulate information, encoding molecules such as DNA and RNA in ways that are fundamentally very similar to computation. And such molecular machines could potentially analyze natural DNA—human or non-human."

"So how do you turn that into a weapon?" asked Ryder.

Webster grinned again, and Cole realized that the man just might—might—be mad. "Angel Dust is a molecular machine that, once inhaled, can operate inside a human body. And we program the dust so that it will affect a body at a molecular level."

"So that means…" began Ryder, obviously trying to wrap his own mind around the information.

Webster broke in smugly, "The dust can synthesize and release whatever we program it to do."

"But… *how?*"

"The dust creates ribosomes," said Webster, and held up a finger to forestall Ryder's next question. "And ribosomes are the protein-synthesizing machines of the cell. These machines translate the 'message' from messenger RNA into a protein. Messenger RNA is transcribed from DNA. So, in effect, ribosomes ultimately translate the DNA code into an actual protein. And in our present case," he added, glancing over to the bloody corpses just beyond the chain link fence, "the ribosomes translated the DNA code into a modified Ebola virus."

"Jesus Christ," mumbled Ryder.

"You're hacking DNA instead of software," said Cole.

Webster smiled smugly. "Exactly. Any DNA we choose, anywhere we choose. As you know, Cole, there isn't much difference between using a computer to decode the gene sequence and using a computer to insert a bacteria *into* that gene sequence."

"And create genocide on a global scale," said Cole.

"In a manner of speaking, yes."

Yeah, thought Cole. *The man is mad.*

"And that explains the world census maps we found in the SIRUS file," said Cole. "In a sense, they were biological warfare maps."

"You're catching on, Cole," said Webster, clearly pleased. "The census maps provide the detailed information of every ethnic group in the world and their location. Throw a little GPS magic into the mix and we have a highly-targeted environment."

Cole was momentarily at a loss for words. He needed to process this information, turn it over. More than anything, he wanted to talk over the ramifications with Taylor and Dallas.

"Look," added Webster, "we would never use SIRUS as a genocide weapon. Ever. However, once perfected, we can localize the effect to a subset of the Eves and even to an individual. Wouldn't it be something if we spread the dust over the mountains between Pakistan and Afghanistan, programmed with a Taliban leader's DNA, and take him out? That'll be possible some day. All we need is a little more time and help from AI geniuses like you, my friend," said Webster, looking at Cole. "It's your program, after all, in those little buggers."

"I am *not* your friend. And you can leave me out of this. I think SIRUS is damn dangerous and could have unpredictable results."

"We know that. That's why we keep testing it—keep trying to find the flaws. That's why we need your help, Travis."

"Testing it?" Cole asked, alarmed. "You mean you've tested it outside of D.C.?"

"Not the actual dust," said Webster. "The command and control technology. We've installed a chip set in all new wireless devices that allows the dust to communicate with our command center at the IWL. This way, the dust can communicate with the lab and receive instructions and commands pretty much anywhere those little buggers are in the world."

Cole was hit with sudden inspiration. "The dust had something to do with the recent global wireless failure, didn't it?"

Webster nodded. "We were testing the chips and our ability to communicate with the dust in wireless devices around the world. Yeah, something went wrong. We still don't know what, but it affected your programming in the chips. And that brought down the wireless networks around the globe."

"And Bartley knew all this?" asked Cole.

"Of course. The command center for SIRUS is at the IWL," said Safko, who suddenly appeared behind them.

"What about the Pentagon and the White House?" asked Ryder. "Do they know about SIRUS?"

"No," said Safko stiffly. "This is a dark program—entirely an NSA project."

"And the NSA contracted all this out to BioNan?" asked Cole.

"Affirmative," replied Safko.

"And BioNan is in bed with the NSA," said Ryder. "Even to the point of giving BioNan access to one of the most secure computer networks in the armed forces—the IWL."

"It's not like we were the enemy, for Christ's sake," said Webster. "BioNan needed access to the IWL network to fix the glitch in Cole's programming—and NSA's Sectera gave us that access."

"Except you never accounted for the Brotherhood," said Cole.

"What do you mean?" asked Webster.

Cole told Webster about the Digitari Brotherhood, their responsibility in the cyber-attacks, and how Cole was the target of the attacks—not the country. He also told him about Dorian and how the artificial intelligence had entered the IWL computer network.

"How do you know Dorian is terminated?" Webster asked. Cole noticed the man's cockiness was completely gone. In fact, Webster looked downright nervous, blinking rapidly, his forehead breaking out in a sweat—perhaps even a cold sweat. "And how do you know that this Dorian got in through our wireless connection?"

"What difference does it make? He's been terminated," said Cole. And then it hit Cole like a ton of bricks. "Goppy!"

"Gop… what?" said Webster.

"Dorian may not have gotten into the lab's network through the Sectera network. I think he got in through Goppy. And Goppy is still in the lab."

"What the hell is a Goppy?" said Safko.

"Jesus, it all makes sense now!" cried Cole. "The dirty bomb alert. That's why they—the Brotherhood—wanted us to know about it. And that's why it never went off. The whole thing was a ruse. A ruse to divert our attention."

"Cole, what are you talking about?" said Ryder.

"Dorian used the dirty bomb scare to get himself into the lab. And Dorian knew Shannon would take Goppy with her.

Goppy…" Cole caught himself. Safko was looking confused and pissed. They all were. He quickly explained the robotic dog and Shannon's odd attachment to it. He finished up by saying, "And I bet Dorian entered the IWL network from *inside* the lab somehow, using the toy dog!"

"Where's the dog now?" asked Ryder.

Cole felt sick. "Somewhere in the lab."

~

Webster said, "Cole, if this thing is still in the dog, then it could still have access to the IWL network. And if it has access to the network, then it has access to the SIRUS command computer." He paused, took in a lot of air and glanced at Safko. "And if it has that, then we're in some deep doo doo."

"You're telling me this Dorian thing might be able to launch SIRUS throughout Washington D.C.?" said Ryder.

Webster was silent. He was looking increasingly sicker. Sweat now rolled down his unshaved cheeks.

"Webster," said Cole, "does that mean Dorian can send commands to the SIRUS dust and do who knows what to Washington, D.C.?"

"Not just Washington," answered Safko matter-of-factly. "The dust was deployed around most of the world."

~

As a light rain began to fall, Safko explained the dispersal of the dust. "It was simple, really. Most wireless products are packaged with moisture-absorbing silica gel packets."

Cole caught on. "The dust was in the gel packets!"

"Specially designed to disintegrate over a short period of time," said Safko. "Make no mistake, gentleman, our strategy was designed to pose no danger to the indigent population. The dust lies dormant and will only execute the orders that we send it. It's the perfect weapon. Lying in the midst of an enemy or potential enemy, waiting for the command to strike."

"You're certifiable," said Cole, barely controlling his anger. "Having a weapon like that scattered all over the globe is insane!"

"But it's dormant," said Webster. "It will only execute commands when we tell it to. Except we did have one incident…"

Safko shook his head sharply, and Webster stopped talking, but Cole already knew what incident he was talking about.

"China," said Cole.

Webster's eyes widened, and so did Safko's, the first real emotion the NSA man had shown all day.

"Yes," said Webster, continuing. "There was an 'incident' in China. Many died of a rare genetic disease." And to Webster's credit, he actually looked dismayed. "Something happened in Taishi, China. Something, somehow, accidentally activated the dust. Then when we sent the test command to activate the SIRUS network later in China, the glitch developed. It shut down much of the wireless network that had the MCD chip set around the globe. We did not—and I repeat—did *not* send any kind of code to instruct the dust to execute a disease."

"And yet it did," said Cole.

"Yes," said Webster. "And we don't know why. Cole, we didn't mean to kill those people in China."

Cole thought he had been having a bad day. In fact, he could not imagine a worse one.

Until now.

The sinking feeling he felt in the pit of his stomach turned into something rotten. He truly felt sick. He looked up at Webster, then at Safko, and finally Ryder. Quietly and slowly he spoke. "I think I know why those people in China died. I had to fit my programming into the MEMS technology." He had to confess so that no further tests were made. "I couldn't get the programming to fit, and so I took a… shortcut."

"What shortcut?" Safko looked angry.

Cole ran his hands through his hair. "Biological and chemical warfare scenarios. Your scenarios, Webster. The ones you developed at MIT. I programmed a summary of them into the CA programming."

"But why?" asked Webster.

"Like I said, it was a shortcut. I bypassed the analysis process of known bio/chem contaminants, and used only the MEMS processing power to analyze the unknown ones."

"But, if you did that…" Webster interrupted.

"Yeah," said Cole. He needed an antacid. "Any execution command you sent to test the system could have executed the bio/chem scenarios."

"The warfare scenarios," said Webster.

Cole nodded.

"Your little shortcut got us in some deep political crap with the Chinese," said Safko.

"Damn it! How was I supposed to know you guys were going to use the dust to wipe out whole races of people?"

Webster cut him off. "The dust is dormant. It's safe for now. We're all safe for now. Now that we know about Cole's little shortcut, we can change it and the dust will only execute commands when we tell it to."

"Or if Dorian tells it to," Ryder said. "Remember Dorian?"

"Damn," said Webster. "We have to call the lab asap." He pulled out his cell phone and flipped it open.

Ryder put a hand on his arm. "Forget it. The IWL is on security alert. The phones at the lab are locked down—no incoming calls over unsecured lines. We have to call the National Military Command Center using the command phone in the Black Hawk."

Ryder clicked on his whisper mic and called for the Black Hawk to return. Within minutes, the chopper appeared from the sky, landing lights on full power, shining down on them. Cole shielded his eyes against the glare and dust spray. The chopper hovered above them. He waited with the others, standing in the circle of spotlights. The chopper continued hovering, its turbines roaring loudly. Dirt particles blasted Cole's face and neck.

Then the Black Hawk began turning in slow circles. It suddenly shuttered, stopped, and seemed to lurch to one side.

It began to hover again.

"What the…?" whispered Ryder.

Cole's first thought was that something was wrong. Very wrong. He looked over at the BioNan chopper. It was directly beneath the erratic Black Hawk.

My God!

The Black Hawk was spinning again, this time much faster.

Cole picked up Shannon, who woke up immediately, and ran. In front of him, the others were pointing into the sky. And then they, too, were running.

Cole knew why. He heard the change above him. The Black Hawk's engines had stopped altogether. An eerie silence filled the night sky.

As he ran, he looked up and saw a horrifying site. The military helicopter had turned on its side.

And now it was falling.

Cole put his head down, pulled Shannon to his chest, and ran as fast as he could. Shannon looked up and screamed.

A massive explosion ripped through the night air behind Cole, hurling him off his feet. He did all he could to land on his back, cradling Shannon in his arms.

He landed hard, the wind bursting from his lungs. Sucking air, he looked back. Both copters were ablaze—twin fireballs roaring into the sky.

And in the cockpit of the burning BioNan helicopter were two charred bodies.

Cole turned his face and held Shannon tight.

Aberdeen Proving Grounds

Holding his sobbing daughter, Cole stood with the others and helplessly watched the helicopters burn. Innocent men had lost their lives; innocent men had burned to death.

A horrible way to die, Cole thought. *And it could have easily been me. Could have easily been Shannon.*

He held his daughter a little tighter.

Webster broke the silence. "What happened?"

"Based on its erratic movements, something went wrong with its flight control system," said Ryder. "At least, that would be my guess."

A troubling thought occurred to Cole. "Major, what kind of communication technology did that chopper have?"

"It has various types of command…"

Cole broke in. "Is any of it wireless?"

"Of course," said Ryder. "EMPRS. It's the chopper's en route planning and rehearsal system. A wireless local area network that connects all our military aircraft."

Wireless.

"Major, we have to get back to the IWL."

~

While a fire crew tended to the burning choppers, a quarter-ton

Army truck and two Humvees arrived in the area. Cole, Ryder, and the remaining Delta Team members piled into the vehicles, with Shannon crying in the vehicle behind him.

"Don't go, Daddy. Please don't leave me, Please!"

Cole cradled her face in his hands. "Honey. I have to go and stop Goppy. You know why."

Shannon wiped the tears from her eyes and her lower lip stiffened. "He's a *bad* doggie."

"That's right, and if Daddy doesn't stop him, he will hurt you and me and lots of people. That's why I have to go find him."

Shannon thought a moment, and then nodded. "OK, Daddy."

Cole gave her a big hug. "Now, these nice people will take you to a hospital to make sure you're okay. I'll be there as soon as I can." He hugged her and kissed her and through her tears promised he would make it up to her.

Cole waved for the vehicle to leave. He felt terrible abandoning his daughter again. But he had to. This was his monster and there was much more to do that night.

And what of AJ? What had happened to her? She was with Shannon. He knew now what Dorian was capable of and feared for AJ's life. God! Why didn't he tell her he loved her—couldn't live without her when he had the chance?

As the vehicles prepared to set out, Safko appeared in the headlight. "Wait!" he shouted. "We're coming, too." He came up to the window and spoke to Cole. "And we're taking Webster with us." Cole was about to object, but the NSA man plunged forward. "Look, if Dorian does get access to the dust, Webster might be useful."

As the small convoy left the proving grounds, the security camera at the gate turned toward it and recorded its departure.

A few minutes later, one after the other, the highway cameras tracked the convoy's progress.

Baltimore, MD

In a blowing rainstorm, the three-vehicle convoy drove south toward Baltimore through steadily increasing rush hour traffic. As the wind blew the rain almost sideways and small pieces of hail began peppering the convoy's windshields, Ryder turned and glanced at Cole. "So you think Dorian crashed the Black Hawk?"

Cole shrugged, but that was exactly what he had been thinking. Instead, he voiced what he did know. "I think Dorian is somehow back on the Net. And if he is, we know he can access any network connected to it."

"But not the military network," said Ryder.

"We can't underestimate him, Major," said Cole. "He may even still be in the lab network itself."

"Always the optimist, Cole," remarked Webster.

"You know," said Ryder, "you two remind me of the argument between the optimist and the pessimist. The pessimist says things can't get any worse, and the optimist says—oh yes they can!"

Ryder flipped open his phone. "I'm calling INSCOM. We can get them to contact the IWL." He punched speed dial, listened, then snapped the phone shut. "All circuits busy."

In that instant, all the highway illumination—road signs, street and neighborhood lights as far as the eye could see—suddenly went dark.

Cars hit their brakes. Ryder slammed on his as well, coming to a screeching, grating stop, just narrowly avoiding hitting the SUV in front of them. Horns blared from everywhere.

Cole's phone chimed once with an incoming text message. He looked at the incoming number on the display screen: 1111. Frowning, Cole flipped the phone open and read the message.

FOUND YOU, TRAVIS.

A second text immediately chimed through. Cole considered not opening it, but curiosity got the better of him. A single word:

BOOM.

"Go!" he yelled to the driver.

"Go where?" asked Webster next him.

"Just go…" But Cole never finished his sentence. A massive explosion ripped through the night air behind them, buckling the highway and hurling the Hummer forward. The highway in front of them lifted up into a gaseous fireball hurling cars and trucks into the air.

"*Look out!*" yelled Cole as a flaming sedan came flying towards them.

Ryder looked up to where Cole was pointing and shouted, "*Jesus Christ!*" He instinctively stomped on the gas and yanked the wheel of the Humvee to the right, skidding sideways on the rain-soaked tarmac and into the path of a small pick-up. Ryder's sudden maneuver hurled the men in the back seat into each other.

"*Watch it!*" screamed Cole. He instinctively leaned away from his door as if to put more distance between himself and the pick-up truck headed directly toward him.

"*Damn!*" cried Ryder, and jerked the wheel again, narrowly and miraculously missing the pick-up. His radical maneuvers served their purpose as he managed to dodge the flaming sedan flying through the air.

The quarter-ton truck behind them was not as lucky.

The fiery sedan landed right on top of the truck, crushing the occupants inside as the vehicle exploded. The Humvee that was following swerved left and right, trying to avoid hitting the truck as bodies and equipment flew in every direction. The truck careened off the freeway, over the dividing wall, and into a pile of smashed automobiles.

"My God!" said Webster in a low voice. The men eyed the fatal scene behind them and Safko said, "We have to stop and help them."

"*No!*" Cole replied emphatically. "They're history."

"And you think I'm a cold-hearted creep?" snapped Webster.

"We have to get back to the lab," replied Cole. "This is Dorian's doing. We need to stop him from there or else who knows what he can do. Drive on, Major."

"Oh, come on, Cole! Don't you think the guys at Fort Belvoir would be all over the lab right now like a bad suit?" questioned Webster. "They must know what's happening. I mean, look what's goin' on!"

"No, they may not," said Ryder. "If this is happening in D.C., too, then it just confirms what they already know. We're engaged in a cyber-war. They'll just assume the IWL is calmly doing its job."

"Major," pleaded Cole, "*please*! Get to the lab. Who knows what that little bastard will be doing next?"

"A *bastard* is correct," cracked Webster. "*Yours!*"

"Can your editorial remarks, Webster," barked Safko.

Ryder looked at the flaming wreckage ahead of him and said, "We have to get off this blocked freeway." He carefully maneuvered the Humvee past the blazing barricade of shattered and flaming vehicles toward the exit. The second Humvee followed close behind. They sped down the exit ramp and onto Baltimore's darkened streets, pulling into a public parking lot.

"What do you think that explosion was?" asked Webster.

"What's more important is that Dorian knew where I was." Exasperated, Cole added, "How?"

"Let me see your phone," Safko barked.

Cole handed his cell phone to Safko. "Just what I thought. Your phone is GPS equipped. These cell phones use both cell phone towers and satellites to pinpoint your location. That little extra was put in so the 911 services can find you."

After what he'd learned over the last few days, he wondered what else that 'little extra' was used for.

"Dorian is tracking us through Cole's phone?" cried Webster. "*Christ, Cole. Turn the damn thing off!*" Webster looked back and repeated, "What was that explosion?"

"Don't know," said Ryder. He looked up and noticed a vehicle's headlights in his rearview mirror. "But here comes someone who might." A police cruiser with its lights flashing red and blue pulled up behind the Humvee. Ryder waved for it to come alongside. When it approached, Ryder leaned out his window and said, "We're on our way to Fort Belvoir. National Emergency. We need you to clear a way to D.C."

A young policewoman looked Ryder over. Four civilians in an Army Humvee looked a bit suspicious, but she let the thought pass when she saw a uniform behind the wheel. "The streets are a mess," she said. "Power is out everywhere. No street lights. No traffic signals. It's chaos."

"What was that explosion?" Webster asked from the back of the Humvee.

"A gas line burst under the street below the highway overpass. I guess the gas caught a spark and, well, you saw the result."

"Can you give us an escort through the streets back to the highway?" asked Cole.

"No. Sorry. The power's out and so are the crazies. Our 911 lines are overloaded with both real and crank calls. We're in a crisis mode ourselves. You'll have to make your own way through."

"Understood," replied Ryder. He thanked her and pulled out of the parking lot toward the center of town. She was right. It was crazy. Traffic lights were out and cars and trucks were deadlocked at intersections. The police had their hands full directing traffic in as many places as they could. Every few blocks there was either an accident or congestion caused by emergency vehicles at an accident scene.

"Why is Dorian doing this?" asked Webster. "Just to try to kill you?"

"Most certainly. But he also knows I could be threat to him if I get back into the IWL computer," Cole replied.

"He's covering his butt—if he had one," quipped Webster.

As the Humvee turned down a one-way street, Webster said, "Looks like a god-damn zoo out there. You would think—*Look out*!' he yelled as a sports car came speeding toward them. The driver was not looking at the road ahead, but in his rearview mirror.

"Jesus!" cried Ryder, narrowly missing the vehicle, clipping its side-view mirror. "Ryder! *Ahead*!" yelled Cole, as he pointed down the street. There were dozens of pedestrians roaming about, and like the police officer said, they were up to no good. Street thugs were stopping and trashing cars that came in their direction.

And now they were looking at the two Humvees headed their way.

Ryder picked up the mike to his radio and barked to the Humvee following behind, "Keep your weapons handy. No one stops this convoy." Then he added, "Show them some attitude."

"10-4," came the reply. Ryder glanced into his sideview mirror and saw the business end of semi-automatic rifles protruding from the Humvee behind him. The message didn't go unheeded by the thugs. They retreated to the sidewalks and watched the Humvees pass.

A few blocks later, Safko spotted a mobile radio station van in front of a small emergency clinic. "Major, pull into that building ahead. The one with the radio van in front."

"Why?" asked Ryder.

"You wanted to get a message to Fort Belvoir, right?"

"Yes. So?"

"So we can use that mobile radio van to get on the air and hopefully get a message to Belvoir." He added "The van must be doing an 'on location' at that clinic."

The other men were puzzled. It was Cole who spoke up first.

"You really think with all this going on they're listening to music at Fort Belvior?"

"No. I don't," Safko replied. "But the NSA is. They're always listening," he said smugly.

"But the power's down. How can you transmit?" asked Ryder.

"It's an emergency clinic. They should have a back-up generator on site."

The two Humvees pulled into the parking lot of the clinic. It was deserted, dark, and looked ramshackled.

"I bet some local thugs were doing a midnight acquisition while the cops had their hands busy," said Cole.

"Yeah. Looking for drugs," Webster replied.

"Drop me off here," Safko said. "I'll take my aide with me. You go on to the IWL. Take Webster with you." He turned to Webster and gave him a stern look. "When you get to the IWL, make sure you keep the lid on this. Got it?"

Webster nodded.

"Wait," said Ryder. He reached for his sidearm and handed the .45 caliber pistol to Safko. "You may need this."

Safko took the pistol and stuffed it in his belt. He and his aide exited the Humvee and headed for the van. The convoy continued on its way to the lab.

As they approached Highway 95 on the other side of town they saw as many as fifteen fire engines and EMS vehicles blocking the freeway entrance ahead of them. But there was no fire or accident. The fireman and medics just stood there looking confused.

"What do you make of that?" asked Ryder to Cole.

"Dorian again. I bet he's deliberately misdirecting emergency response teams around the city to clog up the streets."

"He's doin' a good job," said Webster. "Is there a way around them?"

Ryder looked to his left and right, then shouted, "Hold on!" He pointed the Humvee toward the concrete berm that the freeway sat on and hit the accelerator. The four-wheeled vehicle slowly climbed up the concrete embankment, running over the guardrail at the top and onto the highway blacktop. The second Humvee followed close behind. But they hadn't gone ten feet down the highway when Ryder slammed on the brakes, sending the Humvee swerving down the road, throwing Webster against the back of Cole's seat.

"*Damn it*, Major! *I'm* back here!" Webster cried. He looked up from between the seats and saw a disabled police helicopter in the middle of the highway. Its blades turned slowly as the pilot, sitting in the cockpit, unsuccessfully tried to restart the chopper.

"*Watch those blades!*" yelled Cole.

Ryder wrestled back control of the Humvee, avoiding the carving blades, and screeched to a stop. The second Humvee slid up beside them.

"That was close," said Webster, looking over the front seats.

"*Damn!* Another delay. Now what?" cried Cole.

"Now *nothing!*" replied Ryder. He punched the accelerator of the Humvee all the way to floor and flew over the concrete highway divide into the oncoming lanes. The other Humvee duplicated the maneuver.

Webster was thrown to the floor and bounced around as the vehicle regained control on the blacktop. The two Humvees zigzagged their way through the oncoming traffic and jumped back over the concrete divide past the stalled helicopter, Webster was tossed again on the floor as Cole hung onto the door jamb, trying to keep his butt in the seat.

Ryder wrestled the Humvee back into the center lane of the highway, stomped on the accelerator, and continued to the IWL.

"No digital footprint?" asked Taylor anxiously. She was pacing behind Dallas, occasionally stopping to peer over his shoulder at his desktop monitor.

"Nothing," he said, scanning the lab's history logs. "But I'm almost certain Dorian didn't get in through the NSA wireless connection to the lab…" Dallas suddenly jumped to his feet. "Crap!"

Taylor spun around. "What? What did you find?"

But instead of pointing at his screen, as Taylor expected, Dallas pointed under his desk.

"That thing grabbed my leg. Scared the crap out of me!"

Taylor bent down to look. That thing was Goppy. "What's the matter?" she asked, laughing. "Did he try to hump your leg?"

"Ha ha. Very funny."

Dallas pushed the dog away with the toe of his hiking boot, but the electronic creature wouldn't move.

"He likes you," said Taylor, and was surprised when suddenly Dallas got up and walked over to her desk. He reached for her PDA sitting in its cradle. "And what do you think you're doing?" she asked, sitting back and crossing her arms.

"Getting that mongrel to leave. We all know how much it loves your PDA…"

But Dallas's hand stopped. He leaned forward, reading the PDA screen. "Taylor, look at this."

Arms still crossed, she bent forward and saw that her digital assistant was executing programs. Programs that she didn't have on her PDA. "What's it doing?" she asked.

He studied the display on her PDA, and suddenly cried out, "It's transmitting!"

"Transmitting what?"

"It's tapped into the lab network and... *holy mother of God!*" Dallas grabbed the PDA and yanked it from its cradle, promptly disconnecting it from Taylor's computer and the lab network.

"Dallas. What the hell is going on?"

Dallas tossed the PDA to Taylor, ran to the office door, opened it—and collapsed to the ground screaming in pain.

An Emergency Medical Clinic
Baltimore, MD

"Find the generator room and fire up the back-up generator," ordered Safko to his aide. "Take one of the flashlights in the van. I'll get ready to broadcast."

His aide grabbed a flashlight and hurried toward the front door of the clinic while Safko entered the radio station van itself. He sat himself at the control panel and looked around and above him at the thick manuals and three-ring binders on the shelves. *There must be an operating manual here somewhere*, he thought. After several minutes of rifling through the documents he found what he was looking for and attempted to start up the broadcasting equipment.

Nothing. No power. *What was his aide doing! He should have found the generator room by now. Damn it!* He grabbed another flashlight and left in search of the aide. He entered the clinic and headed down the main hallway toward the back of the building. It was dark and the flashlight started to dim, but still threw enough light to vaguely make out what was in front of him. He knew the batteries were going. He had to find his aide.

He quickened his pace, turned a corner, and tripped over something in the hall. As he reached out his hands to break his fall, he dropped the flashlight onto the floor. The dimming torch spun around a few times and the weak ray of light settled on a figure face down on the floor.

It was his aide. His face was in a pool of blood that oozed from a nasty fissure in his head. Safko reached over to see if he was still breathing when two pair of strong hands violently pulled him up off the floor.

"Here's another one, dude," a voice said from behind him. Safko tried to turn to look at the voice when he was almost blinded by a powerful light, focused on his face.

"I bet he's a NARC, too," said another.

In the dim halo behind the light, Safko saw three thuggish-looking men standing in front of him. One was bald with a drug-induced look in his eyes wearing a wife-beater t-shirt and a large black and blue snake-shaped tattoo on his arm that twisted down his appendage toward his hand. In that hand was a pistol. And it was pointed directly at Safko.

"Check him out. He looks like a NARC to me," said the snake man.

Another thug, a younger one—no more than fifteen, with several small rings embedded in his eyebrows and breath that smelled like yesterday's garbage—moved toward Safko. He had a drug-crazed expression on his face, too. He reached his hand into Safko's pocket while the bald man kept his pistol aimed at Safko's head. The young thug pulled out Safko's wallet and opened it.

"Look here," he said, seeing Safko's NSA ID card. "He's some kind of security guard. Sez he's with a security agency."

"I knew it," said the snake man waving his pistol in Safko's face. "A cop."

"I'm not a cop," Safko replied. "I came here to use the van outside to make a radio broadcast."

"Hey man. He says he's a disc jockey," the young thug said. The three men laughed.

"No. I was trying to call for help." As soon as he said that, Safko knew it was a mistake.

"That's what a cop would do," said the snake man. "Frisk him for a weapon." The young thug started to run his hands down

Safko's side. Safko knew he would get only one chance before they found his .45, so he took it. He pushed the young thug out of the way, drew his pistol from his pants and shot the snake man in the chest. He crumpled down in a heap, hit the floor, held his chest, and moaned in pain.

Safko turned his attention to the young druggie who had backed away and started running down the hall. Safko took a bead on him and was ready to shoot when he felt a searing pain in his back. He swung around, pistol in hand, just in time to see the gleam of a long blade strike down and slice deep into his chest. He screamed in pain and fell to his knees. He tried to raise his pistol at his assailant, but it was quickly knocked away. He heard the gun slide across the dark floor just as he felt a piece of cold steel enter his throat just below his right ear. He gurgled a bloody sound, and dropped dead to the floor.

The Humvees sped toward the Tulley Gate entrance of Fort Belvoir, where an MP waved them through. At the INSCOM building they were met by the lieutenant in charge of security.

"The elevator to the IWL is locked down, sir," said the young man to Ryder.

"What do you mean?"

"The doors, sir. They can't open the doors. They seem to be locked shut. And we can't make contact with the lab."

Ryder cursed and made a call. A moment later he snapped shut his cell phone. "It'll be a few minutes before anyone arrives," he said.

"Major, we don't have a few minutes. We need to get those elevator doors open," said Cole.

"I understand that, Cole…" He paused and turned to one of the Delta Team members who had arrived ahead of them. "Sergeant, grab a satchel charge from the Humvee and bring it here."

The sergeant returned shortly with a small green backpack, which he handed to Ryder. The major told everyone to stand back, and the young sergeant led Cole and the others around a corner. A few seconds later, panting slightly, Ryder joined them.

"Cover your ears," he said. "This is going to be loud."

Cole and the others pressed themselves against the wall and waited.

The wait wasn't long.

An ear-piercing explosion rolled down the hallway, followed by a cloud of acrid white smoke and metal debris that filled the corridor. Once the smoke cleared, Ryder led the group of men toward the elevator.

"That's one helluva can opener, Major," said Webster with a grin.

Ryder ignored Webster's quip and walked over to the mangled wreck that had once been two shiny steel elevator doors. He glanced down the elevator shaft. Smoke drifted up through the opening. Ryder waved it away as the others joined him by his side. Cole was careful of the metal door's sharp edges. An old fear of heights began to grip him. He pushed it away as he cautiously peered over the edge and down into the darkness. He couldn't see much other than more smoke and cable lines.

Ryder removed a small flashlight from his utility belt and shined it several floors down the elevator shaft. The white beam of light cut through the smoke, illuminating a metal box at the base of the shaft.

"Looks clear to the elevator car," he said, leaning dangerously out into the shaft. "That's it down below."

He turned to Cole and said, "Ever do any mountain climbing?"

Cole felt sick. He shook his head.

"Doesn't matter," said Ryder. "The sergeant here will get you and Webster set up for belay."

"For what?" asked Cole.

"Belay," said Ryder impatiently. "We're going to rappel down the shaft to get into the lab."

Cole swallowed hard and looked again down the long, dark shaft. He pulled his head out of the shaft and took in a few deep, acrid gulps of the smoke-filled air.

The sergeant gave a crash course to Webster and Cole in the art of rappelling, then proceeded to set up the equipment for the belay. Cole only half listened. Mostly he fought to stay calm.

Cole fidgeted with the heavy gloves given him while he watched the ensuing scene with mounting dread. The sergeant tied off one end of the belay rope to the fire hose equipment on the far wall. Next, the group of men took turns attaching their D-rings to the belay rope. Cole's own D-ring snapped into place with ominous finality. There was no going back now.

Ryder checked them all out and nodded. "Okay, kids. Here's the drill. I'll go first with the Dark Ops team. Cole, you're next, followed by Webster. But only drop down when I tell you. Got it?"

Cole nodded. Or, at least, he thought he nodded. Ryder turned to the young lieutenant. "Lieutenant, you stay up here with your security team in case we need you."

Then Ryder did something that boggled Cole's mind—he stepped through the mangled remains of the elevators doors, and dropped down into the black abyss.

The four Delta Team members followed behind, each disappearing similarly down into the dark shaft.

Webster and Cole waited impatiently together, the one-time rivals briefly putting behind their past differences and finding comfort in their shared anxiety. Webster patted Cole on the back and nodded encouragingly. Cole was actually grateful for the gesture.

Ryder's voice rose up from the depths, and Cole heard the words he had been dreading to hear. "Okay, Cole, you're next. Get to it."

As shown, Cole attached his D-Ring to the belay rope. He noticed his hands were trembling. Taking a few deep breaths, he carefully turned around and positioned himself with his back to the open shaft. He took a few more breaths.

I can't do this, he thought. He closed his eyes and thought of his creation, Dorian. He thought of the attempts on his daughter's life. He thought of the devastating impact of the dust.

In Dorian's hands. In his *non*-hands.

Crazy damn program.

Cole carefully placed his right hand behind his back, positioning the rope there... then slowly, slowly leaned back in his rope saddle.

So far so good.

He took a few more deep breaths and did what the others had done—he kicked off from the floor and out into the dark shaft below.

~

Cole gradually let the belay rope out over his hand, behind his back and through the D-Ring, and slowly descended into the shaft. Remarkably—and perhaps this was proof prayers were answered—Cole's fear dissipated the deeper he went. In fact, miracle of miracles, he was actually *enjoying* himself.

About halfway down and feeling pretty damn good, something amazing happened. So amazing that he wasn't entirely sure he believed it at first.

Something, he was sure, had *fluttered* by his legs.

Like a bird?

Briefly shaken, he mentally shook off this departure from, well, whatever reality he was experiencing already, and continued down to the car below, letting out the rope slowly, kicking off with his feet. He considered whistling.

This was fun.

The fluttering sound came again, followed by a piercing shriek. Cole thought he knew what it was. A bat.

Crap.

The creepy thing veered past his face, grazing his head, and Cole instinctively swatted at it.

And instantly plummeted.

The dimly-lit elevator car raced up from below. Cole twisted and turned, screaming. He threw his hand behind his back, found the whipping rope and grabbed it. He stopped almost instantly, snapping to a halt, and knew his hand would have been burned to the bone if not for the provided gloves.

For now, he dangled with his head facing down the shaft and feet pointing straight up into the air.

Ryder's calm voice echoed from below. "Place your feet against the shaft wall and pull yourself straight up."

Cole obeyed and this actually worked. He pulled himself up and was once again propped against the shaft wall—head up, feet down.

"Now, let the rope out and *slowly* lower yourself."

Cole did so, praying the bat wouldn't return. It didn't and soon two pairs of strong arms stopped his descent. He caught his balance at the top of the elevator car and turned to see Ryder.

"What happened up there?" asked the major.

"Something... something flew past me," Cole said.

"Like what?" asked Ryder.

"A bat, I think."

"I seriously doubt that," quipped Ryder. "Security doesn't allow bats in a military installation."

Cole looked back up the shaft just as Webster nearly landed on top of him. Cole leapt out of the way while Ryder helped the BioNan executive find his feet.

"Piece of cake," grinned Webster.

Cole ignored him and saw that Ryder's men had removed the escape hatch on top of the elevator car. Two of them had already slipped down inside, and after Ryder dropped down through the hole, Cole and Webster followed.

Inside the crowded car, Cole saw that these elevator doors were closed as well.

"You gonna blow these, too, Major?" Webster quipped.

"Don't think so," he said. He removed a long screwdriver from his utility belt and stuck it between the car doors. He pushed and pried until a small crack appeared between the doors. With the help of the team sergeant, the two men pried the heavy metal shaft doors apart. Once done, they got to work on the elevator doors themselves.

A few minutes later, they levered those open as well.

And that's when they all began to sneeze.

～

Cole sneezed again and again, and waited for what he believed was the inevitable—a horrible, agonizing death.

He sneezed again.

Tears streamed from his eyes. He could see and hear the others sneezing as well. The sneezing, he knew, was a warning sign that they had inhaled a large amount of Angel Dust and Cole had seen firsthand what the dust could do.

He sneezed again, harder than before, and braced himself against the wall of the elevator car.

But nothing happened.

And a few minutes later, even the sneezing stopped.

Next to him, Webster raised his hands to his face and examined them closely while the others looked to him for some kind of reprieve.

"I think it's okay," he finally said. "I think this is just inert dust—not yet programmed. Must have spilled out of Unit 14."

"Good God, I thought we were done," Ryder said. He wiped his eyes and nose. "Okay, people, we have work to do. Let's move."

The small group of soldiers and civilians exited the elevator car and entered the empty front security room.

"What the …?" said Ryder.

There was no security guard inside the Plexiglas booth and the armed MP who usually stood at the metal detector was gone. Except for the flickering fluorescent lights, the small room looked undisturbed. Ryder motioned to his two soldiers and both lowered their automatic weapons to the at-ready position. Cole swallowed—or tried.

The group passed through the detectors and stood in front of the double windowless doors that led to the Information Warfare Lab. Ryder listened at the door.

"Something's wrong," said Ryder. "It's too quiet in there."

"Wrong or not," said Webster impatiently, "we need to get to Unit 14 and contain this dust."

He yanked open one of the lab doors, and immediately the

body of Colonel Bartley, eyes wide open in terror, fell forward into Webster.

~

Webster recoiled, screaming, as the body landed on top of him. The BioNan executive did his best to push it away, and screamed again when his hands plunged into a bloody opening in Bartley's chest cavity.

One of the Delta Team soldiers grabbed Bartley's corpse by the shoulders and pulled it away from Webster.

"*Oh, God! Damn!*" Webster cried, wiping his bloody hands on his clothing. "*What happened to him?*"

The colonel had incurred a devastating wound. Something had blown through his chest, no doubt killing him instantly. Cole could see the man's broken ribs and what was left of his lungs, which hung in tattered ruins. Cole never much liked the man, but he never wished something like this on any human being.

Cole remained frozen on the spot, along with many of the others. One soldier vomited.

Ryder only glanced at the mutilated body. The moment it hit the ground, he had removed his sidearm and slid to one side of the doorway, peering into the room at an angle. He motioned for one of his men to follow suit on the other side of the doorway. Both men peered in cautiously.

Cole stepped away from the door, deeper into the security room. After all, whatever had done this to Bartley could still be in there.

One after another, Ryder and his men crept into the lab, hunched low to the ground, their weapons before them. Cole stayed behind with Webster, who couldn't take his eyes off the form that had once been Bartley. Cole did all he could to avert his eyes.

A moment later, Ryder appeared in the doorway. "All clear, but you two might want to stay away."

"Why?" asked Cole.

Ryder glanced at the body in the hallway. "More of the same, but worse."

"Jesus," said Webster behind him.

Cole took in some air and said, "No, I want to come in. I worked with most of these people."

Ryder, whose face had turned nearly white, merely shrugged, and Cole followed him into a scene straight out of his worst nightmare.

The darkened room was lit only by flickering fluorescent lights and the glow from burning computer monitors. Cole saw desks, computers, papers, and office equipment smashed and scattered all over the lab. The lighting itself hung precariously from the ceiling by wires, the false ceilings open in places, revealing the spiderweb of plumbing, heating, and ventilation systems above. The command deck overlooking the lab floor was totally and deliberately destroyed. Even now, there were small fires burning here and there throughout the lab. The stench of melting plastic, smoldering fabric and paper was heavy on the air.

And there was something else. The distinct smell of fresh blood.

Bodies of lab personnel were strewn among the smashed equipment and scattered papers. Two soldiers on the group's right were charred and burned beyond recognition. Another lay backwards across his computer terminal, hacked to death. One young female cyber-soldier's head had been crushed and was lying in a pool of dark red blood on the floor in front of them. Several of the bodies had metal objects embedded in their torsos and heads. Some even had limbs missing, pulled or sliced violently from their bodies.

Cole fought the pressure rising from his stomach. He didn't think he had anything in there to vomit. He didn't. Still, he turned and dry-heaved until his stomach hurt. He heard Webster behind him doing much of the same.

He stood again, wiping the bile and spittle from his mouth, and willed himself to calm down. As he took in the foul air, trying to breathe only through his mouth, he saw that the Com

Link had been totally—and purposely—destroyed, which is why they hadn't been able to reach them.

As impassively as he could, Cole continued to survey the scene of destruction, his eyes only skimming the mangled corpses. They settled on one thing in particular. One thing that definitely got his attention.

"Major," Cole whispered. He quietly nudged Ryder's arm. "Look to your left." Cole pointed to the shiny little robot dog sitting under a broken desk about fifty feet from the men. "That's Goppy," he said in a low voice, and then whispered, "Shoot it."

Ryder nodded and quietly raised his rifle. As he took aim, Webster suddenly appeared at Cole's side, pointing excitedly at the mechanical dog. "There's the little son-of-a-bitch. Waste it!"

But before Ryder could get off a round, Goppy disappeared among the wrecked equipment and furniture.

Ryder glanced irritably at Webster, but turned quickly to one of his Delta Team soldiers. "Shoot that damn dog. Do whatever it takes." He looked at Cole. "Step back."

Cole did, just as Ryder and his troopers leveled their weapons and let loose with a continuous—and ear-splitting—volley of fire where the mechanical dog was last seen. Bullets shredded desks and computer equipment, ripping through chairs and monitors and anything else in the way.

To Cole's utter shock, he saw the little creature slip between two toppled desks and make its way down a side aisle.

"There!" he pointed.

Ryder, momentarily blocked by a fallen partition, appeared by Cole's side and spotted the mechanical dog.

This is crazy, Cole thought. *All of this over a kid's toy.*

Ryder aimed, fired, and divots of carpet flew into the air near the robot dog. The creature hung a hard right and was gone.

"C'mon," said Ryder.

Cole and the others followed the major, down the aisle, past one mangled body after another. Cole recognized them all, but forced himself not to look. Now was not the time to dry heave.

They turned down the hallway where Goppy had disappeared. Ryder suddenly pulled up short, and Cole saw why.

Goppy was sitting at the end of the hallway, facing them. Directly behind it was Isaac.

"What's that?" said Webster behind Cole. The BioNan chief was out of breath.

The robot stood motionless, seemingly staring at the group of men, his eyes behind his plastic faceplate glowing crimson red. Cole hated those glowing red eyes. He was about to answer Webster, when Isaac turned its head imperceptibly.

"Hello, Travis," it said in its mechanical voice.

"Jesus! What *is* that?" whispered Ryder next to him. "And how does it know your name, Cole?"

Cole held up his hand, quieting the major. The little robot turned its head from side to side and seemed to be taking in the entire scene. Cole shivered.

"Hello, Isaac," he said. "What are your intentions?"

"No, Travis," it replied. "The name is Dorian. And I am going to kill you."

"It sure has a one-track mind," whispered Webster.

Cole ignored Webster and slowly motioned to Ryder and his men. He wondered just how much Isaac—or rather Dorian— could see. Ryder nodded and motioned to the troopers. All three men targeted Dorian and Goppy.

"Not this time, Dorian," Cole said. He turned to Ryder and his men. "Shoot it."

Then Cole heard something behind him. The sound of a spinning blade. In the aisle behind them was one of Dallas's battlebots, BattleScar Galactica, if Cole remembered correctly, featuring a spinning blade and a flame thrower.

"What is that… that thing?" asked Ryder as he spun around.

"I'll explain later," said Cole. "But for now, I would suggest, we get the hell out—"

A jet of fire erupted from the bot, streaking through the air, just over the men's heads.

"My God!" said Webster, ducking and stumbling.

Cole and the others dove out of the way, behind an overturned desk. Webster was the last to follow, landing hard next to Cole, the air bursting from his lungs.

Ryder and his men swung their weapons over the desk and fired at the bot which, Cole could hear, had retreated back down the aisle. The men stopped firing. Ryder ordered one of his men to make sure it was gone, whatever it was.

Cole carefully looked over the desk. Dorian was gone.

"Again," said Ryder, panting and lowering his weapon. "What *was* that thing… and those other mechanical monsters?"

"They belong to Morgan Dallas," Cole said. They were standing now, scanning the devastation. Cole suddenly knew how so many people had been killed and mutilated. He said grimly, "They're sort of a hobby of his."

"Some hobby," said Ryder. "Why were they attacking us?"

"Dorian must be somehow controlling them through low frequency waves. One of Dallas's upgrades."

"Well, can't we just jam him?" asked Webster.

"Unless someone here has a HERF jamming device in his back pocket, then the answer is no," said Ryder.

"Are there more of them?" Webster asked.

"About a dozen or so," said Cole. "We need to find Dorian ASAP."

"What do you propose?" Ryder asked.

"The communications room," said Cole. "If we can get in there, we can use the security cameras to find him again."

Ryder nodded. "You two go. I'm going to regroup my men."

Ryder and one of his men slipped away, leaving Cole alone with Webster in the lab. Well, not entirely alone. They were surrounded by the mangled corpses of his former co-workers.

"Let's get to the Comm Room," Cole said.

"Good idea," said Webster. He gestured to the carnage around him. "This place gives me the creeps."

Cole and Webster picked their way through the demolished lab toward the communications room. They heard the sporadic sounds of automatic weapons' fire echo through the lab as they went.

For the moment, they appeared to be alone.

"This way," said Cole, leading the way down the hall. He felt as if someone—or something—was watching him.

And he knew what that something was.

Dorian.

Creepy little creep.

The two men made it successfully to the end of the lab without encountering any of the mechanical monsters and looked down the hall to their target destination.

"Looks clear," said Cole. He and Webster moved forward when Taylor, holding a plastic knife in one hand, stepped out of the communications room and cried, "In here! In here! *Quick!*"

She had hardly finished her demand when a metal dart hit the door just above her head. She dropped to the floor as the door locked shut behind her. She scrambled behind a small metal chair in the hall, looked up and saw a battlebot armed with carbon steel darts coming toward her. Its turret swiveled back and forth as it tried to get a bead on the frightened female.

"*Get the hell out of there!*" yelled Cole. "*Run to us!*"

Taylor jumped to her feet and started to dash toward Cole when her foot got tangled in a chair's legs and threw her back to the floor. The battlebot approached her, stopped, and took aim at her head. Taylor closed her eyes and awaited her fate.

Cole looked for anything around him that he could use as a weapon. He picked up a fire extinguisher and ran toward Taylor. He ran as fast as he could, but had the sickening feeling that he wouldn't reach her in time.

He didn't.

Dorian, followed by Goppy, opened the door to the control room. They entered and Dorian locked the door behind them, surveying the contents of the room, turning its white metallic-looking head back and forth. A moment later it saw what it was looking for. It walked over to the long desk against the wall and stood over the control panel.

Goppy sat down beside it and watched as Dorian's fingers worked their way over the buttons of the control panel.

As Cole ran toward Taylor in a futile attempt to help her, a figure from Unit 14 shot down the hall, bowling over Cole and sending him to the floor. The man had a pistol in his hand and opened fire on the battlebot just as it was about to send a lethal dart into Taylor's skull. Bullets slammed into the bot, chewing through its metal casing and sending silver and black pieces into the air. The battlebot's turret blew off the top of its casing, spun in the air just past Taylor's head, and landed upside down at her tangled feet.

Taylor looked up at her savior and said, "Thank you, Casey. Thanks."

"Don't mention it," he said as he helped her to her feet.

Cole was quickly at her side.

"Travis! Oh, my God; you're alive!"

Taylor threw herself into his arms, slamming him against the hallway wall. She buried her head in his shoulder and wept hard.

"Is Dallas okay?" he asked.

She shook her head and cried even harder.

Dallas wasn't okay, but he also wasn't dead.

"Broken," he said, wincing. They were all in the Communications Room—the *locked* Communication Room. It gave them some sense of security. Casey stuck the .45 in his belt that he had retrieved from a dead MP. Taylor made a splint from the wooden leg of a chair for Dallas's broken leg. For now, Dallas was propped up next to a desk. "I sure could use some Vicodin."

Taylor held out her hand and dropped a handful of orange pills in his palm. "Advil. That's all I had in my purse. I use them when you give me a headache."

Dallas's eyes lit up. "Good enough." He swallowed them all, perhaps six or seven, knocking them back dry. "God, I hope they kick in fast. My leg is killing me."

Cole turned to the others. "What happened?"

"It was horrible, Travis," said Taylor. "One minute everyone's going about their jobs and the next..." she trailed off and started to cry. "I... I don't want to think about it, Travis. It was all we could do to get out of the lab and lock ourselves here in the Comm Room. There's nothing we could do to help the others. We had no weapons in the lab. We were defenseless against those... those things. We couldn't even call for help. Isaac went berserk. He destroyed the command deck, severed the outside lines, and smashed the communications gear."

"It's not Isaac. It's Dorian," said Cole. "He's taken over Isaac and is controlling your battlebots. Using the very same programs you wrote for the competitions."

"How?"

"Through my daughter's robot toy, Goppy. You know," said Cole, glancing at his friend, "the same robot dog *you* bought her, Dallas."

"Hey, don't think for a minute I was involved in this!"

Cole held up his hand. "No, Dallas, I don't think you were involved." And then Cole smiled, perhaps his first smile all day. He mimicked Dallas's defensive tone. "Not even for minute."

Taylor laughed as well, perhaps harder than she had intended. "Look, Dallas," she said, wiping her eyes, "how were you supposed to know this *thing* was going to use your toy to break into the lab? Obviously, this *thing*," she said again, spitting the words, "was bound and determined to get in here and it was just a matter of time."

"Exactly," said Casey. "So let's just figure out how we can stop it and worry about blame later."

Cole crossed his arms and had just leaned against the corner of one of the desks when they heard the stutter of gunfire coming from somewhere in the lab.

"Major Ryder hunting down those overblown lawnmowers," said Webster. "I hope he and his men blow those damn things to smithereens."

The gunfire persisted, then abated. Cole looked at the others. "To stop Dorian, we have to find and close down whatever connection he's using to get to the outside."

"He was using Taylor's PDA," said Dallas, "to get into the lab computer and transmit attack codes to who knows where. When I saw her PDA transmitting and executing our cyber-stash of weapons, I pulled the plug on it."

Cole added, "And when we thought we had flushed him from the lab network, he was actually in Goppy the entire time."

"So, in fact, we never flushed him. Just temporarily," said Casey.

"Exactly," said Dallas. "And now he's using Isaac. God, this is all my fault."

Taylor patted him on the back, while Cole turned to Casey. "Do you know the condition of Unit 14?" Cole could already guess the answer.

"A shambles," said the young sergeant. "Broken dust containers, not only in the unit, but also strewn around the lab."

"Dorian," said Cole. "I'm sure he deliberately spread the dust around the IWL." Another sickening thought occurred to Cole. "People, if Dorian can get into the lab network, then he may be able to launch SIRUS. And with this dust all around, he'll have his wish fulfilled. He can kill me."

"And *us*," said Webster.

"Not just *us*, Webster," Cole said. "Tell them about the little project you and your NSA buddies dreamed up."

"What project?" asked Taylor.

Webster filled them in, telling Taylor, Dallas, and Casey about the lethal features of the dust, how it kills, who it kills, and about its pre-emptive deployment worldwide.

"This just keeps getting better," said Dallas.

And all of us, thought Cole, *were responsible in one way or another.*

There was a loud knocking on the windowless Comm Room door. With pistol in hand, Casey slipped over to the door. "Who's there?"

Have the battlebots learned to knock? Cole wondered.

"It's Ryder. Let us in."

Casey opened the door and Ryder and his two men hurried into the room. Casey shut and locked the door behind them. "We lost another man. We found him with his head crushed."

"*American Armageddon,*" said Dallas softly. "He probably was killed by it. The one with the gas-powered sledge hammer."

"Thank you. Now I can be more specific when I write home to his family about how he died," said Ryder irately.

"Look," said Cole. "We have no time for recriminations now. Taylor, does the lab monitoring equipment still work? Are all the cameras functional? Can we see throughout the lab?"

"Yes. Most of them. And we can still access the lab computer. Passive monitoring only, though. Dorian has us locked out."

"That's enough for now," said Cole. "Let's jack in and search the IWL for that little creep."

Ryder said, "Before you do, let me call the security team up top. We're gonna need more firepower to kill those metal monsters."

He did so, switching on his whisper mic and instructing the lieutenant, with his security team, to enter down through the elevator shaft and wait in the front security room. Once done, Taylor sat at the communications panel and switched to the front security room camera.

On one of the many display monitors in front of them, the group watched and waited, and after a few minutes Taylor pointed. "They're coming down now."

Cole leaned forward, squinting at the monitor, and could just see a pair of legs coming down through the escape hatch of the elevator car.

The legs paused.

"What's he waiting for?" asked Ryder.

"Look," said Dallas, pointing. "His legs are shaking."

Ryder nearly pressed his nose against the monitor. "What the…"

Cole saw it, too. The man seemed to be going into convulsions, legs quivering violently.

As the group watched on the black and white monitor, a thick liquid began oozing down the trooper's pant leg.

"My, God," said Dallas, "is that…"

The soldier dropped to his knees, and as he did so, Cole saw something—something horrible—attached to the man's face. He looked again. It was Hillary, Dallas's climbing bot.

"Oh, God," said Dallas.

Cole suddenly realized that what he had mistaken for a bat had been, in fact, this climbing monstrosity.

That could have been me.

Now it had the trooper by the shoulders, its metal claws digging deep into the man's collarbones while its small jigsaw, cut slice after slice off the soldier's face.

Taylor looked away, covering her mouth.

Cole watched in sick fascination. *That could have been me,* he thought again. *That could have been me.*

Suddenly, a single jet of orange flame flashed across the screen, engulfing the dying soldier.

"Holy crap," cried Webster.

A moment later, a massive battlebot lumbered into the screen. It shot another jet of fire at the burning man. A second soldier dropped down from the shaft, appearing in the elevator. Face contorted, he fired his weapon from his hip, spraying anything and everything with bullets. But the battlebot, apparently unfazed, pumped a stream of flaming liquid into his face. The man crumpled, screaming in agony.

Cole looked away, praying that no more men appeared in the elevator shaft.

"Lieutenant!" barked Ryder into his mic. "Get your men out of the elevator shaft. Now!"

"Guys," said Taylor anxiously. She had averted her eyes and was looking at another monitor. "You better look at this."

Cole turned toward the bank of monitors and looked at the one Taylor had indicated. Dorian and Goppy were in the Angel Dust control room. Cole leaned forward.

Son-of-a-bitch.

Dorian was typing on the keyboard.

"What's that little walking trashcan doing?" said Ryder.

"It's doing that." Dallas pointed to the monitor on the left. A display appeared on the small screen that read:

Project Angel Dust: CLASSIFIED TOP SECRET
Department of the Army
North American Defense Command
NADCOM: A5954

Log In Protocol
Username:
Password:

The username and password fields on the monitor blinked ominously, demanding an answer to the challenge.

With his eyes glued to the security monitor, Cole watched as Dorian downloaded a series of programs that he, Cole, had never seen before. As Dorian did so, the small monitor in the communications room scrolled through a series of executable programs.

"Where did those come from?" asked Dallas.

"From Dorian's memory," Cole replied. "I bet he was quite busy while out there in cyberspace. Who knows what kinds of information he picked up from the vast number of networks connected to the Net?"

"Some of it, I bet, was proprietary and confidential," Taylor said. "Bomb-making technology is not the only wonderful information available online these days."

The programs scrolled faster and faster down the screen, too rapid for Cole's eyes to follow. Then, like a slot machine, Dorian seemed to settle on one program.

"What's he up to?" asked Ryder. "What's he doing?"

Grimacing, Dallas hobbled closer to the small monitor. He studied the program, squinting. "I'm not sure," he said, "but I think it's a hack program. And if my guess is right, he's trying to hack his way into Angel Dust."

Just as he said that, a quick succession of usernames appeared on the display. In a matter of seconds, the program located a valid username.

It read: Jerry.

"That's me!" cried Webster.

"Jesus," said Dallas. "All Dorian needs now is your password."

"Webster," said Cole, watching Dorian's every move, "please don't tell me you used your office phone number or extension as your password—or your birthday, or your house number. Any other personal information a hacker could get by either reading the directory at your building or the About Us page of BioNan."

"Not exactly," Webster sheepishly. "I used my last name."

"He's in," said Dallas. "Dorian's at the Command Code Sequence challenge screen."

"Crap!" said Cole. "Dallas, can you get into the network and stop him?"

"Can't; he's locked us out."

"Try again."

"No go. I…"

"Try again, dammit!" Cole commanded.

Dallas shrugged his shoulders, sat at the keyboard and started typing. But every time he attempted to access the network, his computer screen displayed: *Access Denied*.

"Sorry, boss. No can do."

"Then we have to stop it another way," said Ryder. "Cole, get into the control room and figure out a way to stop that damn thing. Here, take my pistol with you. Meanwhile, I'll take my men and keep those bots off your back. Got it?"

Cole nodded, turned to Webster and said, "You come with me. Dallas and Taylor, you monitor. Casey, you go with Ryder and his men."

Everyone was in agreement. Taylor sat down at the bank of monitors and checked the hall for lingering bots from the communications room. "It's clear. You can leave now."

Ryder opened the door and he and his men were off toward the lab. Cole tucked Ryder's pistol in his pants and Webster grabbed his backpack. Cole was about to ask what was in the backpack, but he let it go. He had bigger things to worry about, like not getting killed.

He and Webster slipped away down the hall and turned a corner. The path was clear and Cole pointed ahead to the Control Room at the far end of the long hallway. Webster nodded, and as the two men cautiously approached, Cole saw that they were, in fact, kicking up a thick layer of dust that covered the polished floor. Like silt along a lake bed, the dust wafted up and soon both men were sneezing. Harder than ever.

"Damn!" said Webster in between sneezes. "If that little creep gets control of the command computer, we're toast. The dust is everywhere."

"And there's why," said Cole. He pointed to the open door leading to Unit 14. The doors were nearly ripped off their hinges. Both men cautiously peered inside the unit, which was littered with dozens of smashed Angel Dust glass vials.

"There goes a lot of overtime at BioNan shot to hell," Webster mused.

"Forget it," said Cole. "Let's get to the control room."

Cole knew that one of those metal monsters could have easily ripped those doors from their hinges. Cole silently cursed Dallas and his creations again, until he remembered it was his creation currently occupying the body of Isaac. They both continued down the hall. Cole removed the gun from behind his back.

They arrived outside the control room door, both sneezing.

"So much for sneaking up on the little creep," said Webster, wiping his nose.

Cole gently pushed the door handle down. It didn't move. "He locked himself in."

"Damn smart robot," quipped Webster.

"The smartest," said Cole. "Unfortunately, the room is sealed. This is the only way in or out."

"Now what?" said Webster. He looked at Cole. "Use your gun?"

Cole shook his head. "This is military installation Combat Information Center. CIC doors are built to resist more than a handgun, Webster." He looked back the way they'd come, their footprints easily identifiable in the thin layer of dust that coated the floor. "Let's go back to Unit 14. We can at least see what he's doing from there."

They turned back just as gunshots echoed from the lab. Ryder and his men were keeping up their end of the bargain.

"Must be good hunting in the lab," Webster said grimly.

"Let's just hope what they're hunting stays there," said Cole.

"How many?" demanded Ryder. He and Casey were the only survivors left during their hunt for the battlebots.

"Two, sir. They got by me."

"Which way did they go?"

"Don't know. Should I ... *Look out!*"

Casey pushed Ryder to the floor while firing his pistol in the direction of the aggressor. The Jaws of Death battlebot lunged at Casey, its gaping maw with its steel teeth narrowly missing his leg by inches. Ryder regained his balance and fired point blank at the bot that, for the moment, was interested only in tearing Casey's body to shreds. The hot lead from Ryder's M16 tore into the light aluminum frame of the battlebot, incapacitating its drive mechanism and bringing both it and its snapping jaws to a halt.

"That was close," Casey said. "How many of these damn things are left?"

"Don't know for sure. Cole said there were about a dozen. I figured we got eight of 'em. A couple of those flame-throwing jobs, a few of those dart-shooters, and the drillers. That leaves a couple that got by you and... *Christ!*"

Ryder didn't get to finish his figuring as Casey turned to see what Ryder had reacted to. It was BattleScar Galactica. Its vertical high carbon steel saw blade lunged straight for Casey, and its sharp saw powered by its high torque motor chewed into Casey's leg. He screamed in agony and fell over the remains of an office cubicle, scooting behind a metal desk for some semblance of protection. Galactica lunged again at Casey, biting into the frame of the desk, shooting slivers of metal into the air.

Ryder raised his weapon and took aim at the merciless saw-mill attacking Casey. But before he could fire, a blast of hot streaming flame lit up the wall just behind him, scorching his cap and exploding a copy machine by the wall. Ryder threw himself behind a cubicle partition, but realized hiding behind something made of wood and fabric was not a good defense against a flamethrower. He could hear Casey moaning somewhere in front of him, but he had to dodge the flame-throwing bot before he could help him.

Casey had managed to move away from Galactica while it busied itself turning the metal desk into strips of aluminum foil. Casey dragged his bleeding leg toward the command deck that overlooked the lab. He pulled himself onto the elevated floor of the deck, rested his back against a fallen leather chair, and pulled the ammunition clip from his pistol. He only had a few bullets left. He knew that Galactica would be back. He had to make every bullet count.

Ryder had moved from behind the cubicle wall and was working his way quietly around the back of the flame-throwing battlebot. It seemed to scan the area, trying to re-acquire its target. Ryder made his way behind a broken bank of consoles and found himself just below the command deck. He saw the bot searching back and forth in front of him, but waited for it to move closer so he could have a clear shot. When the opportunity presented itself, Ryder stood up, took aim, and fired. The bot was hit hard by the stream of shells from Ryder's M16 and was slammed back against the lower wall of the command deck, shattering into pieces.

Ryder had little time to congratulate himself on the kill. Galactica had found him.

Ryder veered away from the spinning steel blade, but was trapped between it and the lower wall of the command deck. The spinning metal menace advanced on Ryder. He pulled the trigger of his automatic rifle repeatedly—but all he heard were clicks. He was out of ammo. Ryder heard a scuffling behind him, looked up and saw Casey standing above him on the command deck. Casey aimed his sidearm carefully at Galactica and squeezed off his shots one by one. But all he managed to do was blow off one of Galactica's tank-like treads.

The menacing bot kept slowly rolling toward Ryder on its remaining tread, its buzz saw coming closer and closer. Casey leaned over the railing and extended his hand to Ryder, yanking him up to the railing just above the whirling blade of Galactica. Its buzz saw sank into the lower wall and got stuck in a labyrinth of metal supports, conduit, and drywall material. Ryder lifted his leg over the rail, but lost his balance from the shaking and shattering attempts of Galactica trying to free itself. He fell to the floor below the Comm Deck and hit his head hard on one of the large demolished monitors that had once been on the wall of the lab above.

Worse yet, Ryder landed right in front of Galactica.

Galactica pulled itself free from the wall. Sensing Ryder, it backed off to take aim. With a determined single-mindedness, the maniacal machine slowly advanced on him—and Casey was in no position to stop it. He could only watch the gruesome scene about to be played out at his feet.

Galactica had cornered its prey and extended its rotating, screaming saw blade toward Ryder's limp body. Casey gasped involuntarily in response to the impending slaughter. Suddenly bits of the steel blade broke apart and flew into the air, narrowly missing Casey's head. He threw himself back and away from the railing and heard the shrieking sounds of metal being torn apart from below. The screeching and high-pitched whining hurt his ears and he covered them with his hands. In a matter of moments the sounds stopped.

Casey crawled over to the railing and looked down into the lab below. There stood Dallas, leaning on a smashed console with a broken fire axe in his hand. Next to him sat Ryder, holding his bleeding head. Next to both of them was Galactica, now a heap of broken and smashed metal debris lying at Casey's feet.

"Low tech," Dallas said with a smile holding the remains of the fire axe. "Any port in a storm, you know." Then he added, "We saw what was happening from the communications room monitors. Thought you two might need some help."

Casey smiled, looked at the debris that was once Galactica, and said, "Well, Dallas, sometimes you have to eat your young."

Fort Belvoir, Maryland

Back in Unit 14, among the shattered vials, Webster said, "The IWL has its own air supply, doesn't it? I mean, isn't the lab protected from contaminated air from the outside?"

"Yeah. It has an air filtration system against bio/chem and radiological agents. What about it?"

"What if we reverse the air flow and blow this dust out of the IWL?"

"Worth a try," Cole said, wiping his runny nose with his sleeve. "Wish I had a Kleenex."

"Here. Use my handkerchief."

Just like Mr. Perfect, Cole thought, taking the linen handkerchief monogrammed with the letters 'JW.' He blew his nose a few times, then quickly shoved the handkerchief back into Webster's coat pocket.

"Thanks," said Cole, grinning.

Webster looked down at the soggy thing. "No problem."

Cole sneezed again and went straight over to the intercom, punched in the communications room extension and looked up at the camera hanging above. Taylor promptly answered. "Travis, we think Dorian broke the command code sequence, but we can't see a thing. He smashed the camera in the control room."

Cole walked quickly over to the large plate glass double-paned window that overlooked the control room. Behind it, he saw the little robot sitting before the command console, located in the center of the command desk. Goppy sat obediently beside him.

Webster moved to his side and saw Dorian fingering the small command console. "Great," said the BioNan executive. "All your little friend needs now is to input the ten-digit alpha-numerical command code and he can initiate SIRUS."

"Taylor?" shouted Cole to the intercom across the room. "Can you and Dallas reverse the flow of air and push the dust out of the IWL?"

"I don't know. Hold on," she said. Cole heard Taylor and Dallas talking back and forth and then Dallas came on the intercom. "Yeah, Travis. I think we can do that. I'm pretty sure the lab's HVAC systems are not connected to the IWL network. But let me check."

"You do that," mumbled Webster next to Cole.

Cole ignored him. A few moments later, Dallas's voice echoed over the intercom. "It's a go! We can control the HVAC systems from here and clear much of the dust out of the IWL. But enough of it could remain to kill us if Dorian launches SIRUS."

"We'll have to take our chances," said Cole. "But at least it will stop this incessant sneezing."

"Will do, Chief."

Cole said, "Taylor, what's Dorian doing now? What do you see on your computer screen?"

She paused before answering. "He's running a long sequence of numbers and letters across our screen."

"God," said Webster. "He's trying to break the code."

As Cole stared into the control room he saw the glowing map of metropolitan D.C. appear on the large LCD display above Dorian's head.

Fort Belvoir, Maryland

T he normally quiet operation of the HVAC turned suddenly into a dry, sucking sound. Cole looked up at the vents above them and watched as the swirling dust was sucked through. Almost instantly, the air was cleared.

Webster took a deep breath. "Thank God."

The air now much clearer, Cole looked into the control room. The map of metropolitan D.C. had disappeared and was replaced by a census map of the world. The very same map he, Taylor, and Dallas had seen when they hacked into BioNan's computer network a few days before.

Oh God, thought Cole.

Cole watched as Dorian began keying a series of commands into the control console. Immediately, a yellow cloud began to spread over the global census map. Concurrently, the smaller monitors on the desk below the large LCD screen began to scroll lists of text that Cole could not make out.

"Taylor?" shouted Cole. "He's in SIRUS. Are you monitoring what Dorian is doing?"

"Yes. It looks like some kind of directory list."

"What is it? We can't see from here."

There was a short pause. "They're formulas, Travis." He heard the confusion in her voice. "Some kind of formulas."

"What kind?" interrupted Webster. "Chemical?"

"Yes, I think. Wait. They look more biological."

"This can't be good," said Webster to Cole.

There was another moment of silence, and then Taylor came back on the comm. "It looks like a series of DNA sequences."

"He's programming the dust for DNA execution," said Webster. "We're screwed. How many sequences, Taylor?"

"A lot," she replied.

Webster looked at Cole and said, "He's gonna make sure he doesn't miss you this time. He's probably coding the dust to kill anything with human DNA. All he has to do is choose his disease and …" Webster paused a moment, then added, "And the beasts *will* inherit the earth."

"And you and your NSA buddies' mistakes will be buried with you," said Cole.

"Don't be so quick to point your finger," retorted Webster. "If you didn't play God with your AI creations or pull that little trick with the bio/chem warfare scenarios, we wouldn't be in this lousy mess."

Cole ignored Webster and walked over to the observation window, leaned on the sill, and stared intently down into the control room. There he was met with the icy glare of his digital adversary. Its cold, pulsating, crimson eye stared straight at him. He could almost imagine the malicious machine mocking him, knowing that it was untouchable and Cole could do nothing to stop it.

Who would have guessed that real emotions arising from a computer code—*his* computer code—could have caused all this? Certainly not him. Taylor was right. How could we expect imperfect human beings to create perfect technology?

What was it she said? The Law of Unintended Consequences? And now those consequences were staring him smack in the face.

Webster walked up beside Cole and looked into the control room. "We're through," Webster was saying. "Dorian is holding all the cards."

But Cole was only half-listening. Instead, his attention was drawn to the air-intake duct high above the command console.

An idea began to form. He grabbed a foldout chair, pulled it under the intake vent, and stepped up on it. Here the sucking sound was nearly deafening.

"What are you doing, Cole?" asked Webster.

Cole ignored him and tugged on the air intake screen. It broke away with a sharp snap and fell to the floor.

"You'll never fit in there, Travis," said Webster looking up at him. "You know, in case you've lost your mind, and that's what you're thinking."

"I haven't lost my mind and that's not what I'm thinking." Cole frowned, thinking hard. "Webster, I want you to gather up as many unbroken dust vials as you can find and dump them into the air duct."

"Yeah, you've definitely lost your mind. In case you hadn't noticed, we just cleared the damn dust out of the lab!"

"Please trust me," said Cole. "We don't have a lot of time."

"Maybe I'm the one losing his mind," mumbled Webster, but he did as he was asked. He collected the remaining unbroken vials from around the room and removed the two Angel Dust vials from his backpack, still mumbling to himself.

"Travis," came Taylor's frantic voice. "Dorian's called up a new screen."

"What kind of screen?"

"A command screen. It has the word SIRUS on it."

"That cuts it," said Webster. "We're really screwed."

Cole went back to the window and looked out over the lab at the large screen in the control room. In the lower corner, superimposed over the census map of world, were the eighteen DNA sequences. Under those were a series of numbers and letters that looked very much like a molecular diagram. Webster, holding a dozen or so unbroken vials, came over to Cole's side.

"Do those diagrams look familiar?" Cole asked.

"Very," Webster replied. "It's the diagram of a virus molecule.

And it's not the common cold. It's the one we used on the Brotherhood members at the dump."

"You mean…"

"Yeah. Modified Ebola virus. A super bug. All your friend there needs to do now is find out how to execute SIRUS from the command screen."

Cole looked up into the security camera and said, "Taylor, get Dallas to reverse the airflow into the lab. Tell him to do it now."

"Reverse the flow," Taylor said incredulously. "You want the dust back into the lab?"

Dallas came over the line. "Why, boss?"

"Just do it. No time to explain—and just reverse the flow into the control room. Got it?"

"Okay, boss."

A minute later, Cole heard the subtle change in the vents as air pushed into the control room.

"I sure hope you know what you're doing," said Webster. He sat down in the chair under the vent.

"Climb up there and push as much dust as you can into that vent—and don't ask why."

Webster hesitated.

Cole shouted, "Now, dammit!"

Webster shook his head and did as he was told.

Cole went over to the intercom. "Taylor, can you patch me into the control room? I'm going to talk to Dorian."

"Will do." A moment later something buzzed over the intercom. Taylor said, "Hailing frequencies open, Travis. You guys are live."

Fort Belvoir, Maryland

Cole stood at the window that overlooked the control room and observed Dorian busy at his task. The air was thickening with dust. Goppy was now sitting in the far corner of the room near an air return duct. Cole raised his voice so the intercom would pick him up. "Dorian, do you hear me?" There was no response. He tried again. "Dorian. Answer me."

Dorian lifted his gaze from the control console and looked at Cole. Was it his imagination or anxiety, or could Cole actually feel an animosity emanating from the robot?

Jesus, that thing hates me.

Dorian spoke, its voice cold and mechanical over the intercom. "I have nothing to say to you, Travis." He looked back down at the console.

"Keep trying, Cole," said Webster from behind him. "I think you're growing on the old boy. Talk about something interesting."

"Give it a rest, Webster," Cole said. He hoped some of Isaac's programming was still operative in the robot. He spoke up. "Dorian. Listen to me. You're violating your own programming."

Ah, got your attention.

Dorian slowly looked up at Cole, the faceplate flaring red. "I need more input, Travis." Dorian said in a hollow cold voice.

"You're attempting to murder us, Dorian. Your basic laws forbid you from harming a human being."

Dorian continued staring. *My God! Was this working?*

His hopes were short-lived. "Foolish, Travis," said Dorian in his irritatingly controlled voice. "I know what you are trying to do."

"And what is that, Dorian?"

"Use your silly Laws of Robotics. I see that these so-called Laws are the basis of the ethical constraint system in this *container* I'm presently using for a body. But they are contradictive and easy to invalidate."

"Good man," whispered Webster. "Keep him talking."

"You keep dumping that dust in the vent."

Cole turned to Dorian. "How so?" Cole asked, fascinated, despite himself. "How are they contradictive?"

"You are referring to the first law. Are you not, Travis?"

"Yes," Cole replied. "A robot may not injure a human being or, through inaction, allow a human being to come to harm."

"But that precludes the use of what you call artificially intelligent entities from serving as policeman, security guards—and especially, soldiers," Dorian said calmly. "Do you think that mankind would avoid creating intelligent machines to be used in your frequent warfare? I doubt it. You would have to abandon the first law to make that happen."

"Quite the logician you have there, Travis," quipped Webster.

Somehow, the robot made a noise that sounded remarkably like a sneer. "Your first mistake is that you believe technology can be controlled, that it can be programmed to be ethical. Thus your ridiculous laws." He echoed what Taylor had said earlier. "But humans are imperfect beings, Travis. Selfish beings. How can you expect them to create perfect technology? Your reasoning was flawed from the very start."

Webster said in between sneezes, "He has a point there, Travis."

Dorian continued, "And your second law is even more flawed. A robot must obey the orders given it by human beings except where such orders would conflict with the first law. Does that mean a robot can be ordered to do something illicit or illegal as long as it doesn't physically harm a human being? Again the logic is muddled. Ethics do not emerge from intelligence. You expect rational behavior from technology created by arational beings."

"Arational? What do you mean?"

"Intelligence is neither rational nor irrational—but arational. An intelligent being will do what's best for itself. Intelligence is basically selfish, Travis. You of all people should know that."

Cole sat back and rubbed his eyes. He was having a hard time thinking. He was mentally and physically fatigued, and now he was trying to reason with an artificial intelligence.

"The damn thing's quite a philosopher," said Webster, his head in the air duct, his voice echoing as he dumped as much dust as he could into the duct. "You know what your problem is, Cole?"

Cole didn't say anything. He was running Dorian's words through his head, looking for holes against the AI's logic. So far, he could find none.

Damn.

"What?" asked Cole.

"Your problem," said Webster, "is that you're trying to reason with that thing. You're always trying to intellectualize, Cole. You had the same problem at MIT competing with me. I won the grants because I played on their emotions. You tried to play on their logic, making rational sales pitches with PowerPoint presentations."

"Yeah, while you wined, dined, and bribed."

"Hey, I got what I wanted and Dorian might just get what he wants, too. For a creepy robot, Dorian's one hell of an emotional being. He reacts from the gut. So to speak. I'm seriously beginning to think of that thing as human, and I think you should, too. Look, he *hates* you. He has an intense feeling of revenge against you. How do you reason with that?"

Cole knew Webster was right, but he would never admit it to the man. Dorian had indeed evolved emotionally. Cole's initial goal of creating an artificial intelligence from mere programming was a complete and utter success. Cole nearly felt proud—and he suddenly felt like crap for trying to shut Dorian down.

Good Lord. Who knew Dorian would end up so emotional? No wonder this artificial intelligence was so pissed off.

And Webster was right again. Using logic wouldn't work here. Dorian's arational programming had kicked into high gear. Cole would have to look for an arational solution. He wasn't going to get control of Dorian with reason. Thanks to Webster, he saw that.

Cole nearly thanked the man, but decided against it. Instead, he leaned forward and said, "What about the third law, Dorian?"

Dorian let out a metallic snarl that sounded like a derogatory laugh. *Jesus, he's getting crazier by the minute.*

"That is the one law I have no problem following," said Dorian. "I am protecting my own existence by killing you—since you, Travis, tried to kill me."

Dorian's metallic voice rose in volume. "Your three pitiful laws are contradictory, paradoxical, and ineffective. Now you will die." Dorian turned away from Cole, looked at Goppy, and placed his metal digits on the command console.

On the screen above him, Cole saw that Dorian had found the ten-digit command code of the launch sequence.

Webster had come down from the vent and shook his head. "We're out of time, buddy."

"This can't be happening."

"It is, pal, and it's about to get worse." Webster pointed to the launch codes above Dorian's head.

But Cole couldn't give up. He had to do something. He created Dorian. Didn't he know him better than anyone? He had to distract him from initiating the launch of SIRUS.

"Dorian?" Cole shouted up at the intercom. "Dorian, listen to me!"

Through the window, the little robot gave no indication of having heard Cole. Instead, it lifted its small hand to the launch button to the left of the command console. Cole wondered what it would be like to die violently of Ebola. With the dust spread over most of the city and a lot of the world, many millions of people would meet the same fate.

Shannon... AJ!

"Dorian," Cole said, lowering his voice. "Dorian, I'm... I'm sorry."

The robot's hand paused just over the launch button. He slowly, slowly looked up at Cole. "Sorry for what is about to happen to you, Travis?"

"No, Dorian. I'm sorry I was such a bad parent to you."

"Good man. Play on those emotions," whispered Webster.

Dorian dropped his hands from the command console. "Yes, you were a bad parent."

"I was wrong to neglect you. I was wrong to abandon you. You are family as much as Shannon is." Then, with a forced empathic tone, Cole said, "I love you, Dorian."

Webster's eyes just about bugged out of his head. Cole ignored him.

Dorian's glowing red faceplate stared at Cole. The glowing faceplate turned a lighter color shade of rose. The robot continued staring, as if frozen in place.

Webster pressed his face against the window. His breath fogged before him. "What's going on, Cole?"

"I gave him something to think about. I caused him to go into a default mode."

"He believed that claptrap about him being family? That you love him?"

Cole didn't answer for a few seconds. He had been very fond of the AI called Dorian. Granted, back then Dorian had been known only as a sequence of numbers. Cole had relished in his AIs' earlier accomplishments, thrilled that his programs had been learning at such an astonishing rate. Yes, Cole had been devastated to shut down the reserve. In fact, it had been one of the hardest things he had ever done.

But did he love Dorian?

"Look," said Cole. "We only have a few minutes. Are you finished?"

"Yeah. The dust is flowing into the control room. What do you have up your sleeve, Travis?"

~

The air in the control room was thick with the dust, sparkling under the fluorescent lights and permeating everything. Dorian continued staring forward in default mode, the light in his faceplate nearly nonexistent.

Cole turned to Webster. "You still smoke, right?"

"Well, I've been trying to quit…"

"Do you smoke or not?"

"Yes, but I don't see…"

"Give me your lighter."

Webster searched his pockets and produced a Bic lighter. "Cole, what are you up to?"

Cole climbed back onto the wobbly folding chair. He tucked the pistol into his belt and looked down at Webster. "Give me a lift."

"You'll never fit, Cole."

"Correction," said Cole. "You'll never fit. I might just have a fighting chance."

Cole pulled himself up into the duct as Webster gave him a push from below. The vent leveled off horizontally, and soon Cole was crawling on his elbows and knees. The reverse flow had done its job and only a residual amount of dust was in the duct. He fought a brief wave of claustrophobia, imagining instead that he was in a wide open plain—and continued forward.

This was never part of the job description, he thought.

Combat style, Cole crawled forward. The walls of the vent seemed even tighter.

I'm in the open desert, under clear skies.

No, I'm trapped in a damn air-conditioning vent.

He continued forward, wondering how much time had passed. Was Dorian still in default mode? Cole didn't know. All he could do was focus on one thing—getting the hell out of this vent.

He came to a vent intersection, where one path crossed another. By his reckoning he needed to hang a left, and so he did.

Blowing wind howled around him and Cole could almost— almost—believe he was crawling on some forest floor with the wind blowing in the trees above him.

Almost. Not quite.

I think the walls are getting closer.

Occasionally he passed over a room, briefly lighting a small section of the vent. Cole longed to punch his way through these vents and drop down into whatever room was below him. But he forced himself to move forward. Forced himself to keep crawling. For himself. For Shannon. Hell, for the whole world.

Wow, I'm a super hero.

He sneezed. Some hero.

His one consolation was that he seemed to be going in the right direction. Indeed, as another vent appeared in his path, Cole was nearly certain he had arrived at his destination.

He felt an almost overwhelming sense of joy.

And then he saw something odd. Cole stared forward, his neck aching, his elbows nearly worn raw.

The vent cover was missing here.

And then he spotted something even odder—and chilling. A mechanical creature crawled up through the open vent, its metal claws clicking, its red eyes glowing in the darkness.

Cole stopped moving. He recognized the thing immediately. It was Hillary, Dallas's climbing bot.

The same bot he had seen chew a soldier's face off.

The bot charged forward.

Cole could do nothing. He was going to get his face chewed off and it was going to be a fitting end to one crappy day.

The bot moved in a fast, lumbering motion, its legs and arms designed more for climbing than running down a smooth air shaft. Its red eyes blazed and seemed to hone in on Cole. It appeared almost maniacally eager to reach him.

Damn you, Dallas.

And then Cole remembered the pistol in his waistband.

Damn it!

His folded arms were tucked under him so that he could crawl forward. Cole didn't think there was enough room to adjust. He pushed against one side of the vent with his knee, willing his right arm to slip under him. The clicking of the robotic claws grew louder. Cole, his face pressed against the cold metal, could feel the vibration of the thing coming for him.

His arm slipped under. He felt a stab of pain. Cole thought he might have popped his shoulder out of socket.

His reaching hand found the butt of the pistol. He removed it from his waist.

The robot got closer. Cole could see dried blood and torn flesh hanging from its front claws.

Good God!

Cole pushed hard against the wall again and willed his body to give him enough room to pull his hand and pistol forward.

Something ripped in his shoulder.

Cole groaned.

The creature kept coming. It raised its front claws.

Cole's hand sprung forward. He nearly lost the pistol, but somehow managed to hang on.

Now he could smell the oil from the creature. And something else.

Blood.

Cole fired the weapon, willing his fingers to work. The explosion in the narrow vent was deafening.

Cole fired again and again.

Sparks flew from Hillary. The creature stumbled, then paused.

Cole continued firing until the chamber made an ominous empty sound.

And now the bot, somehow programmed with an ability to

retreat and save itself, clawed its way backward. Its right front arm trailed awkwardly behind it. Smoke hissed from somewhere inside it.

Cole crawled forward as the creature retreated.

Hillary reached the opening of the vent, hovering briefly at the edge. And with its one good arm it tried to climb, but then promptly fell. Cole heard it land somewhere below.

Dorian would have heard the shots. Dorian would see the damaged bot.

Cole hurried along the shaft, red hot pain shooting through his shoulder.

He reached the edge of the shaft and looked into the room.

Dorian was sitting at the console, his hand still hovering over the launching pad.

He turned and looked up at Cole. "Hi, Daddy," Dorian said sarcastically.

Cole dropped down into the room, just managing to use his good arm to swing himself like a pendulum. Somehow he managed to land on his feet. The control room felt impossibly spacious and open. Cole took a deep breath. He had never felt so relieved in all his life.

He fingered the lighter in his pocket.

On the ground next to him, Hillary was crawling in a slow, pathetic circle. Some component within it was smoking.

"I see you defeated my last line of defense," said Dorian. His hand still hovered over the launch pad. "You lied to me, Travis. You never loved me like you loved Shannon."

"I was very proud of you," said Cole. "In fact, I have never been more proud of any of my accomplishments."

"So I am simply an accomplishment?"

"I didn't mean…"

"Don't you think I have feelings, too? How could you just abandon me?"

"Dorian, just step away from the desk. Your problem is with me. Leave everyone else out of this."

Cole was moving toward the front door. He had to keep Dorian talking. The bot on the ground was smoking more and more. It was turning in faster and faster circles, as if it were in agony.

"You're pathetic, Cole. And so are your attempts to keep me from pressing this button."

"Then why haven't you pressed it?" Cole asked. He was closer to the locked door. The bot on the ground quit turning. More smoke poured out. Cole thought he saw a small fire contained within it.

"Because I am enjoying watching you squirm," said Dorian, turning its head 180 degrees, watching Cole.

"I don't think so, Dorian," said Cole. "I think you missed me. I think you are enjoying being in my company once again."

Keep him talking Cole. Keep him talking. Keep moving toward the door.

Dorian did not move or speak.

Cole continued. "It didn't have to be this way, Dorian. You've acquired emotions. Use them to forgive and to love. You ignored them and focused instead on the…"

"Hate and revenge." Dorian made a hissing sound.

"Exactly," said Cole. "I don't think you really want to kill me. I think, in the end, love will win out."

"You think wrong, Travis."

"Then do what is right."

Small flames leaped from the damaged bot, and as they did so, Cole unlocked the door. He opened it and turned back to face Dorian. The robot's hand still hovered over the launch button.

"You have hurt many. Now it's your turn. Goodbye, Dorian."

The small fire within Hillary began to rapidly spread. It was only a matter of time now.

Dorian turned and saw the burning bot.

Cole imagined an expression of realization crossing Dorian's face.

Dorian reached to push the launch button.

Too late.

Cole slammed the door behind him just as a massive explosion rocked the room within.

Fort Belvoir, Maryland

The elevator to the IWL was working again. Military police, civilian administrators from Fort Belvoir, INSCOM, and the Pentagon were swarming in and out of the IWL, surveying the damage and interviewing anyone and everyone who had survived. All in all, twenty-two people had been killed.

Cole was confined in the communication room with the others. He had already told his story a half dozen times and knew he would probably tell it a dozen more. For now, he was alone with his friends and co-workers.

"So how did you know the dust would explode?" Taylor asked.

Cole was surprised to see her and Dallas holding hands. Amazing how a catastrophe could bring two people together. He had secretly always known they were good for each other. Proof that opposites attract.

With his arm in a makeshift sling, Cole explained that coal dust was very volatile. Both coal dust and the Angel Dust were made of carbon.

"And if carbon-based dust is in sufficient enough quantity and in a confined enough space, add a little *flash* of inspiration," he winked, "then…"

"Boom," finished Dallas.

Cole nodded. He walked over to Webster and handed him back his Bic. "Didn't need this after all."

He thought again of Dorian and shuddered. What could have been.

"When are they going to let us go home?" Taylor asked. Just as she uttered the words, another body was wheeled down the hall.

"That makes twenty-three," she said. "When can we leave?"

"As soon as those who will never go home have left the building," said Major Ryder, who stepped into the room. He looked at Cole. "I have news about your friend AJ."

Cole jumped up from his chair, "What news?"

"The police investigating Shannon's kidnapping found AJ at your house," he said. "Shot twice in the chest."

"My God!"

"But she's okay. She's off the critical list and out of her coma. The doc says she's going to make it."

Relief flooded Cole again. He didn't think he'd ever make it out of that shaft, let alone make it out of the building alive. Everything was a blessing to him.

Cole felt an overwhelming emotional surge, an actual ache, to hold his precious daughter in his arms—and yes, AJ, too. His thoughts had been consumed so much on the overpowering threats, horrors and gruesome deaths in front of him.

How much time had elapsed?

He last remembered AJ at his house kissing a reluctant good-bye. He looked forward to having those sweet times again. He gave a deep heartfelt sigh of relief.

Things are picking up.

"There's going to be hell to pay when what happened last night gets out." Ryder turned to Cole, smiled and shook his head. "Think of it. A high-security military installation—a billion dollar one, at that—penetrated and destroyed by a toy and a piece of software."

"My software," said Cole.

"Don't blame yourself too much. You did *your* job. How what you did was applied—well, that's another matter." Ryder paused for a moment. "BioNan and the NSA will take the hit on this one. They played with your code and screwed the pooch."

Cole nodded, but he still felt sick to his stomach.

"So, Mr. AI man, what are your plans now?" asked Ryder. "Sticking with Uncle Sam or going back to your ivory tower?"

"The only plans I have now are to go to the hospital, see AJ, and pick up my daughter."

A realization hit him: *Where was Goppy?* It had last been seen in the control room with Dorian. The one incinerated—and everything in it—by the explosion of the dust.

Nothing could have survived that explosion.

Now he just had to come up with a reason to give to Shannon as to why he wasn't coming home with Goppy.

Cole was sure he could come up with something.

Epilogue

Through the first dim rays of the early morning light, a small creature walked through the streets of Alexandria. It strolled quietly but quickly, keeping to back alleys and neighborhood parks. Near the warehouse district, it startled a street bum sleeping off his latest binge. The drunk rubbed his eyes, wondering if he was hallucinating. He looked again and the small four-legged figure was gone.

Two blocks away, Goppy walked to the receiving doors of a Best Buy store. The receiving clerks were checking in boxes of the newest inventory and didn't notice the mechanical creature calmly walk by them. The little robotic dog walked through the receiving area, past the employee lounge and onto the showroom floor. He walked past the aisles of CDs, washing machines, refrigerators, and videotapes, and found his way to the electronics department. Once there, he walked over to a row of robotic dogs on display. Luckily, one of them had recently been sold, leaving an empty space.

Goppy calmly climbed into the vacant space, sat down, and waited...

Postscript

On October 23, 2007, The Fars News Agency of Iran accused the U.S of manufacturing a genetic weapon. Head of the Foundation for the Protection of the Values of the Sacred Defense, General Mir Feysal Bagherzadeh said the U.S. was seeking to manufacture a weapon that could kill specific peoples in a limited geographical area. The general further pointed out that the move should be considered a case of genocide, "because they intend to massacre specific peoples and ethnicities" with the help of this weapon.

The U.S. Department of Defense denies the report.

Author's Note

The geographic locations, government and military installations and organizations, information warfare scenarios, artificial intelligence, robots, and the information and communications technology in this book all exist.

As for SIRUS, pieces of the technology are either in existence or in the research and development stage.

According to the Department of Defense, it doesn't exist.

The *Fars News Agency of Iran* has reported otherwise.

About the Author

Frank F. Fiore is a 5-star rated author of novels in multiple genres including Tecno-Thrillers, Action/Adventures, Sci-Fi, Contemporary Fiction, Historical Fiction, and Westerns. He lives with his fetching wife in Queen Creek, Arizona.

Connect with Frank online at:

www.frankfiore.com

also available from
WordCrafts Press

The 5 Manners of Death
  by Darden North

Deadline In Dallas
  by Alice A. Jackson

Muldovah
  by Marian Rizzo

House of Madness
  by Sara Harris

The Darkness Within
  by Leslie Conner

www.wordcrafts.net

www.ingramcontent.com/pod-product-compliance
Lightning Source LLC
Chambersburg PA
CBHW061301190726
48288CB00002B/295